ANNA'S HOME FRONT

Sara Thomson

To Mark for always believing in all my crazy dreams.
And to Mum for being the first one to show me the beauty of literature.

Hope you enjoy it!

Sara Thomsen

CHAPTER ONE

September 1940 ANNA

A swarm of black flies blotted the early evening sky with angry blemishes. Anna looked up from the grimy window of the Fleet Street office of her newspaper and squinted.

"There's quite a few this time; looks to be about a hundred, maybe 150 bombers up there," she said over her shoulder.

She felt hot breath on the back of her neck followed by the smell of musk and sweat. Turning, she saw leaning over her, narrowing his small piggy eyes through the taped window squares, Frank Delancey. Breathing fast, his chest struggled underneath his slightly overweight frame.

"Not going to get hysterical are you Forrester?" he sneered at her, drops of sweat forming on his temple and in the greying sides of his hair.

"Oh shut up Delancey, you bloody fool."

He scowled at her and went back to his desk muttering something about bloody women, grabbed his pencil and scribbled furiously on the paper in front of him. She ignored him. He wasn't worth her effort.

She scanned the office, noticing that most people were too busy preparing for the next deadline, writing quick, scribbled notes, talking on the phone and sifting through information and dog eared notebooks to go look at the planes. They just nodded at Anna through the clouds of smoke that lingered on the ceiling of the office. They were used to the bombers now. The click of typewriters, the scribble of pencils on paper and the shuffle of notes continued as they all tried to get out of the office and down the basement as quickly as possible. Nazi bombers won't stop this paper, she thought.

It wasn't very long ago, she hadn't been so sure they wouldn't stop the entire newspaper industry. Up until that day they had only had what she heard someone call 'annoyance raids'. But that Saturday, two weeks ago had been different; had changed everything. Now they were calling it 'Black Saturday.' Its memory was forever imprinted on her. It was the shock mirrored on every face as Londoners emerged from shelters. Everyone stood on the street gaping up at the huge fire cloud that hovered above London. That was the beginning. Now, they were used to sirens going off, used to spending their time in shelters so that the bombers coming over today were only worth a nod.

Someone shouting her name brought her back; the last of her colleagues were still in the office collecting their stories and chewed pencils and were hurrying towards the door.

"Forrester, come on. The siren went off ages ago, we should be downstairs by now," Anthony Marcus said over his shoulder as he grabbed a few volumes of books and notes from the dusty shelves and filing cabinets at the back of the office.

Anna gathered her notes and papers from her desk, and balanced them alongside her coat, hat and bag, before following him downstairs to the basement. As she reached the deserted entrance, she stepped out into the street and looked up at the early evening sky, the last of the daylight was now beginning to fade.

Recently the bombers had spread further into London and had stopped concentrating purely on the east. She couldn't take her eyes off the scene developing in the sky. Luftwaffe and RAF planes were circling and diving around one another like angry wasps attacking.

As she watched, the bombers released their loads, little dots at first, a silent eerie threat. Then the thuds sounded as the bombs hit their targets. Bang, bang, bang, causing the ground to vibrate even at this distance.

It reminded her of that first night again - the 7th September - a date she would never forget. She would never forget the horrific expressions on everyone's faces that the Nazis could actually do this to our city, to her London.

Tonight though, Anna didn't rush down to the shelter to take cover like she had that first day. Tonight she remained fascinated by the scene above her head.

She could see the bombers in perfect formation flying in one after another, hitting targets and flying around and another taking its place.

Arms grabbed her shoulders and fixed around her, dragging her backwards.

"Come on Forrester, you bloody fool. What the hell are you doing out here?"

Marcus, although quite slender was actually very strong

and dragged Anna back into the building and down to the basement with the rest of the workers from the office. Anna clutched at the pile of items she was still holding.

"Get off me" she said forcing him away.

As they reached the basement, he let go and she straightened her rumpled clothes with one hand and rubbed her arm where he had held her tightly. He glowered at her before shaking his head, thinking better of what he was about to say and walked off.

Down here the smell of dust and damp lingered but work was carrying

on as normal. The presses still needed to roll and everyone continued to rush around, scribbling, typing and running hands through hair as they all rushed towards the next deadline.

Slightly annoyed at Marcus, she went to the far corner of the dark, dingy room by the bare brick wall. Some of the bricks were crumbling and she had to brush brick dust off the table before she could put her pile of now crumpled papers on it. She sat down and looked around the room. Everyone else was far too busy to listen to the regular thud, thud, thud of the war going on above their heads.

A loud bang close by made the building vibrate and the ceiling plaster dropped a wave of dust on everyone. She brushed some of the dust from the papers, and looked over the story she had been constructing. It was a piece on keeping your home clean. It seemed ironic that she was writing about cleaning when the whole city was in ruins. Cleaning hardly seemed important right now and she just couldn't get interested in the story.

"Forrester? Forrester." Her editor's bark cut through the

dim light in exasperated urgency. She jumped up and went over to the other side of the room where he was squinting through the dim basement looking for her.

"Ah Forrester, there you are. Phone for you. Over there."

He signalled with his thumb behind him.

Anna went over to the table in the corner where a telephone sat next to a pile of folders and notes.

"Hello?"

"Hello, is that Miss Anna Forrester?" came the faint reply through the crackling receiver. The faint northern accent was a shock after the London intonation she was used to.

"Yes. Who is calling?"

"Miss Forrester, I am Nurse Temple, I am from…"

The line crackled and Anna pushed the receiver closer to her ear to hear more clearly.

"Sorry can you repeat that?" A loud bang rang out and the building vibrated again.

"I said, I am from Queens Country Hospital, we have your mother here as a patient. I am calling to urge you to hurry. How soon can you get here Miss Forrester?" The nurse made the word 'hurry' sound like 'herry' when she said it. Anna found that it took her a few minutes to stop thinking about this strange pronunciation to realise what the woman had said. Shouting erupted in the basement making it harder to hear. Anna strained her ear to the phone again.

"I'm sorry, did you say my Mother is in Hospital?"

"Yes Miss, you really must come. When should we expect you?

"But what happened, has she hurt herself?"

"No Miss your mother has been ill for some time; her illness is terminal. I'm sorry Miss Forrester."

"But she never told me she was ill. How can she be ill?" Anna became silent, wondering if she was hearing the woman correctly.

"Miss? Are you still there?"

"Yes, yes. I am on my way. But I am in London, and in the middle of the most horrific bombing raid. These things usually go on all night. I'm not sure how quickly I can get there but I will be as quick as possible. Don't let her go until I get there; do you understand?"

"Don't worry Miss Forrester, we will do our very best but we can't promise. Please do hurry."

Anna put the phone back in its cradle and stared at it. Had that really happened? Had she imagined it?

Her mother was dying? How could she be dying? How could this be?

"Forrester, who was on the phone?" The editor was squinting at her through the smoke from his Woodbine in the dim light.

"Sir, my mother is in hospital in the North of England, near York. That was the hospital telling me to hurry. She's dying."

"Damn. Sorry, I mean sorry. Struggling for staff here at the moment Forrester with this war taking my best men, but you must go to see your mother. Keep me informed Forrester. As soon as the raid is over you can go."

"Thank you sir" she said

"But Forrester, don't take too long."

"Yes sir."

She went back to the corner where she had left her things, the crumbling bricks now taking on a new meaning: the world was crumbling.

The thuds continued.

Only a few moments ago, she was settling down to deal with another night of raids. Damn you mother for moving to the ends of the earth. Why didn't you just stay in London?

She stood for a moment deep in thought, reapplied her auxiliary red lipstick as had become her habit and began gathering her handbag, gas mask, coat and hat, roughly throwing her notebook and a few other bits of paper in her bag. She would take her chances with the bombs.

Staying close to the walls, she crept unnoticed towards the door that led to the stairs. She slipped silently out of the door and hurried up to the main building.

It was now dark outside but not the full, deep blackness it should have been. Fires raged all around lighting the skies over the city, so she could see planes flying overhead, dropping their bombs. Out here the banging was deafening and the ground shook in different degrees as bombs landed both nearby and further away.

Anna began to walk towards her boarding house among the whistling of the bombs, like some creepy song of death. She ran down a street of houses, mostly rubble and destruction, dust and smoke smouldering in amongst the ruins. She tripped over bits of brick, wood, plaster and the remains of people's lives. Acrid black and grey smoke billowed up into the sky from fires somewhere in the distance and the smell of burning was everywhere.

Anna found herself caught in another street as the roar of engines above her grew louder. She crouched in a doorway of a shop feeling unprotected. Here she was very close to the bombs. Flashes lit up the sky like a huge lightning storm.

The house opposite was wrecked. The bedroom on the top floor was still set up with furniture, like a dolls house that had the front removed for a child to play.

A solitary red flower blew across the debris strewn street. It was so out of place amongst this destruction; an echo of what used to be before. The echo of ordinary life, before war came and blotted out the beauty. Anna watched the flower from her crouched position as it blew across the road, over broken glass, over bits of brick and torn stretches of cloth. The brilliant flashes lit up the blood red of the flower. It was only there for a few moments, before another explosion sent more shrapnel raining down. When she looked again the flower was gone.

There was a fog of dust in the air, like a thick pea souper that smelt of plaster, brick, dust and despair.

Anna managed to struggle down the street a little way in short bursts of running, and found one of the shop doors open with the door hanging from its hinges. Inside books were strewn everywhere. There was a narrow space under a large, Victorian counter into which Anna crawled and curled up, hugging herself and wondered if the world was ending. She could hear water running from somewhere nearby. Probably a burst pipe. She remained there for some time - it seemed like days - although she knew it could only have been a matter of hours. Her legs were cramping and she badly wanted to straighten up but she did not dare. Not until the silence and the siren told her it was over.

She emerged dirty, bruised and shaken but otherwise unhurt, her own fear from last night forgotten as she surveyed the streets.

One house had been blown clear from the middle of its row and the remains of the family inside were now spread in pieces across the street. Anna stepped over a young slender arm still wearing an engagement ring, over all the other pieces, covered with a fine, dusty ash as if they had been long buried.

On the corner of the street stood a child clutching a once red, but now dirty, toy rabbit by its ear. He was crying and wiping his little face with the ear, smudging dust and making his face dirtier. He was surrounded by destruction. Anna slowly turned full circle, trying to comprehend the scene.

Faintly she could hear music playing. She knew the song well. It was a ridiculous romantic song about a singing nightingale. It was so out of place. The child continued crying.

Despite this, she had to get away. She couldn't think of these people right now. Nothing mattered but getting to that hospital.

CHAPTER TWO

September 1940 ANNA

Wet heeled footprints followed her up the silent, tiled corridor like the march of death, making its way steadily through the shiny hallways. The stench of carbolic soap infected her lungs and made her want to retch.

Her clicking steps echoed through the stark clinical building as she ran to the dim lit reception desk at the end of the long corridor. Pausing, she caught her breath and tried to stop shivering, while the starched, uniformed nurse with spectacles perched at the end of her nose, peered at her from behind the desk.

A poster behind the nurse told Anna to 'MAKE NURSING YOUR WAR WORK. It's War Work with a future' carried the image of a nurse and some happy cartoon patients in the background.

"Running in the hospital is not allowed." The desk nurse whose accent was out of place and much more proper than she would have expected, twisted her mouth in distaste as she spoke, peering at Anna in a way that would normally have made her feel uncomfortably scrutinised, but right now she was just impatient with this woman.

"Someone telephoned me and told me to hurry, my mother, Bertha Forrester, she's dying. I've just got off the train from London."

The nurse narrowed her eyes raised a bony finger and pointed down a dimly lit corridor to the right.

"Room 5, down there on the left."

Anna hurried down but not quickly enough to miss the nurse's final words.

"I said no running. There is a War on and you're not the only person to lose someone."

Anna knew this all too well. She thought of the family and their strewn body parts across the dust and debris which littered the street that morning when she had crept out from her hiding place in the bookshop - the arm with its engagement ring, the little boy and his rabbit toy, the shock on people's faces on Black Saturday as the whole of London burned alive, and that right now, back in her beloved city, there were people being bombed and dying. This nurse knew nothing.

She ignored the woman and continued on. Reaching room 5, she pushed the shiny, ice cold handle into a dark ward. The smell of carbolic soap was stronger here and Anna tried to hold her breath.

A ward, almost completely dark, stretched out in front of her, except for a tiny lamp on a desk in the centre. A middle aged woman wearing a Matron's uniform and cap was studying papers.

Seeing her enter, the woman gave a warm friendly smile and came to greet Anna. She had what her mother would describe as kind eyes.

"You must be Anna, we've been expecting you." Her voice was soft and breathy and had an instant calming effect. Anna paused to catch her breath and suddenly realised how wet and bedraggled she must look. By the time she had left London and got the train north, it had been late morning. The train had been delayed so it was evening when she finally arrived at the station of her mother's village. A tiny little place called Abbeyfleem.

It had been impossible to find a taxi in such a small village at such a late hour, so she had walked some of the way before managing to flag down a passing car. The driver was on his way home after a late shift and had nearly knocked her down in the blackout, but had kindly dropped her at the hospital entrance on his way.

"How is my mother?"

The Matron must have noticed Anna's anxious look because she patted her arm.

"Don't worry, you're in time. I'm sure it's waiting to see you that's kept her going this long."

She led Anna to the back of the ward where a screen was drawn around a single bed. A faint orange glow escaped from behind a gap in the screen and reflected on the tiled floor.

Anna stood still as if to hold the moment and prevent the inevitable. For as long as she could remember there had only ever been the two of them - her and her mother.

As a child the other children had teased her about being a bastard. She had pretended that it didn't upset her. Since then she had become good at hiding her feelings. The funny thing was she had always felt the need to protect her mother from the truth. It was her mother who wanted more than anything for Anna to believe in a father.

"It's not true my darling," she had said. "You are not one of those, you absolutely had a father. He loved you greatly."

Anna remembered her mother holding her little shoulders firmly as she insisted, willing her to believe. Anna had always known though, she had always known it was a lie but had never had the heart to tell her mother. Her mother's fragile nature meant that she could happily carry on the lie if Anna believed.

The Matron held open the old paint chipped screen. She smiled at Anna as she waited for her to step inside.

Anna took a deep breath. She wanted to turn and run out of the door, back into the rain, back to the sirens, the bombs and the dust fog of London. Back to the world she knew, back to the world where she was an outsider looking and listening to other people's lives. Now however, life and death faced her with all its clinical immediacy. She stood tall, blanked her face and stepped inside. The nurse replaced the screen behind her and Anna heard her footsteps returning to her desk. In the bed was a shrunken, pale faced figure with long greying hair spread out wide across the white puffy pillows. She touched her own hair, she had had it cut to her shoulders and styled in the modern way. Her mother hated it. Anna smiled at the memory of her mother's shock.

"Anna what have you done to your hair?"

"It's not that short mother. All the girls have it like this now. No one has long hair anymore."

Her mother had mumbled something inaudible and had that sad far away look.

The figure in the bed didn't look like the same person.

Everything was familiar, yet different, except the hair. Her mother's hair had always been lovely and even though it greyed now, it remained as beautiful now, to Anna, as it had always been.

Touching the soft slender fingers, she watched her mother drifting away, moment by moment, like the constant dripping of a tap, the water slowly disappearing unnoticed, one slow drip after another.

Anna shut her eyes and took a few shaky breaths of the dense carbolic soap air. The smell made her nauseous again. She sat there for some time, not moving, just holding her mother's hand. Anna wondered where her need to protect her mother had originated. Maybe it was the air of sadness she always had; maybe it was the fragile nature.

The figure in the bed stirred. Anna leaned in closer. "Mama, I'm here, I came as soon as they called me."

"Ah, Anna my darling girl."

Her mother's voice was soft, weak and faint, not the usual rich, elegant sound. It was the voice of someone who had lost. Her eyes though, were the same. Those deep, rich, sad eyes that penetrated.

"Why did you not tell me how ill you really were? I could have been here. I could have looked after you."

"That is precisely the reason I did not tell you my dear girl, because you would have come. But none of this is important now…"

She coughed violently. Anna poured some water from the jug on the nightstand. Her mother clasped her chest and breathed heavily, exhausted. "Mama, you should rest."

Her mother waved her delicate hand impatiently at

Anna. "I have many things to tell you. We have had such an adventure haven't we Anna, the two of us together, free and untied to anyone. I want you to know that I wouldn't change what we've had, or you, in any way. I am so proud of everything you have achieved. But now I am going I wish I had more time. There is something I've never told you… "

"Mama, I already know you were never married, I've known for years and I don't care. I don't want to know what happened. If he doesn't want to know us, then I don't want to know anything about him. We've done fine on our own."

Her mother wheezed and shook her head. "Oh my darling girl, I love you so much. I hope one day you find it in your heart to forgive me. I only ever tried to do what was right. Here take this."

She pulled the necklace she always wore from around her neck and placed it in Anna's warm hands. Anna had seen it many times. It was a small chain with a tiny golden key on the end. Her mother had always worn it for sentimental reasons. Although Anna had never known where it had come from. "And here, take this one too."

She pulled out a small parcel and put it in Anna's hands, her eyes almost closing. "Keep them safe Anna. It's the story of someone that was lost to this world a long time ago. Let her story aid you in your grief."

"What do you mean?" Anna said as she studied the small necklace and parcel in her hands.

But her mother had drifted back off to sleep. Anna fingered the small golden key and parcel. She put the chain around her neck, just as her mother had worn it. It was warm and settled as if it was meant to be there.

The parcel was wrapped in old, brown, paper with string tied in tight knots and was very dusty. On one side a small white envelope had been tucked inside the knots. The envelope was newer, as if added more recently, and the writing was slightly obscured by the string, but still clear enough to read. It was written in her mother's flouncy hand and was addressed to her. She began to pull at the resisting knots and for a long while they wouldn't move. Gradually, Anna felt the pressure release slightly and she was able to pull one of the knots open. She unwrapped the string and picked up the letter. She would read that later. Whatever her mother had to say she didn't want to read in such an exposed space. She unfolded the rough crinkling paper covering the parcel, its length of time being folded in one position made it resistant to being flattened out for later use. Inside was a small pocket sized diary, leather bound and worn. The fat little book looked well used but carefully preserved. The cover cracked and creaked in protest as she opened it. Inside, the book was full, cover to cover, with neat hand writing in long curving arcs - beautifully finished decorative writing. The type of calligraphy that was a dying art. Anna flicked through the pages and found that some had letters, notes and suchlike stuck to them whereas others were pages and pages of handwriting. She turned back to the beginning of the diary where the first entry was dated May, 1908.

May 1908

Dear Journal, my name is Elizabeth Caroline Leyac, today is my birthday. You were given to me by my sister Louisa, and you are my first present of the day.

My maid has told me that all proper young ladies keep a journal but I confess the thought has never appealed to me. But now I have been given you I suppose I must begin to keep you. It seems very silly to own an item intended for a specific purpose and not to use it for that purpose.

But I suppose I should tell you something of myself to begin with. I am the eldest daughter of Lord Ashton Leyac and Lady Catherine Leyac. I have one sister, Miss Louisa Leyac.

I am not too disadvantaged in looks to expect a favourable marriage in the future. My sister is much more forward on this matter than myself. But don't you think it funny, Dear Journal, that I am surrounded by people but often find myself feeling lonely roaming these empty halls. My mother favours my sister, but I spend much of my time in the library where I can go and become someone else through the pages of books.

So here we are, my first entry. Can you tell I know nothing of writing a journal? I can only implore you, Dear Journal, to stay the course with me. I am sure I will have much more interesting adventures shortly. Oh how exciting to think that I might be in my own adventure story, yet to be written, in these now blank pages before me.

Until my next adventure, Dear Journal.
Elizabeth.

Anna tried to recall the name. It was familiar. Wasn't there some story? Anna shook her head, closed the book and inspected the cover. Why had her mother given her the diary of some preening aristocrat? It seemed extremely dull to Anna. She couldn't think why she would ever want to read about such a person and her adventures at the lace and silk shop, or her latest love interest. It was about as far from anything Anna was interested in as it could possibly get. She picked up the letter, diary, cover

17

and string wrapping and put them all in her bag. She shook her head at her mother.

She spoke to the sleeping form. "Why have you given me this?"

With nothing but her thoughts, Anna found herself absently reapplying her auxiliary red lipstick, although she didn't know why when the rest of her looked frightful. Sighing, she went to the dresser cupboard next to the high metal bed, took out the soft hairbrush and began to brush her mother's hair. It was still soft to the touch, although her recent illness had dulled it.

Her mother was dying. The thought jolted her into the reality of her situation again. She hummed softly realising that very soon she wouldn't be able to do this any more. She stroked through each section flowing down onto the pillow, reminding her of the same activity carried out long ago. Her mother had been the one humming by the warmth of a crackling log fire, while brushing Anna's hair. The memory stung. She was glad her mother was sleeping. Her mother relaxed as she hummed and brushed, each stroke releasing calm, while Anna silently shed tears.

CHAPTER THREE
September 1940 ANNA

Anna was shaken awake, the disorientation of where she was and how she'd got there filled her, as a face peered at her with kind eyes and a matron's cap. "Miss Forrester?" the face said.

Anna slowly began to remember. She had sat on the chair to rest for a few moments last night; she must have fallen asleep. The last few weeks of consecutive bombing raids on London had taken its toll. The heavy feeling in her head and the soreness of her eyes told her it was some hours later. She pressed her right palm to her temple and rubbed her eyes with the other hand to disperse the sleep still pulling at her. The Matron was peering over her and the screen curtains had been pulled back. An orderly was wheeling away a squeaky trolley with a white sheet covering the figure laid upon it. The bed her mother had occupied was now empty.

"I'm sorry Miss, she went sometime through the night and was already gone when I came on my rounds."

The kind faced matron squeezed her arm and looked at

her with sympathy in her eyes. Anna said nothing. The deep sleep she had been in was still pulling at her so that nothing seemed quite real. She avoided the Matron's gaze that looked inside her soul. Her gaze with the sickeningly kind eyes irritated Anna. She wanted to slap the woman hard across the face and keep on slapping her until she stopped her invasive gaze and her unwanted sympathy. But instead Anna sat still, both hands tight together and inspected the Matron's white uniform shoes and worn stockings. She noticed the woman's puffed up ankles. Had they always been this way? Anna hadn't noticed before. Did it really matter?

Anna sat as still as she could not wanting to acknowledge reality. Maybe if she kept still it wouldn't be real. Small insignificant objects seemed to draw her attention, the floor, the Matron's shoes, her puffy ankles, the metal leg of the next bed, the fading squeak of the trolley pushing her mother away.

"Do you want me to get you anything Miss?"

"No, I'm fine, I must catch the next train to London." Anna barely registered her own voice and was surprised when she realised that she had in fact spoken.

"But Miss it's not full morning and the weather…"

Anna wasn't listening, as soon as she heard herself speak, she knew it was the only thing to do, to get away from this place, its sterile environment and lingering death. She forced herself to look at the Matron's face. There was that sympathy again. The pungent carbolic smell that seemed to seep from every brick was suffocating.

Gathering her crumpled coat and hat she got up and went towards the door her steps echoing through the ward, getting faster and faster in her eagerness to get away. Ignoring the Matron's protests of the bad weather and waiting for morning, she ran across the corridor and stepped down the stone hospital steps of the large Victorian building and left the place of death behind, one muddy step at a time, down the rain soaked roadway that led through the fields that stretched out as far as she could see. However, unlike her journey the other way the night before, she made no attempt to shield herself from the pouring rain and to stop her city heeled shoes from becoming ruined in the muddy country lanes. Anna didn't care anymore about her shoes or her appearance and walked along the lane, past the waving trees and the sponge like bushes that were soaking up the rain as it fell in a steady flow down the long deserted muddy lane; past field after field, each step taking her further and further away from the country hospital. The rain washed over her as she walked. She welcomed it.

Sunrise was just breaking, creating a pink-orange glow on the horizon, giving the morning a dim twilight feel. The road on which she was walking was a narrow lane that twisted downward, the bad weather making it resemble little more than a mud track. Muddy tractor tyres and other vehicle marks, along with horse hooves crisscrossed and intersected in front of her, from previous travellers. The rain was flowing into a dirty stream down the side and was washing away the tyre marks.

The muddy rain splattered her stockings and inside her shoes, making a squelching sound as she walked. Her chest felt as if she had a belt tied too tight around it. It was hard to breathe, but she didn't cry. The rain continued.

When she put her hat on she hadn't looked in the mirror and could feel that it was slightly askew. She didn't care. Her hair, which she hadn't had time to wash after her night crouched in the remains of the book shop, had been put up roughly in a roll, with bobby pins at the base of her head before she caught the train and had barely survived the soaking it got last night. Now she could feel it was coming loose from the pins. One wet tendril was stuck to the back of her neck like a damp finger, reminding her of her situation. Anna didn't care about anything. The usual impeccable attention to her appearance, topped off with auxiliary red, her favourite lipstick, normally gave her confidence and allowed her to feel like she was able to go and achieve something worthwhile But not today. Today for the first time in her entire life, she felt like she didn't care what she looked like; she didn't care who saw her and she didn't want to try. The wind whistled and although the rain slowed, the wind only served to make her more cold. Anna hated the countryside, unlike her mother who had loved to take her tramping through fields and hills to all manner of cold, muddy places. She had relished in it, breathing in the cold damp air with enthusiasm. Anna had always followed glumly behind, wet and cold.

If only she could get away from this place, things would be better. Get away to a place where she could think. The destruction and despair of the bombed streets of London was preferable to this muddy open space with nowhere to hide.

My mother is dead.

I am completely alone in the world.

She had no idea in which direction she was walking and without road signs to guide her she just kept walking, but she was pretty sure it was just a straight road down towards Abbeyfleem village where her mother had lived. There she could find the railway station to take her to York and then back to London.

The sun had fully risen and the rain had stopped as Anna reached Abbeyfleem station. It was only when she stepped onto the neat, clean paved platform that she noticed how mud caked her shoes and stockings were. Her skirt and coat were soaked through and she could feel that her hair hung in long straight straggles to her shoulder. She knew she looked a sight. She probably looked like one of those bombed out women but without grey plaster and brick all over. She thought of the little boy and his dirty toy rabbit. He had looked how she felt today. In that moment she recognised his despair. Was it worse for him because he didn't understand?

She wasn't sure she understood herself. All she knew was that it was this same dirty, bombed, debris strewn city she now craved; the hustle and her routine of keeping busy with other people's lives with no other thoughts further than the next story, the next article or the next tube junction. Making sure her lipstick was topped up no matter the situation. Absently, she took her lipstick out of her bag and reapplied it although she knew it to be a foolish gesture right then considering the rest of her appearance.

As Anna walked around to the front of the platform, dawn was rising quickly and birds were already singing. The Station Master strolled along whistling to himself, stopped when he saw Anna, the shock at her bedraggled appearance and muddy shoes made his mouth twitch at the corners, his greying eyebrows and watery eyes betraying his thoughts. He must have realised he was staring because he began to fumble for his pocket watch - studying it carefully and without moving his gaze from his watch said:

"You for t' early, Miss?" his heavy Yorkshire accent ending the silence. Anna looked at his face, which was still avoiding looking directly at her. "Yes, could you tell me what time the next train is due?" Her own southern accent jarring oddly to her own ears like something foreign and out of place.

"Bout an hour Miss, you're very early, you want t' wait inside?"

"No thank you, as you can plainly see, I'm already wet and the rain has stopped now, so there seems little point."

"Sxcuse my impertinence Miss, but are yr all right?"

"Yes, fine thank you."

The old man nodded his cheeks pinking, tapped his cap and walked off leaving Anna sitting silently on the platform bench but looking back at her curiously as he went.

The station platform was small and open air. Two sets of tracks sat in-between two identical platforms facing each other. A small victorian footbridge painted in red and white spanned the tracks to allow passengers to cross on either side. There was a small station house on the same side as the one on which Anna was sitting. It was a single storey stone building with a large gabled roof. A white painted fence surrounded the station that led down to the village. After 10 full minutes of sitting on a cold, wet bench, the same red colour as the bridge, and realising just how wet she actually was with nothing for company but her own thoughts, Anna began to wish she could get into a warm bed and not on a long train journey. She considered going inside after all, and as she looked around the deserted platform, she seemed to come out of a trance and had begun to wish she hadn't ran from the hospital. Had it all been real? She didn't have a conscious memory of making a decision, she just seemed to wake up whilst sitting there on the platform.

It was while contemplating this that she noticed the Station Master coming towards her again with a short round-figured woman. The woman was wearing a coat that was unbuttoned and a scarf roughly tied around her head. Anna could see through the open overcoat that she had on a house coat covering her clothes and looked as if she had left home in a hurry. She prepared herself for a conversation with the couple.

The woman sat on the wet bench next to her and put her arms around Anna. So shocked at being handled in this way, Anna just sat stiffly letting the woman hold her, the Station Master shuffling awkwardly behind, his cheeks pinking slightly, uncomfortable at the show of affection he clearly wasn't used to.

"Excuse me." Anna said at last. "But who exactly are you?"

"I'm Mrs Baxter, I'm a friend of yer mother's." The woman smiled at her. Anna just stared rudely at the woman. Her mother had talked of her friends the Baxters before, but Anna had never met the couple.

"Yer are Anna Forrester?" A look of doubt crossing the woman's face.

"Yes, but…"

"How was yer mother? Was it really bad, such a shock to see her se' ill?"

"She died in the night." Anna said simply.

The woman's face changed to a look of distress.

"Oh no! I'm sorry dear. It's a real shame, yer mother was a great friend. I'm se' upset, everyone's been hoping she'll improve.

Come my dear, yer can't go on a train like this. You come with me, a nice cuppa tea is what yer need."

"I'm sorry, no, I'm fine. I want to go back to London."

"Yer can't go like that, yer are soaked to the skin, you'll catch yer death and then yer won't be no use to anyone. How yer going to plan a funeral from London?"

The woman, was almost indignant at Anna's protest. Hand now on her hip shaking her round head in disapproval. But Anna stayed determined, she wanted to get away from this awful countryside to familiar surroundings where she could think clearly.

"Well at least come and eat something before yer go then." She said.

She hesitated under the old woman's gaze. Then on impulse asked "Do you know anything about the Leyacs"

The woman's surprise at such a question was plain to see, but she quickly used it to her advantage. "Aye lass. Come for a cuppa tea and a bite to eat an' I'll tell yer."

Anna was interested and without admitting to the old woman how hungry she actually was, she allowed herself to be taken by the arm down to the far side of the station platform.

The woman turned out to be the Mary Baxter, wife of Arthur Baxter, the Station Master. She made Anna feel safe and warm as she held her.

Anna knew the couple by reputation. Her mother had written to her of them many times so she didn't feel that they were entirely strangers. In her tired, hungry and grief stricken state she couldn't think straight and allowed Mrs Baxter, who insisted on being called Mary, to usher her to her home which was only a little way from the station itself. The woman took her into a large warm kitchen with a big range cooker on one side. She immediately sat Anna down and poured her a cup of hot tea from the brown teapot covered with a knitted cosy, that was sat on the table. Anna nursed the warm teacup in her hands, sipping at the steaming liquid.

"Now" Mrs Baxter said standing over her "Your mother would never fegive me if she knew I'd let yer get off to London in wet clothes and I wouldn't fegive meself if you ended up ill. She'll haunt me if I let yer go like that. Now, none of that" She held up her hand as Anna began to protest. "Yer can take a bath here, Arthur is out until lunch time, so we've plenty of time to get the bath out and get yer cleaned up and wash your clothes. Yer can get the later train, and in a respectable state. Right now yer look like a mud caked, drowned rat."

Anna knew she was not in any state of appearance to travel and a bath did sound wonderful, especially as for some reason she couldn't stop shivering, despite it only being mid September and autumn was only just beginning.

Mrs Baxter had taken her silence as an affirmation and began to get out bathing things. The tin bath from behind the pantry door was set in front of the range cooker, a 5 inch line had been marked, as was regulation.

"I'm thinking yer need a full bath, but I just can't bring meself to do it, I'd feel like I was letting down our Tommy," she said as she began to fill the bath once the water was hot. "So we'll make it nice and hot and that will do yer I think."

Anna wasn't sure who 'our Tommy' was but had vague memories of her mother mentioning the Baxter's son in her letters. She silently stripped down, not really caring about the reality that she was stripping off and taking a bath in the home of a woman she met not half an hour ago, but despite this Mary Baxter had a warm motherly sort of feel. Anna didn't feel Mary was really a stranger, it's just she hadn't visited often to meet the Baxters'.

When was the last time she had visited? She wondered as she stepped into the steaming water.

Despite the meagreness of the bath, she relished the ability to wash and Mrs Baxter had made the water extra hot so, she was soon warmed through. After washing and drying herself Mrs Baxter produced a thick dressing gown for Anna to wear while she washed her mud soaked clothes. Her stockings had been done already and were hanging on the horse to dry while she tackled the rest of Anna's things. Mrs Baxter scrubbed expertly on the washboard and Anna was more than a little impressed with how easily she seemed to get her clothes clean. She had thought that they could just be aired out, but it seemed that Mrs Baxter had other ideas. Once the clothes were washed and drying, they tucked into a bowl of hot breakfast porridge, which Mrs Baxter had ready. Anna was beginning to feel herself again. She had pinned her clean hair into pin curls with her bobby pins and it was drying nicely next to the fire range. Soon she could take them out and style her hair properly, but even without this, she felt as if the last day had been a bad dream. Breaking the silence she asked. "So Mrs Baxter, what is it you can tell me about the Leyacs?"

The woman stopped scrubbing the big porridge pot in the sink for a moment and wiped her forehead with a wet hand and looked up in thought. "Well, not much I'll tell yer," she said shrugging her shoulders and going back to the pot. "But what I do know is that they're a rich family, or were back in the days o' Victoria, God rest 'er soul, from over t'other side of York. But now not so much. But they're more famous now than they used t' be on account of the missin' baby."

"What baby is that?"

"Well, long time ago now, me'be 25 or so years back, Louisa Leyac, had twin sons. But, within hours of the birth a maid at the 'ouse stole one o' them and neither has bin seen again. Well now, Louisa died of some illness or other in the 30s but, the twin left be-ind is now Lord Leyac an' is all that's left o' that family. He still looks fo' his missing brother. Ee won't be found now though. Such a sad story." She shook her head, and started scrubbing again.

Anna contemplated the story. She would have to investigate a bit more, and she had to admit, thinking of it was a nice distraction from the other thoughts that were threatening to take over. "Mrs Baxter, who is Elizabeth Leyac."

"Ah, Elizabeth is the sister, Louisa's sister that is. She would 'ave been Aunt to those twins, had she not died."

"Died?"

"Aye, she 'ad a long illness as I recall aroun' the time of the Great War and died young, unmarried, barely lived that one by all accounts. They not a very lucky family."

Anna thought a bit more and found herself beginning to relax in the warm comfortable atmosphere of Mrs

Baxter's kitchen. She was secretly glad the woman had stopped her getting on that train.

'IS YOUR JOURNEY NECESSARY?' all the posters said accusingly every time she got on the tube in London. Anna was beginning to feel particularly selfish and not just for wanting to go back to London. Is this how all those women felt, all the ones who had been bombed out and lost their husbands and sons to the war? Did they feel this way? Had she been cold and heartless towards them all this time?

Anna pushed the thoughts away. She didn't want to think about that right now so busied herself helping Mrs Baxter.

She spent much of the rest of the morning with Mrs Baxter and hadn't realised until afterwards, but Mary Baxter had cleverly persuaded Anna to stay without actually telling her to. At first it was a little of,

"Could yer just help me with this little job, I find it hard these days now I'm not so young as I was. It won't tek a minute."

And before Anna had realised, it was lunchtime and Arthur Baxter was home from his shift.

Anna had begun to get a little clarity in amongst her shock, and realised that going back to London just wasn't possible. She would have to do what she had preached to so many of those poor bombed out women, she would have to face the reality of her situation. She may have lost her mother, her world may have fallen apart, but the whole world was falling apart around her and she couldn't be so self indulgent. She was going to have to go to her mother's cottage and stay there tonight. Anna dreaded it. There would be so many reminders of her. She didn't want to go, but then she thought of the bombed out women again with their dirty faces and shocked expression, clinging to their crying children. She thought of that little boy again with his dirty rabbit and that stupid romance song.

Mrs Baxter had continued to chatter at her all the while she had been considering this and when she focused on her, she realised that the old woman was looking at her waiting for a response. "I'm sorry?" she said feeling her cheeks go warm in embarrassment but Mrs Baxter didn't seem to notice. "I said, are yer staying for lunch?"

"I think I will be staying a while longer than that. I'm not going to London, I'm going to stay at my mother's cottage."

Mrs Baxter clapped her hands in triumph. "I knew you'd change yer mind. I just knew you'd see sense. Yer mother always said you were a sensible girl, far more sensible than she."

"She did?"

"Aye, she used to sit in that very chair with her posh southern voice and tell me all about you. She used to sit for ages and talk about yer. She was right proud. I'm gonna miss her something terrible."

Mrs Baxter shook her head and went back to preparing lunch. She was obviously one of those get on with it types. Anna had met a few of them before, their homes gone, their families dead and they just pick up and move on with a cheery shrug. Anna had felt an affinity towards these type of women. She had always taken it for granted that she would be one of these types if anything happened to her like this, but now she wasn't so sure. Annoyed at her own weakness, she got up to help Mrs Baxter prepare lunch. She had a slight feeling of contempt for women who fell apart and cried in the face of their tragedies. Why didn't they just get on with it? But now that tragedy was actually happening in her world she was realising that it wasn't as clear as she had thought. The kettle whistled on the range. She poured the boiling water into Mrs Baxter's brown serviceable teapot and covered it with the multicoloured cosy, clearly knitted from old scraps. A few minutes later, after the tea had been poured through the strainer into mis-matched china tea cups, she sat back with her steaming drink and contemplated what to do.

It was some hours later before she managed to tear herself away from the Baxters, having left her ration card with Mrs Baxter who had insisted on providing meals for Anna, from which no amount of protesting would dissuade her. The silent Arthur had advised her it was best to let his Mary have her way. As she was unsure of the way to her mother's cottage, which was a little way out of the village, up a lane on its own, Arthur Baxter walked her all the way to the front door and told her of the key being under the flower pot at the front.

Carrying her parcel of food for her evening meal from Mary Baxter, she entered the silence and closed the door, a little relieved to be alone.

She stood by the door and closed her eyes, listening to the retreating footsteps of Arthur Baxter, the only noise in a thick silence that her bustling London ears weren't used to. She inhaled deeply and the scent of the place filled her. It smelt like home. It was her mother's smell, as if she was in the next room, a mixture of fresh linen, spring mornings, and warmth.

Anna pushed away the tears and went into the sitting

room, trying to distract herself. This was much harder than she had expected. Why was everything so difficult lately? Damn, why was she so weak?

The little living area was exactly the same. The chair sat near the fire, facing the window and her mother's wireless on the mantle. A sofa and a few other pieces of furniture in the room made the little cottage homely. It looked as if her mother had popped out for a few minutes. Anna wanted to cry at the thought that she wouldn't be coming back.

"Oh Mama…" she said out the window and off into the distant Yorkshire countryside. "What am I to do now?"

The silence echoed around the empty cottage and her answer came as the clouds darkened and the pit-pat, drop, drop of the rain started again, plopping on the window sill in large splodges, the only noise to break the deadening silence.

She closed her eyes and a heavy feeling overwhelmed her as the reality of the last few days caught up with her. Events roamed around her brain like bees buzzing, putting events into the wrong order.

Sitting down on the chair, she wondered what to do next. This was a feeling she didn't like. Used to being organised, busy, having deadlines, somewhere to be, noise and people, this silence, this nothing was almost intolerable. She flung her handbag onto the sofa opposite in frustration, missed and it bounced off the sofa and thumped on the floor, the contents spilling all over and rolling around the rag rug carpet Anna remembered seeing her mother make.

"Damn." Getting on her hands and knees, she collected

her things and shoved them irritably back in her bag. She noticed the paper package her mother had given her in the hospital which she had forgotten about in her haste to leave. The wrapping was now crumpled and the string was wrapped around a number of other items from her bag, her identity card, her lipstick, her purse, her tissues. The diary and the unopened letter were strewn among the little pile of items. She hastily picked up the rest of the things from her handbag and settled down with the diary and letter. Maybe now was the time to read it, now she was alone. She sat and held it for a few minutes unsure what to do. Curiosity took over and she put the diary in her lap. It settled there, a small weight while she turned the letter over and over in her hands fingering the smooth paper, tracing the letters of her name. Ripping open the envelope she unfolded the letter and began to read the words.

My Dearest Anna,

You have been a wonder and a saviour in my life, more than you know, and through all my sadness and melancholia over the years, you were always able to cheer me and make me feel glad to be alive.

I hope you are not too angry with me for not disclosing my illness. I made the decision not to burden you and I stand by that decision.

As time gets closer to the end, I find myself wondering; I would like to think that I always did what was best for you, but like all parents, I suppose I am destined never to know the truth of this. However, given my choices again, I would make the same ones - I stand by my decisions, I hope you can understand that.

I am not worried about dying it is my time. I have seen so many of my generation lost in the Great War and afterwards as the ripples of that War continued long after the guns fell silent, and still are if you know where to look. And now we are facing yet another war, but at least for this one I am grateful I won't be around to see its destruction. I haven't the energy for another. In many ways my whole life has been one big war.

What I am trying to say my darling girl is that I don't want you to feel sad for me, shed tears for my loss or let this spoil your wonderful career. I am so proud of you, just keep holding up your nerve with those men. You were born to do that job and don't let any man tell you that you should be home cooking with a brood of children.

However, despite my words I know you. I know you will find this difficult to deal with, so here is a little reading material, which may help a little by taking your mind off it.

It is the diary of someone who was lost a long time ago now.

I entrust her story to you in the hope that, as you lose me, she may give you comfort.

With my dearest love and sincere affection.

Mama

Anna folded up the letter and not for the first time thought how much more to her mother there was than she had ever realised. How much of the real woman had she actually ever known? Taking another deep breath to calm her emotions, she swiped at the threatening tears, briefly looked out the window at the world crying tears of rain and looked down at the letter again.

Looking up from the page once more, she realised she would need to make the fire up and make sure there was material at the windows for the blackout before it got much later, or she would be sat in the dark. Glad of the distraction she started at the front window and discovered that her mother had made a special set of curtains that sat inside her own, closer to the window, which just had to be pulled across when it got dark. She had always been able to make things from any old scrap of material. Anna however, was useless at anything remotely crafty. After a quick assessment of all the cottage windows, she discovered that her mother had blackout curtains at each of the windows. Where had she found so much material? It was scarce in the city and expensive.

She found some kindling and cut logs for burning on the fire and before long had set the thing ablaze. After she had pulled the curtains for the blackout and lit the cottage's old fashioned oil lamps, she was feeling quite hungry so opened Mrs Baxter's parcel of food. Shortly, with a fresh pot of tea from the store in her mother's larder, and the crochet blanket from the back of the sofa, she sat cosily sheltered from the darkness outside and re-read her mother's letter. She still couldn't understand why she had given her the diary of such a person.

To take her mind off her own thoughts and the desperate silence outside, which was making her uneasy, she decided to give the diary another try. Sighing resignedly she picked up the leather book which cracked in protest again as she opened it and turned the old pages to the next entry. This one was also dated 1908.

CHAPTER FOUR
May 1908 ELIZABETH

I can scarce believe it to be true but my father is dead. It was very sudden, the maids found him last night and the doctor has confirmed it this morning. Even though I have been informed it still does not seem real.

I was in his study talking with him only yesterday. If only I had known then what was coming. The thought that I will never ever, throughout the length of my entire life, see his face or hear his voice speak is unthinkable. I cannot contemplate the endlessness of that. He will never roam these rooms again. I do not know what to do first, I sit and am restless, I keep busy and am tired and distracted. I cannot get comfort in anything except writing here in this journal. Thank the heavens Louisa gifted it to me.

Do not misunderstand me, my father and I were not close but there was something he said to me yesterday through the dying embers of his study fire with its rose coloured glow gently stroking the side of his face. Now I think about it he did look fatigued, but in that moment all I could see was the connection we could have had, the one we should have had, if he had allowed it.

The only kindly words he ever spoke to me were that night, the only thing he had ever uttered which made me realise that there was something beneath the blank exterior, something underneath beating and beautiful. But it had always been hidden, except for a brief moment when his melancholy eyes looked deep into my soul and he said:

"You are just as beautiful as your mother. Do you know that Elizabeth?"

Just a flicker before it faded and he sent me away. I was too stunned to utter any answer and stood there confounded before turning to retire. I wish now I had answered, I wish I had given some reply, any reply. I did not know that would be my last opportunity to delve beneath the exterior and discover the man beneath. This man I have lived beside all my life who is a stranger to me, who finds my presence irritating and could never wait to leave a room in which I was present.

'If only' is a terrible phrase, it tells so much of the cruelty of reality, of never being able to go back and alter mistakes, of never being able to discover who the real man actually was. I am left with a tantalising snippet of what could have been, of him pushing me on a swing as a child, teaching me to ride my pony, walking and discussing books and poetry. So much lost, that I did not know I had to lose until that brief moment when he revealed in that short phrase, that there was more to him than he had ever allowed me to know.

My mother is grief stricken and the maid told me she has cried every moment since we were informed. I know she loved him dearly and I am greatly saddened for her. I am trying to stay away from her though, I seem to have a propensity for annoying her without meaning to. I really must try not to get things so wrong all the time.

And so I find myself idling with the view from my top floor bedroom window watching the wind blow the trees, I can see so far. It always makes me wish I was a bird and able to fly all over the county free and at one with nature. Life continues in its customary way, a farmer in the distance is ploughing his field with his horse. There are sheep further still on a hill, and down in the distance is the top of the church spire and the beginning of Heathfield village, where people go about their business as if nothing were any different to any other. It does not seem right somehow.

I have just been disturbed from my view and writing by a young maid, who anxiously cleared her throat behind me before bobbing a rather amusingly clumsy curtsey and touching her cap, which I must say looked as if it were about to topple from her head. She informed me that Lord Moorlass has come to pay his respects to the family and that he is presently waiting in the drawing room.

"Has my mother been informed?" was my reply to this remark - to which she then says that she has and is far too distressed to see anyone and also gave instruction that Miss Louisa should be allowed to rest. I inform the girl I will attend shortly.

But I confess to sitting here idling at my view once more. The wind is blowing the distant trees quite considerably, it must be extremely windy. I have just realised I did not enquire as to the young maid's name, but it is too late now she is gone. I suppose I must stop putting off the inevitable, and go down and receive my visitor. I will be back soon, Dear Journal…

I have returned from receiving Lord Moorlass a meeting that went better than I anticipated. However, I must tell you that on leaving to go and attend him I caught sight of myself in the large mirror on my dressing table and was shocked at how frightfully pale, fatigued and a little stunned I looked. My large eyes were frog-like and my hair, wild untamed curls, was protruding up from its pins stubbornly. So lord knows what my visitor thought of me.

When I did get to the drawing room I found myself pausing at the door before entering, but when I did go in Lord Moorlass, who had been pacing the floor strode over and took both my hands in his, looking deep into my face with a rather friendly open expression.

Lord Moorlass is one of my father's oldest friends and owner of the nearest neighbouring estate. He is elderly, with a large bushy white moustache and always stands upright as someone with a military background.

He began by offering condolences at my loss and said he had been hoping to commiserate with my dear mother. I naturally informed him that she was unwell and unable to receive visitors but that I would convey his message. This appeared to satisfy him for he then began discussing how she had been such a devoted wife to my father Ashton, (he calls my father by his first name due to their long friendship).

I asked him if he would like me to ring for tea, but he said that it was not necessary and something else rather interesting, "I know what it is like to lose someone suddenly. The last thing you need is to entertain visitors."

I also noticed more than usual, his habit of twisting his moustache as he spoke. He offered to help with the running of the estate or provide advice and consultation to us 'ladies' and told me to inform my mother of his offer directly.

And so, now following this encounter I am back sitting idling at my view again, feeling more than a little apprehensive because I will have to go and inform my mother of this meeting, and seeing her today was not what I had wished to do. But there is nothing for it, I must do as instructed.

I have been to see my mother, Dear Journal, and I can barely think, for she has told me something shocking, something I cannot believe. My heart races and my hand shakes as I write this, but the whole encounter is spinning round my head in a whirl so I will set it out in full for you in hope of making some sense of it. Here is what happened:

My mother's rooms are on the first floor of the house, through the round gallery where one can view the hallway below from an oval shaped balcony, and along the long gallery, which has windows at either end. Dark panelled walls with portraits line these walls, including one of King Charles I and King Charles II, and a great number of ladies, lords and others in which I have little interest . Suffice to say that one of my ancestors collected portraits. I despise them, they watch me with their beady eyes and intense frowns.

However, this is also the way to the library, my most favoured part of the house, so I usually endure the portraits for that sake.

My footsteps echoed along the parquet floor and I slowed my pace as I get nearer to the door at the end.

Quietly I entered her antechamber and paused, my back pressed against the door. This is where she entertains her visitors. It was empty apart from a small fire in the grate. A door directly in front of me leads to her private bedchamber; this door was also shut firmly. I listened for movement. There was silence. A shadow flitted across the floor as a bird flew past the window at speed. It looked like rain. I crept slowly across the room and pushed open the narrow double doors ahead.

This room is the most grand in the house with colossal tapestry carpet pictures on the walls, one of ladies at a ball and another of ladies on a swing. Gilded crowns surround the chimney piece encasing another giant portrait. A large bed with silk hangings dominates the room and the figure bundled on the bedstead was so still, it took me some moments to realise this was my mother and not a pile of gowns.

"Mama?" I enquired softly, unsure of my welcome.

The figure on the bed jumped in startlement, she had not heard me enter. My heart began to leap and I prepared myself for her tirade.

The bundle stirred and sat upright, turning she directed her gaze at me with narrowed eyes, her face puffed up from weeping. Her pink complexion red, her blue eyes slits and her once blond hair hanging in messy limp tendrils down her face, so uncustomary from her usual

41

neat bun and much more like my own untameable dark mass of curls.

"You. Why are you here? I did not send for you." She wiped her face in a vain attempt to gain control.

"Mama, I just came to say that Lord Moorlass has gone, he asked me to convey…"

"Good. Odious man, why on earth would he want to visit? To gloat I suppose." She got up from the bed and thrashed at her dress in vexation as it got in her way, before she marched to the window of her room and looked out.

"No Mama, he…"

"Is that why you're here to gloat at my suffering girl?" She directed with her back to me.

I swallowed. I did not know how to construct an answer so I confess, Dear Journal, that I remained dumbly silent in hope that my misgiving did not show.

"You know your trouble Elizabeth? You think you are so perfect." She turned to face me, her vexation now aimed directly, her hands in fists of rage at her sides.

"No Mama, truly…"

But my words only served to fuel the anger and she launched into a tirade of how despicable I am. It seems I stood there ages as she continued her relentless attack. Her face changing colour to purple as she contorted it into expressions of distaste. She did not appear to be able to stop herself. She did not appear to want to.

Then, as she begins to slow and I prepare myself to make my escape, she delivers her final blow. I can see in her face she enjoyed viewing my reaction to her words. Her eyes sparkled with greed as she inspected my reaction. I poised in horror, mouth open. Forgetting all my propriety and upbringing, I stood as if a common maid unable to speak.

I cannot believe it to be accurate, Dear Journal. I cannot believe she could tell me something that could alter my life in such a way so harshly. How could she be so cruel? I cannot comprehend. It simply cannot be right. It is the grief, it must be.

I cannot write the words, not yet, but soon, Dear Journal, I will. Soon I will be brave enough to admit what she told me. Right now I feel nauseous with it. My stomach flips over and my heart will not stop pounding. My head is filled with too many thoughts for one small girl.

I do not know what to do first. I need to contemplate. I cannot write any more, my weeping blurs the words.

Today truly is the worst day of my life.

CHAPTER FIVE
September 1940 ANNA

Anna got in her mother's bed thankful for the distraction of Elizabeth's words which helped her ignore the strange yet familiar room. It was filled with items that only served to remind her that her mother was gone. She was beginning to think her mother had been clever in giving her such a thing to distract her thoughts. Although worlds apart, she recognised the familiar numbness that Elizabeth didn't say but, which clearly emanated from the pages - the words between the words. Maybe Elizabeth might be interesting after all. Had she misjudged her? Perhaps there was more to this girl than just a flighty, insubstantial, privileged heiress. Anna closed her eyes as the sleep called, still considering Elizabeth.

She dreamt she was a small child, her little legs half running, half flying as her mother pulled her along faster than she thought possible to go. Her mother's long dark hair flying free, so unlike her normally pinned up style.

Little Anna was extremely cross to be woken in

darkness and made to go out in the cold scary night. And she'd left her favourite dolly behind. She wanted to go back for it but Mama had said no.

She pulled an irritated face. She didn't see why they couldn't go back. She felt tears coming, her arm hurt and her feet were sore, she didn't want to run in the darkness anymore.

Suddenly her mother stopped running but they were nowhere she had seen before, this place was near a river with big metal pillars on either side and big boxes everywhere.

Mama bent down, picked her up by the waist and put her behind some boxes. "Now Anna darling, we're going to play a game, a hiding game. It'll be so much fun, you must stay there and be as quiet as a mouse. OK darling?"

Anna pulled a face she didn't like Mama's games and thought this one especially silly, but she did as she was told crouching down and sticking her thumb defiantly in her mouth in silent protest. She waited quietly in the darkness snuggling down in the corner of an upturned box just the right size for her to crawl inside and curl up with her eyes closed and thumb for comfort.

She put her free hand over her head as she listened to the nearby footsteps. Were they Mama's? She really wanted her dolly.

Waking with a start, Anna was disorientated for a moment before she realised she was in her Mother's cottage, then the memories of the day before slowly came back. Her mother was dead. Somehow the dream seemed to make her mother's loss worse, even though the dream wasn't real. Anna had no memory of running anywhere in the night, although she partially wished it were true. It would make an interesting story, a lone woman and her child running in the night, but from what?

Shaking off the silly dream she set about getting herself ready. She didn't know where to start and thought that getting up would be a good beginning.

She noticed the diary on the table beside her and fingered its old leather cover. Elizabeth was suffering too. She felt comforted to know that there was someone who was also feeling as she did. It didn't matter that it was long ago. To Anna, it was right now.

Beginning to dress, she wondered about Elizabeth's mother. What was it she had told the girl that had horrified her so much?

She had barely finished getting ready when a knock at the door and a shout from downstairs shook her out of her thoughts. She smiled at her reflection. In her boarding house in London, it was Olivia who always popped in early on a morning after her night shift at the hospital, where she worked as a nurse. Here it appeared it would be Mrs Baxter giving her a morning wake up call.

She watched her reflection apply familiar auxiliary red before going downstairs. Mrs Baxter had brought breakfast.

Anna protested, "Mrs Baxter, I mean Mary, you mustn't keep feeding me like this. Surely you're giving me more than my ration book allows for."

"Nay don't worry. Each allowed scrap all works in together to make a big bit that goes further. Besides, we fair better with supply hereabouts. We've all heard of how starved yer all are up London way. When the evacuees first came they were half starved little retches, both the children and the mothers." She shook her head in disapproval as she set up mis-matched bowls on the little wobbly table. Then her expression changed and she smiled at Anna. "Now girl, what you going to do today? I was thinking we could go up the hospital…"

"Do you have many evacuees?" she asked, keen not to discuss her mother or the hospital.

"Aye, some. Although many went back to the cities when the bombs didn't come. I'll bet they regret that now. We heard about the bombing in London. Is it really every night?"

"Yes it's been every night and in the daytime too, so far, and they are saying that it is set to continue. That's one of the reasons I wanted to get back. You see, I sometimes get to report on the bombings and the families, how they are doing and what help they get. At the moment there are quite a lot. I'm missing a lot of work."

"Well it seems to me that it's a strange thing to long for, the misery o' others."

"Oh I don't long for the misery of others. I just think the rest of the world should know what's going on. Anyway, back to these evacuees, do you think I could get to interview some of them? It would make a nice piece, especially if there's any from London. I could do a piece on escaping the bombing and readjusting to life in the country, maybe some kind of war effort in the country article. However, with the paper being cut down to a very limited number of pages, it's only because all the young men have gone to fight that I still have a job, otherwise there would be no job at all. Less pages in the paper means less stories and less work. Not less news though, there's more than enough of that, and most of it bad."

Anna was thinking aloud and wasn't looking at Mrs Baxter, but stopped when she noticed her expression, one hand on her rounded hips as Anna had noticed she had a tendency for when she disapproved of something.

"Now all this is well and good, but yer still have a funeral to plan and I'm happy to help out, but yer can't go gallivanting all across the country. Yesterday yer were going back to London, now thankfully yer not but yer going chasing stories, when yer poor mother needs yer to sort out her place of rest. People will be asking shortly."

"I know you are right of course. I have no intention of gallivanting anywhere. However, I do still need to keep my hand in, my career is an industry where they can't wait for anything, it needs constant nurturing. If I take too much time off, someone else will start getting the good leads."

"Too much time off. Girl yer have only been here a day." Mrs Baxter shook her head and went off to the little kitchen muttering to herself, presumably to make tea. Evidently she knew her way around because before long the little kettle was whistling and Mrs Baxter returned with a teapot and cups.

Anna knew that she was using her career as a way to take her mind off everything, and why shouldn't she? How else was she to get on? She realised just how unprepared she was for the loss of her mother and had nothing but her job to focus on to keep her mind from going mad.

"Now, tell me, what is it yer are going to do today? Are yer going to come up the hospital?" Mrs Baxter asked her hand on her hip again.

An hour later she was standing on the train platform having persuaded Mrs Baxter that she didn't need to go to the hospital and that a day in York was much better. She told Mrs Baxter she needed a break, that a bit of sightseeing would do her the world of good. Mrs Baxter had looked unconvinced by her motives, but had relented with her lips in a tight thin line. And it hadn't entirely been a lie. York was a beautiful city and unmarked by the all-night and every-day bombing that London had endured in recent weeks. Anna just wanted to go somewhere and feel like there were still places that weren't in ruins, as her own life felt right now - and she would do absolutely anything to avoid going to that hospital.

She shuddered as the train drew in and Arthur Baxter gave her a wave as she stepped inside the carriage. He closed the door behind her. Abbeyfleem village, although small, was on the direct route out from York to the western towns, so the trains stopped there regularly on their way back and forth. The trains were often busy as people travelled back to the main line at York and on to London or Scotland in the opposite direction.

She settled in the compartment, and opened the stiff window a little way, to dissipate the thick heavy smell of pipe tobacco. The countryside rushed passed in a blur of sickeningly endless green horizons broken by snippets of villages. There were a number of stops before they got to York itself and one station had many more people getting on the already busy train. Through the open window Anna could see a handful of fresh uniformed youths kissing their sweethearts and calling their mothers a fool as they waved goodbye teary-eyed to their sons, off to do their bit for King and country.

Proud fathers stood on the platform with stiff military backs and sticks for damaged legs, imparting what little advice they could to their boys before comforting their wives. All these fathers and mothers had a far away scared look. It was the look her mother had had when there was talk of another war and now it was here, they all seemed to be in on some secret that she and her generation didn't know.

Some of these youths entered Anna's carriage noisily, throwing the window open wide and letting in more of the noise from the platform. Talking excitedly between themselves, they hardly noticed her sat in the corner by the window.

A small group of Wrens got on chattering in excited tones as they jostled for space. Most of them looked very young, the one nearest Anna was tall, awkward with a large frame and thick arms. She had a shy plain face but beautiful deep blue eyes. Her hair was mostly hidden under her wren's hat and she stood out because her companions were all much smaller than she. One of the girls was a small curvy blond with a very pretty face but she seemed to Anna to be a bit too aware of her attractiveness from the way she made eyes at any man who walked by their compartment door. As she sat watching them discretely, she couldn't help but hear their conversation.

"Well, my Ma said he was trouble and I shouldn't ought to step out with him, and at first I had a mind that she was right, but then he went and signed up for me. Well, he said it was for me, to make me proud of him, he said. So what could I do? I couldn't very well say no after he had gone and done that now could I? So I let him take me dancing." The small dark haired girl with the wide mouth gestured with her hands as she spoke and patted her hair below her wrens cap in a satisfied way.

The other girl in the group was red haired and fair skinned and was looking horrified. "What? You mean you went anyway even though your Ma didn't like him?"

"Well of course I did, my mum doesn't tell me what to do. She might try but I always get my way. Anyway are you telling me you would have refused the poor chap after he went and joined up for you"

"Well, no when you put it like that... It's terribly romantic, just like in a film." The red haired girl clasped her chest and sighed.

The dark haired girl, shrugged, superior. "Yes I suppose it is. He's terribly nice when you get to know him. We're going to write."

"Oh you're so lucky. I wish I had a chap to step out with." The red haired girl looked sadly at the other as she said this.

The blond who had been making eyes at some young man who happened to walk by a few moments before, was looking thoroughly bored now and turned back to her companions rolling her eyes.

"You're all mad," she said arms folded. "Why on earth would you want to tie yourself to just one man when there are so many others around? I wouldn't let any man keep me and call me his."

The dark haired girl narrowed her eyes. "No because you like to have them falling at your feet."

"And what's so wrong with that?" the blond opened her eyes wide in mock innocence.

"Only that you're in that uniform now and you'll have to behave properly."

"Ah pooh, I'm going for a look around. You girls are

becoming dreary."

After the blond had left and moved along the train, the others huddled together and Anna couldn't hear their conversation anymore.

She thought about them for a while as she watched the green horizon change to small villages as they got closer to York. Why had she never had girl-friends to be companionable with? Anna had never got on well with other girls and her constant moving around as a child hadn't helped much. She had always just had Mama. Girls always seemed to be very like these girls, superficial and silly and Anna had never worked out if it was other girls, or if it was her that was somehow strange.

And now, as she thought about it more, the friends she did make had always been men, although she mistrusted their motives too as a general rule. Many resented her being in the job she had and either wanted her fired, or to teach her a woman's place. She had always been very much a loner. Anna didn't mind, she liked being left to her own thoughts, except that at the moment her own thoughts were full of her mother and she desperately wanted to think of other things.

As the train began to pull into York station and slow its movement as it edged towards the platform, she got up and left the compartment, jostling for space to leave the train, sighing at herself. Would she ever learn to control her feelings?

CHAPTER SIX

September 1940 ANNA

The station was busy but despite this, she couldn't help feeling she was being followed. Although, when she stopped and turned around there was just the usual mass of people going about their business, rushing to catch their train, waiting to meet sweethearts. Nevertheless, she couldn't shake the feeling there was an unseen shadow just outside of view, always behind every last corner. It was a strange feeling but one she had felt many times before. She ignored it as she had all the previous times and made a mental note to not be so paranoid.

York station had a canteen built on one of the platforms with a long wooden counter and panelled sides, two large white urns sat on the top surrounded by lines of white mugs for making tea. It was filled with soldiers, sailors and airmen all eating and drinking tea served by the WVS girls behind the counter. Anna walked on past them feeling slightly distanced from her surroundings. As she passed she heard a saxophone begin to play. One group of soldiers in the far corner were huddled around the player who had his eyes screwed in concentration.

She glanced up at the large arching roof that gave the station a kind of aircraft hanger feel, rather than a station. At least it wasn't raining today. She dodged a man running towards her, carrying suitcases, his hat flying off as he ran. He smelt strongly of pipe tobacco.

Going across the bridge towards the way out, Anna looked down at the trains below her, their big, steaming engines pulling carriages at the back. The steam rose and billowed upwards as she walked on.

Down by the station exit there was a collection of telephone boxes, many of which were already in use, but she managed to find an empty one. Closing the heavy door, the noise of the station, soldiers going off to war, weeping wives and mothers, busy people and children all rushing about their business muffled to a quiet calm.

Once she was connected the crackling ring of the phone at the other end went on for a few minutes before it was answered. The abrupt voice of her editor barked a hello down the phone at her. She imagined him in his usual chair in his corner office in her building, a Woodbine stuck at the side of his mouth, his shirt sleeves rolled up and running his hands through his hair. She imagined her own desk empty and alone.

"Sir, it's Forrester, I'm calling you from York station. I'm going to have to stay up here for a while, my mother… she died yesterday. I'll try and get back as soon as possible, Sir, but I'm going to have to organise the funeral and empty her cottage of things."

"Forrester. Damn. Oh I mean Sorry. Sorry for your loss."

"Do you need me to come back to London?"

"No, no Forrester. Stay there. I need you back in top form. So get everything ship shape and get back as soon as. Clear?"

"Yes sir, if you're sure."

"Was there anything else Forrester?"

"How are things down there?" Anna began to absently twist the phone cord around her finger.

He made a kind of laughing snort noise. "I lost two to conscripts this morning. One of my best. These bloody raids are making it impossible to get any stories. We're spending day and night in the damn basement. I'm being tied in knots over what we can and can't print. And my paper is going to be a one page pamphlet if these cuts get any worse. So business as usual Forrester."

"Sir, are you all right?"

"Yes. Yes Forrester forget I said any of that."

"Sir I have an idea for a story, I was thinking of doing an interview with some of the evacuees up here from London and writing a piece on how well they are doing. What do you think?"

She could hear him audibly sigh, and pictured him running his hands through his hair. It was clearly a bad day. "No Forrester, I can't think about that right now. I don't like it. You know we have to be careful what we print."

"But Sir, it would be a positive story."

"No Forrester, I said no. Blast. That bleedin' siren's going off again. Get your family responsibilities in order and get back here as soon as possible. I need a woman on some of these leads, some of these mothers and wives will talk to another girl."

55

"all right Sir, I'll hurry back."

She heard the click and the line went dead silencing the faint air raid siren in the background. She sighed and put her head on the phone dial and shut her eyes. Now what?

There was a tap tap at the door. Opening her eyes, a suited man was frowning at her. She opened the door and he went inside giving her a scowl as he did.

She left the station and went out into the daylight, the rain was still holding off as she walked into the City. In the distance the Minster rose above the tops of the buildings and trees. Turning towards it, she inhaled the fresh autumn morning as she walked under the archway that was cut into the city walls, before going across the bridge that straddled the River Ouse.

The imposing structure of the Minster grew in front of her and she noticed the many intricate details and carvings in the stonework. It was a building which looked magnificent from a distance but more intricately magnificent on closer examination. Anna knew very little of architecture or the specific names given to the arches, pillars and structures that made up the interior of the Minster. She hadn't planned to visit the Minster at all and wasn't remotely religious, but now she was here, the sheer magnificence of the place and its imposing, yet quietly sedate structure, seemed to draw her in. She was unable to resist.

Inside, the light shone through the round window above the doors. The outside intricate stonework continued on the inside walls but the stonework, not having been exposed to the elements, was much cleaner and whiter creating a regal atmosphere.

Anna stood for a few moments looking down the length of the structure. Huge archways lined either side and looking up, a massive white vaulted ceiling extended the length, inlaid with golden flowers that from this distance looked tiny, but which were obviously much larger in scale than they appeared to her far below.

She began to walk slowly along the central aisle, looking at the windows on either side, the daylight streaming in casting dancing shadows on the floor below.

The floor itself had a black geometric design that snaked around the lighter coloured floor and Anna's shoes echoed loudly as she walked.

She wondered whether she had ever stopped to take in the great sights of London and realised that she had passed by many of them every day, taking little notice throughout the length of her time there. She wondered how many of them were now in piles of bombed-out rubble, gone forever.

A little further down she found a seat. The peacefulness calmed her. The minster had an air of serene calm and she just sat and enjoyed the beauty of the place.

After leaving the Minster she walked along High Petergate, then turned right and enjoyed the sight of the old, drunken looking shops on either side. At the intersection larger paving gave way to smaller cobbles. In front of her was a smaller, but wider, street in a square. Buildings of differing architectural styles made up the square; a church building, a building with columns and another painted red and white. Slightly to the left of the corner of the street was a building with small stone columns and large glass window walls. The sign across the top read Betty's Cafe Tea Rooms. Now was a good time for a hot drink.

Anna entered the tea rooms and was shortly brought a pot of tea in a shiny pot, served on a gleaming tray with matching milk jug and tea cups of delicate, fine china. The place had an air of luxury; crisp white table cloths lined each table and bright, shiny cutlery on each place setting. The waitress smiled at Anna and she handed her the tea.

Anna returned the smile and thanked the girl. As the girl left, her thoughts again returned to Elizabeth Leyac. She absently stirred the tea she had poured herself. The teaspoon clunked on the sides of the cup as the tea swirled around in the cup.

What was it about Elizabeth?

The elderly gentleman at the table across from her looked at her above his round reading glasses and cleared his throat frowning. His moustache quivered and she realised that she had been stirring her tea for far too long. She put the spoon down and picked up the teacup and sipped her tea.

Anna knew there wasn't much she could do to find out anything about Elizabeth until the funeral and the cottage had been dealt with. She dreaded both tasks. Now was the only time in her entire life she wished she had a sibling with whom to share this task. Mrs Baxter was lovely, but right now, what she wanted, more than anything, other than her mother not to be dead, was a sibling to share her grief with, to have someone there to help deal with everything.

If she was honest, she didn't know what to do or where to start. She could do a man's job and work alongside people who resented her. She could interview people who had lost everything. She could stay impartial and closed off from most things, but this, this she just couldn't control and no matter how angry she was with herself, or how much she tried, she couldn't stop herself feeling.

Anna spent a few more hours in York wandering around the streets looking in the shops, walking along the Shambles with its old overhanging buildings and large bowed windows. Then, down at the river she watched the water gently float by, living up to its name, a few leaves bobbing on the surface like tiny insect boats.

Anna wandered aimlessly, enjoying the feeling of just having nothing to do, for a short while at least. She wandered enjoying the sights of this lovely old city until the clouds darkened and the rain began again.

Then she admitted defeat and returned to Abbeyfleem village. When she stepped off the train onto the wet platform, Arthur Baxter was on shift again.

"Mary's waiting on you, she's been up the hospital this mornin' for yer."

"Thanks Arthur, I'll go see her now."

The hospital had told Mrs Baxter that they would only give out information to relatives and that her mother's doctor himself was planning to visit and bring the death certificate directly. Mrs Baxter had told her he was named Doctor Laker and was apparently, according to Mrs Baxter, "…a very nice man, and such a good doctor" so she was to look out for his visit shortly.

She climbed into bed that night weary from indecision. Tomorrow, she decided, she would start getting things organised.

* * *

She was awoken much later by a noise. It was still pitch black. Yawning she stretched out for her bedside clock. Anna could just make out the time by the moonlight when she opened her curtains.

The street outside was empty and her clock said 4.30am. Throwing on her mother's old worn dressing gown, Anna walked softly, barefoot out to the landing and down the stairway, feeling her way down the darkest part of the staircase to the sitting room.

She drew back one of the curtains to provide a welcome relief from the darkness   letting in a clear moonlit cloudless sky, casting long silver streams across the furniture. The sky was full of stars and she looked across towards the small lobby with it's tiled floor and noticed a small rectangular shaped envelope on the floor.

She was certain it hadn't been there when she had gone to bed and was a little relieved that the noise that woke her was the letter box and nothing else. The thought crossed her mind that anyone posting a letter at this time of the morning can't be delivering good news, unless the postman was doing his rounds early, which was possible. Maybe they delivered mail earlier in the countryside. Even as she thought it, she knew that this was a ludicrous idea.

She began to feel cold so picked up the letter, closed the curtains and returned to the warmth of her bed. She lit the lantern beside her, pulled up the woven blankets further and looked at the rectangular envelope. It was light and flat, and addressed to her in an unfamiliar hand. Her curiosity piqued, she opened the envelope, tucking the blankets further to her as she did.

* * *

Dear Miss Forrester,

You do not know me. However, I know you recently lost your mother. I know not what she may have told you about her past and what went on before you were born, but I would advise that it will be best for all parties involved if you did not pursue the past and any connections you may feel you have.

For your own sake, and mine, I would very much like the past to remain hidden. I see little sense and no gain in bringing up things which happened long ago.

The financial arrangement with your mother has been in place for a long time and will continue with the same arrangement terms for you. This is obviously on the same understanding.

You would be very wise to take my advice. I am not used to people crossing me and I would recommend that you do not do so.

Good day.

The note was not signed and Anna had to read it a number of times before she began to understand what it meant. Once the shock of such a threat had subsided, she began to wonder who could have written it. Perhaps some disgruntled person she had written an article about, but no, it mentioned a financial arrangement between the person and her mother. Someone who wanted something in the past to remain hidden. But what? She knew nothing of her mother's past, not a thing, except that she had kept hidden the fact that she had never married Anna's father, and that whatever had happened to result in Anna herself, her mother had always felt she could never discuss it with Anna at all. There was no doubt her mother had been brokenhearted by whoever her father had been, but Anna had always felt, with some degree of dread, that whatever happened must have been horrific for her to not be able to confide in her only child.

But then a white hot wave washed over her as she came to the only logical conclusion. If ever she needed proof that the man who abandoned her mother was already married, as she had suspected for many years, this was it. Who else knew about her mother's past other than the man whose secret it also is? In all her life, Anna had told no one of her mother's unmarried state, and her mother had spent many years convincing everyone of the carefully constructed lie that she was a widow. Who else had something to lose from the secret exposure of her true birth but her father? And most galling of all is that there had been some kind of financial arrangement between them. Had he been paying her mother to keep quiet? Who was this man?

Knowing that he was still alive after all this time, and worse still, that he had been watching her made her hate him more than she did when he was just a faceless person.

How long had he been watching her? Had it been all her life? The letter implied that he was desperate to keep the secret, in which case he could have another family or be some kind of public figure. Anna felt nauseous at the thought of him being there, but never being there. Did this explain her feeling of being followed that she had experienced all her life? Had it been him all along?

Well, he needn't have bothered. She had never had any intention of finding a man who could abandon a pregnant woman and never be around throughout her life, except for some secret 'financial arrangement'.

Anna had no intention of ever pursuing any financial claim, or whatever he had written. The fact that he felt the need to write such a letter told Anna that he knew nothing of her character at all. "He must be worried I might write an article about him or expose him." She laughed aloud.

She felt nothing but anger. Anger at him for his audacity; anger at her mother for accepting financial help. Was that what had paid for her education? My God. Was it his money that had paid for everything? She had never questioned it before but there had always been enough money for as long as she could remember. She and her mother had faired better than some, when rightly as a single mother shouldn't they have been worse off? Mother had worked too, but still. Was this the reason they had been comfortable and that Anna could get an education and that she had been able to get the start in her career she had needed?

Good grief. She knew the answer was that it had been. They had both lived off him, from his 'financial arrangement' whatever that was, for years.

She screwed the paper up and threw it across the room. Her chest became tight again. She threw the heavy blankets across the bed.

"Oh mother how could you take money from such a blighter? What did he have over you? Oh how could you? Damn you both."

She cried then, and once the tears started they wouldn't stop.

CHAPTER SEVEN
September 1940 ANNA

Anna woke much later to a clattering downstairs. She rubbed her eyes which were sore from crying.

The room was in darkness because of the blackout curtains and she sat for a few moments as her mind woke up and processed what was happening.

The clattering was Mrs Baxter letting herself in. "Anna, Anna, come quickly you'll not believe the paper this morning." The excited shout came up the stairs.

She covered her face with her hands and sat on the edge of the bed, pausing to muster up the energy to stand. She had fallen asleep after laying awake in anger and tears for a while, the note from her mysterious feckless father playing on her mind, and now she had a headache. She shouldn't have gone back to sleep.

Getting up slowly she sighed and went to the window, the floorboards squeaking with each step, and opened the blackouts. Daylight poured in and made her screw up her face and cover her eyes.

"Anna , Anna, you up girl?" Mrs Baxter's voice was

urgent and excited.

"Yes." She said. "I'm coming."

She picked up the old dressing gown from the floor where she had left it and put it on again. As her eyes adjusted to the light, she was able to straighten her face slightly from the squint she had been wearing. Birds were tweeting outside. They seemed to make a damn lot of noise.

The note from last night was still in the corner where she had thrown it in temper. She picked it up, smoothed it down and put it in the pocket of the dressing gown.

She could hear Mrs Baxter downstairs opening curtains and decided that she couldn't hide upstairs much longer.

Walking across the bedroom's squeaky floorboards she opened the paint chipped door and stepped out on to the staircase.

Going down she could hear Mrs Baxter who was now in the kitchen. Anna presumed she was making tea.

"On the table." Came the shout from the kitchen. Anna looked, there was a newspaper folded on the coffee table. Opening it the headline was striking and bold in big black letters. "ALMOST 200 NAZI PLANES DOWN"

She continued to scan the rest of the front headlines, "BUCKINGHAM PALACE IS BOMBED", "BOMBERS CHASED BACK ACROSS THE CHANNEL" then she saw it, in big dark type towards the bottom of the front page.

LEYAC TWIN IS DEAD!
I have the unfortunate duty of informing you that Lord Thomas Leyac, the remaining Leyac

twin, is missing in action.

What makes the loss of Lord Thomas such a sad affair is that he has died before managing to restore his missing twin brother to the family. It is well known that Lord Leyac never gave up the search for his missing twin, and the story has become famous...

CONTINUED ON BACK PAGE.

Anna quickly turned the paper over to the back page and continued to read the rest of the article.

A 25 year old mystery, which so captured the nation's heart at a time of war. The story is a thing one would expect to see in a work of fiction - It's 1915, in the grips of war, a baby heir stolen from his crib by a dastardly maid never to be seen again. I defy even the most deft of fiction authors to come up with such a story.

But Lord Thomas Leyac was the last surviving member of his family and without knowledge of the whereabouts of his brother, stolen from their crib only a few hours after their birth, the Leyac line dies out.

But many of the nation are losing their families, brothers, sons, fathers. Why does the nation continue to care about this family?

Well, it was Lord Thomas' continuing connection to the people, his innovation at opening his estate to the public and virtually turning his family home into a museum for anyone to go and visit, whether you be young, old, poor or wealthy.

But it was his brother who truly brought the name Leyac to the nation's lips when, during the Great War, among hardship and struggle, he was taken from his crib. The thief, reportedly a maid in the employ of the family, stole to the nursery and took the child from under the noses of the Leyacs, their staff and subsequently, the nation.

In the early days it was thought there would be a ransom request but no such request ever came. It was as if the little boy and the maid just vanished into thin air.

What also makes this case strange, is the loss of only one of the boys. Why take just one child, why not both? Why choose a privileged child at all?

So many questions surround this case, and now with the tragic loss of Lord Thomas, we will never find out what happened at Leyac House all those years ago.

But without finding the missing brother, it is unclear what will happen to the Leyac estate. It is expected that it will be closed to visitors until further notice, but the long term future remains uncertain.

However, don't let this family's tragedy make you too sorry for them. They have kept another secret for nearly 40 years.

* * *

The infamous Lady Catherine Leyac, Grandmother to the twins, was Lord Ashton Leyac's second wife. Not only this but Elizabeth Leyac, the twin's Aunt, isn't Catherine's daughter at all. She is the daughter of Lord Ashton's first wife. This first wife has been virtually forgotten, some say by design. But however it happened the name Eliza Leyac has been almost erased from existence by the family themselves. Why? Well some say, because Catherine was insatiably jealous of her. It was reported that Catherine had been Lord Ashton's mistress before he married Eliza, but this was never proven.

Whatever the family truth behind the stories, what we do know is the story of the Leyac family stops here. The questions remain frustratingly unanswered and we must end the book on the lives of this fascinating family and say goodbye not only to Thomas Leyac, but to the search for his brother too.

Anna closed the paper thoughtfully contemplating the story. The name of the reporter wasn't printed, as was usual for some articles. But she made a mental note to ask who had written it when she was back in London. She wondered if the story had been watered down at all to save space. After all, in the middle of daily bombings across the country, the death of one aristocrat, no matter how famous, was hardly important. But she did know news, and this was something that would get people buying the paper. She knew what a story like this could do.

What is it about this family that keeps coming back to me? First the diary now this. However, it was a welcome distraction from the shock of the threatening letter from her father during the night. And the more a story of this calibre pulled at her, the further away that letter seemed to get, so to Anna, it was just the distraction she was looking for that morning. What had happened to that baby boy all those years ago? And just how was she supposed to find answers to a mystery that many more experienced people had spent years trying to solve. If Thomas Leyac himself, with all his resources, couldn't find his own brother what hope did she have? The twin was most likely dead anyway. There was no other way someone could remain concealed like that for so long, she was certain of that.

But Elizabeth did interest her. Maybe looking at both mysteries may help find out her mother's connection. There was no doubt more information in the diary itself and she made a point of deciding to spend some hours reading it, but she also needed to visit Leyac House.

The death of Thomas Leyac meant that it may soon be even more difficult to find out any information about Elizabeth at the house itself. It made going there not something to do at some point but something she should do as a matter of urgency. Who knew what was to be done with the estate and all its contents. She needed to get over there and find out what she could before it was too late.

Looking up as Mrs Baxter entered the room with tea, she wasn't relishing the thought of telling her plans. However, she was beginning to feel that Mary Baxter was just a little too helpful. She knew she meant well but she had never been used to this kind of mothering. She had always been an independent soul.

It's not that she was running away from the loss of her mother, well maybe a little, but her mother had given her that diary for a reason. The death of Thomas Leyac only made her visit to the house more urgent than anything else right now.

And then there was the note from her estranged father. She didn't want to think about him either, or his reference to the 'financial arrangement' whatever that meant. She decided to keep her little night visitor a secret from Mrs Baxter. She didn't expect her mother would have told her anything at all about her past. She hadn't even told Anna so it was highly unlikely Mary Baxter would know anything, and Anna found trusting strangers difficult.

First of all she needed to walk to the village and phone her office again.

Mrs Baxter had now poured the tea and was settling herself comfortably on the sofa clutching the little china cup and saucer.

"Eee I can't believe that story, such a tragedy an' him only 25." She shook her head in a tight lipped shake of disapproval.

"It says he's missing presumed dead, but that could mean he's alive," said Anna.

"Na, he's dead all right. My friend Mrs Silver, she had one of those telegrams sayin' that her boy was missing presumed dead, and she keeps on believin' he might be out there somewhere, but he's not he's dead, everyone knows it. It's just a fancy way of saying they don't know what happened to' body. It might have been blown to bits, or lost in the sea, anything could have happened. They don't like to say this to folk, so they say missin' presumed dead, when really they mean, he's dead and there ain't no body to come home. In the Great War, my brother was one of those missing presumed dead uns. Me Ma always hoped he'd be back but he never did come home. Broke 'er heart that did."

"I'm sorry." Anna said.

Mrs Baxter seemed to come out of a trance when she said this. "Ah, don't worry lass. It were a long time ago now and Ma's been dead fo' years. But it's a real shame about that young man, especially as there's no more of them Leyacs left and he never did find his brother."

"Yes, it is. I wonder Mrs Baxter did my mother ever mention that family to you? The Leyacs I mean?"

The old woman looked puzzled. "No, no. Why, should she 'ave?"

"No, it's all right I just wondered whether she'd mentioned them in passing, or in particular, Elizabeth Leyac?"

"No, as far as I know yer mother didn't take any interest in the rich folk. What would people like us have to do with any of them lot?"

"Yes, you are right of course, but as I'm up here and this is my newspaper…" She held the paper up to Mrs Baxter as she spoke. "I will have to go to visit the house and see what other information it might hold. It will save them sending someone, you see. I'm already up here and it seems silly when I can be useful."

"Aye, I suppose yer are right, but I don't like it. That paper of yours should give you some time off to grieve. Ye've just lost yer mother. But nothing I say has any bearing on it, so I suppose I shall be off and let you get ready."

Anna felt slightly guilty at the deception, but she

couldn't tell Mrs Baxter about the diary or the letter from her father. She just knew she needed to get over to that house today and she didn't want to incur anymore of her tight lipped disapproval.

She reached the station in plenty of time for the next train, so went to the phone box at the entrance below the platform steps and went inside the heavy red door.

Hearing the familiar ring and crackle before the tired voice of her editor answered in his familiar bark.

"Hello Sir, it's me, Forrester. I've just read today's news."

"Forrester. If ever I needed all hands to the pump, today is the day. I've been on the blower all day and people are banging down my door to find out information. The whole country's going mad for the story of this fancy Lord getting killed. The world is falling down around us. Every day, people are dying and they are all bothered about some privileged toff who's probably never worked a day in his life."

Sir, I'm up here anyway and Leyac House is a train ride from York, so I'm going to go over and see what information I can find."

"Yes, Forrester, that's good. I'm not one to argue with people buying my paper and this toff is selling them like hotcakes, so anything you can find out will be good for business. But don't expect too much. These well to do types close ranks at this sort of thing and especially to reporters. And this family is particularly guarded. Anyway, get off over and report back anything you find. Good, good well done, keep up the good work Forrester."

"Yes, Sir. Thank you Sir. Sir, Can I ask, who wrote the

piece?"

"That would be Marcus, Anthony Marcus. He has a contact at the University who researches these families, or some such thing."

"Thank you Sir."

"Right then Forrester, go to it. And get back to me with any information you find out. And Forrester?"

"Yes Sir?"

"I appreciate you taking time away from your grieving and the funeral and what not."

"You are welcome Sir."

She waited for the click at the other end before she replaced the handset and left the phone box, glad at last to at least have something to do other than rattle around in her mother's cottage and arrange a funeral, which she really didn't want to do.

She went up the steps onto the platform and when the train pulled in it was a relief to feel like she was off on an assignment. This she knew. This she could do.

As an afterthought she had grabbed Elizabeth Leyac's diary on her way out of the cottage. It would make the journey go quicker if she had reading material to pass the time, and it was a welcome distraction from all the despicable countryside.

Settling into the unusually empty compartment, she opened the cracking leather book. It creaked as usual. She flicked through the pages following the first few she had read. As she did so, the book naturally fell open at a page with a letter stuck in the middle of the text, the fatness of the extra pages making the book open there. She stopped and began to read this entry.

CHAPTER EIGHT
August 1908 ELIZABETH

I have a small confession to make.

I have been keeping secrets, even from you, Dear Journal. Some things I just could not bring myself to write until I was certain. Well now I am certain and can tell you the particulars.

Since that day back in May, when my father died and my mother informed me of something I could not bring myself to confess, I found over the following days that my mind wandered of its own accord to the possibility of it.

At first I told myself I was being fanciful, but once I began seriously looking into the possibility of truth in her words, I found that investigating engaged a sense of purpose, which has helped me come to terms with my father's death.

In the beginning I was concerned my mother might discover, but I find that since carrying out this research and discovering the truth, I am less frightened of her than I was. I have realised she is never going to give me approval, she is never going to accept or approve anything I have to say or feel, and now I know why.

Finally after years of feeling like I was wicked, like I was a disappointment, like every wrong was my fault, I have been given the knowledge that there was nothing good I could ever have done to make her happy. Catherine hates me because she is my stepmother. I am the reminder that there was someone else in my father's life.

When I look now it is difficult to see how I could never have known the truth, my hair so thick, wild and untameable - a mass of curls. It is so unlike Catherine and Louisa's straight strawberry blond hair and pink complexion. Even my father had dark blond sandy coloured hair and green eyes. I am the odd one of the family and now I know the reason.

That day and her words haunt me. They replay over in my mind again and again. The woman I had always looked to for approval, told me she had always hated the very sight of me, that she had brought me up as her daughter to spite my own mother and to punish her for stealing Ashton, my father, from her in the first place. She had laughed in my face then and told me I was a failure the moment I was born, that I had killed my own mother and it was the one thing she thought I had ever done right in my entire life.

No amount of will could erase those words. They continue to replay. But somewhere inside a small bud began to bloom, one I had not known existed and I have been nurturing that little bud.

I began by considering my father's youth. He had been a society boy and went through a period where he was in the society pages at parties and events in London, sometimes there was a picture of a group of them, some even with Catherine in the early days. She was young and beautiful back then with long hair pinned up, her eyes wide, staring at Ashton devotedly.

Then the society pages were of him with his friends and the gentlemen from his club rather than Catherine. After searching for weeks through the society pages, where he would appear some weeks and not others, I began to discover a pattern with one particular name that kept appearing with my father.

Investigating further into this name, I learned that this gentleman was now a prominent barrister in London, his address available for all to view. So with nothing to lose, I wrote him and informed him my investigation.

Today with the early post as the birds sung and the sun shone rosy I received his reply in a tiny square envelope with his business address printed on the reverse. I have included his letter below:

My dear Elizabeth,

I must confess myself very surprised to hear from you my dear. I have not had contact with your family for many years now. However, I am very pleased that you did write to me my dear and would like to express my condolences as to your father's recent passing. Although I was not at the funeral, I paid my respects to my old friend in my own way.

I hope my dear that in writing and asking me your searching questions, you realise what a long buried history you are unearthing and I warn you Catherine will not make it pleasant for you if you were to unearth any of the secrets she has spent many years hiding.

The reason you do not know me personally is that I am not welcome at Leyac House any more and haven't been for many years. This was Catherine's doing not your father's. He remains blameless in my eyes in this matter.

Now, as to the further contents of this letter. I am going to lay bare the facts of the history of your father, mother, Catherine and myself. I hope you are not easily shocked my dear, as I intend to be blunt.

Ashton met Catherine in 1881 - she was 16 years old at the time. From the very beginning she marked Ashton as someone for her and in the beginning he was very taken with her. He asked his father if he could make a match of her but his father refused saying she was unsuitable and would bring nothing of value to the estate and their name.

You see, Catherine had been the daughter of an Earl, but when the Earl died, his son from his first marriage inherited the land, title and money. He subsequently disinherited Catherine and her mother. Ashton, from a titled family and heir to his father's estate, was an ideal target for her to regain what she had lost.

But old Lord Leyac saw through this and told his son point blank that he would never give consent. Catherine however was, even then, very determined.

As time went on, Ashton grew bored with her but kept her on maybe out of habit rather than anything else and, against my own advice, put her up in an apartment. It appeared that Catherine had decided to be content with being Ashton's mistress.

When Ashton's father died he took it pretty badly. However, things changed in 1889 when one evening at a party in London, Ashton met the very beautiful Eliza Victoria Fairfax. Her father had been some important military man and had spent many years in India. The family were now back to find Eliza a good husband.

From the very first moment the pair were besotted with each other. I have never seen two people more in love than Ashton and Eliza. Her family were more than pleased to marry her off to someone titled, so it seemed that everything would go right for Ashton.

But, when he told Catherine that their relationship was over she was completely outraged throwing things around the apartment and screaming that she wouldn't let him go. He told me he had to quickly duck out the door, but not before she had hit him in the head with a vase. I saw him afterwards and he did indeed have a cut on his head, so I do not believe this story was a falsehood. He was pretty offended by the experience. We had to go for a couple of strong whiskey's.

After the wedding and the news that they were expecting a child, everything seemed to be well for my friend. Then on that fateful night in 1891 a year following their marriage, Eliza died in childbirth. I know not the particulars, but I travelled straight up to see Ashton. He was a broken man. I couldn't get any sense out of him and he wouldn't see you. He said you looked too much like her and it hurt to look in your face.

I tried many times to coax him out of it but within a few weeks he had secretly married Catherine and she made it perfectly clear I was not welcome at the house any longer. Ashton was so broken over Eliza he let Catherine do what she wanted with the estate and every aspect of his life.

Over time people forgot about Eliza. She had been a part of the Leyac family for such a short time and seen rarely due to her pregnancy that it was easy to forget that there had ever been any other wife to Ashton than Catherine.

As to what happened between Catherine and Ashton following this or any other aspect of life at Leyac House, I cannot say. After I was made unwelcome I wrote to Ashton to let him know I would be in London in the usual haunts when he wanted to come back. He never did. I lost my friend the day Eliza died.

If you would like to meet me to discuss the above further, I am in London at the address marked on this letter. I would be very happy to see you my dear, and I wish you every happiness.

Regards and fond wishes,

Toby Blackwood

More than anything else, apart from explaining my family history, this letter informs me of something far more important. It tells why my father had been distant with me. Toby Blackwood says my father would not see me because I reminded him of Eliza.

And so with this new information I find myself stopping writing to idle once more at my view of the lush green fields and bright sunshine seemingly that much brighter today. On a whim I have just thrown open my window letting in all the glorious summer freshness, which now cascades down onto this page as I write. Today I almost feel free.

When I think back to that evening when my father died, when in his study he said to me "You are as beautiful as your mother," it was Eliza he was talking of not Catherine. Had he been trying at last to tell me, to make amends?

I will never know but I wish I had known and had been able to ask him of her. Now I know she existed, all I want to do is discover more about her, who she was, what she took pleasure in. I know not what Catherine's intentions were when she told me in that cruel way she was not my mother, but the reality is that it has given me freedom. I no longer blame myself for all the trouble I get into, for all the times I get shouted at. I am guilty of nothing more than being Eliza's daughter.

CHAPTER NINE

September 1940 ANNA

Anna's thoughts were so preoccupied with Elizabeth that the journey to Heathfield village, where Leyac House was situated, passed quickly. She was glad that there weren't any irritating stops along the way, as in the journey to Abbeyfleem village. She was surprised to see that Heathfield was, in fact, larger than she had imagined.

On the platform, people were milling around rushing past each other and a great number of uniforms from all services were hurrying on and off the train, kit bags slung over their shoulders and excitement in their eyes.

A teenage boy with a sandwich board and leaflets was trying to keep his balance as people knocked into his gangly frame. He was waving leaflets and shouting something that at first she couldn't make out. But as he came nearer to her carriage window, she heard his squeaky voice shouting;

"Heathfield. Home of the Leyac Estate and Gardens. See where the twin was taken and mourn for the loss of our local hero Lord Thomas Leyac."

She thought it interesting that they actually had leaflets printed for such a thing at such times when everything is precious, but maybe it was old stock, she reflected.

She thought about the diary entry she had just read. The coincidence that both she and Elizabeth were investigating didn't escape her. Elizabeth's words echoed Marcus' news article and Anna made a mental note to discuss his source with him when she returned to London - whenever that would be. It would be a bloody long time if she continued to avoid dealing with the funeral arrangements. She shook her head at herself. Picking up her jacket from the seat where she had discarded it, she left the compartment and stepped onto the platform.

Outside the station she looked up and, despite the fresh chill, the skies were blue with cloud puffs floating by. The big tree on the common in front of her was waving its golden and orange leaves as the wind rushed through it. Anna shivered. Autumn was definitely here and she buttoned her wool jacket to the top.

She wasn't sure what story she was chasing but couldn't help wondering how her mother, a commoner from London, had ended up with a diary from a long dead member of a wealthy family. Anna wondered if the new revelations that Eliza Leyac had been Elizabeth's mother meant that there would be nothing left of Elizabeth at Leyac House. If what Marcus had said in the article was true, that Catherine had been jealous of Eliza, and certainly what she had read of the diary corroborated this, maybe she would find nothing of either Eliza or Elizabeth at the house, but still it was the obvious place to begin.

Anna decided to start in the main village area. Most of

the activity seemed to be located in a central semicircle around the main green. Clearly the place was used to getting visitors and tourists as she passed little knick knack shops selling photographs of Leyac House and others selling an abundance of tourist souvenirs and a little further on, a cafe.

Peering through the taped up windows, she could see there were a number of people already in the little Victorian style tea room so Anna decided to go in. A bouncy girl with blond curls brought Anna a pot of tea gave a smile and bounced off to the next table. Sitting in a cafe often meant gleaning useful information from the conversations going on around her. She had, in the past, got some useful information on people and what was happening from this strategy. It was a good tactic as people tend to start clamming up when someone starts asking questions, especially now with the fear of invasion and spies. Today, everyone seemed to be avoiding discussing the one subject Anna wanted to hear about.

Today seemed one of those bad luck days and she had almost finished her entire pot of tea when three women and two men entered the cafe. Anna could tell they were local as they were dressed simply and in what Anna's London filter would call a 'country way'- the complete opposite to her own two piece suit. She supposed she should dress more conservatively now she was out of the city.

The group all sat together and Anna guessed they were all about middle 50s. About her mother's age she thought with a shock, as the realisation appeared without warning.

The men had on working clothes and Anna guessed they must either own local farms, or work on them. The three ladies had simple dresses, which looked quite out of style to Anna but which were smart, clean and appropriate.

"It's such a tragedy," said one lady shaking her head. "I just can't believe what's 'appened to that poor young man," she said.

"Well war has a habit of doing that to yer whether you be high born or low. In any case that family were cursed," said a second woman.

"Oh hush Alice, you're always preaching doom and gloom. They were just unlucky." The third woman folded her arms as she spoke.

"Well whether you call it unlucky or cursed, it's all the same thing. Even you, Eleanor Grey, can't deny that that family has had an accursed number of things happen to it. Children goin' missing and never seen again, people dyin'. Now the young Lord dead. All that family has been wiped out and if that's not a curse then I don't know what is," said the one called Alice, with a sniff at her two friends.

"Do you really think there could be a curse?" asked the first woman sounding a little awestruck.

The men in the group had until this point been ordering drinks. Now however, coming back to the table, they overheard this last remark. "What's cursed?" said the balding one taking a seat with a flop.

"Oh, Alice here thinks that the Leyacs were cursed and that's why they are all dead" The second lady, Eleanor Grey, almost laughed as she told the story.

"Oh you women," said the other man, "Yer can't be happy unless you're yapping. Yes 'ee's dead, yes it's sad but 'ee died serving his country. An honour. None of us knows who's gettin' the 'ouse. We'll have to wait an' see. You're as bad as those London papers for gossip. More importantly is how I'm ever goin' to plough that top field." He shook his head and wagged his finger at the women.

Their conversation then turned to other topics, which didn't interest Anna. She had heard enough anyway, so paid for her tea and left. Local gossip mongering was always going to find superstition in things and she hadn't learnt anything she didn't already know, but it had told her that the locals had no idea what would happen to the house any more than anyone else.

Outside, she stopped a young girl and an older woman, who looked as if she might be the girl's mother and asked them the way to Leyac House.

"Oh, it's that way, up the hill out the village and keep goin'. Turn left, it's a bit of a distance from the main town, but there's a horse pulled wagon over there that goes up regular like." The girl beamed at her enthusiastically pointing across the green towards the railway station.

Her mother nudged her and gave Anna a suspicious look. "Daisy, hush so. You shouldn't tell people these things. You don' know who they are. She could be a spy."

"I can assure you I am not a spy."

"Humph" said the woman, pulling her daughter by the arm and continuing on her way, the girl protesting that she didn't think Anna looked anything like a spy.

She laughed at the woman's suspicions and rushed over to where the wagon was waiting. It looked rickety and old, and she wasn't sure it was safe but got on anyway, along with some other people. Some of the men in the group looked suspiciously like reporters, but she didn't recognise them. The horse set off and Anna, not liking animals much, found the journey bumpy and uncomfortable. The twisty roads making it worse than she ever imagined.

Once the wagon arrived and she paid her entrance, she walked along the driveway. The house was concealed by an arched tunnel of trees. Light sprinkled down in bursts, but once through the trees a walled entrance and gates led to the main, brick built house.

The house was nothing like she had imagined. Where she had imagined a gothic castle, this was in fact much more sedate. It had matching twin towers on either side of the rectangular building, with matching bow windows on each tower. The main door in the centre nestled behind a circular garden and cobbled driveway.

The walls around the edge of the front circular garden had recessed oval shapes, at head height, spaced along the entire length. Inside each recess were busts. These were duplicated along the house above each window. The place was calm and still, except for the creaking of trees in the wind and the odd bird tweeting somewhere behind her. Where she had imagined a gloomy, imposing building, she was surprised that instead it was in fact, such a peaceful place.

Anna took the first opportunity to separate from the other passengers in her group and instead of going in the house, went towards a small gate, almost hidden, in the walled area to the right. She crossed over a courtyard, walked past the side entrance and through the gate opposite, which led into the main gardens at the rear of the house.

The rear facade was flat-fronted apart from two miniature versions of the bowed window towers at the front. Following the garden paths, Anna made her way to the top left corner, where iron fencing marked the area of family tombs. A large crypt lay in the centre containing all the previous Leyac Lords. All except one she thought. The rest of the family members had individual graves.

She began wandering through the headstones, some old and worn with fading words, some more recent with names she recognised. Finally, at the end, under the overhanging of an ancient creaking, weeping willow tree was a tiny headstone marking the grave of Elizabeth. She would have missed it if the wind hadn't blown away the branches of the willow tree.

"So there you are, "she said in the stillness of the place, except for the rustling of the trees. It was almost as if she was being watched by the gravestones.

It made Elizabeth more real somehow, to see her place of rest. However after a further search, Anna did find it interesting that there was no grave belonging to Eliza. This suggested that the diary entries and Marcus' article, which said that Catherine had been jealous of Eliza, was in fact true. The little she had read of the diary, certainly corroborated this. She thought of the beginning entry where Catherine tells her of her true parentage in such a cruel way. No that wasn't the actions of someone rational. Yes she was grieving, but Elizabeth had described her as enjoying it. Only someone with a deep sense of hatred and jealousy would do such a thing.

She wandered back towards the house and retraced her steps to the main entrance. A young girl dressed in black was welcoming visitors, so Anna asked if she knew what was going to happen to the house now. The girl tilted her head slightly.

"Might be we'll all be out of a job."

The main hallway in which Anna was now stood extended left from the front door. On the wall opposite there was a large cast iron black fireplace with a marble surround and ornate scrolls. Looking above she could see there was a large oval shape cut out of the ceiling to show the room above.

It was odd to be in the place where Elizabeth had been, where she had spent her life; this mysterious girl whose life, so far as she was reading, was parallel to Anna's in many ways.

She went towards the impressive staircase which was very ornate and had large baskets of fruit carved onto each corner post as it went up and turned to the upper floors. The balustrades had carved depictions of war, swords, shields, armour and other such details, all intricately worked in minute detail. Anna had never seen such elaborate workmanship on what should simply be a functional thing.

Her heeled shoes echoed on the wooden floor as she walked. The wall of the stairs, from bottom top, was lined with portraits and paintings of scenes. On the first floor, the staircase behind led up still further, but this part of the house was excluded from the tour by a roped private sign strung across the stairs.

Turning to the room on the left, she read the sign.

The bedchamber of Louisa Leyac up until her death in 1935. This room is where Lord Thomas and his brother were born.

The room itself was nothing out of the ordinary for a family such as this. A large four poster bed dominated the room, twin windows with matching heavy curtains were tied back with thick, heavy rope ties.

The wallpaper was blue flowered and the room had pictures of Louisa, mostly in London from what she could make out, at parties and posing outside of theatres. In all, she was wearing her elegant white dresses for which she had been famous. The text on the wall next to the pictures told her how Louisa was very much a fashion icon of her day, always in white in the latest style. She was often talked about in the press relating to her dress and what new style she was sporting that season. Louisa, it said, had been happily married to her husband and they had waited a while before having children. She wandered across the hall to the room opposite. This, said the sign, was the nursery from where Lord Thomas' brother had been stolen. The room was still decorated as such with an old fashioned cot in the centre. The walls were covered in stories, clippings and other information about the hunt for the missing twin. Anna peered at a tiny photograph of the beautiful Louisa Leyac in an easy chair relaxing, all dressed in white, with a wide eyed stunned look on her face. Her two babies by her side in a cradle. They are not clearly visible but the tops of two fuzzy heads can be seen in the picture. Anna studied the text next to the photograph.

This picture was taken by a reporter, who seeing his opportune moment, took an unauthorised picture of Louisa and her newborn twins. No one knew at the time this photo would become the only photograph in existence of the twins together with their mother, as only hours

**after this was taken, one of them would be
stolen.**

Anna was very impressed that the plucky reporter had
been able to steal into a house like this and get a picture
of this magnitude and get away with it, inside the house,
no less.

She took notes in her notebook on some of the
clippings, names of people Lord Thomas had talked to,
had help from, bits of information to pass on to her editor.
However, all of it was common knowledge so she moved
on. She went through the third door, which led to the
round gallery. This was directly above the hallway and the
large oval cut out floor in the centre looked down to the
black and white tiles below. The entire length of one side
of the room was lined with windows, directly opposite was
lined with portraits. Anna looked into the eyes of the
family staring back at her, frozen in their scene. The
current, recently deceased, Lord Thomas' portrait was
young with an intense, determined look about the eyes.
His hair had been tamed into a side parting and looked as
if it had a mild wave. There was another of Louisa. She
really had been beautiful, big blue eyes and golden blond
hair with an ever so slight hint of red. She looked wide
eyed and serene, but Anna detected a hint of stubbornness
behind that serene countenance. Lady Catherine and
Lord Ashton's portraits stood alongside each other. His
portrait had been done when he was young and depicted
him in fine late Victorian clothes, looking masculine and
strong, his fair hair wavy. Catherine's portrait showed a
woman in her mid 20s. You could see the resemblance
between her and Louisa, but she didn't have Louisa's

beauty. The features were similar but on Louisa they were just enhanced somehow. Catherine's eyes had a look of superior satisfaction in them.

There was no portrait of Elizabeth and the text on the stand said that there had never been one commissioned due to her illness and early death. Anna was disappointed, but not surprised, however she had still hoped to set eyes on the girl whose diary she was now reading.

She moved on. The sign told her the next room was the North Drawing Room and was used by the family to entertain guests. This must have been the room where Elizabeth met Lord Moorlass, on the morning her father died. The room contained a large red patterned rug, virtually the size of the room, some of the red fading to pink due to its age. The walls had great tapestry pictures hung from floor to ceiling, all the way around depicting different scenes of people working in the countryside. Anna didn't stop to read any of the information, she wasn't interested in the furniture or its history

The next room was the long gallery, which she remembered Elizabeth saying how much she hated the portraits. Dark wood panels down both sides of the long room gave it a gloomy appearance. This gloom was relieved by matching windows at either end. Anna glanced at the portraits, but found the faces to be intriguing, full of character with lines of life creasing their expressions. What stories could these faces tell through the lines mapped out on the canvas? She didn't at all find them how Elizabeth had described them. To her they were the faces that stretched back to endless lives and interesting stories. However, she reluctantly moved on. None of this was relevant to her own investigation.

She skipped through the rest of the rooms briefly, none of them were really relevant to her. She noted the things Elizabeth had described about Catherine's rooms. They were indeed the grandest in the house. And she noted the library, which Elizabeth had said was her favourite room but was surprised at how much smaller it was than she had imagined. Really, it was the top floor she needed to see, the section of the house that had been Elizabeth's room.

But she also needed to remember that her editor was expecting her to ask about what would happen to the house and the investigation into the missing twin now that Lord Thomas was dead. He wasn't expecting anything at all on Elizabeth Leyac. However, Anna was far more interested in that, than anything else and couldn't resist going back to the staircase and pretending to examine the portrait at the top of the stairs, while she waited for a brief moment alone. After a while, the visitors close by had moved on and she could hear that some others were still downstairs, so she quickly slipped off her shoes and carrying them in one hand, lifted the rope with its 'private' sign and dashed up the stairs to the next floor. Up here it was dark and the rooms immediately to the left and right were locked. She went down the long corridor. This corridor was dark, with doors on either side, all the way along to the end where, in the distance was a window with its curtains drawn, adding to the gloom. Each of the doors she tried were locked, except one. She could tell this one was a man's room. Men's shaving equipment and fragrance stood on the drawers. It wasn't ornately dressed like the rooms downstairs and had a modern feel, with modern blankets on the bed. Anna wondered if this had been Thomas' room. She left and went further down the corridor.

"Just what do you think you are doing up here? This area is private and is not open to the public."

She turned to find a man about five years older than herself standing with arms folded glaring at her. His hair was slicked back and he had a thin face and pointed nose. His grim expression made him look pinched.

"You. You're a reporter aren't you?"

"Yes, I was just…"

"I knew it. I know what you people are like." He marched her down both flights of stairs by the arm. "Tell me, what did you expect to find up here?"

"Nothing." She decided not to give away her real reason for being here. "Who are you?" she said as they continued down the hall towards the door.

"I am Mr Julien Flynn, Estate Manager of Leyac House and long time friend of Lord Thomas Leyac. So, you see, I have the right to escort you off my property."

"Could you tell me, Mr Flynn, what will happen to the house, and the search for the missing twin now that Lord Thomas has died?"

"Nothing is finalised yet. And even if it was, why would I tell someone who would rather trespass on my property than come and ask plainly for an interview."

"Would you have granted an interview?"

"No I most certainly would not have. Not to you in any case. Just what are you doing here Miss Forrester?"

"I am here to talk to you, to find out what your plans are for the house and the search. The public would like to know what will happen to Leyac House now. Will you remain open, as you have today?"

"Like I said, nothing is finalised yet." He looked at her suspiciously. "Are you certain that is the only reason you are here?"

"Yes of course. Look, I am sorry about trespassing, I thought there might be some information about your future plans up there."

He looked at her through narrowed eyes. They had reached the main entrance at the top of the driveway now.

"Leave, please Miss Forrester. And do not return here. You are not welcome, no matter what capacity you come in, or claim to come in. Do not pursue this, there is nothing here to find." He began to walk away.

"So you will not give me a quotation for my article?"

He turned around on his heel then and came close to her face holding her arm tightly. "I warn you. I am not someone to be crossed. You stay away. Do you understand. I have lost enough. I will not have the likes of you coming and upsetting everything."

"All right, I understand. I am going," she said.

He nodded and strode away. She watched him march away agitated. Gosh he really doesn't like journalists that man, or maybe it was just the ones who trespass on private property. She wondered if she would have been able to get any information from him had he not caught her trespassing.

She put her shoes back on and began to walk away but turned to look at the top of the house again. It would seem that Leyac House wanted to hold on to its secrets a little longer.

CHAPTER TEN

September 1940 ANNA

Anna rang her editor from Heathfield railway station and reported that she hadn't gleaned any new information. He wasn't surprised, but still sounded a little disappointed. He was however, amused when she told him how she had been thrown off the premises for trespassing in the private quarters.

She left Heathfield that afternoon determined to put the Leyacs' and Elizabeth to the back of her mind. She was really going to have to start to get the funeral organised and decide what to do with her mother's possessions.

The task of going through it all would be difficult enough and she could do without the distraction of the Leyac family, if she was to have any hope of ever getting it done and getting back to London where she belonged. She really couldn't avoid it any longer. And maybe her mother had some other clue about Elizabeth amongst her things. There had been very little mention of her at Leyac House other than to say that she had been Thomas' Aunt and had died before he was born.

And other than Marcus' report and the few pages she had read of the diary, she knew little and less of Elizabeth, let alone how her mother had come to be in possession of the little fat book.

The following morning she woke with a sense of trepidation at the task ahead. And in hope of putting it off a little longer, went to the kitchen to make a pot of tea.

She poured the tea through the strainer into her cup slowly, trying to make time stop. Sighing she nursed the chipped teacup with the blue flower design her mother had loved. Out of the front window, the country road wound into the distance from her mother's front garden and the rising mound of the field opposite drifted further still into fields of farm land. Right at the top she could see tiny white blobs dawdling along the hillside.

She shivered. She was definitely not a country girl. In determination she set her cup down in its saucer with a bang more forceful than she had intended and swallowed the urge to avoid the task ahead. There would be no avoidance today. She felt more ready than ever to tackle this cottage.

Just as she was wondering where to begin, while looking over the large bookshelf with stacks of books piled high, pushed into every available space, Mrs Baxter popped her head round the door. "How did it go at the big 'ouse up the way?"

"Terrible. And, I've decided that I'm going to get on with things today. All this 'gallivanting' as you put it, isn't going to bring my mother back. So, let's just get on with it. What do you think Mary?"

"Oh, I'm glad. I knew yer just needed to come to terms with it. I don't mind saying that I've been proper worried, yer would never get things sorted, and your poor ma would never get buried."

For once, she was glad Mrs Baxter wanted to stay and help. She could not only get through the task quicker but would be far less likely to have an emotional episode with another person around. Anna, as always, was most afraid of letting her emotions get the better of her.

So she set Mrs Baxter to clearing the kitchen of everything surplus to requirements except for a few essentials while she was staying at the cottage.

When the daylight from the window began to change and she realised they had been clearing and sorting all day, she was surprised at how little they had managed to get done. How much stuff did mother have?

Mrs Baxter heated up the pie she had brought for Anna before leaving to go home. "Now yer will be all right on your own tomorrow won't yer? I can't come and help out tomorrow, yer know how it is."

She nodded, not really understanding 'how it is' but smiled at Mrs Baxter all the same. "I will be fine Mrs Baxter, thank you for your help today."

Mrs Baxter smiled a satisfied smile and patted her arm. Shutting the door she felt a sense of relief to be alone again. She was surprised at how easy sorting out all the things had been. If she concentrated on the mundaneness of the task and removed herself emotionally from it, treating it as an exercise in spring cleaning, she found the task much easier to deal with and began to make good progress.

She went to her mother's wardrobe and opened the door, all her clothes were neatly lined up. Surprisingly she had collected a good deal of clothes, much more than Anna had known. She wasn't sure what she wanted to do with them yet. Throwing them away would be unthinkable, but there were probably a few she could get made into more modern dresses for herself and some could go to somewhere in need. She closed the door and went and sat on the bed. She didn't want to think about the clothes yet.

Then she remembered her mother had always kept a box of her most precious things under the bed. On impulse Anna reached underneath and pulled out the big dusty trunk with all their memories inside.

The trunk was one her mother had kept for years. In her childhood Anna remembered it being used as a suitcase on one of their numerous journeys.

Brushing the dust away from the worn leather case, she unlocked the front catch and opened the lid of the now battered trunk. Inside were piles and piles of letters, pictures and trinkets. She picked up a pile of old crumpled pages on the right hand side. Some were pictures she had drawn as a child. One was a picture of herself, her mother and a sunshine alongside the words 'to mama' on the top in childish handwriting. The two little stick figures had huge smiles and lopsided features. She smiled and put it aside.

There were piles of letters in her own handwriting, all the letters she had ever written to her mother from London. Anna couldn't believe her mother had kept so many letters. She stacked them all together beside her on the floor.

Next she spied a small tissue wrapped shape in the corner. It turned out to be the pile of seashells she had collected on one of their trips to the seaside when she was a girl. Anna remembered the trip well. It was one of their great little holidays and Anna had meticulously collected the seashells, discarding the damaged or ugly ones, only collecting the very best. She had presented them to her mother saying that they were very precious and must be kept in a special place. She laughed at the memory.

She put the pile of seashells with the letters and delved further into the trunk. There were a few things she had not seen before. Some strange old trinkets and an ornament of a girl with some ducks. Right at the bottom of the trunk was a black folder. She picked up the folder and opened it. Inside were a lot of newspaper clippings. She lined them up on the bed. Every one was something to do with the Leyac family; messages about deaths many years ago, Lord Ashton Leyac's, Elizabeth's, Catherine's, and even Eliza's. Anna scrutinised the Eliza death notice. It was very small.

This was before the twin mystery had made the family a household name, so hadn't got much coverage. There were other news articles. The opening of Leyac House to the public, Thomas Leyac's various adventures and the search for his brother.

It seemed her mother had an interest in the mystery. Why hadn't she shared her interest? Maybe she had given her the diary so she could finish the investigation.

She closed the file and put it with the clippings on the bed to investigate thoroughly later. She reached for another bundle of letters, and as she did she heard a pinging of metal. She caught a flash of something shiny and she followed the object as it rolled along the bare floorboards pinging as it did.

Once it settled, she reached for it. It was a ring. The ring was a delicate golden band with a single large ruby at the top clasped in golden fingers and inlaid with delicate tiny diamonds. Anna had never seen a more beautiful ring and had no idea where her mother had got something so lovely. She had never seen her wear it. It was small and would only fit on her ring finger. She put it on. It glittered and she admired it for a few moments until she realised that the ring looked like an engagement ring. She went cold at the thought of an engagement ring on her finger and took it off almost throwing the beautiful ring back in the trunk, shuddering as she did.

CHAPTER ELEVEN

September 1940 ANNA

It took a few days to go through the cottage and get rid of her mother's possessions. During the process she managed to get out into the village and meet some of the local people. Most were kind and said how much they had liked her mother. Only one woman with tight lips and a thin face looked at her with disapproval. Mrs Baxter told Anna later that she was Mrs Lynn and disliked everyone. She had begun to find that the villagers were very nosey. Being used to the city where everyone went about their own business, she was not used to such behaviour. Mrs Baxter assured her it was only because they never got new people in the village and that her mother had talked about her such a lot.

She was beginning to feel like she was getting to know country life but some things would always seem strange. She still chuckled when she thought how Mr Baxter had told her he was in a Pig club, which apparently meant that he and the others in the club were raising a pig. Anna thought it very strange indeed, but it apparently was normal behaviour here in the countryside. Alongside this she had discovered that the local farmer was someone everyone was nice too, in the hopes of a few extras no doubt. Most people kept chickens and grew their own vegetables, a concept wholly alien to her. She had no idea what to do with a garden. In the city a garden was a luxury, so she left her mother's vegetables to Mr Baxter. She also thought it strange how much the villagers seemed to know, or suspect about each other. Even Mrs Baxter, who suspected that the Post Mistress was steaming open her letters! However, Anna thought she looked a jolly nice woman.

Then there were the other things: the young lad she'd seen smoking behind the post office who had disappeared when Anna saw him. This had been strangely comforting - despite their oddities, these people were just like everyone else. However, these brief breaks from the clearing didn't make her feel rested and once most things were gone, other than a few sticks of furniture for Anna to use while she remained in the village, she felt thoroughly exhausted. She had found the clothing the hardest to deal with. Each item reminding her of her mother, memory snatches that she cherished but which also left her with an emptiness. However, she kept a few pieces, which she thought could be made into more modern styles and the rest she parcelled up and donated. She had sorted through the rest of the collection in her mother's chest and had resigned herself to the fact that keeping everything was impossible. In the end she only kept Elizabeth's letter, her mother's newspaper clippings, a few sentimental trinkets and the ring, although she hardly knew why she had kept the ring. It still made her shudder when she thought of how it looked on her finger. She shut that away firmly out of sight.

Everything was organised for the funeral now, but Anna was trying not to think about it. Clearing the cottage would be nothing to that. Mrs Baxter had organised the wake and Anna was grateful for one less thing to do. The more Anna got to know the old lady, the more she was warming to her, despite her bossiness and stubborn attitude that her way was the only proper way. Anna knew she had relied heavily on her and she was quietly grateful. Today however, there was little for her to do so, being frightened of the thoughts that sitting still would bring, she donned some appropriate footwear saved from her mother's stash of winter shoes and went for a walk.

She wrapped her warm coat around her as the wind whipped around the fields and followed her as she walked. The mildly warmer climate of London still had the last warmth of summer when she had left, but here it felt like autumn had arrived early.

She stepped over the little white picket fence around the tiny grass area that separated the cottage from the lane. Turning right she headed down the winding road. There were no road signs of course but after a few false starts she had thankfully learnt the way around the area.

She strolled round the bends and twists, up and down hills and gentle inclines. Her mother would have called it beautiful. She remembered a letter from her mother who had described how the autumn leaves were falling, the gold and orange raining of crisp leaves. That must have been last year she thought.

But Anna didn't see the beauty. She thought the

branches twisty and gnarly, the wind blowy and the leaves messy. As she got nearer the main village, the trees on either side had grown to meet in the middle, forming an arched tunnel. Her mother had described it as being like intertwined lovers, but Anna thought the trees looked as if they were locked in a battle of wills. It reminded her of the similar arch of trees on the way to Leyac House.

The main village began with a row of stone cottages with bowed, warped windows and low door frames. In the centre of the village, outside the shop, there was a young woman with blond curls and rosy cheeks in a Land Army uniform.

"Hello there Miss. Have you thought about joining the Land Army?" She handed Anna a leaflet. "We need to keep ol' England on its feet and we can't do that if our Farmers aren't getting help. Free up the boys and help win the war."

The girl had clearly been practising the speech and looked very proud of herself.

"I'm sorry, I can't, but if I was able to join any service, yours would be top of my list."

The girl beamed at her and Anna felt better about the lie.

"So what do you do then miss?"

"I'm a journalist from London."

"Oh. Are you the one whose mother has just died? I heard about you. You write for some fancy newspaper in London. Ooh, what's it like?"

"It seems everyone knows who I am." Anna said ignoring the last question.

"Oh sorry, I'm Betty. I'm a land girl up at the farm." The girl smiled widely at Anna. "You simply must come dancing with us, one day. The other girls would love to hear all about London. I've always wanted to go."

"Yes we must do that one day. Maybe when I'm not burying my mother." Anna smiled back before she left the girl and crossed the road.

Passing the local pub, she went in on impulse. This was something she often did in London. People tended to let themselves go a bit more in the pub. It was a great place for picking up information for a story, but today she just wanted to look at different walls.

The pub was traditional looking with old fashioned furniture and an open fire at one side. The barman looked at her suspiciously but didn't say anything as he served her a drink. She sat at the far side of the bar away from the old men propping it up at the opposite end. They paid no attention to her.

She sighed at herself swirling her finger around the rim of her glass. She was beginning to feel as if she was drowning one minute and flying the next. It was difficult to know what to make of her own feelings. She was most upset that everything she had thought of the world, the precise order she had created for herself seemed so far away, broken in little pieces and she didn't know how to put them back together.

Anna had been so lost in her thoughts, staring at her glass that she hadn't noticed anyone was behind her until she heard someone speak.

"Excuse me Miss, but you're in my seat"

Irritated at being interrupted from her contemplations by such a silly remark, she gave the young man with sandy hair a look of disdain.

"I'm sorry sir, but this seat was vacant when I arrived

and there was no indication it was taken." She replied with every attempt at mock politeness she could muster.

"No miss, you see, us regulars we have our own seats and you're in mine."

"Well as you can see, I'm not a regular and had no idea, nor have I any intention of moving. There is a pub full of empty seats. Why is this one so important? This is likely the only time I will ever be here and you can have your seat any time you wish."

"I am sorry miss, I didn't mean to offend you, it's just a village tradition that's all."

"Oh for goodness sake, go and do something useful will you. Join the Army, fight for your country instead of sitting in this God forsaken village arguing over bloody seats. Do you know what?" She stood up and downed the rest of her drink before slamming the glass down hard on the polished counter. "You can have your seat." She stormed out of the pub and back up the road.

Damn him. Who was he to interrupt her over something so silly? She knew she had been exceptionally hard on the young man, but he was being so petty she couldn't abide listening to insignificant arguments when her mother was dead and her life seemed to be in pieces.

She was so wrapped up in her thoughts she made it back to her mother's cottage in what seemed like half the time it took to go the opposite way. The walk hadn't worn off her anger though so she decided to tackle her neglected laundry. She was in just the mood for scrubbing. She turned the wireless on loud and vented her frustrations out on her clothing, scrubbing them more forcefully than necessary as the wireless played that blasted nightingale song.

"Damn it," she said to the empty kitchen but left the wireless on anyway.

She didn't hear the knock at the door, nor the person enter until she heard a voice behind her.

"Hello there Miss Forrester, I'm Dr Laker. I was your mother's doctor throughout her illness. I wanted to…"

She turned around elbows soaked with suds and her hair all floppy and damp to face the young man from the pub. "You?"

"Yes, I suspected it was you in the pub just now, but you ran off so quickly I hardly had time to say," he said.

"Just what are you doing in my mother's house. I don't believe it is customary to walk in without invitation."

"I did knock but there was no answer. As I said, I was your mother's doctor throughout her illness and wanted to come around in person to offer my condolences and answer any questions personally. And to apologise for the delay, I've had an urgent case to deal with. I would also like to explain about our encounter just now."

"There is nothing to explain. You clearly are the rudest, most impolite man I have ever had the displeasure to meet. I wish you to leave."

"I think you have misunderstood me. I didn't mean anything by the incident in the pub, I am sorry you have taken offence, but I was trying to meet you."

"Meet me. Well I don't know what is customary up here, but in London we tend to say hello and are polite to people. You are clearly devoid of all propriety." She couldn't stop the rage inside her, she really disliked this man and she didn't care whether she was being fair.

"All right, I can see this is a bad time and you are

clearly busy. I did hope you might be interested in hearing the things I wanted to say about your mother. But I suppose, you were too busy to visit then, you're probably too busy to hear about it now." He looked back at her, shrugged dismissively and went towards the door.

She stood at the sink for a few minutes before following. "Just wait one moment, just what are you suggesting? That I didn't care for my mother because I was in London?"

The doctor turned around as Anna's hands dripped water and suds on the lounge floor of the cottage.

"I must keep an air of professionalism. I have said too much already. You, for some reason appear to bring out the worst in me," he said.

"That doesn't answer my question."

"I'd rather not say, Miss Forrester if its all the same to you."

"Actually, no it's not all the same to me, I want to know your meaning?" Anna said.

He ran his hands through his hair and down towards his neck, closing his eyes briefly. "I must apologise, this is no way to treat a grieving relative of one of my patients and my respect for your mother meant I came around in person to speak to her daughter and tell her that I thought her mother was a truly gracious lady who didn't get what she deserved. I was fond of her, hence why I am here. Is there anything you would like to know about your mother's case?"

"No I believe not," she said in defiance. Folding her arms.

The doctor's face hardened and he clenched his jaw.

"Fine then, Miss Forrester I will leave you to your soap

suds."

The doctor put the envelope he was carrying on the side table and turned to leave.

Anna sighed, as she watched him leave, she didn't know why this doctor made her so angry, but he did have information about her mother. Of course she wanted to know what he had to say. Swallowing her pride, she called after him.

"I'm sorry, doctor, of course I would like to hear what you have to say. Can you forgive me and come back inside?"

He hesitated, looking at her. "I can make us some dinner and you can tell me all you know," she said putting on her false smile so that he relented.

Once he had given her what she needed, she would never have to see him again. She decided to treat the situation as if she were conducting an interview with someone for a story. Anna watched him walk towards the window and look out, his arms folded. She must try to keep her temper, she thought watching his back rise and fall as he breathed. It was very unlike her to be so angry.

Anna made him some tea while she finished off her laundry. To her relief, he was happy to sit in the lounge area away from her while she finished off.

Once her laundry had been hung out on her mother's garden washing line, she busied herself beginning dinner. One of her best meals, probably because it was easy to do and not too taxing for Anna's limited cooking skills, was stew. Just chopping up ingredients and throwing them in was great as far as Anna was concerned. Once the stew was cooking, Anna was just about to go into the lounge and sit down when the door knocked. The doctor was letting in Mr Baxter when she entered the room.

"Why doctor, what a surprise it is t'see yer here. Yer are not ill are yer Anna?" Mr Baxter looked anxiously at Anna. She smiled and shook her head. Mr Baxter looked relieved but looked from the doctor to Anna and back again. "Oh," he said, "Oh I see now," his colour rising. He stammered and shuffled one foot.

Anna began to protest that it was nothing like that, as did the doctor but Mr Baxter wasn't listening.

"Oh I almost forgot, our Essie's having the baby so the Mrs won't be seeing yer for a bit. She said that if yer need anything yer are to let me know, but I can see the good doctor has it all taken care of."

Mr Baxter went red again and quickly left the cottage in a hurry of stammers and almost tripping over in his embarrassment.

The doctor watched Mr Baxter disappear up the road. "It'll be all round Abbeyfleem we're an item once he tells his wife."

"Oh surely not. Mr and Mrs Baxter are lovely, but who is Essie?" she asked watching Mr Baxter disappear up the lane over the doctor's shoulder.

"Yes but they do love to gossip. And Essie is their daughter, did they not tell you?" he said.

"No they didn't, but then I didn't ask. I knew they had a son." She paused thoughtfully. "What shall we do about it?" she continued.

"About what?" he asked turning to face her.

"About the gossiping."

"Oh" he said turning back to the window. "Not a thing, let the villagers have their fun. You and I both know that we are the most unlikely couple that could ever be. I mean it's simply laughable."

Anna agreed, the notion was ludicrous. Changing the subject she told him that dinner would be an hour.

"I hope you like casserole. It's likely the only decent thing I can actually make."

"Why does that not surprise me, but yes I thank you. I enjoy the lovely winter taste of a casserole in autumn."

She couldn't quite tell if the comment was meant to offend her or not, but she kept her tongue, wanting to get the whole process finished with as soon as possible. Why had she invited him for dinner?

He had attempted to tame his hair into a side parting but there was a stubborn bit at the back that was sticking up. She studied his face. His green eyes were dark, and in some lights could be mistaken as being darker than they were. They had a strange intensity about them, which Anna thought gave him a cold look. She didn't like him. He sent a chill down her back and she found him opinionated. Again she wondered what on earth had possessed her to ask him to stay for dinner. She could have just apologised and got the information without offering to feed him, but then possibly he would have remained stubborn and left anyway. He seemed the type. Whichever way, he was the most unprofessional and arrogant man she had ever met and she knew a lot of those.

"Maybe while the food is cooking we should discuss your mother?" he said after a silence.

She sat down on the sofa and waved a hand towards the opposite chair for him to sit also in acknowledgment of his suggestion. "Well as I've never seen you before today I would guess you didn't often visit your mother so have little idea of the nature of her illness."

She bit the backlash of comments that came to mind in reply to that dig at her. He was clearly one of those men who had specific ideas about what women should do. She suspected that living alone in London while your mother was ill wasn't one of them.

He continued, fiddling with the small fraying edge of the chair as he spoke.

"She came to see me about some pain and discomfort, Without going into details of everything we did, we ran tests and discovered she was suffering from a specific kind of cancer. In the beginning we attempted to treat the cancer, which made your mother extremely sick, so I took a personal interest in her case and made it my business to check on her progress. However, the treatment was soon stopped - at your mother's request as it was having little effect and was causing her great distress. I attempted to dissuade her from this decision, but she was firm in her insistence. I had thought that this would be the time her daughter, and only relative, would come to nurse her in the last few months of her life. However, she remained alone so I took care of everything she needed. She became a great friend to me in our short acquaintance and she didn't deserve the end she got."

He looked at her for a reaction. She was in shock. Why had her mother not told her she was so ill?

"Your mother was an amazing woman and you can do nothing but sit there in silence when faced with your guilt and neglect of her in her final months. I posted letters to you myself, so why, can you explain why a daughter can neglect her mother in such a despicable manner and then have the audacity to show up right at the end just to get rid of the stuff and get back to her own life as quickly as possible. What sort of woman are you?"

"How dare you presume to claim knowledge of me or my relationship with my mother. You have no right to judge me after a few months of knowing her. Even if what you say were true it would be of no concern of yours as our relationship answers to no one and certainly not an opinionated person such as yourself. I was unaware that my mother was ill, and believe me those letters contained nothing whatsoever about being ill in the way you have just described. She was a very secretive woman. There are a lot of things about her even I have never known. Do not presume to know or understand my family. You neither have the knowledge nor the right."

She left the room and went to the kitchen to stir the casserole. Damn the man, she thought stirring furiously. She went outside and sat on the chair facing the garden and looked out to the fields stretching out before her. She was seriously thinking of taking up smoking. It was supposed to be a great calmer for the nerves.

A great friend to my mother? Why would she want him as a friend? He's a complete idiot. Anna shook her head. No she couldn't see her mother getting to know this doctor.

Anna was very good at portraying indifference when actually she was in pieces inside and this was one of those instances. So that once the food was ready, she went back to the doctor with steaming plates and found him scrutinising the newspaper clippings from the folder she had found in her mother's trunk.

He looked up startled. "I'm sorry."

She wasn't sure if the sorry was for what he said or that he had been snooping, and to be honest she didn't really care so just ignored the remark.

"I didn't realise you weren't aware and should never have judged you," he said in a gentle tone.

She was keen to get off this topic. She pointed at the article he'd been reading. "Find anything interesting?"

He at least had the decency to look slightly ashamed.

"I'm sorry, it was just there... I take it that you're interested in the mystery?" He waved his hand to indicate the rest of the Leyac stories.

"Actually those are my mother's."

The surprise on the doctor's face was genuine. "She didn't strike me as the type to be interested in silly old tales."

"Me neither, but theres a lot I'm learning about my mother that I didn't know."

"Really?" the doctor asked "It's such a story of conspiracy. It's simply there to make people interested in the family and make them money to prop up their money pit of a house. You can't surely think there's anything in this do you?"

"Well my mother did, or she seemed to, from the things she collected. I mean she's got some stuff here I would bet are very rare. According to the article by a colleague of mine, Catherine, Thomas Leyac's Grandmother, was Lord Ashton Leyac's second wife. His first wife was actually Elizabeth's mother and died in childbirth. However, with the young Lord Thomas dead a few days ago, I went to the house to see what would happen but they weren't very forthcoming."

The doctor was surprised and mildly interested but he still dismissed the idea as such a silly story.

"But, if mother was interested in it, I want to find out

more. It's what she wanted me to do I'm sure of it. Breaking something this big and this famous could make me." Anna hadn't even spoken the words to herself before she found herself telling the doctor, but she realised that it would do exactly that. No more cleaning and laundry articles if she broke this one.

"Maybe she wanted to give you a mystery to investigate that seemed impossible to solve, to take your mind off losing her and keep you doing what you clearly are very good at," he said, distracting her from her thoughts.

"And what is that?" Anna wasn't sure if he was trying to insult her again.

"Being a reporter of course."

Once the doctor left and she had cleared away the pots, her discussion of the Leyacs made her think of Elizabeth's diary again. Being so busy with the cottage recently, she hadn't picked it up for a few days and she wondered whether now was a good time to begin again.

She liked having this as her little secret and wasn't sure why she hadn't told the doctor of the diary, but she felt it was the right thing to do for the moment. In fact she was pretty angry at herself for the things she had revealed to him. She was usually very guarded.

Now a little more used to the peace and darkness outside, she made herself comfortable and poked at the fire a little before opening the book, skipping forward about a month from the last entry she had read. One day she would read it properly, but it was so long and she was too impatient.

She waited for the familiar crack of the leather.

CHAPTER TWELVE
September 1908 ELIZABETH

My hair is my sole curse. It has wild dark, thick untameable curls that thrust up in all directions. It refuses to lie precisely in fashionable styles like my sister Louisa's.

However, I detest it a fraction less than usual this morning. Yesterday, while roaming through the treasure trove that is the attics of Leyac House, in search of clues, old pictures, letters, anything to aid my investigation, I arrived upon a large flat wrapping which appeared as if it could be a portrait of some kind, tied with knotted binds and partially hidden at the rearmost corner of the large attic behind an ancient dresser, a dismantled chair and various items of furniture. I relocated the dismantled chair with its wobbly legs and succeeded in pushing the dresser with my weight using my hip to push. It was most undignified. It shifted with a rather loud screech of protest, but did provide enough room for me to move behind and withdraw the large wrapped frame. The package was at least as large as my person and heavy, I could only move the thing by an ungainly drag across the floor. Slowly I managed to remove it from behind the dresser and lean it against a wall. I was most curious as it was the only one amongst a further stack of pictures laid together, that was wrapped with tied up knots of twine. It was most dusty. I untied the tight old knots, which ripped at my fingers in their protest at being unbound. I shall have to hide their state from Catherine. They really do look like a common scullery maid's hands. Brushing away the cobwebs with a shudder, I withdrew the layers of paper wrappings surrounding the frame. Once the picture was free, there gazing out at me was a china doll-like face, with vast dark eyes and a mass of wild dark hair - my hair. At the bottom a miniature gold engraved square informed me that the portrait was Lady Eliza Leyac.

I situated myself on the floor before the portrait in amongst the dusty boards, my dress filthy and dusty. I cared not. Here was my mother. It was the first time I had looked on her face. I recognised the curve of my own eyes and the form of her chin, but it was the unmistakable hair. The mass of hair, hers was thrusting out of her attempt to create a neat style and the artist had captured that familiar wildness perfectly. I wondered whether she had viewed it as a curse as I did.

I wrapped the portrait in its coverings once more and placed an old screen in front to conceal it. To think that all these years she had been sat there is unfathomable.

I confess, Dear Journal, to being unable to stop myself smiling secretly when I think of my discovery yesterday. But now I must tear myself from this window seat and my usual view, for I must finish dressing for breakfast. Until later, Dear Journal.

I am back from my breakfast with the most startling of news. I have received the most interesting of correspondence, but before I tell it I will discuss the particulars leading up to the letter arriving.

It was early when I went into the dining room and the morning light had not yet fully risen through the tall doors that opened to the gardens. I glanced up to the sky, that I had just moments before viewed from my own window, and saw grey clouds floating across the skyline, blocking out the sunrise. It looked like rain again.

I seated myself in my usual place with my back to the window and one of the staff in his starched uniform and rather neat haircut quietly came up behind me and poured tea into the teacup set by my place. Other than him, I was alone in the room. I listened to the silence and thought how pleasant it was to enjoy breakfast in peace without the family. I am seriously considering getting up early far more often to enjoy the quiet stillness of the morning. Because of this peacefulness, I took my time eating, it would be a while before any of the others joined me.

A young footman entered with letters on a silver tray and held the tray toward me. I took the pile of little squares and he waited half bent for me to return the ones that were not marked for my attention. A few for Catherine, one for Louisa from a London postmark. She had a large number of friends in the city and travelled often for parties. There was one for me in an unfamiliar hand. My heart leapt, I had been waiting on just such a correspondence.

I placed the remaining letters on the tray and the footman retreated. My letter was a small square envelope in a plain simple hand. It was a rather fat letter and the envelope bore a West Country postmark.

I knew who it was from before even reading the contents. I have written to the elderly woman who had been housekeeper here for many years before Catherine became my mother. I had only half expected a reply due to her probable advanced age.

So in anticipation I abandoned the remainder of my breakfast, replaced the teacup I had been holding in its saucer and rushed upstairs feeling the weight of the small, fat, rough paper between my finger and thumb as I hurried.

Now here I am, Dear Journal, having read the letter. Here is what it said:

Miss Elizabeth Leyac,

I was surprised to receive your letter. You must forgive me, my eyesight is failing in my old age, so my niece is writing the words as I dictate them. She has a good hand.

Anyway, as to the business you wrote me of. I remember clearly the time you are referring to and the incident which has led to your enquiry. Let me first address that.

The reason you cannot find anyone who knew your mother on your staff, or anyone who knows the staff who were there when your mother was mistress is because Lady Catherine dismissed all Leyac staff a few days after arriving at the estate.

No one knew she was coming and we weren't told by the master he was marrying. She just arrived one day and things changed.

Many of the staff had been with the family for some years - I, and some others, had been there since Lord Ashton's father had been master of the estate. The gardner, Glover I think his name was, had got the position from his own father, who had been gardner at Leyac House before him.

None of this made no matter to Lady Catherine, she sacked the entire staff one morning. I remember the day clearly, it was less than a month after Mistress Eliza had sadly died.

The morning it happened we had a new girl in the kitchen, who cook was training up. She was a jittery girl and kept dropping things. Cook was beside herself and had come to discuss the girl's future with me. We were contemplating the issue when Lady Catherine came down to speak to me. I remember it clearly as she had never struck me as one who would come downstairs and I was stunned at what she could want.

She looked at myself and cook coldly, with distaste and told me to have all the staff brought up to the long gallery, as she had an announcement to make. She then made it clear that she really did mean every member of staff who worked at the house from ourselves right down to the scullery maid.

Unsure what to say I told her I would do as she asked, but Cook had some bread needing her attention and asked to be excused, but she wouldn't hear of it, just said everyone had to come.

We both agreed to her request. She was determined and seemed someone not to get on the wrong side of. Half an hour later, Cook and I had gathered everyone in the long gallery with some difficulty.

Some of the young ones and the ones who didn't venture upstairs were awed by the sight of the house and chatted excitedly amongst themselves over the portraits and the furniture. We looked an unusual bunch, some in uniform for working upstairs, some in outside gardening and groom's clothes, some of the kitchen maids were dirty from cleaning and blacking up. We didn't look presentable and I was worried the new mistress would be annoyed at everyone's appearance. If only I had known then.

Shortly, Lady Catherine walked in from the green closet on the right and stood in front of the bowed window seat area facing us. As soon as she entered, everyone stopped talking and stood a little straighter facing her. She could control people with a single look that woman. Anyway, she stood staring at us all for a moment narrowing her eyes greedily as if she was enjoying the moment, before she began to speak. I will never forget the words she said then. She said we were there for one reason only and that some of us will no doubt be unhappy with what she had to say but we must know that it is necessary. She continued by saying that the following morning a workforce replacement was arriving at 8am to replace the entire Leyac Household and we were to all leave that very day without exception. She said she had written us all a good reference and included a week's wages in lieu of notice. She also said, as if she were being generous to us all, that she had included a little extra to get us to London or wherever there were jobs but I knew it was bribe money. We were only to get this money and reference on condition we were gone from the village by morning or we would face arrest.

There were sharp intakes of breath across the whole room at these words. I can still hear them now. I could tell from her face that she was serious and having heard of her past dealings, I knew she wasn't someone to be crossed.

Mutterings of disbelief went round the staff as they stood staring at her. A few were brave enough to question her, but it was to no avail, she just enjoyed being the cat with its mouse in her trap. She didn't care that some of the staff had lived in the village for years.

She put on a face of sympathy, but I could see through that sympathy. Her eyes showed the truth, there she couldn't lie. There was a silence of disbelief across the gallery then, so she took up the little basket of letters from behind her on the window seat and began calling out names.

The first name looked around at his companions next to him and the realisation was mirrored on their faces that was written on his own. He meekly went to collect his letter and when he did, the entire staff knew they had lost before they had even had chance to fight. As he took his letter and walked away, she told us we were not to disturb Lord Ashton with this news. But I doubt he would have cared. He was far to grief stricken over Eliza and I knew Catherine was fooling herself if she thought he would love her. I saw how he had looked at Eliza. A man doesn't look at every woman that way. I was old enough to realise what she didn't, that the Master would never be the husband to her that he was to Eliza and no amount of staff sacking would change that.

Her eyes glowed with a strange greedy pleasure but she didn't like the sympathy she found in my own. Her smiles didn't fool me.

I left the house that evening and travelled to the West Country where I stayed with my brother and his family. I have remained here ever since. I lost the stomach for service that day.

However, I have replied to you, Miss Elizabeth, out of respect for your dear dead mother. She wasn't like the rest. She was different. I can only hope that you inherited some of her and that Catherine didn't ruin you with her decayed and twisted poison.

I am sorry if this shocks you Elizabeth, but I am too old and too angry, even now, to have any sort of respect for that woman.

I wish you every happiness and good fortune in your life,

Kind regards,

Josephine Hill

The correspondence was not at all the sort I had expected and I confess to having read it through a number of times before I could quite believe it. The old housekeeper, all the staff, all removed from service at once. Why would Catherine do such a ludicrous thing? It explained the reason I had never found anyone who remembered my mother or who worked here before, or even anyone who knew the staff who had worked here. The more I had attempted to find out, the more it appeared no one remembered an Eliza Leyac, but she did exist. I had discovered the portrait that proves it undoubtedly.

It was one of those happy chances, when I was at the library in York searching for information through old newspapers, that I discovered an article about a summer open day at Leyac House in 1896, which mentioned the housekeeper by name. This allowed me to find the woman after a few false trails, so I wrote her and asked if she had been housekeeper at Leyac House before Catherine was mistress.

Initially my enquiry into old members of staff was to discover information about Eliza, but the longer I searched the more I found it extremely mysterious that there was no one who had worked here before I was born, not a single elderly staff member, but now I had the answer as to why that was. It appeared Catherine had not even wanted the staff to remember Eliza. It seems she had attempted to erase my mother from existence.

If it had not been for her mistake, her outburst that day, I would never have known she was not my mother and would have continued in my belief that all my troubles were my own doing.

Catherine has done me a good turn informing me of the truth. Just see, Dear Journal, what I have already achieved. What more could I possibly discover with more work?

CHAPTER THIRTEEN
October 1940 ANNA

The morning of the funeral came all too quickly and Anna couldn't avoid thinking about it any longer. Opening her eyes, the first thing that greeted her when she woke was the black dress hanging on the door of the wardrobe.

Her heart lurched. She didn't want to get up. Why had it come so quickly? She turned over and pulled the blanket over her head in a vain attempt to protect herself.

She heard the front door open and Mrs Baxter shout upstairs.

Does that woman get up before dawn?

Forcing herself out of bed, she pulled back the blackout curtains, the daylight making her squint. It looked a windy day and falling leaves were blowing around in billows. Further still, trees were swaying on the hill. The sky was dotted with white puffs of cloud, but on the horizon, there was a black cloud.

She closed the curtain just as Mrs Baxter knocked on her bedroom door and opened it a crack.

"Are yer up Anna dear?" Seeing that she was, she came

in with a steaming cup of tea. "Here yer are. Just what yer need to get yer through today. How are yer feelin'?"

She sat on the edge of the bed again and sipped at the steaming liquid the old woman handed her.

"I'm all right," she said, wondering if it were true or if it was just the thing to say.

"Well no matter, I'm here and so will Arthur be in his own way. And, I'm sure the good doctor will make sure yer are all right."

Mrs Baxter gave her a sly look but she ignored it. Today everything seemed insignificant. Everything was unimportant. How could she get through it? How could she face all those people and keep it together. Damn why was it so hard?

She dressed in a trance and felt as if her head were underwater, as if she were watching the world through a watery glass bubble, so much so that as she sat down in front of the mirror to do her hair, she was almost surprised to see that she was dressed.

She applied her usual auxiliary red lipstick, a habit which had lapsed recently. Taking a few minutes to study her reflection, she noted how she looked pale and that the blood red of her lips lifted the dreary black she was wearing, which all but washed her out.

Once she had finished putting up her hair, she pulled out her black heeled shoes that she only wore in London now she had learnt that country folk didn't dress up, unless there was a reason. Today however, it was important to look perfect for her mother's sake.

Anna stood at the bedroom door for a few moments, holding the cool, firm door knob in her hand, feeling its smoothness and the ridges where the screws fitted. She was wasting time. She knew as soon as she went downstairs it would be real. Here, alone, she could almost pretend that today wasn't happening, that none of this was real.

She closed her eyes, held her breath and took a step forward and quickly descended trying to hold her nerve.

Mrs Baxter handed her a bowl of something hot and gloopy, in a chipped round bowl. It didn't look appetising but this, she suspected was due to the feeling of rocks in her stomach rather than Mrs Baxter's cooking. She spooned some into her mouth and the taste of watery glue told her it was porridge. With an effort she swallowed and looked down at the remaining contents of the bowl stirring it absently, watching as the gloopy mixture moved slowly around the bowl.

She looked up when she heard her name mentioned and seemed to notice for the first time that there was a number of people in the cottage. Where had they come from?

Mrs Baxter was in the kitchen chatting with another lady Anna recognised as Mrs Long, a member of the local WI. Mr Baxter and another gentleman were in the garden examining her mother's vegetable patch, which Mr Baxter had tended. There were a few other people going in and out from the lounge to the kitchen, some she had met or been introduced to, others she didn't know. Everyone was wearing the same black uniform as she and a girl of around 14 was ushering in and out of the kitchen with tea cups. She placed one in front of Anna at the dining table as she absently continued to stir her porridge. She only registered the movement at the back of her mind so that when Anna realised the girl had given her tea, she had already walked away. Her faint "Thank you" echoed in the empty space the girl had occupied, her own southern accent jarring against her ears like it had that first day.

All too soon someone was bringing her coat and helping her into it. She had refused any kind of funeral procession through Abeyfleem village. For mother it was wrong. She would never have liked that and Anna couldn't, when she thought of all the men fighting and all those dying in the bombing back in London, have something like that. The coffin was to be brought directly to the church and she and the rest of her mother's friends would meet them there.

Outside the wind was still blowing and it blew at Anna's hat. She held it to stop it moving. Some people began the walk towards the main village through the snaking roads that led there.

Anna was bundled by someone into a car, maybe more than one someone, she didn't really notice. Mrs Baxter was in the back, she thought without turning to see. Yes it was definitely her. She was chatting in a strained, high pitched way. Trying to lighten the mood she supposed.

It was only as the car started that she noticed the driver was the doctor. She considered getting out, but couldn't in all honesty fight anyone today, so instead sat there watching the leaves blowing, billowing around as they drove, feeling the smooth cool of the leather seats, icy and strange beneath her touch, the faint smell of disinfectant reminding her of that blasted hospital.

She felt a kind of strange gratitude to these almost strangers, this small community who had done nothing but help her since she arrived. Mrs Baxter had adopted her as a kind of daughter and Anna, although unable to say so, was immeasurably grateful. It was a strange feeling. She had never had people like this before and it was something she hadn't even realised was missing in her life. She wasn't sure whether to like it, or hate it.

Outside the church a number of people were standing around waiting below the swaying trees and the floating orange and gold leaves that were falling.

The small church was a delicate thing with a spire and a curved side entrance like a picture from a Christmas card. Many people stared at her as she walked up the little pathway supported on one side by someone, the doctor again, she realised. Someone else was sniffing close behind her.

They stood for a few moments and when the coffin arrived, many people went inside and took their seats in the church. She turned then and saw that it was Mrs Baxter who was sniffing. She looked away the cold making her face feel frozen in a single blank expression.

The men who had volunteered to carry the coffin included Mr Baxter, the local publican, the tall youth who helped run errands for people and a few men from the local home guard.

Still, they all walked straight and stiffly as they carried the coffin, she noted, as if they had been in the military and had done this many times before. It reminded her of her mother's words in the letter that she was glad she wasn't facing another war - a war in which she had seen her generation broken. Anna wondered, following, as they walked bearing the coffin, what horrors these men had seen in that war; how many of their friends they had buried; how many coffins had they carried for them, like they did now for her mother.

As they entered, music began to play, a melodic tune she had heard her mother hum many times. She seemed to wake up then and come to herself all of a sudden. This was real. She stopped walking for a few moments, and the doctor next to her whispered. "It's all right, hold onto my arm."

She did so, although in her head she really wanted to tell him to go away but the words wouldn't come, so instead she concentrated all her effort on each foot walking one before the other.

Taking her seat at the front next to Mrs Baxter, the doctor on her other side, she felt slightly claustrophobic and comforted at the same time. The priest began to open and close his mouth, but she had no idea what words he was saying. Even as she looked at his face, it was as if he spoke in a foreign tongue.

By the time the service was finished and they were again lifting the coffin to leave the church, she felt a mixture of relief, that it was over and guilt that she couldn't remember any of it. The funeral procession went out to the back of the church yard where the grave site was already waiting. People gathered around the hole as the coffin was lowered into it with long wide straps while the priest continued to speak prayers. Anna stood at the end and was first to throw soil into the grave. She picked up the cold damp earth and threw it onto the casket, making a light thud as it landed. Others followed suit but she began to walk away. They would not see her cry. They would not. Good Bye Mother. She quickened her pace.

* * *

As she moved around to the front of the church she noticed a man ahead of her also leaving. She thought it strange because she didn't recognise him. Even from this distance she could see his suit was fine and well tailored, but it was more than that. He looked out of place here in this sleepy village, his hat pulled firmly down, his shoes shiny and black.

She called to him, he stopped but didn't turn.

"Who are you?" she said. "Did you know my mother?"

Without turning the man began to walk off again, this time at a faster pace. She followed but by the time she reached the covered wooden gate that marked the entrance to the church, he had gone.

Strange. She thought.

She continued on to the hall where the wake had been organised. She wanted to be first there. Mrs Baxter had organised everything and she had no idea what to expect. She thought it wise to make sure everything was ready. Plus a little walk alone was a welcome relief. The dark clouds had firmly planted themselves overhead now and the day was almost like evening. She felt a few faint plops of rain.

As she entered the little hall, Mrs Baxter and the other WI ladies looked up surprised.

"Why Anna, yer a little early?" one lady said over her half moon spectacles.

"Oh I left before everyone else," she replied looking around the room. Between the ladies they had managed to put on a buffet with much more food than she had expected.

"How ever did you get all this food?" she asked disbelieving.

"Well everyone hereabouts chipped in. We've all been making things for yer. Everyone wanted to make sure yer mother got a good send off." Mrs Baxter patted her on the arm. "Well now you sit, here have a drink of this. I reckon yer need it, but don't tell anyone. It's strictly for medicinal."

She handed Anna a small, old, battered hip flask that she had produced from her handbag. She took a swig of the strong smelling liquid and it burned her throat, making her cough. She was certainly not new to alcohol but didn't often drink it that strong. Still it wasn't long before the liquid gave her a fuzzy, numb feeling.

By the time everyone had started to arrive from the church, she was able to quite gracefully, with the help of the detached numb feeling from the alcohol, greet them at the door. She particularly thanked the men who had carried the coffin. She also, despite her inner sick feeling at the thought of it, thanked the doctor. He had been good to her today and even if she didn't want to admit it to him, she had needed the support he provided.

"You are welcome Anna, I was happy to be there. Like I said before, your mother was a special person to me. But, I can't stay long," he said examining his watch." I've got a patient to visit in a little while so, it's back to work for me. But the service was good and Mrs Baxter has clearly done a great job with the food." He smiled and moved towards the table.

The rest of the day passed in a strange dream and later as the last few guests left the church hall and headed to the pub, she began the laborious task of cleaning up.

"You coming across to the pub Anna?" a few people asked her.

She said she would but needed to finish tidying first. They left saying they would see her there.

Mrs Baxter had remained behind and was currently packaging up the food to take home.

Anna began to sweep the floor with the brush from the cupboard at the back of the hall, where she also found a mop and bucket. She had promised that the hall would be left clean and tidy after the wake and she thought it was a good trade for the use of the place.

So, quietly cleaning the floor, she had the first opportunity to reflect on the day. It was supposed to have been about saying goodbye, but had she really said goodbye? Running through the events only intensified her headache. She was sure it was the alcohol Mrs Baxter had given her.

Mrs Baxter finished clearing the food and had packaged a small pile of things for Anna to take back to the cottage to eat before she had even half finished the floor.

"There are a few little things there for yer tea, I must dash now. Mr Baxter will be expecting his tea. There's nothing left to do once you've finished with that floor. Will yer be all right?"

"Yes, I'll be fine, thank you for all your help. I'm meeting some of the others in the pub."

Mrs Baxter smiled a satisfied smile and patted her arm, nodded and left. She was glad of the silence and continued the task of sweeping and mopping the large expanse of the hall. Once completed she locked the hall and turned away with a last look down towards the church pathway that led to the small plot in which her mother was now buried.

She looked over at the pub and hesitated. She was

suddenly very tired and now that she thought of it, she just wanted to go home, have a hot cup of tea and go to bed.

So, as Abbeyfleem village receded behind her, she strode back towards her mother's cottage in the fading light, thinking about how everything was done and she could now go back to London. But strangely, it didn't seem as appealing as it once had.

CHAPTER FOURTEEN
October 1940 ANNA

By the time she had begun her ascent up the final hill that led to her mother's cottage it was fully dark and with the blackout, there was little to let her know if she was walking along the side of the road, or the middle.

She still hadn't got used to the blackness of the countryside. It was intense somehow, like the inside of a black void surrounding her. Here the blackness was darker, thicker, deeper, just more of it, or maybe it was the openness of the space. In London there were buildings to find your way in the darkness. Here there was nothing but black, empty air. The blackness only intensified the brightness of the stars, and tonight's clear sky allowed them to shine brightly, like the sparkles on the ring she had found. The cool damp air smelt of wet leaves and grass and a faint smell of animals, and something else she couldn't quite describe.

A mixture of wet and dry leaves squelched and crunched beneath her feet, but as she moved beyond the trees, the leaves thinned and she could once again hear the click, click, click of her heels. Her feet were beginning to hurt and she was looking forward to taking off her shoes.

As she walked the familiar feeling of being followed returned. She turned to look and saw nothing but darkness. She ignored the prickling on her neck and her own rapid breathing. This was not a new feeling and it always turned out to be nothing. Perhaps it's just the darkness she told herself.

She stopped. The silence was broken only by leaves swirling, the wind blowing and whistling gently through the bushes. She held her breath. What was that? She imagined footsteps behind her, faint, quiet. Short, quick tapping steps, like a distant drum beating, becoming louder with each tap; low heavy taps of something wide and flat, like a man's shoe, but quick and fast as if someone was running.

The tapping increased to where she was certain it wasn't her imagination. The footsteps were just behind now, closer than ever. She stood squinting down the lane into the blackness but couldn't see beyond her imagination. Maybe she had forgotten something. She waited, then called out a greeting.

A dark shape formed and for a moment Anna thought it was going to run right past her, but instead it ran up to her wrapped one vice like arm around the front of her waist and another around her neck and held her tight.

The figure smelt of musk and sweat and had a rough stubbly face. He leaned in next to her ear. His voice deep and raspy, his breath fast from running.

"Little girls like you shouldn't be out at night alone in the dark."

Anna struggled against his grip but the more she struggled the more he squeezed, his thick meat-like arm becoming tighter around her neck, so she stopped when the world began to spin.

The man took his arm from around her neck and grabbed at her handbag. She took the opportunity to hit out at him with her elbow and managed to make contact just below the ribcage. She heard him grunt. His grip loosened, but with one giant shove from his large paw he sent her falling and then ran off into the darkness with her handbag. Anna sat on the road listening to the sound of his footsteps growing fainter.

Anna was left on the rough, damp muddy ground with the cold wind wrapping around her and claw like branches grasping above her.

She could feel her stockings were torn and the pain shooting round her right knee told her she had hurt it badly when she fell. A wet stickiness trickled down the other leg and when Anna wiped it, the soreness told her that this probably wasn't just wet mud from the damp ground.

Her dress seemed to be very loose at the skirt and as she felt the area she could feel lose threads of a giant tear. Her jacket too, was ripped at the arms from when she had put out her arms to save her falling into a bush.

She staggered to her feet and tried to hobble along the road but the pain that shot up through her knee meant she could barely stand. Hopping was extremely difficult and Anna was beginning to think that she would be there all night when she heard the engine of a car coming towards her.

Anna stood in a position where she thought she might

be able to attract the attention of the driver. She waved her arms frantically at the car as it drove past. The car carried on past and Anna shouted "Stop, STOP, you bloody fool."

Anna heard a squeal of brakes and the noise of the engine changed abruptly as the car reversed towards her. The window was wound down and Anna peered into the darkness at the shape of the driver.

"I'm sorry, can you help me. I've just been attacked. I need to get home?"

"Anna?"

She peered closely at the driver and recognised the doctor. Her heart sank. Of all the people, it had to be him. She cursed whatever God there may be for sending him of all people to rescue her. She was just wondering if she could make it to the cottage without his help after all, when he got out of the car and moved quickly towards her, steadying her as she hobbled on one foot. With his slender, but strong arm, warm against the cold air, he helped her move round to the passenger side of the car.

"Good grief Anna how did this happen?" he said with a note of disbelief.

She felt the anger return again and paused for a moment putting one hand on the warm car bonnet. "Well it's not like I invited someone to come along, take my handbag and shove me into the bushes whilst he was at it. I thought the countryside was safer than the city. This has never happened to me in London. I am in the country for less than two weeks and I'm attacked."

"Well that's as maybe, but I'm beginning to wonder if you have a knack for getting into trouble. I'll take you back to the cottage and take a look at your injuries."

"No, I am fine doctor I just need dropping off."

"Miss Forrester, you may not like me very much and I can assure you the feeling is mutual, but I am a doctor and I will not leave a patient in such a state."

She did not protest any further, not because she didn't want to but because frustratingly, she knew he was right. Not that I will allow him to know that of course, she thought, looking at his profile in the darkness. The smell of iodine, wax and oil mixed with a faint smell of carbolic soap inside the car made Anna gag and took her thoughts right back to the hospital again.

The car vibrated as the engine started, humming a low sound and adding a smell of fuel to the mixture. She began to feel claustrophobic as Doctor Laker turned his car around in the dark narrow lane. There was a faint clunk as branches hit the back of the car. He cursed under his breath, and jammed at the gear stick in a fit of temper, which vanished as quickly as it came. He spoke in his annoyingly calm voice.

"You were very lucky I was along here. I was paying a house call to a patient recently discharged from hospital. I am almost never out at this time along this road unless there is an emergency somewhere."

"It seems I must thank you again today doctor." Twice in one day she had had to rely on this blasted man. Damn it all. She thought as the car juddered up the dark lane.

The doctor pulled what looked like a smile, or was it a grimace? She couldn't see properly in the blackness. He had one of his arms at the top of the steering wheel lazily holding on while the other was resting on his lap his hand holding the edges of the base of the wheel.

Anna felt the smooth leather of the seat beneath her

with one hand and how its coolness gradually warmed.

The car squealed as it came to a stop outside the cottage. The doctor got out and rushed to her side. Her attempt at getting out before he got there was hindered by the pain in her knee. Without a word, he lifted her expertly under the arms to a standing position. She leaned on him heavily. Her knee was beginning to throb, a pulse of pain shooting up, affecting her ability to protest. She was thankful that she had kept to the tradition of storing a key under the plant pot, so that, even with the loss of her handbag, she could still get in to the cottage.

The doctor opened the door with one hand, as someone used to juggling things. He shuffled with her through the door and into the sitting room, helping her on to the sofa and sat her down, gently placing her leg out straight, propped up on a nearby cushion.

"I'll be back in a minute, my bag is in the car. I'll just get it and we'll have a look at that leg."

He disappeared outside and came back with his black medical bag. He set it down on the floor.

"I'll just sort out your blackouts so we can have a bit of light," he said already doing so.

"Really there's no need I can manage." She protested at his familiarity with the cottage.

"I need light with which to see, Miss Forrester. How else would I be able to take a look at you?" There was a tone of irritation in his voice.

Anna really hated being indebted to people and today she had had enough of having to thank this man. Why was he so helpful?

Once the light was on and he had lit the fire, a warm

burning smell filled the room and made it much more comfortable. She watched the fire pop and crackle for a few moments before she removed her jacket, and saw that it was in fact, not in pieces as she had thought, but that a few of the seams were torn. There was a rip along the left sleeve which she was sure was salvageable. Her dress however had a huge tear down the side where she had fallen and she was certain that any repairs would make it all the more obvious. The dress was ruined.

The doctor disappeared into the kitchen and Anna heard the clattering of cupboards and running water before he came back with a bowl of water, which he set gently on the floor beside him. Peering down at Anna's knee he frowned and opened his bag.

"We will need to remove your stockings, so that I can clean the wounds properly and get a good look at the knee."

Anna struggled to lift the skirt of her dress with some embarrassment as she tried to reach for the top of her stockings and unhook them. Struggling for a few moments because of the pain the movement caused, she eventually gave up admitting defeat.

"You will have to help me. Every time I move it sends a shooting pain down my leg."

"Oh, ah, all right, are you sure?" he said stammering a little.

"Yes I'm sure, why is that a problem?"

His face betrayed how uncomfortable he was with this. Was this man not a doctor? Did he not do this every day? She watched his face change as he toyed with the idea.

"No no, nothing like that." he said quietly.

He looked at Anna for a few minutes and then frowned,

cleared his throat and set his face in a mask of clinical and professional indifference. Gently he reached for the edge of Anna's torn skirt and slowly raised it as she wriggled to help him. His fingers were warm and soft and Anna ignored the strange feeling she was getting at his touch. She hated this man. She became aware of how much the sofa arm was digging into her back.

Once her skirt was out of the way, Anna easily unhooked the stocking top. The doctor took the top of the stocking lightly brushing his fingers against hers as he began to roll it down in an impeccably slow and gentle way; it was a practised motion. She watched him as he did so, through the silence, broken only by the popping and crackling of the fire. He seemed oblivious to her gaze, a small lock of hair falling down into his face as he repeated the same movement on the other leg which, although not hurting, showed a large gash down the shin.

The doctor discarded the stockings and frowned again while concentrating on Anna's injuries, his face close enough for her to feel his cool breath on her legs. His forehead creased as he rummaged in his bag with one hand and rubbed his temple with the other.

She glared at him. Why was he irritating her so much? This man, this irritating doctor. She hated him more than she had ever hated anyone and it wasn't just his arrogance either. It was more than that, but something that Anna couldn't put into words.

He irritated her with every little thing he did. The way he ran his hands through his hair, the way he muttered under his breath when he was thinking, the frowning as he concentrated. What is it about you, she thought as she watched him work? His warm fingers and hands continued gently feeling around her knee, his face still frowning in concentration.

Damn, she was annoyed for allowing herself to become indebted to him. But then, she hadn't been given the choice. She had been bundled into the car that morning without being asked, he had held her arm as they followed the coffin into the church without asking, and he was again being helpful now.

God, why all this kindness? Anna didn't know what to say, and the fact that she knew she needed his professional help right then irritated her more.

She rubbed her hand up and down the bumpy fabric of the sofa in an attempt to distract herself from her own thoughts, concentrating on the rising and falling of the bumps underneath her fingertips as she gently ran them over the sofa back in a similar motion to what the doctor was doing with her knee.

He sat up straight suddenly and looked at Anna directly, declaring in his usual calm way that she had a knee sprain before getting up. He went off to the kitchen and came back with cold damp cloths which he put around the knee.

"This should help with the swelling," he told her as he worked methodically.

He then began cleaning the scratches and the large gash, which stung as he dabbed at it with a cold clinical iodine solution, his hand gently holding hers as he cleaned the wounds around her hand and wrist.

Once all her minor wounds were treated, he stood up and folding his arms. He frowned down at her. "Well Miss Forrester, I think you will be staying in Yorkshire for a little while longer. You need to rest that leg and you can't go rushing round London with an injury like that. No, you are staying put while your knee heals. Doctor's orders."

"Rest? You can't be serious. I have to get back to my job. If I don't go soon I won't have one to go back to at all," she said looking up at him, not liking the change in eye level. It made her feel as if she was back at school.

"The fact is, your knee is injured and you must rest it if you want it to get better any time soon. I understand you want to get back to London, but your knee has other ideas." He grinned, which exasperated Anna more.

She sighed and leaned her head to the side on the back of the sofa, its bumpy fabric pressing into her head a little. This was all she needed after today. It was bad enough burying your mother without this to end the day.

"We need to report this to the Police," he continued. "It's very unusual for this kind of thing to happen here. I'll drive over there and get someone out to see you. They'll probably want a list of things that are missing and a description of the attacker. Will you be all right for a little while, while I go to the Police Station?"

"Yes," she said in a defiant way. "And why wouldn't I be?"

"Don't worry, I'll be back shortly, I won't leave you alone long. I'll be ten minutes at the most."

"Doctor, I am perfectly capable of being alone. I do not need you to treat me like a child. You needn't bother coming back. Don't let me trouble you any further. Thank you for your help. And don't forget to prepare your bill and send it over tomorrow."

"Nonsense, Anna, you can barely walk." He laughed then as he went out and slammed the front door of the cottage, not allowing her to reply. She listened to his footsteps receding down the pathway towards the car.

Anna pictured him getting in as she heard the car door open and close, and the engine start then he turned the car around to drive towards the village.

Anna became aware of the deep silence in the cottage. She listened as the sound of the car engine grew fainter and fainter until she could no longer hear it, and all that was left was the silence of the cottage and the darkness outside, the flames jumping and the fire popping and crackling.

Looking around the cottage, she began to wonder whether her attacker could have been watching her and the doctor and followed them. Even though her rational mind told her to stop being such a little fool, she couldn't help wondering what if he was outside now. She was alone completely. In London her boarding house was full of people, her street was full of people and houses. There were people everywhere. Here there was no one. It was a good walk back to the main village, to her nearest neighbour. This cottage was isolated, surrounded by fields and hills. The attacker could just walk in and there was no one to come and rescue her. Her hearing heightened and her heart pounded. She listened as she thought of those meat-like arms around her neck.

Leaves were rustling and made a clicking noise as they tumbled along the road outside in the wind. Or was it footsteps? The door to the cottage creaked and rattled and sounded as if someone was trying to come in. Anna's heart began to bang as she considered the possibility that, in her incapacitated state, if he did come in, she couldn't do anything to defend herself.

When the noise of an engine and squeaking brakes told her the doctor had come back, Anna's heart was pounding

Sara Thomson

in her ears and she found it hard to catch her breath. What if it wasn't the doctor?

A wave of relief poured over her when the doctor came through the door, pulling off his hat and running his hands through his hair, making it stick up in part. He stopped and looked. Relief must have showed plainly on her face because he came rushing over.

"Anna are you all right, you're as white as a sheet?"

"Yes, I'm quite all right thank you," she said primly not wanting him to know how foolish she felt or how relieved she was in seeing him again. She began to fiddle with the bumps on the back of the sofa again to avoid looking at him.

"Oh Anna, I'm sorry, it's perfectly normal for you to feel like this. You've had a terrible shock. It's my fault. I should have called out that it was me."

Anna felt that familiar anger again rise up inside. Damn she was so sick today, she couldn't stop it spilling over and once opened she couldn't stop it.

"Feel like what exactly? And just who are you to tell me how to feel. What would you know of any of it? And why are you being so helpful? What are you after? I don't need you or anyone." She paused as emotions spilled out. "I've just buried my mother. I need to go to London," she said her voice rising. She couldn't help herself and despite her best effort to stop it, the tears began to fall for the first time that day. "Damn it, damn you, damn everyone," she raged through her tears.

Without a word the Doctor sat next to her on the edge of the sofa and leaned in, putting his arms around her and holding her in silence for a few minutes. Anna let him, closing her eyes and breathing in the smell of fresh musk

144

mixed with damp rain, Brylcreem and a faint odour of sterilisation.

"I will stay with you here in the cottage tonight so you can be sure you are safe from harm and that the attacker won't come back," he said, his voice muffled in to her hair, his breath hot on her neck as he spoke.

Anna pulled away from his embrace to look up at his face, her eyes feeling hot and swollen, her face wet. She was about to tell him he was not welcome, when she noticed that his green eyes looked darker almost grey in the dim light. Unusual, she thought, distracted from the protest that had been forming inside her.

He was looking down at her with a strange expression on his face that she couldn't read, his breath warm as he breathed in and out.

Reaching up, he gently brushed the tears from her cheek with the warmth of his thumb.

Anna watched him, silent and unmoving. She wanted to hate him.

He leaned forward slowly gazing at her. She watched, right up to the moment when he closed his eyes and his warm soft mouth gently pressed against her lips. A feeling of electricity ran through her body, like a channel that seemed to wake her from a long, dead sleep.

She shut her eyes instinctively, but he pulled away and her mouth felt cold where his had been a moment before. She felt the loss of his kiss but looked up into his face for his reaction.

He put his hand to the bridge of his nose and screwed up his eyes. "I'm sorry, I took advantage of you, it was completely unprofessional of me and I can't comprehend what came over me." He took his hand away then and stood up suddenly, pacing around the room. "I never do this kind of thing, never, never ever. It's completely unprofessional." He said again putting his hand to his forehead. He sighed again then. "This never happens to me, I mean... who would do such a thing." He sighed again. "I'm sorry" he repeated looking directly into her eyes for the first time.

Anna was attempting to make sense of it in her own mind and trying to decide if this changed her feelings towards him, so sat in silence for a few moments, before realising that he was expecting her to speak.

"I probably should have..." she paused not knowing what to say.

He nodded in some kind of acknowledgement. "I should leave." He said.

Anna felt a wrench of panic swell up inside her. She wasn't sure if it was that she didn't want him to leave, or if she just didn't want to be alone.

"Please don't leave" she heard herself say and rolled her eyes inwardly at how pathetic she sounded. Damn you weak fool she told herself.

"Are you sure?" he said.

"I don't care about what happened, I just don't want to be alone, what if the attacker comes back?" She said in a panic to say anything so he wouldn't leave her alone.

She saw his face relent. "All right then, but I think you should go up to bed and get some rest. I'll stay down here and sleep."

Anna knew he was sending her to bed so they could be separated but she didn't mind. It had been a long day and she was very tired and only too glad to be away from the doctor's company.

CHAPTER FIFTEEN
October 1940 ANNA

Anna slept peacefully through the night and woke next morning feeling refreshed and laid for a few moments content, until she remembered the events of the night before. Rolling her eyes, she put one hand to her face to hide the world. The smell of food wafted up the stairs, a mixture of warm bacon and runny eggs, but it couldn't be. Those were impossible to get these days. She had a feeling of dread that it was the doctor and he had made himself at home downstairs, she felt slightly sick at the thought of him being comfortable in her space. She pulled herself out of bed and tried to stand. Her knee was very swollen and bruised and she couldn't put any weight on it. Hanging onto the end of the bed she tried to hop along the floor, each footstep thudding on the boards.

"Damn it," she cursed aloud to the silent room.

The doctor must have heard her shuffling about because a few minutes later he burst through the door.

"What are you doing?" he demanded.

"Trying to get up. What does it look like?" she said,

ignoring the fact that he'd just walked into her bedroom without knocking.

As there wasn't much option, she allowed the doctor to support her. This was becoming a habit, she thought, irritated that she was in need of assistance and couldn't manage on her own.

He helped her to the door and she paused holding onto the frame while they adjusted positions to follow the turn, as the stairs moved down to the right.

The dark narrow staircase forced them to squeeze uncomfortably closer as they descended awkwardly together.

This is ridiculous thought Anna, as she used the cold uneven surface of the wall to help her balance, uncomfortably aware of how tight she was gripping his warm shoulders.

What should have been minutes, seemed to take an age and Anna decided that she would have to find a way to help herself in future. She couldn't go through this every day.

The doctor sat her at the table and gently propped her leg on the opposite chair, frowning down at her knee as he did.

"I've prepared breakfast," he said smiling up at her suddenly. "I was going to bring it up to you but you're up now so…"

"You shouldn't have done that. Surely you have patients to see?" Anna tried, unsuccessfully to hide her anxiety for him to leave out of her voice and said it much more sharply than she intended. He didn't seem to notice, or ignored it and continued as if oblivious.

"Not just yet, besides I was hungry. I never start the day

148

without a good breakfast," he said smiling, and went off to the kitchen, returning a few moments later with plates of food.

He put one of the plates in front of her. "I had a jolly difficult time finding things to cook with Anna. Where are all your cooking pans and pots. I'm sure your mother had much more than is left in that kitchen?"

"Oh I got rid of it all, I was supposed to be leaving today, remember? Anyway, never mind about that. Where on earth did you get this bacon, and the eggs? This stuff is impossible to get, I haven't had bacon and eggs in... well I can't remember when," she said.

He gave her a sly grin, as he picked up the battered knife and fork and began cutting up his food. "This is the country. It's easier to get all sorts of things out here than in town," he said forking a large portion of egg and bacon into his mouth together and beginning to chew. "From what I've heard anyway. Besides the local farmer's wife is a patient of mine. They're always happy to spare me a few bits."

"Black market food?" Anna took no trouble to hide the shock on her face. Was he not a doctor? Weren't people like him supposed to be upright and law abiding or some such thing?

He laughed, "Not exactly. The farmer had some from a pig that they recently had to slaughter so, I knew he would let me have some."

Anna didn't answer him. It still sounded black market to her. Still she wasn't about to turn down the delicious smelling food and began to methodically cut up and eat her bacon, cutting into the egg and watching the yolk spill over and run across the plate, pooling on one side next to a bacon slice. She ate in silence firmly concentrating on her plate and avoiding looking at the doctor altogether.

"I really am sorry about last night…" he said quietly breaking the silence.

She jumped. He had brought up the subject she had been hoping to avoid. She sighed, pushing her bacon piece into the pool of egg and mixing it round a little.

She didn't want to look up at him hoping that staring at her plate would make the words unsaid. Eventually she said, "You don't need to worry about that. It's all forgotten now. It never happened. Let's not mention it again," she said continuing to swamp her bacon piece in egg yolk.

"I'm glad you feel that way but I would understand if you felt you needed to report me," he said in that exasperatingly calm voice.

She looked up at his face then, shocked. How could he say such a thing in a calm way. He would understand if she wanted to ruin his career, have him struck off? How could he just sit there and take such a thing? Anna shook her head at him.

"There's no need for that. I'd rather just forget it."

She may not like him, but she knew what it was to love your career, to spend your life focusing on it, trying to achieve. She couldn't, in all honesty ruin that, even for someone she didn't like. That would be the worst kind of punishment for anyone.

"I appreciate it Anna. Your mother meant a lot to me." He paused before continuing. "While we're on the subject of your mother, it's because of my affection for her that I feel I must say something."

She looked up at him questioningly, now chewing the yolk soaked bacon piece.

"Whilst I was tidying up a few things last night, I noticed this." He produced a folded piece of paper.

Anna knew instantly what it was and went cold. "How dare you go through my things." She said slamming her fork on her plate.

"I did not go through anything. It fell out of your pocket. Anna please don't shout, listen to me. This is important." He said in a tone she had never heard him use before. It surprised her so that she stopped the tirade of insults she was preparing and instead, chose to sit glowering. She silently cursed herself for not burning the note the night she found it on her doormat. But no, she had folded the letter and put it in her pocket and forgotten about it. And now he knew. Now he had read those words from that delinquent man that was her father. Now she was going to have to tell him. Blast him for finding it. Now she was going to have to expose herself to his judgement.

"I know you think I'm infringing on your privacy and I realise that you are someone who doesn't accept that lightly. However, after reading the contents of this letter, I'm glad I did. This letter is clearly a warning for you to stop. The letter is a threat. Surely you see that investigating whatever it is you're into is causing you serious harm. This person clearly wants you to stop whatever story you're chasing. You must stop for your own sake and your mother's," he said his calm tone disappeared, urgency creeping in.

"Doctor, you have once again seen the evidence and come to the wrong conclusion, but since you seem to take a keen interest in my personal life I will tell you. That letter is merely a threat from someone insignificant and I do not respond to threats," she said folding her arms and narrowing her eyes at him, enjoying the fact that for once she was the one with the calm, even tone.

"But considering you were assaulted last night surely that proves you are in danger." He ran his hands through his hair.

"That was nothing to do with this letter either," she said leaning back in her chair. "The writer of this letter is my father. I have never met him, nor do I wish to. He is simply warning me not to look for him now that my mother is dead. There is nothing more to it than that. He wants nothing to do with me and I certainly have no intention of having anything to do with him. He has offered to pay me to stay quiet. Why would I want such a person in my life? I can assure you I am not investigating him at all."

The doctor hung his head into his hands for a few moments before looking directly at her again. "It seems Anna I must apologise to you again," he said his calm voice back. "I should not have pried into your personal life and I am sorry I did so. I just saw the letter and assumed that it was something to do with your job and you getting involved in something dangerous. I see it's a silly notion. I'm sorry. I was just, well… I was worried about you that's all."

"Do not mention the letter or that man ever again. He is not someone I or my mother ever talked about and I have no intention of allowing even the mere thought of him to remain alive in my mind. He has nothing to worry about. I will not be looking for him. So you see, there is no danger whatsoever. Except from nosey doctors. "

Anna spent the rest of the meal eating in silence. The

thrilling taste of the bacon and softness of the egg, losing their appeal and all she wanted was to get rid of the doctor as quickly as possible. How could she ever have let him kiss her. She really hated him. Damn him for being so nosey.

The police came and took her statement and brought back her now battered and dirty handbag, which they had found abandoned near the wooded area. Much of the contents had been rifled through but the only things removed were money, so luckily her identity card was still there. Her ration card was still at Mrs Baxter's so she knew that was safe. Her notebook had been taken too, which she thought odd, but there wasn't anything in it that she needed at the moment so she was not bothered about its loss.

Mrs Baxter came mothering in when she found out what had happened and declared that Anna needed nursing, so very quickly packed all her things and installed her at her own house while her knee heeled. "I' keep an eye on yer," she had said to Anna with a shake of her head. Anna didn't mind. She was supposed to have been travelling back to London, so had nothing much left in the cottage with which to live on, and she was secretly glad that she wouldn't have to stay alone in the cottage and that there would be no more awkward encounters with the doctor while Mrs Baxter was around.

Anna hated sitting resting, unused to doing nothing and finding nothing of use to help with, even though Mrs Baxter was always busy. Anna, began to read Elizabeth's diary again. Over the days while her knee heeled she read on going back over the entries she had skipped over. Many of the entries were uneventful and although entertaining, nothing really related to anything so far that she considered helpful to her investigation. Until she found one entry in 1912 and suddenly things became interesting again.

CHAPTER SIXTEEN
April 1912 ELIZABETH

I have had such a day, Dear Journal. I am simply giddy with excitement, but if you had asked me this morning I would not have thought it would be such a happy day. To preserve this memory I am going to recount it as best as I can recall.

It began early this morning with the most ungracious slamming noise that woke me in such a shock. I rose from my bed disorientated. As my vision cleared I could see Louisa stood over my bed observing me.

Presumably the slamming noise had been her entering my room. It was not a pleasant way to be woken, but I remained silent under her impatient stare.

"Elizabeth you simply must get up, I am so excited I am going to burst." She did a little dance around the room before she lurched herself ungraciously on my bed.

"Oh Louisa. What on earth is the time?" I rubbed at my smarting eyes then and attempted to focus my vision on the clock

"Oh it is so late it is practically lunchtime. You must get up I want you to come along to town to shop with me. I am getting married Elizabeth isn't it wonderful?"

By this point my watering eyes had now focused on the clock on the wall. "Louisa it is only half past the hour of eight. I would hardly view that as late." So, I positioned myself back against my pillows.

Louisa then waved her hand impatiently before she seized me by the shoulders and shook. "Come on Elizabeth get up. You must help me shop for my wedding."

"But Louisa are you certain this is a wise decision? You do not love this man to whom you are engaged."

"But what on earth has love to do with the matter?" Louisa looked at me with genuine astonishment, her blond hair bouncing as she shook her head. Clearly this thought had never occurred to her.

"He is a respectable gentleman and will sort out our money issues. We need a man. Well I do. Especially when mother drops off. I cannot be expected to run things here."

It did not escape my notice that I was never mentioned in this, assuming that she would be given responsibility for running the house and estate, which was very true. There was no mode or method that would ever persuade Catherine to pass over her precious Louisa for me, even though I am older and arguably more entitled. I will never be forgiven for the crime of being Eliza's child. Anyway this is beside the point, Dear Journal, back to my story…

"Well, come on get up, hurry, there is no time to be lolling in bed" Louisa rose, impatiently viewing me from above again, hands on the hips of her customary white dress.

This one was rather nice and sported a large stripe of black across the bottom hem. Over it she had a black and white striped coat of the same length that fastened tight at the waistband and opened out at the collar to reveal a red and white pattern across the chest. In her hand she had a matching parasol and a large hat with a white feather trim. She would have looked at home amongst the ladies of London.

However, one thing I do know of my sister is that there is little use resisting and I could see she was unlikely to give in this time either. She was dressed for attention and clearly determined that I was to be a part of it.

I did have a prior engagement to visit some of the poor in the village, but it was obvious that would be postponed. Once Louisa decided on a course of action, there was no deterring her. So I gave in Dear Journal, with a sigh of defeat and rose from my bed.

Satisfied she had won, Louisa then rested herself on the stool of the dressing table and examined her reflection, poking at her perfectly styled blond hair while I hurried to get ready under her impatient glances through the mirror.

One hour later Louisa, whose best virtue was not patience, virtually pushed me through the door. Catherine stopped us as we were about to leave and gave me a cold glance.

"Louisa dear, surely this is a task for a mother and daughter to do. Why do you not wait and let me come with you?"

Happy at the opportunity to miss wedding shopping, I seized this chance moment. "Yes, Louisa really it should be Mama going with you."

"Oh tosh." Louisa stamped her foot "What a lot of rubbish. What better person to come with me than my sister. Mother I know you would probably like to be there, but I simply cannot go walking down the aisle in something you would choose. I love you dearly but your tastes are so old fashioned. No mother I am determined, this is a young ladies' job."

Even Catherine knew better than to argue with Louisa when she was in as stubborn a mood as this, so she simply nodded and left, waving her arm in a non-committal way. "As you wish dear."

But for my mind it was not the first time I had witnessed Louisa's apparent power over Catherine and it always, still impressed me. She was the only one who never had the displeasure of Catherine's harsh tongue directed at her. Anyone else would have felt a harsh backlash for speaking so. Almost as incredulous was that Louisa did not appear to notice any difference.

Louisa then hooked her arm through mine and marched out of the front doorway, up the cobbled front lawn to the waiting carriage.

But I was not impressed by the sight I saw. Louisa had ordered the large ornate carriage we used for my father's funeral. But when I enquired as to her reasoning, she simply tossed her head and said "It is such a pretty carriage to be always cooped up and never see the light of day. And besides, it is a special occasion. Why not do it in style? We cannot very well shop for the biggest event of my life in the standard buggy now can we?"

She then hopped into the carriage as if to say that there would be no negotiation and took up the whole seat facing and leaving the rear facing seat for me. I was already dreading the day ahead, especially as Louisa insisted on travelling the entire way to York by carriage instead of train as is usual. But just as I began to think things couldn't get worse, she decided to break in Heathfield village to show off her engagement ring. I asked her whether we really had to do this but she insisted that I was just being miserable and that I will do the same when it is my turn. I am absolutely positive I will not do anything remotely the same as Louisa. However, I kept quiet and allowed Louisa to draw me out of the carriage.

She proceeded to flutter down the main street where all the shops are collected along one side of the village square with the large oak tree marking the centre. She pretended to fix her hair, smooth her clothes or generally do anything that would mean she could wave her hand and show off her ring to absolutely anyone who would give her the attention she craved.

The village shops consist of a number of small boutiques each with their name in large letters along the top of the colourful windows. Mock columns and Victorian moulded frames mark the entrance ways. Each of the windows is filled with an array of *different items, clothing in one, ironmongery in another, pottery and bric-a-brac, food and dry goods in others. The village also boasts a post office, police station and a small tea room, so you see we do not live quite in the wilderness, Dear Journal.*

Anyway, back to Louisa. She suddenly became exceedingly excited over the amount of people in the tea rooms, and said they would all be dying to see her ring. Observing through the bowed tea room window above the lace half curtains, it was plain to see that there were indeed a number of people exactly the type Louisa wanted to see her ring. Let me just say, Dear Journal, that these people take an irregular interest in the business of others and we'll say no more for the sake of propriety.

So I will admit to being proud of myself in that moment, I thought quickly and came up with a very plausible excuse as to why she should go in the tea rooms alone and I should not. I told her I had a book on order at the library, which I simply must collect that day. I even went further with my lie and told her that Mrs Hughes had left word to expressly tell me to fetch it this very day. I apologised wholeheartedly told her she did not need my tiresome presence getting in her way, she should go show them her ring. Louisa was not entirely happy with this answer and said "Sometimes you really do vex me considerably. What you find so interesting in the pages of dusty old books I will never know. They are such a bore. Really, you are an odd sort of girl Elizabeth. But all right if you really insist, but I must say I am very put out. Now hurry along and don't be all day about it. We have an extremely busy schedule."

Relieved and elated to be provided with a fraction of freedom I departed, leaving Louisa to enter the tea rooms alone. I quickened my pace on the chance she may change her mind. I had got off lightly with Louisa's temper and was more than certain to pay for it later, but right then I was just happy not to have to go and sit with the rather dull ladies and their oh-so-false smiles and congratulations. I do not like that sort of game play. It makes my stomach churn with nausea, but Louisa cares not a jot. She just wants attention.

I strolled away from the cafe and the main village circle and along the top corner towards the wilderness and the poorer homes. I was so contented, Dear Journal, that I could not help but hum to myself at the tranquility of this part of the village and enjoyed the odd tweet of birds and rustle of leaves blowing. So much so that I simply had to breathe it all in. I inhaled the freshness indulging deeply and closing my eyes as I did. I simply adore spring and how the promise of warmer days lingers in the very air.

But it was at this moment, as I stood with my eyes shut enjoying the freshness of the air, that strong warm arms came and clasped me firmly by the shoulders and I must confess to my heart beating wildly in surprise. I opened my eyes and to find Harry stood before me. His golden amber eyes smiling at my own in that almost mischievous way of his. His dark blond hair shining golden as the sun cascaded down from behind.

I can see now, Dear Journal, that this reads like Harry is some unscrupulous person who goes around wrapping his arms around young women, but now I must make yet another confession, Dear Journal. Harry is not a stranger but our acquaintance is not an old one. However, I know with absolute certainty that my family would definitely not approve. He is an ordinary young man from the village and not at all the sort of young man a lady should be associating with. I would never be given permission to marry someone like Harry, so I have been trying to keep him at a distance, but my heart leaps when he is near and my duty to my family and station seem less important when I look into his eyes.

Harry looked at me in that moment and again, I found myself drawn to him despite my rational reservations. He leaned forward and kissed my forehead then and said in his funny way "There's ma girl."

I told him to hush and reminded him of what would happen if we were discovered.

"Don't ya worry, I'm going to look after ya, I can't give ya what you have at the big house and can only offer ma humble self, but once I've joined up and got a bit o' money saved, ah can get a nice place and we can settle and be happy as peas in pods." He smiled and winked at me with mischief in his eyes.

Harry is so much more certain than I am. I have never gone against Catherine before and even with this fact she still hates the very sight of me. He has a plan. I just need to be the one to be brave and agree. He is considering following his father, a naval man, into the services. His mother resides in the village, so currently I could see a great deal of him if I was ever given the freedom to do as I pleased.

However instead of giving him the answer he wants, I instead say "It makes little difference. I will never be granted permission to marry you and now Louisa has announced her engagement, there is even less likelihood than previously. Do you not see how hopeless it is? We cannot be together no matter the plans you make."

"But ma dear Lilly of course we can be together, ya are free t' marry me whenever ya wish to. We can do it in secret and then once it's done they can't do anything t' stop us because ye'll belong to me, exactly where ya should be. And I'm going to make ya the happiest wife in all the world, I'll give ya everything."

I still resist him, Dear Journal, but my resolve was weakening by this time and even my response "I'm aware you would, but I cannot view a solution" was only half hearted.

He seemed to decide something then and drew me around a corner and down a narrow street, along a row of quaint one storey brick terraced houses, with one door and one window for each little residence. Some women on hands and knees were cleaning the front steps of these little houses, their skirts tucked up high out the way as they scrubbed but they did not pay much heed to me. I was often along here, so my presence among the poor of the village was not in any way unusual.

We walked a little way, Harry's shoulders now had an agitated stance about them. He paused before saying, "Your trouble is that ye've lived too long under Lady Catherine an' Louisa's shadow. It's about time ya decided something for yourself. Do you really think they will let ya marry anyone decent if you asked them? No they're probably planning t' marry you off t' some decrepit old Earl from some awful place who can't even sit astride his own horse anymore, but will make them some kind o' wealthy connection or some other ridiculous reason rich people get married for. All ah know is that ye'll be thoroughly miserable. Ya said yourself Catherine is going to make sure Louisa inherits the estate, so what have ya got to lose apart from a big bedroom?"

"Harry the truth of it is I am frightened of what will arise. I have never before defied my family. Catherine is used to getting what she wants. How will I be able to go against that in defiance of everything? What you require of me Harry is a large undertaking."

"But ma darling, I'll be there t' protect you and we'll move closer t' wherever I get stationed so ya won't need to see them at all. It'll be nice. Our own little place together."

He wrapped his arms around me then and kissed me. I regarded his smiling amber eyes looking on me expectantly and all I could see then, Dear Journal, was the life I might lead with Harry at my side. Despite the money and Leyac House, in that moment all I desired, and all that appeared to be significant was that he became mine. Right in that instance it was as if there was nothing more vital than Harry and I being together and my fear of Catherine melted away.

In my desperate attempt to hold back tears, I uttered no words and merely nodded my answer.

"Is that a yes then? Are ya finally agreeing?"

"Yes, Harry." I said finally. "Yes I will marry you."

"We're getting married." He whispered into my cheek with soft breath before he proceeded to kiss my face repeatedly in excitement.

It was infectious and I began to feel elated at our future together. No longer would I be required to think of ways of avoiding members of my family. I could be content and happy. I allowed myself the indulgence of closing my eyes and hugging Harry's strong body to mine. I felt secure and more blissful than I was aware it was possible to feel. Harry was mine, my own little secret. I would not allow them to spoil this.

And so, I find myself smiling as I write this, staring out of my window towards the village and where Harry is right now. I cannot contain myself, Dear Journal. I am going to be the happiest wife. I am certain of it.

CHAPTER SEVENTEEN
October 1940 ANNA

Once her knee was healed enough to walk, Anna was more than glad to get rid of the responsibility of the cottage and to be finally going back to the life she knew in London.

No-one seemed to know who the owner of her mother's cottage was and all contact was care of an agent in York. She had no idea what was to be done with it and assumed it would be let again, but didn't care so long as she could get back to her career.

Just before leaving, with her bags by the Baxter's door, she went for one last look around the cottage that had been her mother's life for the last few years. She still didn't understand what had made her mother come to a place like this and, especially now the cottage was empty, it looked tired and sad. Where once she had seen simple understated homeliness, she now saw forlorn shabbiness; where before she would have overlooked the damp in the corners and the worn arms of the chairs, now they seemed immediate and stark. Where before the cottage looked cosy and simply comfortable, now it seemed plain, worn and tired.

She ran her finger along the top of the mantel, already gathering dust from being empty, before rubbing her fingers together to remove the layer that had stuck to them.

It was almost a shell now. Before the smell of her mother's cottage would have made her think of childhood memories, of playing and hot drinks by the fire while her mother read aloud. Now the scent was of damp and abandonment. It didn't smell like home any more. It smelt like loss.

However, she had found that she had enjoyed having a whole house to herself during her time here. In London she had a room in a boarding house along with a number of other girls, but having an entire cottage with a garden had been nice. She still hated the country and was even less fond of its twisty roads and deadening silence, but she did enjoy being able to sleep a night through without bombers overhead or having to hide in dank holes and dusty cellars. She hated the countryside a little less.

She wandered around the almost empty rooms now, her shoes echoing on the floors. This was the last thing of her mother's. This really was goodbye.

Yet, being back here only reminded her of the night of the attack and even more so when the doctor had kissed her. She had to put those thoughts away, so leaving the cottage locked up, she replaced the key under the plant pot and walked away without a backward glance. She became more self assured with each step that took her back to London, the world she understood.

* * *

At the station she said goodbye to Mrs Baxter, who had insisted on waving her off from the platform, despite Anna's protests that it wasn't necessary.

"Well now yer will write won't yer? I will be waiting on the post for yer letter. Although don't put anything secret in them because yer know I think her at the post office opens my letters," she said frowning and folding her arms in disapproval. "And I'll visit yer mother's grave regular like, teking flowers and such for yer." She reached out and patted Anna's arm.

"Yes Mrs Baxter I will keep in touch, I can't thank you enough for all you have done for me."

Mrs Baxter smiled briefly and sniffed turning away slightly as if she had other things to be getting on with. "Well now. Be off with yer then. Yer don't want to be missin' yer train," she said a little sternly.

Anna got into the carriage and opened the window and leaned out.

"Good bye Anna luv." Mr Baxter said in his quiet unassuming way, as he put his whistle to his lips.

Mrs Baxter stepped back and waved at her. Anna returned the wave glad that today she was going back to the familiar life she knew.

The train lurched and juddered as it began to move, slowly at first then gathering speed, she watched her mother's village disappear for the final time.

But she had one stop to go before. One she hadn't told anyone about. In one of the newspaper clippings she had kept from her mother's collection there had been mention of the maid who had stolen the Leyac baby. It had said that the maid, Sissy Jenkins, was from a farming family in the area. She had decided she would stop and speak to the family before continuing her journey to London. Anna thought it unlikely they would talk to her, or even if anyone was around who remembered the case, but she wasn't going to let that stop her trying.

She didn't expect to solve the missing twin case when so many had failed over the 25 years, but it was Elizabeth she was really interested in, not the missing baby, although this baby case seemed to get in the way. However, she did know that Sissy Jenkins had come to work at the house as a personal nursemaid to Elizabeth when she became ill. She was hoping that Sissy may have written to her family about Elizabeth with information she was hoping may give her a lead.

She wasn't really expecting anything from the Jenkins family and, would a girl who was willing to steal someone's child really be the kind of girl who wrote home to her family? Still, Anna felt she had to start somewhere now that she was free of funerals, cottage clearing and village life. Now she was actually able to pursue some kind of investigation, no matter how remote her chances of success, she still felt much better than she had in weeks.

She watched the fields and hills rise and fall in the distance as the train snaked through tiny villages, through larger ones, through farmlands and onwards as it sped towards York city.

She was certain her mother had left her Elizabeth's diary and the other things for a purpose, but that damn missing twin was all that anyone was interested in. All the information about that family was centred around that mystery. There didn't seem to be any interest in any other aspect of their lives at all.

So as she sat there staring out the window

contemplating all she didn't know, she decided that it may just be possible that the only way to find out more about Elizabeth was to also look at the missing baby case at the same time, and even if she didn't want to admit it, she was intrigued as to what had happened to that little boy.

A few hours later Anna eventually found the Jenkins farm down a winding trail at the bottom of a hill, after the complete lack of road signs meant she had initially gone in the wrong direction.

The road to the farmhouse was on a steep decline that turned and twisted. On one side was a small woodland area and on the other a large field hidden by a hedge. The road had deep parallel rivets and channels all the way along and Anna, cursing that she was yet again wearing the wrong shoes, made her way awkwardly, hopping from one flat grassy knoll to another, as she tried to avoid becoming covered in mud.

The hedge to her right gave way to a large gate and Anna could see properly into the field. On the very far side was the tiny speck of a person bent over doing something. Anna called out to the person but the wind, blowing in the opposite direction carried her words away so that they sounded thin and feeble. The speck of a person continued at their work without standing up so she gave up and turned back towards the farmhouse, continuing to pick her way gingerly along the steep lane.

The house itself was stone built and rundown. Dirt seemed to be ingrained into every aspect of the whole farm. Dogs and chickens were running wildly around the yard and the whole place held the stench of horses and pigs. Anna went to knock at the dirty battered farm door, stepping over some abandoned muddy boots as she did, just as the door was flung open by a woman a few years older than herself. Anna still had her arm raised about to knock and the surprise on the woman's face was evident as she took a step back making a surprised O with her mouth.

"Hello there, I'm sorry to bother you. Is this the Jenkins farm?" She smiled putting on her professional expression.

"Who's askin'?" the woman said suspiciously, changing her face to an expression of mistrust and folding her arms.

"I'm Anna Forrester, I'm a journalist from London, I was wondering if there was anyone available to speak about the Leyac family."

The woman rolled her eyes. "You people, Ah wondered if this nonsense would start again once the news broke of Thomas Leyac's death. My Aunt had nothing to do with the baby's disappearance and ah won't have you goin' upsetting ma mother again," she said wagging a finger at her accusingly and shutting the door against her back her blocking the way to the inside of the farmhouse.

"I'm not here to go over old ground about the twin disappearance. I'm actually interested in one of the other Leyacs, Elizabeth. She died before the twins were born. I'm investigating her life. I'm not interested in whether your aunt did or didn't take the baby. I was just wondering if she had ever told your family anything about Elizabeth. What kind of person she was? You see I'm having trouble finding anything out about Elizabeth because of this missing baby case."

The woman looked at her suspiciously for a few moments, an undecided expression on her face, before finally saying. "If ah let you in and you start badgering ma mother, I'll be annoyed. Ah don't trust you reporters. You say anything to get in the house, but we've never had a woman before, and since you say it's Elizabeth you're interested in, I'll ask ma mother if she'll see you, but if she says no, you're to go straight away or ah'll send for the police. You understand?"

She nodded at the woman and was led into a long kitchen area with a large fire and sitting area at one side, and a range and kitchen working area at the other. It was a little like Mrs Baxter's but on a much larger scale. There were more abandoned muddy boots by the door in here and Anna gingerly stepped over the clumps of mud around the doorway.

The woman told her to stay where she was and went out of the room through a connecting door banging it shut as she did. After a few minutes she returned and said her mother was willing to see her and she would be in presently. She indicated that Anna should sit down and set about making tea, setting the kettle on the range to boil.

Soon a hunched, elderly woman with a rounded figure came shuffling in and peered at her. Her hair was all different colours ranging from dark black to white and was pulled up into a soft bun, a few strands escaping and gently touching the side of her loose fleshy cheeks. Anna stood and introduced herself. The old lady indicated that she was Sissy Jenkins' elder sister and had been ten years her senior, so remembered what happened well. The old lady's name was Margaret and had been Jenkins until she married and her name was now Brown.

"Mi daughter tells me you are interested in Elizabeth Leyac?" the woman said peering down at her.

"Yes that's correct, my mother passed away recently

and left me the diary of Elizabeth Leyac with no other information about her or how she had got such an item. The problem I have is, that there seems to be little known about Elizabeth. It's all about the twins and their mother. Elizabeth's entire life and death seems to have been overshadowed by the twin disappearance. I was hoping your sister may have mentioned Elizabeth to you in her letters home - any small bit of information may help."

"Well now, that is interestin', I've never had a reporter ask mi that before. They usually come looking for scandal. But we haven't been bothered in a few years now. Still there's always the odd one. But as t' your question, can I just ask, what meks you think she wrote home?"

"Well, a young girl away from home for the first time, it's usual to write home or get someone to write for her if she couldn't write herself. Are you telling me she didn't write home all the time she was at Leyac House?"

"No, I'm not sayin' that." The woman leaned back in her chair and viewed her, as if deciding something, her hands pressed together at each fingertip in an inverted V.

She was just about to ask another question when the woman suddenly spoke again.

"Yes she did talk of Elizabeth in 'er letters." The woman was looking at her as if trying to assess what impact those words would have, but Anna knew her face betrayed nothing of the lurch she felt when the woman had said that.

"Could I ask what she said." Anna replied calmly, scribbling in her notebook and avoiding the woman's eye.

The woman remained silent for a few moments forcing her to again look up and meet her gaze.

"Well y'see. Sissy was taken on with the specific purpose

of nursin' Elizabeth during the illness which eventually killed her. She was 'er personal maid and the only member o' staff permitted to tend Elizabeth and see to 'er. From what I understand she spent much of 'er time with the sick girl."

"Did she ever tell you anything about Elizabeth?" Anna rephrased the same question, but the woman seemed intent on telling her story her own way. She had unclasped her hands now and put them in her lap. Her head was resting lightly on the side of the chair as she spoke, her eyes glazed and far away.

"She loved that girl, that much were obvious from 'er letters. She did once say that she thought Elizabeth the best o' the lot. That Catherine favoured Louisa an' poor Elizabeth was always bottom o' t' list."

"Really? How so?" Anna said to encourage the woman to continue.

"Yes, apparently Catherine favoured Louisa openly an' made a point o' ensuring that everyone, especially Elizabeth, knew abou' it."

She sat in silence and watched the woman, the clock above the mantel ticking through the silence. Outside she heard a dog begin to bark in the distance.

"From what our Sissy said, that poor girl 'ad a miserable life in that family. For my mind God blessed her by tekin' her young as he did. But I know mi little Sissy was fond of Elizabeth. She would often write about how she and Elizabeth had shared some joke or other, how they had become friends. But I'm not sure that Sissy wasn't over actin' the friendship, or whether they really were as good friends as she said the' were."

"So, Sissy implied that her and Elizabeth were very

close?"

"It was more than implied, she outright said it openly." The woman nodded, her loose cheeks quivering as she did. "But that's why I'm sayin' I think that the friendship may have been more in Sissy's head than in reality. I can well imagine that Elizabeth paid Sissy attention and gev her a friendly word or two, but the likes of Elizabeth Leyac wouldn't mek friends with a common maid like our Sissy, it just wasn't the done thing. You see mi sister was a fanciful girl, she used to let people tek advantage of 'er, an' she would imagine that people were nicer than the' really were. People would prey on 'er good nature y'see and she would blindly let them do it without thinkin'. If someone like Elizabeth had been nice to 'er, I can see how Sissy would imagine that they were close, but even though Elizabeth had a miserable time with her family, she was still a Leyac, and the likes of the Leyacs would never befriend a farm girl like our Sissy."

Anna instantly thought of the entry she had read about Elizabeth's secret love affair with a common village boy. Maybe she and Sissy had been friends. Maybe Elizabeth hadn't been the way Margaret Jenkins assumed, maybe Sissy had been right when she said her and Elizabeth were close. However, she kept this to herself and instead asked. "Do you think Elizabeth took advantage of Sissy's good nature?"

"No I can't say as I believe that bu' I will say I think the idea of friendship in the wey Sissy said were fantasy, but from what she used to say about Elizabeth, I got the impression she were a kind and thoughtful girl. If she hadn't died when she did, I would like to think she would 'ave stood up for our Sissy's name when they accused her of tekin' that babe."

"So you think Elizabeth was an honest sort of person?"

"Yes, as much as it pains mi to say anythin' nice about them Leyacs, I do think she was."

"What about the rest of the Leyac family?"

"No, them lot 'ad more money than sense they did. I think they used our Sissy as a scape goat. She was a common farm girl. Nothin' t' the likes o' them. They would a just used 'er an' thought nothin' of it, as if she was an ol' rag t' be thrown out." Her tone had changed and a touch of anger had crept into her voice.

"Do you mind my asking you about Sissy?" Anna asked.

The woman looked at her with calculating eyes, assessing her. Anna looked back with a blank expression to put the woman at ease. She needed the woman to believe she wasn't after printing some scandal.

"You're an unusual sort o' reporter. Do you 'ave a husband?" The woman asked squinting down at Anna's left hand.

"No, I am not married."

"Hmm, an' you're from London y'say?"

"Yes I work in the city, mostly writing the women's columns, domestic problems, family articles, rationing - such as how wives can make meals without certain foods, that sort of thing."

"I see. So this is a very different sort o' story t' what you usually write then?"

"Yes in some ways it is, but like I told your daughter I'm interested in Elizabeth Leyac and how my mother may have come across her diary. So it's more of a personal investigation rather than something for my job."

"I see." The woman leaned forward in her chair and narrowed her eyes at Anna shrewdly. "Y'know there's one vital piece o' evidence, which everyone forgets that proves our Sissy didn't tek that babe."

"Really, what's that?" She asked trying to keep her voice calm and professional. She leaned forward in her chair mimicking the older woman's pose.

"Well, Elizabeth Leyac was very ill at the time our Sissy started workin' at the house, her job was to look after Elizabeth, mopping her brow during fever, clearing up after 'er mekin' sure she was clean. Now what everyone forgets is that Elizabeth Leyac's illness were bad, the girl were dying. So, while Sissy were busy dealin' wi-this, she wouldn't a had time t' see Louisa durin' her pregnancy, or even those babes when they were born as she would a been s' busy wi' Elizabeth. Now I know from what Sissy used t' say about Elizabeth, and regardless of whether Elizabeth reciprocated the friendship or not, Sissy loved that girl an' would never leave her just as she were dying. I think what 'appened is that Elizabeth died an' our Sissy was so devastated she left an' disappeared somewhere."

"What makes you believe that?" Anna asked intrigued by the theory. Her pencil stopped mid sentence and now wandered aimlessly as her concentration left her notes and focused on the woman.

Margaret Jenkins sat back in her chair a satisfied smile on her lips. "Well our Sissy 'ad already faced tragedy in her life an' was a delicate soul. She would 'ave taken Elizabeth's death hard on top of the loss of 'er own…"

The woman's daughter, who Anna had almost forgotten was there, had been silently moving around the kitchen listening to the conversation and dropped a pot in the sink with a loud thud as Margaret Jenkins said this. Anna looked over at her blinking, but the younger woman's expression made her stop. She was looking at her mother sharply, her eyes giving a silent private message. Anna looked again at the old woman's face and realised that whatever she had been about to say must have been important and was information she hadn't meant her to find out.

Her heart was beating, she knew there was something in this. "The loss of her own what?" Anna asked gently.

Within second the younger woman was at her mother's side. "Mother! What are you saying. Ah think that's enough now." Turning to Anna she said "You've got your information about Elizabeth, I think it's time you left."

The old woman patted her daughter on the arm, who was trying to help her mother to rise. Margaret Jenkins however, didn't seem inclined to move. "Now now Dorothy, I don't believe that you can repair the damage mi old loose tongue has done. The girl 'as heard now, an' you know yoursel' what these reporters are like. She'll sniff around until she digs it out."

"That's what concerns me mother. She needs to leave now before you say anythin' else." The younger woman again attempted to make her mother rise to her feet.

"Now now Dorothy, I'm going t' tell the girl." She swatted at her daughter like an annoying fly, a frown of irritation crossing her face.

"What? She's a reporter. She'll twist your words and make Aunt Sissy out to be a monster." The younger woman's face was beginning to turn a deep purple red and she waved her arms as she shouted in exasperation.

"I assure you I have no intention of any such thing."

Anna said holding her hands up in a surrender.

"Y'see Dorothy she 'as no intention." The old woman said.

"Mother, of course she'll say that." Dorothy said putting both hands to her cheeks.

"Now Dorothy, that is enough. It's my story t' tell and I will decide, not you, so kindly unhand me girl." The old woman had lost her own temper now, but her stern words worked and Dorothy stalked to the connecting door, but turned to Anna just as she was leaving wagging her finger at her.

"You print any o' this an' drag my family name through the mud again an' you'll have me t' deal with. We've had enough of your types over the years." She left slamming the door behind her. It vibrated in its hinges for a few moments.

The old lady smiled at Anna, all her anger forgotten.

"I want to tell you because you have trustin' eyes. Mi ma always said you can tell a person by looking into their eyes an' it's about time the truth came out."

She sat silently waiting for the old lady to begin, not wanting to speak in case it broke the spell and the woman changed her mind.

"Mi sister, was a very naive girl an' like I said before was led astray by many. One such occasion was when she was no more than 15 year ol. A wealthy landowner's son took a shine to 'er. She was flattered and thought it was the start of somethin'. She believed that ee loved her an' he told her as much, but ee was doing it for one reason and mi sister, believin' herself engaged, let him tek her on the promise of a ring and a life, for she loved the scoundrel. Well once he 'ad his way, he grew tired and left 'er." The old woman shook her head in disapproval.

"There was a bit of trouble as Sissy wouldn't believe it of him fo' ever such a long time. Well, after a few months of her sitting waitin' an' believin' he would come back, she found she was with child. She thought this would be the thing to bring him back. Well she were wrong there too, as we all knew she were. When she told him abou' the child, ee told her straight what he thought of 'er. He called her a 'common little whore' an' said that she had never been anythin' but a little amusement. She were heartbroken.

Our ma said she would bring the babe up as 'er own because Sissy, stubborn that she were, insisted she would keep the child. Anyway, that's exactly what 'appened, but the babe was sickly and got scarlet fever when it were but a few months old an' died. Our Sissy were heartbroken again." She sighed and shifted positions in her chair.

"It wasn't long after that our ma found the advert for a maid at Heathfield, this was in t' days before the Leyacs were well known. Back then they were just another rich family. The benefit of it was that it were far enough away that Sissy would be able to go an' start a new life. No one knew her and no one cared, she was just another young maid at a big 'ouse.

Now y'see this is why I know she would never have teken that babe. She loved her own too much to tek another from its mother.

But we never said this when the Leyac twin went missing an' our Sissy were accused, as our ma said it would only add fuel t' fire and Sissy's name had been dragged through t' mud enough."

The old woman leaned back, resting her head on the side of the chair again, the glassy far away look back in her eyes.

Anna wasn't so sure of Sissy's innocence and especially with the knowledge that she had lost a child herself. Once, at the beginning of her career, she had come across the story of a woman who lost her baby and took another woman's child to replace that loss. It was common in cases like this wasn't it?

Anna looked at the old woman's face again. She could understand her belief in her sister's innocence and her desire for it not to be true, almost like a desperate hope.

But being an outsider looking in on the case, the evidence almost indisputably pointed to Sissy as the culprit. She and the twin boy went missing together, no one had found a substantial trace of either of them since. Where Sissy had taken the boy Anna had no clue but she did suspect that she had somehow managed to get the baby out of the country. With an entire country poised for the last twenty five years looking for this missing child, it's not possible that the child could still be in this country and there be no real substantial evidence of him. And for Sissy, a poor farm girl to have concocted a plan and carried it out, she must have had help and money from someone with an interest in one of those twins going missing, and to be able to pull all this off during a War. Yes, Anna was certain Sissy had been given help from someone with money. But who? However, she kept these thoughts to herself and instead said to the old woman:

"I thank you for your time and for sharing your story and thoughts of your sister and Elizabeth with me. I can assure you I have no intention of printing the information about Sissy's loss. I can see you have suffered enough over the years because of this case. I am only sorry we don't know where Sissy is."

She rose and held out her hand to shake the old woman's. The woman took it and looked up at her and with an intense look, thanked her. She smiled and pulled her hand away.

As she went back outside the cold wind hit her face and she shivered as once again, she stepped over the muddy boots abandoned at the doorway. She began the more difficult journey of making her way back up the steep lane, through the deep muddy channels made by tractor tyres.

Dorothy came running up behind her, having no such problem with stepping in mud. It squelched and oozed around her already mud-caked boots. She didn't seem to notice.

"If you print one word of the story about mi Aunt Sissy's baby I'll come lookin' for you, I'm not afraid of you reporters and ah won't allow you t' ruin my family anymore. Stay away from here. My family is not your ticket to success."

She stalked off before Anna could answer, her boots kicking up mud as she marched her feet back towards the farmhouse.

On the train towards London that afternoon, she watched the country rush past her window and thought of the old lady's words. She had been convinced of Sissy's innocence. But this was just her affection for her sister clouding her judgement. The evidence was clear, Sissy took that child, but why and where. Anna sighed, there was only one piece of evidence she could consult right then, so took out the little, fat book and opened it at the last read entry. There was still a lot of the book to read.

She skipped ahead about a year and opened the page at June 1913. Anna wondered what had happened to the young man to whom Elizabeth had become engaged.

CHAPTER EIGHTEEN
June 1913 ELIZABETH

I am so desperately tired, but before I lay to sleep I feel I must record what has happened today otherwise, despite my tiredness I know I won't sleep. I still cannot believe it but I must get the thoughts out of my head. I must tell you, Dear Journal, of this horrendous day.

I was awoken early in that dim moment between darkness and daylight. A young freckled face had been peering down at me and was rather too close, so that when I opened my eyes I got a fright.

"Miss, Miss, ye' mus' come quickly. It's Louisa, she's asking for ye." The face told me, which by now I had deciphered as being that of the new ladies maid Bess, still it took me a few moments of cloudy judgement before I registered her words.

"Is she well, is it the babe?" I replied.

"No miss she just asks for ye'." The maid shook her head, her rather neat red curls bobbing where they had escaped from beneath her cap. It appeared she had put it on in something of a hurry.

In the time it took me to rise, she had already procured my robe and I wrapped myself in its light cool material, its coolness allowing me to further distance myself from the sleep which at this point was still pulling at my memory.

Louisa was once again having a problematic pregnancy, however, she had made it further than ever before this time, and although the baby was not expected for some while, yet she called often for me in some discomfort and suffering.

Being the socialite she was, Louisa was finding it a considerable difficulty being incarcerated from her society friends in London, and remaining cooped up at Leyac House was rather a tiresome bore for her. She relied on my comfort and I confess to spending many a night sitting reading to her to aid her in sleep.

In the interests of what is proper, Dear Journal, I will not say unkind things about my brother-in-law, however, it is not gossip to speak the truth and he has been virtually useless during this time and has kept himself away from his suffering wife, as if he may catch some dreadful disease.

His distaste is plain to see in the curve of his eye as he appears almost in panic when conversation finds its way to Louisa, or even in instances where he has to be in company with her. She however, appears scarcely concerned by his absence. For her, he had only ever been a trophy; someone to dangle from her arm, another possession. And, although I recognised her great capacity to love underneath her flighty exterior, I was not entirely convinced having a baby of her own was not just another toy for her to possess, like the dolls we pushed around the gardens as children. Louisa always with the most grand and luxurious baby carriage.

For Louisa, every aspect of her being was seeking fun and enjoyment, and as such pregnancy was particularly difficult for her to come to terms with. But despite this, I had observed her absently stroking her silken gowned stomach as she laid on her bed, her feet elevated as I read. She appeared to occasionally allow her hidden self to escape in those brief encounters and I longed for her to drop all the superficial ornaments and allow the real Louisa to surface, but I was wholly conscious that, by no means would she ever allow this.

I had found myself quietly observing Catherine, and Louisa's husband carefully in recent weeks. Catherine had quickly won him to her side when he first arrived, as I suspected she would. She would on no account give control of the estate to another, this I was most certain of.

However, I frequently speculated whether Louisa had been purposely steered towards him by Catherine. He was exceedingly her variety of character and had an air of conceit, a certainty about himself that he was entitled to regard people as well, or as ill, as he wished. He contrived with Catherine and I frequently suspected him of an ulterior motive. Countless times over dinner, I had discovered him viewing me with narrowed eyes, assessing me, wondering. It caused me to shiver and I took great pains to examine the silver crowns at the ends of my cutlery and the golden scrolls on the edge of my plate in order to avoid meeting his gaze.

Catherine however, appeared to retain control of him for the present. I, however, have no reservation in saying that he is hardly the kind of gentleman who would remain under a woman's control for long.

I sidetrack, Dear Journal, back to my story. Having descended the dark ornate staircase in my bare feet (which was quite a freeing revelation, Dear Journal) what remained of the clear night moon was shining through the staircase window, but the advancing dawn that was beginning to break provided a strange light across the carved war trophy balustrades.

I halted momentarily at Louisa's door to offer a brief knock but went in without pausing for a reply. I knew that on no account would Louisa's husband be there, it was a rare instance when he ever was.

I found Louisa bellowing at her maid and creating a rather loud din. Just as I crossed the threshold, she propelled a glass of water at the girl, which cuffed the wall behind and smashed. Glass fragments and water droplets trickled down the blue flowered wallpaper to create an extremely interesting effect of watered plants on the pattern.

The maid hastened from the room in tearful hysterics without halting to clear the disarray on the floor. I glanced at Louisa searing with rage and breathing heavily before quietly bending to do the maid's job for her, by retrieving the fragments of glass and collecting them on a small silver tray on the nearest table.

"Honestly, Elizabeth where do they find these fools? That girl is utterly useless. She could not aid me with a single useful task if she set her mind to it, I am certain."

"Louisa, what is wrong?"

"It is this baby, my stomach is paining me. I am certain it is coming this time."

"But Louisa, the child is not expected for another eight weeks, it cannot be now. Are you quite certain?"

"Oh yes, I am certain."

Although sceptical, I had no point of reference having never experienced being with child myself. Louisa however, had been this way for a number of weeks now, certain the child was imminent in its arrival but, so far, she had always been mistaken. Not for the first time I considered whether this concern over the child's arrival was an unfortunate consequence of all the miscarriages she had endured.

However, do not think, Dear Journal, that this means my concern for her wellbeing is nominal. In fact, although I did not inform her, I was concerned. Her doctor had given instructions that she was to rest her swollen feet, elevate her legs and above all remain calm. She did not seem to be able to manage this and increasingly got herself into states of distress, which seemed to worsen her condition somewhat. I peered closely into her face and noted her normally sparkly blue eyes were considerably dulled, her eye rims red and swollen in a most unattractive manner, and her face sported a flush around her cheeks and down her neck. I placed my cool hand on her forehead. It felt warm and clammy to the touch, too warm in truth.

"Come now, Louisa lie yourself down." I tucked the blankets around her, pulling back the top layer to cool her and rang for a maid to fetch a bowl of cool water and sponge.

Once the maid returned with a substantial porcelain bowl and round sponge, I dipped my already cool hands into the cold water and sponged her forehead and face for a while, feeling myself quite the nursemaid, before reading for a time while she drifted back off to sleep. If the child was coming, she would require rest.

The dawn sun had risen fully in the time it took her to descend into sleep and its warmth flooded through the window, shaded only by the heavy drapes pulled open with curtain ties. A square of criss-crossed light spread across the room and against the far wall like the outside infecting the interior, wilfully attempting to get in.

Birds sang faintly and the distant bang of doors in other parts of the house was the only other indication of life. Other than this there was silence, so I clambered into the far side of Louisa's substantial bed and descended into sleep beside her in the peace and tranquility of the morning. I confess I was somewhat bemused at how comforting it was to lay beside another.

It cannot have been more than a few hours we slept there beside one another, but when I awoke and viewed the window I wondered what the hour could be. It could not be more than an hour past breakfast I considered. I was however acutely aware of my hunger.

Louisa had rotated on her side away from me and I began to quietly raise myself. As I drew back the blankets, I observed a curious shadow emanating from around Louisa.

Gently lifting the starched white sheet, it was plain to see that the shadow was in fact a circle of blood. My heart rose and my mouth tingled with trepidation as a white heat of fearfulness swept up my chest in waves.

I placed one foot on the floor and silently rose, I hastily moved to the long cord and pulled its heavy roughness repeatedly. It silently *moved with my force and I pictured the little bell frantically tinkling in the servants area.*

Leaving the cord I attempted to encourage my breathing to slow and moved toward the door. Knowing not what should be done, my initial concern was to ensure Louisa did not wake prior to someone with more knowledge of these situations being beside her.

I had a rather unusual sensation then, the strange yearning that I had never wanted to lay eyes on Catherine more. I lingered just outside Louisa's room and waited rather impatiently on the staircase for a servant, who eventually ascended recklessly, white faced and breathless.

"Fetch my mother immediately, inform her it is Louisa. Then return here and wait for her instructions. She will require you to telephone the doctor but will need to give you proper directions first. Hurry, run. What are you waiting for?"

The maid nodded like a puppet on a string and ran off in a flurry, picking up her skirts high and showing her thick black stockings and flat black shoes her feet tapping like a drum as she ran.

It appeared to be an age before Catherine arrived and I had almost given up and become resigned to fetching her myself, as I paced the floor outside Louisa's room in my bare feet and nightgown. I noticed insignificant details then as I paced, how there were a great many small cracks between the floorboards and how the swords, armour and canons carved ornately into the balustrades on the staircase had darker sections in each of the crevices.

When Catherine did appear it was in a state of undress herself, her hair not yet fully dressed was down and flowing behind her, her face overflowing with concern.

"What is it? What is awry?"

"I cannot say. I am certain, she is sleeping soundly but Mama, she is covered in blood."

It did not escape my notice how visibly Catherine swallowed.

Then a scream emanated from behind the closed door and appeared to almost shake the house within its very foundations. Louisa had awakened.

Catherine flung the door wide and it rocked in its hinges. Louisa was half sitting half laying on the bed her swollen stomach taught through the straining seams of her nightdress. She had removed the sheet to reveal a vast stain of blood surrounding her, far larger than I had initially thought. She continued to scream at the blood in apparent hysteria.

Catherine directed immediate instructions at the maid who rushed off to do as directed. She then turned her attention to Louisa and set about cleaning her and making her comfortable. Without feeling like I had a particular purpose, I took it upon myself to attempt to calm Louisa from her distressed state.

However, once she had comprehended that Catherine had full charge of the situation and I was there to provide comfort, she discontinued with the hysteria and I, in my naivety, began to have faith that everything would be well.

However, in an instant she went from being calm and appearing much improved to writhing on the bed, the blood appearing to seep and expand out ever more with each passing minute.

When the doctor did arrive in a most calm and leisurely manner, he peered down at Louisa crying and writhing on the bed with interest, as if he had just walked into the tea rooms and they had served him a dish of strawberries and cream.

He observed me beside Louisa clasping her hand and simply lowered his grey head slightly, held aloft his wrinkled hand toward the door and voiced through his bushy moustache "Out."

He appeared to be a person most used to giving orders to others and his tone and presence immediately made me feel it necessary that I obeyed. I rose to vacate the room, but Louisa had a firm grip of my hand, and indeed her knuckles were white with the tightness of her grasp. So, I seated myself once again and glanced at him in resignation. He frowned at me in silent disapproval but said nothing further.

He removed items from his rather old and worn leather bag and lined up instruments of varying degrees and curious shapes along a white cloth, before providing Catherine with directions on the items he required from downstairs.

Catherine proved herself an excellent nurse to Louisa and I confess I was more than impressed by her ability to recognise almost instinctively what the doctor required. I was fascinated with her attentiveness to a man she would otherwise view as beneath her. However, her ill concealed concern and the doctor's strain at the eye area, alongside the tiny drops of sweat on his forehead did not escape my attention. I was fully in possession of the fact that both Louisa and her child were in grave danger.

Louisa clasped my hand tighter, my healthy one only serving to make Louisa's appear even greyer, our two hands together fiercely as one. She hardly seemed like Louisa, her beautiful straight golden hair now limp and lifeless. Anyone viewing it now would scarce believe its usual sleek glow.

It was a great many hours before any progress was made but despite this, Louisa's eyes remained closed throughout.

I confess, Dear Journal, that I have never before seen anyone in such pain and never wish to again. It was a relentless attack of torture. Just when poor Louisa reached the summit and it began to fade away, another would begin greater than the previous. I do not have reservations in confessing that the whole process alarmed me considerably.

When the child was born, a boy, he appeared to arrive all at once and was very slight, far smaller than other new babies. His eyes remained firmly shut despite my wishing him to open them. He did not stir. Not even a little, not even when I almost dreamed he had. It was the fancies of my wishful imagination willing him to cry out. He did not. He lay motionless like a doll, his porcelain skin so resembling his mother's.

The doctor wrapped the little boy in a blanket and shook his head at Catherine. I comprehended instantly that I was correct and no amount of imaginings would alter this. Only then did I glance at Louisa. Her eyes now firmly open, she was observing the process calmly, a new darkness around her once bright blue eyes.

An oppressiveness then descended on the entire room. It suddenly appeared stuffy, the scent of blood and birth becoming almost intolerable.

Catherine despatched me to inform Louisa's husband his son had been born dead. I rose, still regarding Louisa whose cold, dead eyes were intently viewing the small still bundle. What unnerved me was not the aspect in her eyes but the uncharacteristic way she remained silent. Louisa was never silent and it made me wonder whether the loss of this boy, at such a late stage, would change things for everyone. I began to suspect we were bereaved of more than a little boy, but also of something else I was not privy to yet.

So here I am, now returned to my room to recount this story. It is one that I cannot rectify and it frustrates me more than I can ever communicate.

CHAPTER NINETEEN

October 1940 ANNA

With Anna's stop at the Jenkins farm, she was much later getting into London. However, there had been no delays on this journey and as she stepped off the tube the familiar cool stale air brought her back home and she smiled to herself.

She inhaled the dank smell of khaki uniforms, sweat and cold. The platform filled with soldiers, seaman and airman all hurrying off and on the train. The sides of the tiled platform walls were already beginning to pile up with people ready to shelter for the night.

Anna almost fell on a woman in the corner with a baby and a little boy of about three, when a soldier, running to get on the train knocked into her at speed.

"Ere, watch yorsewf, Miss." The heavy London accent, familiar but strange to her ears after the last few weeks of Yorkshire.

"Sorry," she said giving the woman an apologetic look.

She moved slowly with the crowd out of the platform and up the narrow tunnelled steps towards the exit, the wind from outside blowing down and along the tunnel as the crowd moved. A man with a large umbrella and old fashioned black hat was trying unsuccessfully to push past the crowd. His repeated throat clearing and tutting didn't have any effect on the large group ahead of him and they continued to move along patiently. Anna knew from experience it was best to just go with the crowd. London wasn't the place to be impatient.

When the throng of people began to disperse into the street, she was able to skip up the last few steps and emerge onto the damp main street and into the people moving past in a hurry.

It was almost dark and she rushed on through the crowds of people and with every step felt more confident in herself and her surroundings. This strange familiarity was something that, if she let herself, could almost make her believe that nothing had changed; that her mother was still in the north and would write to her any day now. Almost.

This was her world and she relished in it, almost skipping down the street past the people rushing about their business before darkness fell and the bombers came. She glanced at the darkening sky. She hadn't missed those, however.

She did notice that the city looked much more worn and run down with broken buildings, blocked off streets and some roads that were piles of rubble. People were scrambling around the mess and destruction unconcerned as if they were nothing more than annoying deposits left by stray dogs.

She couldn't decide whether her stint in the country, with nothing but green fields and animals, had made

London's destruction all the more a shocking reality. When she was here daily, she, like those scrambling over the rubble, continued her day regardless, but now she seemed to notice every little missing piece of her city. Buildings had chunks missing from their corners, some were barely standing and some seemed as if they would topple any moment and amazingly some were stood next to buildings that looked as if they hadn't been touched.

She quickened her pace as the sky darkened to an inky blue. As she turned off the main streets and down the familiar roads that would lead her home, the darkness came in faster and soon she would not able to see. However, she was pretty sure she could find her way back. She had left the crowds behind on the main street, and these narrower streets with their tall close buildings and dark alleys enhanced the quietness, but not the same deadening silence of the country. She could still hear London. It was never truly silent, thankfully. Her footsteps echoed on the pavement as she shifted her bags from one hand to the other.

Arms from behind grabbed at her and a rough dark cloth which smelt of stale cabbage was thrust over her head. She dropped her bags and put her hands up to remove the hood, but she was picked up roughly by two people. She was aware of being thrust into a vehicle when she heard the doors banging shut and the floor beneath her began to vibrate with the sound of an engine. Someone grabbed at both of her hands and she fought back hitting out at whoever it was. She felt a blow to her stomach, which made her eyes water and she fought to recover her breath.

"Now shut up, and keep still," a rough throaty voice

said.

"Get off me, who are you? Why are you doing this?" she shouted, hitting out again between gasps for air.

She felt a hand come up inside the hood and soft cloth was forced around her mouth and nose. The acrid smell made her head swim and she felt dizzy.

She woke some time later, not in a vehicle, but instead tied to a hard chair, her hands bound behind her back. The cabbage hood was still on but now she had a headache and felt slightly nauseous.

Little squares of light filtered through the rough weave of the sacking. She pulled at the binds tying her to the chair but they were firm and cut into her arms and wrists. Her feet were also tied and wouldn't budge. She moved her eyes from the light beam at the centre to the darker part on the left and squinted to see the shapes around her. There was nothing but darkness and specks of dim light no matter how hard she tried to make the shapes form into a person.

"Ah, you're awake. Good," said a voice with a dark gravel tone. She wondered if he was the one she had hit earlier.

"Who are you? Why am I here? Let me go at once." She made an attempt to sound commanding and tried to steady her thumping heart as she began to wonder if he was a Nazi spy. Didn't they do things like this?

"I first need to ask you some questions," said the voice.

"What sort of questions?" she replied warily, wondering if she was going to be interrogated about her newspaper or forced to write messages for the enemy.

That was treason, she thought, her heart hammering faster. I could get shot for that.

"Did your mother ever tell you anything of her past?" The voice was calm and direct.

She was so unprepared for such a question that she remained in stunned silence for a few moments before indignation took over.

"My Mother? What have you to do with my mother? Who are you."

"Answer the question."

"No, not until you tell me who you are." She felt braver now as a suspicion began to form in her mind.

Anna heard movement and within seconds searing pain shot up from her hand. She screamed and tried to catch her breath. Her heart was thundering now and there wasn't enough air in the room no matter how hard she tried to breathe normally.

She felt him close to her left shoulder as he whispered in her ear, his breath hot though the fabric of the hood. "Did your mother ever tell you anything of her past?" his voice was menacingly calm.

"No she never talked about it. But you must tell me why you want to know. Who are you?" Her bravery all but gone and the fear returning.

The pain shot up her other hand this time and she screamed again. "I ask the questions, you answer. Understand?" he said in his calm menacing voice.

"Yes," she said, now learning that he wasn't going to answer anything she asked. He had all the power and could do whatever he wished. "Good." She felt him move away again but couldn't tell in which direction he now stood. "What did she tell you about her life?"

"Nothing." Anna answered with a tone of irritation.

The pain this time was the side of her leg. She

screamed.

"Are you lying to me?" he said, this time from her right side.

"No, stop doing that. What is that? Why are you doing this to me? My mother is dead? What does it matter now." Anna's temper was getting the better of her. Who was this idiot and why did he think he had the right to question her like this.

"My employer thinks it matters a great deal. Now tell me what did she tell you?"

His consistently calm tone irritated her more. "NOTHING, I tell you. Nothing. She never spoke of her life. But I have always known I was a bastard."

"You have always known? How, if she never told you?" His voice changed slightly this time a tone of interest creeping in.

"I just did. It was the way she always was. How much she wanted me to believe she had a husband, it was desperate. It made it obvious and I wasn't the only one to know the truth. I suspect that is why we had to move so often, because people kept finding out she hadn't been married to my father. She was a good mother, she always tried to shield me from it, but she never could. Children can be cruel to a bastard."

There was silence in the room. She could stand it no longer, she had to ask the question. "Did he send you?"

"Did who send me?" His tone was different now, less menacing.

"My damn father."

"Your father? I can't tell you that information." He seemed flustered now.

"You didn't know did you?" she said feeling braver

again.

"What don't I know?" he asked a little defensively.

"You didn't know that your employer was my father? What did you think this was, a quick roughing up of some reporter getting too close to a story?"

"I can't tell you that. Now shut up. I'm asking the questions here." She heard him move and the searing pain shot up her leg again.

"I'll just tell you one more thing. You can tell him from me I got his damn letter warning me off finding him. He has nothing to worry about. I have no intention of finding him, or ruining whatever life he has built up for himself. I don't care who he is or what he does. I don't want him in my life any more than he wants me. If abandoning a pregnant woman wasn't bad enough, but paying my mother to stay away, offering to pay me to stay away, why would I want such poison in my life? No, you can tell him he has nothing to worry about. I have no intention of pursuing him or any connection I have to him at all."

"That's a very nice speech Miss Forrester, but I need to be sure you're telling me the truth." His tone had changed back to the calm intimidating one again and Anna knew she had lost. But she didn't care. She was fed up of this man, this so called father.

"Oh really. Well, damn you too. I am just about fed up of you and your damn employer. Tell him to stay away from me and I will happily stay away from him. Damn you all to hell. My mother was worth a thousand of you. What sort of person does this to someone?"

"I can make a deal with you Miss Forrester. If you agree to leave the past alone and not pursue the matter further, I can report back to my employer that you are willing to agree to his terms. If you can give me your word that this won't go any further, I can let you go. If you don't agree, then things will be a little different."

"However did my mother get involved with such a person? Tell me, if I agree not to pursue him or look for him, will he agree not to follow and watch me either?"

"I can't say either way Miss, but I think you can be certain he will definitely keep an eye on you."

"All right, I agree. Of course I agree. I want nothing to do with him. You be sure to tell him that I don't want anything to do with him."

"Good, then Miss Forrester, we have an agreement. The agreed payment will continue as before, the arrangement stays the same."

"No I don't want his money."

"You have no choice Miss Forrester, it is part of the agreement."

"Is this to make it look like I've taken some sort of bribe if things should go wrong?"

"Everything will be all right if you keep up your terms."

Anna felt him loosening the binds around her ankles and pulling her to her feet, she walked forward unsteadily as he pushed her from behind.

They went forward for some distance, probably only a few yards, but Anna, struggling with temporary blindness from the hood, found it was difficult to be sure how far they had walked. Each footstep echoed, thudding on stone, like a countdown as she walked.

A door squeaked to her right and she was pushed in that same direction. The faint light she had detected from under the hood was now gone and there was nothing but darkness. The cold air flowing through the holes in the sacking and through her clothes told her she was now outside.

He was behind her now, loosening the binds around her wrists. "Remember Miss Forrester, he'll be watching you. Keep your end of the bargain up and you'll be left alone. Otherwise he might send me again and next time I won't be so generous."

She felt the thud of something heavy hit the floor on her left side and heard his footsteps fade away quickly as he disappeared. She stood for a few moments waiting and listening before raising her hands to the rough sacking material and lifting it away.

As she did the air raid siren began to wail its ghost song and Anna instinctively looked up. There were no stars, just blackness, and she remembered the clear sky she had seen while at the cottage. The London stars were hidden behind clouds and it began to drizzle. She bent down in the darkness and feeling to see what the thud next to her feet had been. It was her bags. She relaxed a little, relieved that at least her things were still there. The only problem she had now was that she had no idea where she was and she was in the middle of a blackout, with rain falling and an air raid had just started. She moved forward slowly, hoping she wouldn't step in debris or fall in a bomb crater. As she reached the end of what was an alleyway and moved out into a main street, she felt along the wall to her right, past the square, bowed windows and down the street, with the hope she would run into someone who could tell her where she was, before the bombers started dropping their loads.

She thought back to that night she had wilfully gone out in the raid. What had she been thinking? She shook her head at herself in the darkness. She had learnt that night what a bombing raid really was. It seemed so long ago now. So much had changed since then. Her mother had gone, and some lunatic was sending thugs to kidnap and threaten her.

She wasn't usually the sort of person to agree to the terms of someone like that, but she had no intention of looking for that man, whoever he was. He had to be either someone important, dangerous or a criminal, or he wouldn't have gone to such lengths to hide his identity. She was beginning to think he was a criminal. What sane person would send someone to kidnap and torture their own daughter?

She didn't care.

"Damn him," she said out loud in the darkness.

"Excuse me," said an amused soft voice. "I hope you are referring to Mr. Hitler, because if you are referring to me I take issue with being damned for no good reason."

"Oh sorry, I didn't realise anyone was there."

"No matter. And I quite agree."

"Agree with what?"

"To damn Mr. Hitler. Bloody inconvenience this bombing lark, isn't it? I mean, one can't walk down the street without running into other fellows."

"Oh I see. Yes, well, I'd best be off. Oh just a moment, could you tell me where exactly I am? I appear to have got myself hopelessly lost in this blackout." She sounded a little more hopeful than she would have liked to a completely unknown and unseen stranger in the dark, especially after what had just happened.

"Yes I understand. It's a darn nuisance. You're on the

corner of Christchurch Street, on the way towards Arthur street."

"Good grief I have no idea where that is." She fought to keep the dismay out of her voice.

"Where do you want to go?"

Being reluctant to tell the stranger where she lived, she instead decided to tell him where her work was. At least if she got there, she could either find her way home or shelter at the office.

"Fleet Street."

"Gracious Miss, you are a long way from there. Here I'll help you find the way if you like."

"No, I'd rather not put you out." She was a little reluctant to trust a strange man after her last encounter, especially one she couldn't see, but he did have a kind voice.

"No it's no trouble, I'm only going home to sit on my own. I'd rather help a lost damsel."

She agreed reluctantly, to allow him to walk her once she realised she had little choice. What was going on lately? She seemed to be turning into someone who needed help from men. It wasn't like her at all. She really needed to put recent weeks behind her and get back to normal. She liked the way her life had been and didn't really want it to change. Deciding she would let this man help her was the last act of reliance. From now on she was going to live as she had before, as someone who stood on her own and didn't go around kissing doctors and getting assaulted, kidnapped and interrogated by criminals.

No. She was going to have to pull herself together but she was very glad the blackout disguised the flush in her cheeks, which must have been a deep blush of annoyance and embarrassment.

It wasn't long before the first, faint roar of the bombers began to grow louder, alongside the sound of the ack-ack guns - our only defence. She looked up but couldn't see the enemy. It was too dark. The only light was from searchlights criss-crossing the sky, hunting the elusive Luftwaffe.

Anna stumbled along with the man, through the darkness for a little while longer, bumping up and down curbs as they crept along side by side. Once, she tripped over something hard in the road but a supporting arm from the man stopped her falling. A car, with its lights dimmed, almost knocked them down but just at the last moment, they managed to jump out of the way. After that incident they stayed hugging the buildings, feeling their way along using the solidness of brick and glass.

Soon the roar of the engines above grew to a familiar deafening sound and the man said he was pretty certain the planes were Messerschmitt's. An eerie whistling scream began and she was again reminded of that night hiding in the broken book shop.

They turned a corner and an ARP warden, wearing his tin hat, came up and said, "ey you, get down the shelter now. What you doing up 'ere?"

"Oh sorry warden, my wife and I got caught on the way home. We only live up this road here, so will rush on up to our shelter now," said the man before Anna could speak.

"Just up there you say?" The warden peered up the road behind him.

"Yes, not more than a few seconds."

"Well, I shouldn't ought to let you go, but as you say it's only just up the way I will this once. But mind you get yourself back before the raid next time. I don't want to see you wandering around here in a raid again."

"Yes, thank you. We will be sure to be better organised next time my good man," he said rushing past quickly.

"Quite an accomplished liar aren't you?" she said once they were a little further up the road.

"Well sometimes, there's a jolly good need for a little white lie," he said.

The whistling continued, as did the thudding, like a drum beat, making the ground vibrate with each successive thud.

"Luckily for us they're not directly overhead," he said.

She felt his movement as he tilted his head to look up. She mirrored his movement but still could see nothing but blackness, interspaced with searchlights scanning the sky.

A small van came up behind them as they crossed a street and the breaks squealed as the driver tried to stop. It stopped just short of them and the driver put her head out the window.

"Oi get off the road. I almost flattened you."

"Sorry," replied Anna. "Are you going anywhere near Fleet Street?"

"Yes, hop in, I'll take you."

She thanked the man for walking her so far and jumped in the van.

The clouds drifted momentarily so she could just make out the silhouette of a petite young woman who could barely see over the steering wheel. She wore trousers and had her hair tied in a scarf with a small, stray curl poking out the top.

The man she had left on the street tipped his hat at her

as he began to walk back the way they had come. It was only then she realised she hadn't even asked his name.

"So what you going to Fleet Street for then?" said the girl as she struggled to put the van in gear.

"I work there," she said, "but actually, would you mind taking me back home? I've had a hell of a day."

"Yes course, where's that?"

She gave the young woman directions and they drove on, the girl peering into the darkness ahead of the van.

"So who's the fella then?" The girl nodded her head towards the man walking the opposite way.

"No idea, he found me in the blackout. I'm actually glad to get away if I'm honest."

"Why was he the wandering hands type? I've met a few of those."

The girl's directness shocked her, but she liked it and felt comfortable with her.

"No, not at all. It's just different, I wouldn't want to tell him where I live, that's all."

"You not trust him then?" the woman asked.

"No I suppose not," she admitted, realising that she hadn't thought about it being a matter of trust, but she supposed it must be. "But you trust me then?"

"Well yes, you're a girl," Anna said, surprised. The question seemed a silly one, the answer was obvious wasn't it?

The young woman laughed. "That makes a difference does it?"

"Yes of course it does," Anna said, not admitting that the girl had made her think.

"You're a funny one. I've met plenty of women who aren't trustworthy at all. I knew one girl whose landlady held her prisoner by keeping her ration book and using all the rations in it. Can you believe such a thing? I know another who sells black market stockings at extortionate prices, making herself a tidy profit as she goes. And worst of all, a friend of mine told me about one woman who entertains other men while her husband is away at sea, although this friend does like to exaggerate, so I'm not sure how true that one is."

Anna did suppose it seemed a naive thing to only trust women, and she wasn't a naive sort of person, but she couldn't help but automatically be suspicious of men and trusting of women, especially after her two recent attacks. She did however know that the girl was right. This wasn't always the case, but she somehow couldn't help herself.

The young woman continued laughing and chatting to her about her job, but Anna was still thinking about their earlier conversation. She did however catch that the girl was driving for the WVS, but hadn't got her uniform yet, they were so short of drivers, they sent her out as she was, but she did have the little WVS badge on her collar.

Sitting on that seat, inside the old dirty van, with a stranger beside her, she relaxed more than she had in the last two weeks. What a strange day. What a strange few weeks. Had it really all happened?

"I'm Emily by the way," the woman said. "Emily Borrows."

CHAPTER TWENTY
October 1940 ANNA

Going up the misshapen stone steps to the darkened doorway of her boarding house, she took one last look at the sky, the searchlights were still scanning, the bombs still whistling, London was still vibrating under her feet alongside the return fire from the ack-ack guns.

In a strange way, now that she was home, she didn't feel quite as scared anymore. Maybe it was the attacks, maybe it was the loss of her mother, maybe it was that she had become used to danger. Maybe it was something else. She didn't want to think about it. She was only thankful not to be scared any more. If there was a bomb with her name on it, so be it. Let it come she thought, facing the dark sky.

There hadn't been enough light anywhere for her to see what damage the earlier kidnapping had left and she tried to ignore the pain in her hands and leg where she had been wounded with something hot and burning. In some ways she was thankful for the blackout. She put her hands around the cold, firm door handle, relief washing over her as she turned it.

Shutting the door behind her, she listened for a few moments. There was silence. Then she heard footsteps on the cellar steps and the under stairs door that led down to the basement, where everyone gathered during a raid, was flung open letting a beam of light into the dark hallway.

"Anna darling, it's you. Where on earth have you been? I was expecting you hours ago." Olivia, clutching a mug of something hot and steamy, had a net wrapped around her head and her blond tresses wound around curlers which poked through the sides.

She was dressed in silken pyjamas and leaned on the door to the cellar in a way that unconsciously showed off her curvy figure. Even when she was in her nurse's uniform Olivia looked like she was dressed a little provocatively. It was just Olivia. She had the look of a Hollywood film star and all the confidence of one too. She often popped into Anna's room on a morning, just as she was getting in from a night shift with some of the most unusual stories.

Olivia stopped and looked at her, "Gracious Anna, have you been caught in the raid again? You look frightful. Lord come downstairs. All the girls are here and we've got hot cocoa on the go."

"Olivia, I need to go to my room, I'm dreadfully tired and I can't face anyone right now. I don't care that it's in the middle of a raid. Frankly I think I'd sleep through an invasion right now."

"Well, if you're sure, but if you get bombed in your bed, don't expect me to nurse you back to health. I'll bring you up a cup of cocoa to warm you up. It's getting frightfully cold out there now."

Anna didn't reply but began to walk up the familiar

creaking stairs, stepping over the worn bit of carpet in the dim light, which often tripped her up. Anna felt like she had spent so much time travelling recently, all she wanted to do was get back to her familiar way of life.

And so, when she opened the door she could barely be bothered to get undressed, but knew she must look at her hands and leg, which were painful. Her room was exactly as she left it. Simple with no fancy extras, or Hollywood pictures like Olivia's.

Once the blackouts were drawn and the lights on, Anna surveyed herself in the battered mirror on her wall. Her stockings were in shreds and her skirt and jacket were covered in dirt. Her hair was a disheveled mess, sticking out everywhere. She had lost her hat somewhere along the way and her bobby pins had abandoned ship. She inspected her hands. Both had identical red, oval-shaped welts on them, like burns and Anna's memory of the pain told her she was right. She remembered burning herself while cooking once and it had been a similar pain, but less intense because that time she had immediately taken her hand away. He, however, had held whatever implement it was on her skin for a time. When she looked at her leg, the burn was bigger, where he had burnt her in the same place twice.

Damn it. She thought. She abandoned her stockings to the waste bin and removed her clothes down to her underwear, dropping her clothes in a heap on the floor.

There was a knock at the door and Olivia came bustling in with a steaming mug of cocoa in one hand and balancing a porcelain bowl and jug in the other, rather expertly Anna noticed.

"Darling, I'm so glad to see you. I've brought you

something to wash with. I thought you might like to freshen up before going to bed. I'm dreadfully sorry about your mother. It's such a shame and her so far away. Did you see her before hand? I suppose you didn't make it. Oh such a shame. Well I suppose you'd rather not discuss it. That's all right. How was the north? I've heard that the northern people are nothing short of folk who live in little tumble down houses. Is that true? We've had a dreadful time here while you've been gone. Bombs every night. Lord when will it ever stop. We have all learnt to ignore it now and often sit having a sing song down in the cellar. It's quite jolly really. Oh but when I'm on shift at the hospital, oh that's simply terrible. The injuries they come in with. Anyway, I'm rambling on. Sorry Anna."

"It's all right Olivia, I don't mind, I just want a good, long sleep."

Olivia looked at her sideways "Before you do, I want to hear about this doctor you wrote to me about."

"I did not write to you about Doctor Laker. I wrote to tell you I was going to be staying there a while longer due to my knee injury. Believe me, there was no pleasure in it and certainly not in the way you're implying." Anna pulled a face as the kiss came to mind more clearly than she was comfortable with. She certainly wasn't going to tell Olivia about that. She would never let it go. It would be the next big romance, for Olivia was a hopeless romantic. Anna simply couldn't understand what was so appealing about being in love.

Olivia looked at her suspiciously. "Well, I'm not convinced that there isn't something you're not telling me, but I know you well enough to understand that you're not going to give it up easily. However, you know I'll get it out of you in the end. I always do," she said retreating to the door and blowing her a kiss as she left. "It's good to have you back darling Anna."

She woke early the following morning to the familiar sound of the city. The familiar noises of busses, bicycle bells, the footsteps of people rushing to work and the constant buzz of voices at a level too inaudible to make out. After the silence of the country it seemed strange and unreal, but familiar and oddly comforting.

The journey to work allowed her to enjoy normality and the closer she got, the more the North, the doctor and the last few weeks seemed to be little more than a strange nightmare. Pushing those thoughts away, she picked her way through the dirty, bombed out streets. Why did the destruction shock her so much more than before?

The difference was startling. She hadn't noticed before that even the buildings not touched by bombs looked tired. The whole city looked like it was hanging by a thread. She could almost believe that if she blew hard enough the whole city would collapse, and it made her feel sad and angry at the same time. What had they done to her city?

When she walked in she was greeted by a cold glance from Frank Delancey. Unusually, it made her smile. Some things didn't change.

She nodded at him in greeting all the same, but he just stared at her through his piggy eyes, while mopping his sweaty brow.

She paused at her own desk only to deposit her bag and coat before moving directly to the Editor's office. He was rooting through a filing cabinet and had his back to the door. The room was filled with a familiar cloud of smoke, which swirled around the ceiling and off the peeling paint in the corner of the walls.

Anna coughed and he turned to look at her, his customary Woodbine clamped firmly between his teeth.

"Forrester, you back then? Good! I'm seriously lacking in decent journalists. And I'm probably going to have to promote you to bigger stories, even though you are a woman. But I reckon you could handle it.

In the meantime, I've got something I want you to go over today. If you get straight on it that would be good. I want it going in as soon as possible. It's about cooking, so something you should know what to do with. Go to it then Forrester, you've had enough time off. Here's the information on the article I want."

He handed her a small pile of documents and papers and she left with a sigh. She was glad to be back, but somehow she felt different, yet here she was back to the same old stories.

She found her thoughts strayed to Elizabeth Leyac once again as she thumbed through the information her Editor had given her. She felt removed from her surroundings and found it difficult to concentrate. It just didn't seem important. Why did a story about cooking matter? Had she really just buried her mother?

Anna didn't get the opportunity to seek out Marcus until almost the end of the day. She wanted to ask him about his article and his source. He had his own office tucked away down a corridor away from everyone else. He always said it was because he liked to be alone to research, but Anna suspected he had been put there to keep him out the way as Marcus seemed to horde papers, research, information and books. Anna found him buried under a pile of dusty old papers. He was surprised and pleased to see her.

"Forrester, he said, did you know that the Ministry of Defence is taking over many of the country's large estates? It's compulsory and is not particularly popular with many of the landowners, who are finding themselves effectively kicked out of their own homes."

"No Marcus, I had no idea. Is it going to happen to all the estates?"

"No, I doubt it but it's fascinating. I am interested in how this new turn of events will change the estates' heritage and preservation."

"Marcus, I've come to pick your brains on the Leyacs."

He looked up at her over his spectacles and rubbed the side of his temple. He was interested, she could tell by the way he was fidgeting.

"What do you want to know? Most of the general information about them is freely available."

"Ah that's just it, I don't want to know just general information. I want to know about Elizabeth Leyac."

"Elizabeth Leyac? Hmmm, there's not a lot of information available about that particular Leyac, and as she died so young, there isn't much of a life to speak of. What is it in particular that interests you?"

She hesitated unsure of how much to tell him. "Well, you see Marcus, since I read your article about Lord Thomas' death and the family's history, I have found myself interested in Elizabeth. I'd like to know what happened to her?"

"As far as I understand it from my source, there isn't a lot known about the girl. She died young, and unmarried."

"Would you be willing, Marcus, to take me to see your source?"

"I don't think so Anna. I'm sorry, I can't see how this could be of benefit to anyone. There is nothing to learn about Elizabeth Leyac that isn't already public knowledge. And my source is keen to stay anonymous. He doesn't want any repercussions with regards his information. I can't just let you see him without good reason."

"The thing is Marcus, I believe I do have a good reason. When my mother was dying, she left me something. Something which belonged to someone. When I opened this package, inside was the personal diary of Elizabeth Leayc dating from 1908. It is a huge fat book filled to the brim with writing, letters, notes and other things the girl recorded. I'd like to speak to your source and show him this item and ask him what he thinks of it."

Marcus sat up in his seat and pushed his spectacles further up on his face his eyes widening in surprise. "Really? And do you in fact know where you mother came to find such an item? It's a very rare item, I would imagine. I didn't even know Elizabeth Leyac kept a diary. You're certain it's genuine?"

"I've no reason to suspect that it's not. Do you think your source would be interested? What I've been reading of her life so far is very interesting indeed."

"Yes, he would be. Just wait one moment. Let me telephone him. He might agree to meet us tomorrow."

Marcus shifted the mess of old papers and ancient sources of information on his desk and dug out his black heavy phone from beneath, moving one pile on top of another pile. Some of the papers toppled and rained down on the floor. He didn't seem to notice.

She waited while Marcus was connected to his mysterious source.

"Hello... Yes, It's Anthony Marcus from the newspaper... yes... yes I've got something you might be interested in... a very rare item belonging to one of the Leyac family... yes... yes how does tomorrow morning suit?... yes, I'll see you then. Good bye."

He replaced the receiver. "We're meeting him tomorrow. He's a professor at Oxford, so we need to travel up there tomorrow morning. You all right to come in a bit early?"

Anna agreed that she would and left that evening with the prospect of finally meeting someone who might be able to give her some information on the Leyac family. Finally she would be meeting an expert.

CHAPTER TWENTY-ONE
October 1940 ANNA

Next morning she met Marcus at their office and they went off to catch the train to Oxford. Not really having spoken to him much, she was unsure what to talk about. He was a quiet person, someone who would watch people unobserved in the corner of a room, and as such was often overlooked by many of their louder, more extroverted colleagues, but she knew that there was a quick intelligent mind behind that exterior. One which she didn't underestimate, as did some others. The journey was a quiet one and she was glad when it was over and she didn't have to make pointless conversation with him.

As the entered the grounds of Oxford University, he suddenly turned to her. "So how do you think your mother came across this diary?"

"I'm not sure," Anna said, careful not to give too much away, but in truth she still had no idea.

Whatever he was about to say in reply was lost as he was distracted by a figure coming towards them.

He lifted his hand and waved in greeting. "Ah there's

my source now," he said.

The professor, a small man, slightly overweight, was wearing a jumper with fraying edges and patched elbows. His shirt collar was turned up slightly at the back. He had grey curly hair which had been left untamed and was sticking up wildly. He walked as if in a hurry and looked flustered.

"Hello professor." Marcus held out his hand and shook the older man's chubby wrinkled one.

"Is this the girl with the item?" the professor asked, peering at Anna through his small eyes that had a tendency to shortsightedness, making him squint giving his face a screwed up, peering expression.

"Yes professor, this is Anna Forrester. Anna this is Professor Williams."

She held out her hand and shook the older man's clammy one.

"She's trustworthy is she Anthony?" the professor asked Marcus as if she wasn't there.

She thought it odd hearing the professor use Marcus's first name, and she wondered what their relationship was.

"Yes professor. I wouldn't have brought her if she wasn't."

"Well then, let's get on shall we."

He walked on without waiting for a response and led them, at a fast pace, through a number of different buildings, doors, corridors and up a set of stairs, until she was quite confused as to where she was.

The professor led them into an office cluttered with books, papers and files piled up in every corner. A huge bookshelf lined one side of the office was groaning under the weight of books that were crammed into all corners, and more papers were stacked on top of these books. The floor had various piles of items and folders laid around. A line of dirty cups lined one side of the desk and an ashtray was full of the butt ends of cigars, the lingering smell of cigar smoke mingling with the smell of dust and damp. He moved a few piles of papers on to other piles to reveal two dirty chairs. Anna and Marcus sat and the professor sat at his desk chair, looking at her expectantly.

She pulled the diary out of her bag. "Here it is," she said handing him the small fat book.

He took it in his hands, roughly putting on the glasses from his desk as he peered at it.

It made that familiar crack as he pulled back the cover and it opened naturally where she had placed a book marker. He turned the diary to the beginning and looked over the first few pages and read the initial entry. He then began to flick through the pages of the book, stopping at certain intervals, flicking on.

"Fascinating," he said eventually. "I don't mind saying that as far as we knew, this item didn't exist." He looked over, assessing her.

"Is it genuine then professor?" Marcus asked.

"Oh yes Anthony, I am pretty certain it is the real thing. You can tell by the handwriting. You see how she flounces the edges of her R's and F's. That was common for her. I've seen Elizabeth's handwriting before and I'm pretty sure this is genuine." He looked over at her again. "So could you tell me how you came to be in possession of such an item?"

She told him then of her mother giving it to her as she died and of the news cuttings she had found under her mother's bed.

"How interesting. Could you tell me Anna, was your mother ever in service?"

"No never. She had me quite young, and she's never told me anything about being in service. She didn't tell me much, but I'm pretty certain she wasn't in service."

"Hmm, well if she wasn't in service, does she have a wealthy background? Someone who could have been a friend of Elizabeth's in her childhood perhaps?" he asked overlooking her joke and rubbing the greying edges of his beard as he frowned at the book.

"No she has no family."

"What about your father?"

"I never knew my father. There was always just mother and me."

He looked at her and she expected to see the usual disapproval in his eyes, but instead there was only curiosity.

"Do you have any idea at all how your mother came to have such an item?"

"That's what I've been trying to find out. While I was in Yorkshire I went to Leyac House and I must confess I did sneak into the private part of the house in search of, well I'm not sure, but something. Anyway before I could find anything interesting, I was stopped and thrown off the grounds."

"Really? Well how exciting," he said pushing his glasses further up his face.

"I didn't know this Anna. Did you really trespass?" Marcus asked, sounding slightly impressed.

"None of that is important now Anthony." The professor waved his hand at him in dismissal. He looked down at the little book in his hands again.

"This is certainly an interesting document, especially one correlating to such an unknown member of that family. There is little information about her and records and personal accounts are even rarer."

"Is there anything you can tell me about her?" she asked.

"Not a lot unfortunately, but, what I can tell you is that she was different from the rest of her family in that she kept herself modestly and tried to do well by others in the surrounding village. It seems she had been fairly popular with the locals but only as far as any rich, young girl can be popular with common folk. Unfortunately the illness that took her, means whatever life she might have had will never be known."

She was slightly disappointed. It seemed no one knew anything at all about Elizabeth. "Do you think that the lack of information about her life is simply due to the fact that she died so young, so therefore she didn't get the opportunity to do anything worth remembering?"

"Yes partially, although I do suspect that it is also partly due to the family history and that Elizabeth was not Catherine's daughter. I suspect that Catherine, who I have had reports was a cold, calculating and vicious person, favoured her own daughter and pushed Elizabeth aside as she was the daughter of the other woman. The woman, I suspect Ashton Leyac loved to the day he died. You see there are a lot of reports about Lord Ashton being a cold and brooding sort of person who had no real affection or love for his wife or his daughters. However, reports of the person he was in his youth tell a different story, almost as if it were talking about two different people. I know people change as they age but this is such a dramatic change that I can only conclude it is due to the loss of his first wife Eliza. But getting back to Elizabeth, with no real love from either of her parents, she may have been a kind of family outcast, although the lavishness of her funeral tells a different story. The problem with someone like Elizabeth is that it is all guesswork. We have no source information on which to base our conclusions and can only build a picture of who she was using information from her family and people who met and saw her. That is why such a diary is a great find indeed and one I would give my right eye to examine further. Would you allow me to examine it Anna?"

"I am happy to let you examine it, but I want to read it myself first, if you don't mind."

He looked slightly disappointed. "Yes, of course, I quite understand, but you must promise me that I can be the first to examine it once you have finished?"

"Yes of course, but I did want to tell you. I have read a few entries already, and what you say about Catherine is right. If you turn to the first main entry at the beginning and read that one, you should get the first hand evidence you're looking for."

He read aloud the entry she had read all those weeks ago, about Elizabeth losing her father and Catherine's reaction, it took her back to that night in the cottage and the correlation between Elizabeth's life and her own. In that moment she suddenly felt exposed, as if it were her diary they were reading, but she pushed that thought to the back of her mind.

She then showed him the entry with the letter from Lord Ashton's friend Toby Blackwood. By the time he had finished reading this entry he was almost jumping around in excitement.

He looked up at her and mopped his perspiring brow, despite the coolness of the room.

"You must forgive me Anna. You see I have spent much of my life researching families such as the Leyacs and to find such an item as this about such a famous family is rare indeed, one that possibly even the family themselves don't know about. This diary may shed some light on many of my theories of that family and give the evidence I have lacked, straight from one of the members themselves. It's an almost unprecedented find. But I must warn you Anna, you must keep the existence of this diary a secret. If the family were to find out that you possessed such an item, they would take measures to get it back and without the evidence you need that your mother legally had the right to hold such an item, I fear it may be taken and we will never find out what Elizabeth has to say."

"But with Thomas dead, there is no family left. How can that possibly matter now? Surely, they can't do anything like this, with no family members to contest it." Anna replied.

"Don't underestimate that family. There are no Leyacs as such, yes you are right, but there are others who still look out for their interests. Just because the master is dead, don't make the mistake of thinking that the dog is too. The dog, so to speak will defend the home even when the master is gone," he said with a little chuckle.

Anna thought of Mr Flynn who threw her off the estate. "People like Julien Flynn?"

He looked up at her surprised, "You are a clever girl, Anna Forrester. Yes that's exactly the kind of person I mean."

"Never mind about that, is there any other information about the Leyacs that you can tell us professor?" Marcus asked with a slight note of impatience.

She glanced over at him. It hadn't escaped her that he had phrased it as 'us' as if he were also a part of her investigation.

The professor rubbed his chin, "I did come across a letter many years ago, which may be of interest. Let me see, where did I put it?"

He started to shift papers around on his desk muttering to himself as he did. After a couple of minutes he tapped his fingers on a folder aimlessly, while he stood and thought. Then his face changed with an expression of realisation and he went over to his filing cabinet in the corner, sidestepping piles of folders and books lined up in a higgledy piggledy line across his floor. He rooted through the filing cabinet for a few minutes before producing a brown folder with tatty corners and dirty marks from years of opening and closing. From the folder he produced a set of small notepaper sized sheets written in a hand Anna didn't recognise.

He handed it to Anna. "This is a letter from one of the maids working at Leyac House when Louisa and Elizabeth were children. It is written to her mother."

She sat back to read the letter, with Marcus peering over her shoulder. It was written fairly well but by someone without the training of eloquent writing, so someone from a common background whose family had had the good foresight and opportunity to teach their children to read and write.

My dear mama,

I hope this letter finds you and Pa well. I thank you for your kind words and news in your recent letter, I only wish I could be a part of the lambing this season. I remember fondly our time in the not so distant past when we sat up all night waiting for ol-Bessie. Anyway, I am sure you will manage fine without me and I know we had great need of the money that my being in service brings.

Speaking of my time here. I have a problem, which is concerning me greatly and I confess I am struggling to keep my place and not step in and do something about the situation. The two children, Miss Elizabeth and Miss Louisa are both sweet girls in their own way, however the younger of the two, Louisa, is much favoured by their mother and I fear this has led her to become spoilt. I have caught her on a number of occasions getting her sister into trouble for things she has done herself. It would not matter quite so much if Elizabeth would defend herself and stand up against her sister, but she is a strange brooding sort of child prone to silence and I must admit I often want to shake her and instil some kind of self defence in the girl, as she just seems to accept whatever is thrown her way.

For all that Louisa needs taking in hand (and a good dose of discipline would do her wonders) I fear Elizabeth is more of a difficult case. I cannot understand a child who would appear to just give up and accept her fate. Surely all children would, in the very least, defend themselves from injustices?

What I want to know is what I should do about these two strange children. I fear Louisa's antics are making Elizabeth's life miserable not to mention that her continued behaviour will not serve her well in the future, despite all her money.

Dear mama please write and tell me what I should do, if anything. It's difficult for me to sit back and say nothing of these observations, but equally I must remember that I am the maid here and not their equal, so with that in mind, would it be proper of me to say something or would it just jeopardise my position?

Help me mama, I am all in a muddle. Your dearest daughter Polly

"An interesting letter professor, but what does this tell me, other than Louisa was spoilt and Elizabeth didn't stand up to her. We already know Louisa was favoured, you've just read us a passage that says so."

"Ah Anna, you must learn to read what is not said." The professor sat back in his chair and leaned back folding his arms in satisfaction.

She just stared at him, then glanced at Marcus who was looking equally perplexed.

"It tells us, of Elizabeth's character. She was a child who this maid says was brooding and silent, she didn't stand up against her sister but took her treatment silently. Why would a child do such a thing?"

Anna lifted her shoulders in a shrug and shook her head. She was getting impatient now and was beginning to feel like she was in a lesson. She could see why the professor was a university lecturer. She watched his eyes sparkle with information and passion for knowledge.

"Because, Anna, if she was silent, it means she kept her thoughts and feelings to herself. Not that she didn't get upset with her sister's treatment of her, but that it was better to not get in the way. She was good at keeping her own thoughts and feelings to herself, she was good at keeping secrets. And, this is important because it means that she probably had secrets. Secrets about her life that we don't know but which she may have written in this diary."

"That is certainly true professor, she was courting a boy."

He nearly fell off his chair, when she said this. And she secretly enjoyed being the one with information.

"Yes In 1912 she talks in her diary of a boy she was courting, in secret because he was a villager, a commoner who joins the Navy. She talks of how she's torn between what is right and what she wants to do herself, so she keeps him a secret, but she does agree to his marriage proposal. But the last entry I read was a year later in 1913 and they still aren't married. Harry is his name. He is away a lot and she hasn't married him because her sister has many miscarriages, some awful ones from what I read. I don't yet know what happened between them."

He was perspiring now, clutching the little book like a treasure, his mouth open in shock.

"I, I mean… I knew she… gracious. Are you certain?" He stumbled over his words almost as an extension of what was going on in his private thoughts.

"But professor, the family weren't as well known back then were they?" Marcus interrupted.

"Gracious no, they were just a moderately wealthy family in the north with an ancestral estate," he said almost absently.

"So Elizabeth never knew or experienced the kind of attention and fame the family now has. And therefore may have been able to keep all manner of secrets?" Marcus continued.

"That's right. Her world would have been very different indeed. She was the daughter of the local landowner and that would have been the sum of her world. If she came to London or went out in society, she would have had a close circle of acquaintants and that would have been it. However, there is little evidence that Elizabeth went into

225

society much.

Louisa, on the other hand was another matter entirely. There are countless articles and photographs in the society pages of her in London partying, sometimes with her husband and some from before she was married. Knowing what we know of Catherine, though, this could be due to her influence and her control over Elizabeth, but this is just speculation. Maybe Elizabeth just wasn't a party girl in the same way her sister was.

However, it has been speculated over the years that Louisa was sent to the point of madness with all the miscarriages she suffered before she finally conceived the twins. I am inclined to believe this could have been exaggerated a little, but it would have had an effect on her, there's no doubt about that.

This brings me to the important point in my theory. With the knowledge that Catherine was capable of almost anything, including attempting to erase Eliza and keeping the fact that she wasn't Elizabeth's mother from the girl herself, until she could use it against her. It's my belief, that to save her favourite daughter from further hurt and so called 'madness,' what would she do if, for instance, the missing twin had actually died?

The answer I believe is nothing. I think Catherine faked the kidnapping and somehow managed to get rid of the maid by paying her off. It would be very easy to dispose of the baby, especially as there was now a coffin for Elizabeth. All she had to do was hide the baby in the coffin with Elizabeth and voila, no one would ever find the child. It certainly explains why the child has never been found despite extensive searching. However, it is just one theory and completely unprovable, unless we would be allowed to dig up the graves of the Leyacs, but that would be wholly frowned upon and very difficult to get permission to do, so alas it remains just that, a theory. Very exciting one though don't you think?"

He shrugged his shoulders in a kind of resignation, which no doubt had come from years of trying to fathom out mysteries of this type and failing to find all the evidence and clues to prove them.

She nodded holding out her hand for the book back. He looked at it for a few moments as if he didn't want to let it go, before slowly holding it out in a shaking hand. As she took it, he held it for a few moments more than was necessary and she was almost certain she might have to prise it from him before he let go with a sudden flurry.

"I'm sorry professor, we have to get back. Our Editor wants me on an RAF story this afternoon. We need to get back before we lose our jobs," Marcus said. "We'll be in touch."

The professor nodded at Marcus and patted his arm. "Good to see you Anthony my boy."

They thanked him and left, but not before he made her promise once again to let him examine the diary more closely.

On the return journey to London they sat in silence, Marcus seemingly deep in thought, so she took out the diary and skipped through some of the entries, until she came to one particularly long one, much longer than some of the other entries. It was dated July 1914.

CHAPTER TWENTY-TWO
July 1914 ELIZABETH

It has been two years complete from the time when I first accepted Harry's marriage proposal and we are still yet to succeed in becoming man and wife. Following Harry's joining of the Navy, he has been absent considerably and Louisa has been so desperately ill trying to become a mother, it hardly seemed the appropriate time for a wedding. With Louisa's needs, making such a startling announcement to my family would not be met with great revelry. In truth it would be met with great disdain.

However, I have begun to speculate whether there ever would be an appropriate time. I was abundantly conscious that one day I would have to rupture the manacles of my life here, set myself free and hang the consequences. There would be an upsurge of vexation when they discovered our attachment, but I am not wholly certain I am prepared to handle such an encounter at this time.

Is it just cowardice? I cannot say with any degree of certainty. I long to be with Harry to set forth on our life together, but cannot abide their contempt. Even Louisa would certainly not understand, her husband would ridicule and Catherine - well I shudder at the mere mention of what she might do.

Today however, I find myself giddy with excitement once more for Harry is expected home. His latest correspondence contained a slightly apprehensive promise of his wish to 'discuss matters with me.' I suspect these matters are to decisively settle on a date for our marriage and to inform my family. However, this is concerning me somewhat. I find myself fearing greatly what Catherine will do to make my existence difficult when she discovers our secret. It is imperative my family does not find out about our engagement until they cannot do a thing to alter it.

I halted my writing for a moment there, Dear Journal, to feel the realness of Harry's letter. It is true, he really is coming home but I notice my constant feeling of the letter to reassure myself of this reality was making the edges become rough. I really must stop handling it or the words will become illegible.

I am determined, Dear Journal, that thoughts of my family and their disapproval will not spoil today. Harry is returning and I refuse to allow fanciful ideas to spoil this reunion. Although I find that my heart is hammering considerably, my breath comes in quickly and the butterflies dance in my stomach so much that I have to place a palm across my abdomen to attempt to control myself.

I suppose I am just full of nervous excitement. Harry has been away for considerable months and I want him to be happy when he sees me. I have spent a good deal of time this morning trying to decide what to wear and attempting to tame my wild hair into a respectable style, but as usual its obstinate tendency to freely do as it pleases remains, despite all my efforts, so I have given up on it in exasperation and am now purposely avoiding looking at myself.

Oh and another new thing I have achieved today, I have dressed myself. If I am honest, Dear Journal, it proved to be a considerably harder task than it appeared to be. But if I am to be Harry's wife, I must learn to do tasks for myself and my new husband who would expect me to be able to manage without staff to attend me. However,

I do not mind admitting that the thought of this does make me smile and on quick glance at my reflection I notice a slight pink tinge to my cheeks.

Well, that is it, Dear Journal. I am off to meet Harry. Being so early, the house is silent. Catherine never rises early and Louisa, in the grips of yet another pregnancy, has been ordered bed rest. Her husband spends much of his days in my father's study. I suppose it is his study now. So I am safe to steal away unnoticed. I shall update you later on my day.

Gracious, Dear Journal, you will not believe what has happened. I have not been able to continue where I left off for some days, things have been so frantic and so many demands on my time that I simply haven't had a moment.

I left you a few days ago about to leave early in the morning to meet Harry. Well let me pick up the story from there and recount what has happened over the last few days. And be prepared because the story is long and I'm going to tell it as I recall it to have happened.

On that morning, after finishing writing, I departed the house and moved across the driveway to the main gates and out into the covered, wooded pathway that leads away from the house. But I must pause to tell you how exquisite and fresh the warm July sun was, as it had not yet reached the full heat of midday. It poked through the openings in the branches and created little flashes as I walked, intermittently, feeling heat and cool on my cheeks as I passed. I simply adore spending time outdoors. It is the only period I ever feel truly free and nature seems to welcome me in its embrace throughout all seasons of the year.

So, back to my story. I was early for my scheduled meeting with Harry, so took my time strolling through the fields and hills, taking the long route towards Heathfield village. The morning was so delightful I found myself relaxing, my concerns melting away into the fields like rain drops seeping into the earth.

By the time I reached the village, had strolled through the green area and passed the big tree marking the centre, and by the rows of small one storey cottages toward the wilderness and lake that marked the furthest part of the village, it was close to the scheduled time Harry and I were to meet.

I was first to arrive and I confess to feeling a sense of mild disappointment and an inconvenient wave of fear as I considered whether he would arrive at all.

I only had to stand alone for a few moments however, as I saw Harry approach, a playful smile about his lips.

"My Lilly, I've missed ya." He wrapped his arms around me and kissed my face in quite a bold fashion.

I felt so secure and contented wrapped in his arms.

"I've brought us a picnic Lilly, I thought we could walk t' the river and spend a bit of time alone." He waved the basket and smiled expectantly.

"What a lovely idea, but we need to go separately. I cannot risk Catherine discovering us."

"I'm not scared of her, I think we should tell the world." He tossed his free arm wide then and grinned cheekily, his eyes twinkled with mischief.

"Please Harry, she has the power to separate us. Believe me, you know not what she is really capable of." I caressed his arm as I pleaded with him, his touch sending unusual tingles through my fingers.

Harry did reluctantly agree to co-operate but his grin disappeared and a serious expression took its place.

We set off towards the river and wilderness area that marked the end of the village, Harry looped rearwards and I through the more secluded nature route.

Sara Thomson

The river streams through a most beautiful unspoilt part of Heathfield, Dear Journal, that is popular with couples and fishermen. My family owns a river boat that sailed up and down many years ago, but it had not been operated for a considerable period. The river walk consists of a trail beside bushes, undergrowth and overhanging trees, which create a secluded and private walkway. It cascades down one side of the river and across a small bridge and loops back up the opposite side.

Adjacent to the riverside are breaks in the undergrowth, which are popular areas for local fishermen to sit and enjoy the pleasant climate on their days off.

It was as I was walking along this part of the river that Harry caught me up. After a short walk he navigated us from the pathway into the small clutch of considerably pretty trees lining one side of the river. Once it had been an extensive forest with the river just a small part of it snaking through, but that had been centuries prior and now lives only in the history books Nanny had made Louisa and I study as children. Now however, all that remained were trifling patches of tree groups where local children played games of Robin Hood.

Harry appeared to have significant knowledge of this clutch of forest and escorted me deep into what remained of it. He halted beneath an ancient oak, where the sunshine pattered through the trees forming a delightful light show, like a child's glass mobile catching the light. I was touched at the beauty. I asked him how he knew this place, to which he replied "I used t' play here as a child. In fact I spent a lot of ma boyhood here in these trees playing heroes an' villains. I know the area well and knew that you would like this spot. It's perfect for a picnic don't ya think?"

He had been rummaging through his basket as he spoke and had spread a rather large but well worn cloth on the ground. He then told me to sit, which I did and watched him arrange the food and drink he had brought.

On bold impulse I leaned forward and kissed him. He rather quickly raised his hand and held my face, preventing me from drawing back and kissed me himself in a rather longer and deeper manner than I had first anticipated. As he leaned away somewhat, he regarded me intensely frowning in a searching manner before breaking into an extensive smile his eyes twinkling, and produced a sandwich in his left hand. I looked at it and smiled before taking the sandwich and biting into it rather rapidly, still viewing him.

"Good?" he asked.

"Perfect."

He smiled in acknowledgement then and retrieved a sandwich for himself before also taking a large bite, regarding me as he did, his eyes shining with mischievousness.

After a few moments his face grew serious and his golden fiery eyes viewed mine with a sense of urgency.

"We need t' talk about something important."

I immediately had feelings of apprehension, as Catherine's face appeared in my mind. "I know it has been a long time since we were first engaged and that we need to change this, however with Louisa's current state of health, I fear greatly that they would make it extremely difficult for me to leave."

"Lilly, it's not just that we need t' talk about. Remember we talked before about a war comin', a big one?"

I nodded my head, now with my mouth full of cake in a most undignified manner, but Harry did not appear to notice.

"Well, it's happening. Any day now they'll announce it an' once it finally is I'll be going away for a long while and it'll be difficult for me to get back. Actually, it was very difficult to get back this time, but that's not important now."

"Louisa's husband was discussing something regarding this over dinner, but I must confess to not paying attention. How are you certain it will mean war?"

"Oh my dear Lilly, ya live a sheltered life all the way up there in your big house. You will just have t' trust me that there will be an announcement any day now and we will be at war. It's just a case of officially announcing it. But I don't want t' talk about the ins and outs of the political situation. What I want t' discuss is us."

He paused and took hold of my hand in his before continuing. "As I'm going t' be away and because we have no idea how long this war will last or how long I'll be gone, we need to get married right away. Otherwise it could be years before we're together again and I just can't face going away again without knowing you're my wife. It's been two years Lilly, we need to do this now. Ya cannot live in fear of Catherine anymore. And Louisa has her mother and husband to take care of her. I am here for ya now. Let's get married while I'm home on leave. I'm only here until the day after tomorrow, we can get married tomorrow and spend the day after together as husband and wife before I leave t' go back to Queenstown. What do you say?" His large hands warm and rough in mine, urged me to agree.

Despite my considerable fears, whenever I was with Harry I felt I was able to accomplish anything, so heard my voice declare, before I had time to think. "I believe we should do it Harry. With you going away to war, I should be able to postpone informing my family by at least a number of months and with luck, by this time you may know when you are due home."

"That is the best thing t' do I think. Keep it quiet until I can get back and sort out living accommodation for us. You will have t' live up there for a little longer until I can get something organised. I will try t' make it as short as possible. And, there's something else."

He paused weighing me up as if he had been attempting to gauge my reaction. "I also think we should tell my mother about us. She will help you while I'm away and any letters I will address to Lilly and send t' my mother. She will keep them for you and it is less risky than using the gardener at your place. I know I can trust my mother.

We don't know we can trust the gardener. I know he's been good so far, but who's t' say that won't change?"

"I will admit it would be pleasant to meet your mother and to have someone to talk to about you. We have kept the secret for such a long period, I find I am quite apprehensive about the prospect of informing others. But as it is your mother and as I trust your judgement implicitly, we should go ahead."

He nodded at my words. "I've already spoken to the priest at the church in Lowsbury and he has agreed t' marry us tomorrow. We can tell my mother this afternoon and she will be one of our witnesses."

A strange combination of disbelief and excitement washed around me at that moment. I was truly to be married the next day. I would have the right to distinguish myself as 'wife' albeit in secret, but that was no matter. I will belong to another and that other will belong to me. This thought alone made me believe I could overcome whatever punishment Catherine could deliver.

As the afternoon sun sidled across the sky we discussed our future together in a blur of excited chatter. As the light finally changed to spell the lateness of the hour, I was barely able to wait until its rise again.

Strange is it not, Dear Journal, that it is the very thing that spells destruction, which spurs us to finally fulfill our promise to each other. War is a strange being.

Once we had collected the remnants of the picnic and set off in the direction of Harry's mother's cottage, I was in turmoil with butterflies fluttering and dancing a jig in my stomach. I made an attempt, as best I was able, to ignore this and clung to Harry's warm arm for a considerable degree of comfort.

I suspected this meeting would be a difficult affair when his mother discovered my identity, but I confess to a degree of hope that the woman would see past the name and view me as Harry did, simply Lilly, a girl who loves her son dearly. I shuddered involuntarily and Harry held me tighter. I suspect in belief that I was cold, but I did not feel cold and could not say why I had shuddered.

We retraced the same route back and met one another at the top most row of cottages where Harry's mother lived.

The cottages themselves were quaint single storey houses all joined together in a long row. Each house consisted of a single crossed sash window, slightly recessed into the light-coloured stone brickwork, and a single black door also surrounded by the same light stone frame, but this had the added advantage of an interspaced darker brick, creating a pretty chequerboard pattern.

Harry and I sidled down this row like common thieves keeping to the shadows as much as was possible in our attempt at being unobserved.

He halted at one of these quaint houses and entered. The door Harry opened led directly into the main portion of the little house. I had been in a number of these quaint houses prior to this, so was not in the least shocked at the arrangement.

A sizeable open fire had chairs huddled around one aspect of the room and the other consisted of a large table, where a woman dressed in apron and rather outdated day dress, had sleeves rolled up and hair pulled back with a scarf, was busily kneading dough extremely vigorously. She halted her work as we entered and glanced up, the smile she had on her lips halted abruptly and remained there half formed when she saw that it was I who accompanied her son.

She gazed at Harry inquiringly. He immediately kissed her cheek and drew her from the dough and in the direction of the seats by the fireplace.

"Come Mother sit. We must speak with ya."

She whipped up a nearby tea towel in a practiced motion and wiped her hands on it with an expression of confused bewilderment, but nevertheless she sat herself where Harry instructed, viewing us both expectantly.

He had been blessed with his mother's eyes, the resemblance was plain to view now I was close enough to examine the woman. However, despite this I could not find any other semblance of familiarity between them.

Harry, having ungraciously abandoned me in the doorway, returned and steered me to a seat opposite his mother. I felt his warm fingers through the folds of my dress as he pressed my shoulder briefly. It was a great comfort.

"Mother remember we talked last night and I told ya a war was coming?"

"An' I told yer I'd been married to the Navy long enough t' never be shocked by anythin' that might be comin'."

Harry smiled and continued. "Well, this is Lilly. we're getting married tomorrow and would like ya t' be there."

"When yer said there was a girl and 'er name was Lilly, I didn't think yer meant Elizabeth Leyac. I can see now why yer didn't tell me her real name." She crossed her arms and viewed me, a serious mistrust on her face, her golden eyes narrowing.

"Mother, Lilly is the name I gave her. It's short for Elizabeth," he said with extreme patience and a note of resigned exasperation, as someone used to arguing in this manner.

"Yes, well. Why on earth d' yer want to marry a Leyac in any case? That family is notorious. I'm surprised Lady Catherine will allow it. We all know what sort o' woman she is." She inclined her head in agreement with herself and folded her arms yet more tightly, her lips in a most disagreeable thin line.

"That's just it Mother, Lady Catherine and the rest o' the Leyacs know nothing of our plans. Lilly and I have been engaged for two years and in all that time her family have known nothing of me."

"Two years? Yer tell me now yer have been engaged to Elizabeth

Leyac for two years and her family know nothing of it? Two-years. Why call yer'self a son of mine. Why I've a good mind…" She stopped herself mid sentence, her indignation suddenly dissipated before ending with. "Well in any case that doesn't matter."

She remained in her seat huffing for a number of moments. Her eyes sharp with shock and anger at the information with which she had been provided.

When she did speak once more, her tone had considerably softened.

"Son, don't yer see how dangerous this is? Her family are rich an' mean. They aren't the kind o' people to take this lightly. It's a mistake to get tangled up wi' that family. The likes o' us have no business courtin' daughters of Lords. Please reconsider Harry."

Harry shook his head, at this moment giving his mother a glance of determination. "Mother everything is in place and nothing will dissuade me from Lilly. She's the one for me and I'm not scared o' her family. What can they do once she's my wife? The law is on my side regardless of who they are an' how much money they have."

She plainly realised that her son would not be dissuaded so she turned her attention to me.

"I'm sorry Miss, but I just don't trust yer family or you. What can yer get from marryin' my son other than to ruin his life? I don't understand why a girl like you would choose a boy like my son. Are yer seriously saying yer could spend your life living like this and doin' everything for yer'self, with no servants?"

She huffed again in annoyance as I remained still and silent at a severe loss for words to know how to make my answer.

Seemingly frustrated at my lack of response she spoke angrily.

"Why, I'll bet yer don't know one end of a mop to t' other. If yer are doing this because yer want some play thing, please don't, I beg yer. He's my son."

I found my voice then as indignation at the wretched suggestion I was using Harry as a toy. "I can assure you madam I have no intention whatever of hurting Harry, or using him as a plaything. The idea is preposterous. I do understand your distrust and reluctance, but my affection for your son is genuine. I care little where we live so long as we can be together. However, in one aspect you are correct. I have had every advantage in my life but try, if you will, and imagine what it is like to have Lady Catherine as your mother."

"Mother the wedding is tomorrow. I want Lilly as my wife before I leave an' we'd like your blessing. We're keeping it quiet from her family for a little while longer, until I can organise somewhere for us t' live and I can find out how for long I'm going to be away. I suspect it may be a long time."

She heaved a sigh of defeat then, her golden eyes, that matched her son's, moist as she glanced deeply into her son's face with a fascinating look of such deep affection that I had never experienced from my own parents. She must have seen something in his eyes then, something unspoken that passed between mother and son because a sad, resigned expression came across her face and she blinked away the moistness at her eyes.

"I don't want t' spend our last days fightin' when I haven't seen yer for so long. But I want yer to know that I don't like it. I hope yer know what yer doin'."

She rose then and moved towards where her dough was waiting. "Now I need t' rescue this dough otherwise the bread won't rise."

She began to beat the dough in what appeared to be an even more deliberate fashion than she had before. I was fascinated and watched her practised hands moving swiftly.

"Thank you mother, and don't worry. I know what I'm doing."

He moved towards her and kissed her forehead in a brief motion. She closed her eyes for a flicker before continuing to beat the dough.

"Go on then, be off wi' yer. I've work to do," she replied rather gruffly.

Harry clasped my hand in his own and escorted me in the direction of the door.

As time was now progressing and the light was indeed fading, we concluded that we were secure enough to stroll together without suspicion. We travelled in silence for a time, I quietly assessing Harry's mother's reaction. It had been somewhat of a problematic meeting, as I had feared, but it had not been as severe as the encounter I had yet to endure with Catherine. I am only thankful, Dear Journal, this event is some distance off yet.

"She'll come round, Lilly. It's just the shock o' the way we told her and how quickly we're doing it. Once she's had time t' process the idea she'll be thrilled and it'll be nice for her t' have someone to talk to while Dad and I are away." He embraced me into a hug and kissed my forehead. "I can't wait until we're able t' tell the world. Tomorrow you'll officially be mine. I could not be happier."

"When are we scheduled to arrive at the church?"

"Eleven am. It'll give us time t' get over to Lowsbury. It's a good two hour buggy ride from here and I've managed t' get a horse and cart to drive us there. So you'll need t' get up early tomorrow so we have time to travel. We need to allow time for any problems we may encounter on the way."

I allowed myself to relax at that point and succumbed to Harry's infectious excitement. In that moment I thought to myself, tomorrow, I would own the title of wife

CHAPTER TWENTY-THREE

October 1940 ANNA

Anna had to stop reading Elizabeth's diary as the train pulled into London. As they left the tube and she had the distraction of negotiating people to avoid Marcus' eye, she felt brave enough to ask him a question that had been burning since they left Oxford.

"What do you think of what the professor said?"

What she really wanted to know was what he thought of the existence of the diary. She wanted to know whether in his professional opinion he thought there was something worth looking into or whether he, like the doctor, thought it was a fools errand, but she didn't dare ask that outright. "Well, it's certainly an interesting one. I would never have considered such an item to be so important, but what do I know I'm just a reporter. The professor's the expert. I knew he'd be fascinated but he's far more interested than even I expected. Although, it could have something to do with the revelations you revealed about what you have read in it."

She nodded. She had been surprised at his reaction

too. "What do you know yourself of the Leyacs?"

"Only what the professor told me for my article and what everyone knows. They are only well known because Louisa's twin son was stolen, Elizabeth died young and unmarried, but I know from what you said in the professor's office today that she didn't entirely live a nun's life."

He looked at her with a smile and continued.

"Catherine wasn't Lord Ashton's first wife and wasn't the mother of Elizabeth, but she was Louisa's mother. Lord Thomas was the only surviving member and he spent most of his life searching for his missing twin brother until his recent death. I think that's about it. To be honest, these sorts of families and their history doesn't really interest me. It's only because of my assignment I made contact with the professor again. Personally, I think there are far more important war stories we should be writing about."

She ignored his last comment and continued her questions. "And what do you think of the professor's theory about the disappearance of the twin?"

He sighed as they skirted around a large amount of rubble, broken bricks, glass and other debris covering almost the whole of one side of the street. Men were scratching their heads as they tried to contemplate how to begin clearing up. Marcus was walking quickly and she had to trot along to keep up.

"Anna you have to understand. I love the professor, he's my old University Lecturer and is extremely good at his job, but he's been almost ridiculed in professional circles for his many crack pot ideas. This is just another in a long line."

"So you don't think it has any merit?" She was a little breathless now.

He stopped suddenly then and looked directly at her. "No, I didn't say that. What I'm saying is that you need to take what he says with a pinch of salt."

She nodded and followed as he continued to walk at his brisk pace, the collar of his jacket now turned up.

The professor's suggestions certainly were one theory, but not one she had considered before, however it would explain why, as the professor said, there was no trace of the missing boy whatsoever. There had been no evidence. Nothing of any significance had been seen or heard of the missing boy. So the question remained, how would Catherine have gone about doing such a thing and, if indeed she had paid the maid off, where had the girl gone? Abroad surely? There was nowhere else she could have been so well concealed.

Anna thought back to her conversation at the Jenkins farm with Sissy's sister Margaret and knew that she would instantly say Sissy would never have run away and been paid off like that. But Anna wasn't so sure. A young girl given a sum of money, more than she had ever seen before, and the chance to start again and travel to places she never would have dreamed of. She could see how such a proposition would be appealing to such a young girl.

As they got to their office building, they made their way upstairs directly to their Editor's office.

"Forrester. Marcus. Come here. Where have you been?" His woodbine quivered as he spoke, arms folded while he stood in the doorway of his office, his eyes slightly squinting at the smoke rising into them from the end of his woodbine. He turned around and walked back inside presumably expecting them to follow.

Delancey was sitting in one of the chairs opposite the Editor's desk looking very angry, his arms crossed and one foot jiggling around. The room's usual fog of smoke hung about three inches from the ceiling.

"Marcus, as you've been mentoring young Forrester here lately, I want you to take her with you and Delancey to cover the RAF story," he said sitting down and leaning back in his chair.

"Sir, I've hardly been mentoring her. She's just been helping with the Leyac story developments that's all."

"Ah, and do you have any developments I can print?" he asked in a tone of voice which indicated he already knew the answer to this question. "No Sir."

"Well, that's what I thought, so now you can do as you're told and cover this story, and take her with you."

"Sir, is it really appropriate for a woman to come along to an RAF base?" Delancey piped in.

"Delancey, you really are an idiot sometimes. You do know there are women in the services these days?" He looked over at Delancey, as if he'd like to beat him around the head.

Anna folded her arms, she didn't like being discussed as if she wasn't there and was some kind of child in need of attention. Both Delancey's and Marcus's faces had a sulky look. Apparently she was a great hindrance to them.

She looked from one to the other, her temper rising. She couldn't contain the outburst any longer.

"Blast you both. I am a good journalist and I can do the job as well as either of you. I'm damn well going whether you two like it or not, and what's more I'll bet either of you I can get the story before you do."

She stalked off slamming the Editor's door behind her. She bloody well would go and prove them wrong. They were both fools.

"Forrester, get back in here," her Editor barked from his door.

She flinched at his tone and got up from her chair, which gave a squeak of protest. She wondered if she was going to be fired. He went behind his desk and took his time lighting another cigarette before squinting at them all in turn, as the smoke cascaded around his eyes.

"Now, as you've thrown a challenge Forrester, I've decided to make things a bit interesting. None of you are doing the RAF story, I'll send someone else."

"But Sir," both Delancey and Marcus said together.

He held his hand up and they both went quiet. "Instead I want you all to go out and find a story."

"Find a story?" Delancey asked bewildered.

"Yes Frank Delancey, find one" he said more slowly. "I want you to go out into the city find a good story and write it by the end of today to go in tomorrow's paper. I want you all to go and find something that you think is one, interesting and newsworthy, two, will get approved by the censors, and three, is something I'm going to like. I don't care what it is, you decide. The decision's up to you."

"Sir aren't I a little advanced for this kind of thing?" Delancey said.

"You know Delancey, sometimes I wonder why I have you around. No one is too advanced for a bit of good old-fashioned, real journalism. Whichever story I like the best is going in tomorrow's paper, so whoever finds the best story wins."

"So you want us to compete against each other?" Delancey asked.

"Yes Delancey, that's the nature of what I'm saying. Forrester here reckons she can get the story before either of you, so here's your chance to prove her wrong. Off you go then?"

"And it can be about anything at all?" Marcus asked.

"Yes, think of it as an adventure. A bit of fun in your lives to lighten the darkness of this war. Go on then, get out of my office." He leaned back in his chair again.

They all left the office, the men looking angry. Anna however was feeling quite excited at this new prospect. At last she was getting her chance to prove herself. She sat at her desk, leaning forward in her chair considering.

She felt hot breath on the side of her face and the faint smell of whiskey drifted past her nose. "You Forrester. You lost me a great story. I'll not forget this." Delancey straightened up and pointed his finger at her threateningly.

"Oh buzz off Delancey. You really are a bloody fool."

He walked away his shoulders tight with tension and rage. She sighed watching him. No matter what she did, she would always be the outsider.

She sat for a few moments wondering where she could find an interesting story. What would make the Editor print her story over theirs? She stared out the window, grey cloudy skies were dropping intermittent blobs of rain. Absently, she ran her finger along the blemishes and dents in her desk as she thought, allowing her fingertip to explore the arrow shaped crevices and points. Trying not to think how much that cloudy sky reminded her of Yorkshire, where her mother did not exist anymore.

"Anna?"

She jumped at the voice and turned. It was Marcus. She didn't want to talk to him so scowled and turned back to the window.

"Anna, I wanted to apologise to you," he said to her back.

She turned and looked at him surprised.

"There was no need for me to behave the way I did. I know you are a good reporter. I was just so worried about losing that story, but we lost it anyway, so it makes no sense falling out."

"Well, Delancey seems to think it was my fault," she said looking over at him, now on the telephone at his own desk.

"No, I think we are all partly to blame. I do want to work with you and I am glad to be your mentor if you would like me to be. Plus, if I don't apologise, how will you ever get to speak to my contact again?" He raised his eyebrows at her.

She gave him the faint flicker of a smile. She would need access to the professor again, she was sure of that.

"So, what were you thinking of doing for your story?" he asked.

"I'm not telling you, you're the competition."

"Well I think we should work together." He told her, his eyes wide with interest and expectation.

"That's not what we've been told to do."

"I know but I think we can beat Delancey if we work on this together and we'll do a better piece with two heads. What do you say?" he said grinning.

She nodded. "all right, but I don't know where to start looking for a story."

Sara Thomson

But even as she spoke, it came to her. The girl who gave her the lift home in the raid, the WVS driver with her supplies. What had she been carrying? She realised she'd never asked.

"I've got it. I know where to go," she told him jumping up and grabbing her coat. "Come on," she said over her shoulder already running for the door.

Marcus ran to catch up, bewildered. "Where are we going?"

"Wait until we're out of here and I'll tell you," she said.

Outside Marcus turned up the collar of his coat and pulled his hat down to further shield him from the drizzling rain.

At a small WVS canteen Anna asked after the girl who had taken her home the night before. The other WVS girls told her she should try the shelter set up for those bombed out.

Half an hour later they were stood outside a church hall building, with people queueing in a long line outside, clutching dirty children. Some had a sad, desolate look in their eyes, some a more defiant one. These were the faces she saw in her dreams. The faces of people who had lost everything. She turned away as they made her think of what she had lost and she couldn't think about mother right now.

An elderly woman in a pristine WVS uniform behind the desk in the entrance was taking down information from each person in turn. Other ladies were giving out blankets and some were giving food and cups of tea. Anna went over to the lady with the blankets, who peered at her through her thick glasses.

"Excuse me I'm looking for a girl, Emily Borrows. She's a driver."

"Oh yes I know who you mean. She's one of only two who can drive. She's a rare one is Emily, always off to fetch more supplies, even during raids. She's not scared of nuthin' that one."

The woman peered at her seeming to remember that she didn't know who Anna was.

"Why who are you, what you want her for?"

"She helped me the other night when I was caught in the raid and took me home. I wanted to thank her. Also, I'm a reporter and I'd like to know if she'd consent to let me write a piece about her."

"Oh, Oh I see. Elsie. Elsie."

The woman began shouting into the main hall where camp beds were set up for families who had all their worldly goods beside them. Small picture frames, little trinket boxes, piles of letters, each person masking the same shock on their face, some better than others.

A woman who walked with a slight limp appeared.

"Yes, I'm here, what you shouting about?" said this woman.

"Reporters to see Emily."

She pointed with her thumb at Anna and Marcus before going back to dishing out blankets to the newcomers.

The woman, who presumably was Elsie, led them through the main hallway, past all the makeshift beds, through the tangle of people, children and possessions, to a little office in the back corner. Inside she went behind the desk and sat down, both hands pressed together in a kind of prayer stance.

"Now what can I do for you?"

Anna explained again about how she had met Emily and that she wanted to write a piece on her.

"Well it seems to me, you have all the material you could ever want outside that wall."

She pointed at the door which led back to the main hallway. "Those families, have lost everything some of them. They're the ones you should be writing about, they're the ones that the country should be taking notice of."

"Oh don't worry, I intend to speak to them too with your permission, but I do want to speak to Emily, if that's all right with you?"

"Well so long as you aren't going to print any lies, I don't mind. God knows we could do with the publicity. We need all the help we can get. Miss Borrows is out at the moment picking up supplies but we are expecting her back shortly. In the meantime you have my permission to talk to some of the families here, but only the ones who are willing mind you. I don't want no one being hassled. You understand me?"

Anna nodded and she and Marcus thanked the woman.

As they left the office to begin talking to the people, Marcus leaned across and whispered in her ear.

"Nicely handled there Forrester."

"Thank you. I was thinking we should take the angle that the piece is about Emily of the WVS and what she does, then talk about these people that Emily is helping. What do you think? Not too much doom and gloom but still getting in the facts?"

"Good idea Forrester I like it. I'll start at the far end and you start here, between us we should get some good information."

She began to wander around looking at each of the beds, where to start was now the problem. At the far end of the room, Marcus was already in conversation with an elderly man who was talking while Marcus nodded and made notes. This was the bit she needed more practice at - striking up a conversation. She wandered slowly towards the table where tea was being made in big urns and picked up two mismatched cups, one with a crack. Taking them down one of the rows of beds she saw a young woman. She was about her own age was sitting cradling a baby, who was fussing but not crying. A little boy was playing nearby holding a tiny carved wooden car that he was pretending to drive around the bed. The woman was sitting there alone, staring at nothing.

Anna approached. "Would you like some tea?" she asked.

The woman looked startled to see her and blinked as if she only just realised she wasn't alone.

She looked blankly at the tea Anna was holding out to her. Then, in an instant she seemed to shake herself.

"Sorry," she said. "I was miles away. Thank you."

She took the tea with her free hand, continuing to jiggle the baby with the other.

"Are you all right?" Anna asked.

"Yes, it's just such a shock, I seem to wake up and find myself here and then I remember. I keep expecting to wake up back at home and it's all been some hideous dream."

The girl stared out of the window above her at the floating grey clouds. "Who are you anyway?" she asked suddenly.

"I'm a reporter. If you'll let me I'd like to talk to you about what's happened. I think it's important we don't forget about people like you and what's happening. Would you be willing to talk to me?"

"Yes, I don't mind. But I want to make it clear, that this isn't important. I can find another place to live. My children and I are safe. The important thing is the boys fighting. That's what really matters; the boys fighting for our freedom."

Anna took out her notebook and began making notes having balanced her tea on the wobbly floor next to her foot.

"Is your husband in the services?"

"Yes. He's in the Army fighting abroad. That's what matters, that's what's important. Not any of this."

"When did you last see him?"

"Six months ago now. I've no idea when I'll see him again, but it doesn't matter where we are, so long as we are all right at the end and can be together. It's just a house. It's just possessions."

Anna considered the woman's attitude and wondered if she herself could be like this. Before losing her mother she would have thought the woman a little stupid for not being concerned about the loss of her home. However, now she understood what loss felt like. And despite still thinking romance a silly notion, she knew then that the reason this woman wasn't bothered about losing her home was that there was something else she was much more afraid of losing. Something she was so afraid of losing that she could sit calmly at the loss of her home, if it meant that she could keep that something, or should that be someone.

Anna sat with the woman a little while longer sipping tea and gained what information she could before she moved away and met up with Marcus.

She felt a swift pat her on the back. "I hear you're looking for me," said a voice.

She turned to find Emily Borrows. She was wearing a scarf tied around her hair as she had the night they met, but this one was scarlet red. Her lips matched with the same scarlet colour. She had big oval shaped eyes of hazel and a curl poked from her scarf and down one side of her forehead. She stood with her hand on her hip, in old dungarees and a shirt with WVS badges on the collar. She had one eyebrow raised in a kind of mocking laugh.

"Emily, yes I have. I was wondering, would you give me an interview about your work at the WVS?"

"Well does it mean I'll get my picture taken?" she said doing a mock pose.

She laughed then. "Don't look so worried I'm kidding. Of course I'd love to. We need all the publicity we can get here. But I hope you don't mind if we do it on the go. I've got a lot to do. And you…" she said turning to Marcus. "You're a strong looking chap. You can help lift these supplies off the back of my van. Come on then, there's no time to dawdle at the WVS," she shouted, already walking off swinging her hips as she went.

She turned, gave them both a low hooded eye look and grinned, a cheeky twinkle in her eye as she did, and turned a corner laughing.

Anna and Marcus looked at each other and followed her. Outside she handed Marcus a huge pile of blankets. He struggled to see above the top of the pile. She instructed him to take them inside. She leaned back against her van then and laughed at him before lighting up a cigarette and offering one to Anna.

"So what you want to know then?" she asked lifting her head skywards and blowing smoke into the air.

CHAPTER TWENTY-FOUR
October 1940 ANNA

As they left the WVS following Emily's interview, they discussed how to begin their story.

"I think we really have something here Anna, I think he's really going to like it. He'll surely print it. It has everything. The war effort, how women are helping the men win the war. It's ideal," he said tapping his notebook as he listed the things he had written.

He stopped walking and held her arm for a few moments. "There's something I want us to go and look at before we go back to the office."

"What is it, what do you want to look at?"

"I want to go to the library and look at the old newspapers. I'd like to check the coverage of Elizabeth Leyac's funeral. If we hurry, we'll still have time to write the piece."

"Why?" was all she could think of to ask.

She could see from the frown lines that creased his forehead he was deep in thought and she began to wonder if there was something she had missed, that he hadn't. He was also walking fast again and she was trotting along to keep up.

"It's just something the professor said. He said that her funeral was a lavish affair. But, from that diary entry the professor read and the things you mentioned reading, what I don't understand is why the funeral was such a lavish affair when Catherine didn't like her stepdaughter. And when the family had just suffered the injustice of having their baby stolen from his own nursery by a woman on their payroll. It doesn't make sense to me."

"It does. Catherine probably felt sorry for Elizabeth, after all the girl died a young woman without having lived much life at all. Maybe she wanted to show the world the family would uphold their honour. That class of people think family honour and how they are viewed in society is very important don't they? Catherine simply gave Elizabeth the funeral any member of that family would expect."

"Maybe, but it just doesn't seem right to me. I can't quite believe that someone who was insatiably jealous of Eliza and the daughter that came from that marriage, would suddenly soften to her and throw her a lavish funeral. But maybe I am cynical and you are right. Either way, I won't be able to concentrate all day unless we go and look at the details of what exactly a 'lavish funeral' means," he said crossing the road quickly before a taxi came rushing round the corner.

She had to wait until the taxi had passed before she could cross. She ran to catch up with him, dodging puddles as she did.

"So does this mean you want to help me discover why my mother gave me that diary?"

"Of course Anna, you're going to need someone's help," he said surprised.

"Really? What makes you think I'm going to let you help?"

He turned and faced her then and she nearly ran into him as he stopped so suddenly. "Oh Anna don't be awkward about this. I am offering to help with your investigation. I'm good. Surely you want someone who has a bit of experience with investigating stories."

He continued to walk on without waiting for an answer. She ran to keep up with his quick strides again. She was slightly agitated that he seemed to be taking over what had been her own secret until recently. This was precisely why she had kept it a secret.

But, she was interested in the newspapers and knew Marcus would continue the investigation himself without her or the diary, so maybe he was right, she should let him help her.

"I suppose I could let you help me," she said grabbing his arm and stopping him in the street so that everyone walking along had to dodge out of their way, while they stood blocking the middle of the pavement. "But, you must remember that this is *my* investigation. I'm the lead on it, you are there to advise and help, but you cannot take over or go off and carry on without me. The diary was given to me. I will only let you help if you agree to this."

He looked at her as if he was assessing whether she meant it.

"I'm serious Marcus, if you want to be involved you do it on my terms."

He nodded at her then and she held out her hand. He

looked down at it.

"Shake on the bargain then to make it official." She smiled at him and he took her hand and shook it, shaking his head at her as if she were a silly child.

She felt elated, she hadn't expected him to agree, at least not so easily, but now that he had, she was determined to keep him to their agreement.

He continued to rush off though and she was beginning to feel that her choice of shoes that day had been a mistake.

Eventually they entered the library and found the floor where newspaper archives were stored. He shook off his coat in a hurry and abandoned it in a damp heap in the direction of nearby chairs. After spending a little time going through the archive list, he selected a title and propped it up on the large board along the reading benches and flicked through the paper until he reached the correct page. "Ah, here it is, Anna," he said leaning forward and peering at the faded old print on the page in front of him.

"What does it say?" she asked trying to see over his shoulder.

He was scanning the lines of text with his finger. "It says the reporter saw the carriage first pull into the grounds of the house that morning. It was a huge glass carriage with a polished wooden casket inside." He paused as he scanned some more, his finger tracing the type on the page. "It was drawn by four black horses with big black plumes on their heads. Shiny black leather straps…" He paused again. "Oh here, it says the family and staff had a private service in the family chapel, before the coffin was brought out again, and another carriage for the family followed behind the carriage containing the coffin."

He scanned the article some more. "It talks of the family's expressions, grim, sad, worried. The reporter is trying to gauge whether that is from the loss of the baby, or the death of Elizabeth. It then moves on to say something about how Louisa looked, elegant, etc. Yes, we're not interested in her... Oh then it says that after Louisa and the one twin go into the church, Lady Catherine comes to talk to the reporters."

He looked at Anna in surprise. "Well, what did she say?" Anna asked him impatiently again trying to see over his shoulder.

He scanned the document again. "It says they asked her about the missing child and she said, and they've quoted her 'There has been no further developments in the case. We will inform you immediately that we are given news from the Police. Thank you Gentlemen, I must go and bury my daughter who has just lost her young life.' That's it, that's all she said. It describes her dress and goes on to discuss how some people thought the lavishness of the funeral a disgrace during a time of war and suffering."

He sat back disappointed, "I was hoping for something more."

"Well, you should get used to disappointments with this investigation. I've had nothing but disappointments from the beginning. The only thing that I have found out about the girl is what I've read in her diary and that was given to me. Nothing I have investigated has come to fruition, nothing at all. The only thing that's made sense to me is that there is nothing to find out about Elizabeth. She had no life to speak of due to her early death, and the more I think of it, what the professor said this morning is probably true."

"What is that?"

"That the twin probably died and was buried in the coffin with Elizabeth."

"That doesn't explain the maid."

"It does if they paid her to keep quiet and gave her more money than a young girl like that had ever seen before. It would be appealing to a young girl. The prospect of going abroad to... somewhere like America."

"Hmm maybe," he said shrugging into his long coat and replacing his hat, looking deep in thought.

"Well, if it's any consolation, there is something else I haven't told you," she said with a tiny smile.

"What's that?" he looked at her then interested.

"The last entry I read, her young man, Harry, has just come back on leave and told Elizabeth there is going to be a war and they should finally get married while he is home. I had to stop reading on the train earlier, but it seems Elizabeth is about to be married."

His eyes widened in surprise. "I wonder Anna, would you let me read that entry?"

"Well, let's get this article written and beat Delancey this afternoon and after work we can go and have a drink and we'll read it together."

"Great idea. Come on now, we need to hurry and make this article brilliant," he said already walking off. She trotted to catch up yet again.

They rushed from the building and out into the pouring rain. He turned up his collar again and pulled down his hat. Anna tipped her head lower and wished she had put on a larger hat and better shoes earlier that morning. Her feet were getting very wet as they splashed along the damp pavements.

Once again she put the Elizabeth Leyac issue to the back of her mind and concentrated on her article. Beating Delancey was the most important thing at the moment. She was beginning to like Marcus, if their day together was something to go on. He was certainly far more experienced than she, and was definitely someone she could learn from.

As she slowly began drying out in the office, with the rain still beating frantically on the window, she sorted through the notes she had taken at the WVS centre and read through Marcus's scrawled handwriting. After a little thought she formed an angle for the article.

In the heart of London, pounded by bombers nightly, the WVS girls stand strong helping our boys win the war.

There are people like Mrs Long and her two young children, her house flattened, but the WVS girls were there to give her a hot cup of tea and help her on her feet again. Mrs Long says 'None of this matters. What matters is the boys fighting for our freedom.'

It's a sentiment echoed by all the bombed out Londoners in the WVS station today. But who are these WVS girls? Well, they are ordinary women, wives, daughters and single girls who want to help. One such girl, Emily Borrows, drives a van through the streets of London, even in the middle of an air raid to make sure people who have lost everything, have something.

* * *

Anna stopped and thought about what to say next. She was enjoying this piece. It was so much more interesting than the cleaning and household tips she had been reporting on before.

The hand on her shoulder made her jump.

"How are you getting on?" Marcus asked.

"Good," she said and showed him what she had so far.

"I like it. It's a good start. Here's what I would do next."

He showed her some ways to improve what she had and between them they created an article that had all the important elements the Editor liked: human interest, positive reporting on the war effort and the home front.

When they were finished he pushed the finished piece towards her. "Come on then, let's see what he thinks."

They went into the Editor's office after a quick knock. He was on the phone and had his chair turned around facing the wall as he spoke. He stopped when they entered and swung round to face them. He beckoned them over while continuing to listen to the phone.

Once finished, he slammed the black receiver down in its cradle and looked at them expectantly.

"Well, what have you got for me?" he asked.

Anna handed him the article. And he took it looking at them both before beginning to read.

As he read he stroked his chin and frowned in places, nodded in others. Anna looked at Marcus who looked calm and unconcerned. Finally he put the article down and looked up at them.

"I like this, I like this a lot. It's positive, it talks of the issues but without being negative. Well done. Well done both of you. It seems working together is a good thing.

Marcus I want you to take Forrester with you on your assignments. It's about time she learnt how to chase real stories like this one."

He turned to Anna then. "I want you following leads and using your initiative. But remember, the censor will only let us print certain things and there's no point you wasting my time and yours bringing me stories that won't get printed." He waved his finger as if to scold.

"Marcus, you can show her what to do. It seems that even though you are a woman, you can write decent articles with a man's help of course. But maybe, in time you can learn to do it yourself. I'm going to have to bring in more female staff, so you'll have some company Forrester. That'll be nice for you won't it? God help the rest of us though. Anyway, I've work to do off you go."

"Sir when will we find out who won the challenge?"

"I'm waiting on Delancey, and then... Oh here he is now."

Delancey came up and walked into the office without knocking and slapped his news article on the desk and smirked at Anna.

The room fell silent with a strained tension as everyone watched the Editor as he read Delancey's article.

Finally he looked up at Delancey. "This is good. Very good as usual Delancey."

Delancey gave her a satisfied look.

He put both articles beside each other on the desk.

"Do you know what. I like them both, I'm going to run both articles."

"But Sir?" Delancey said jumping from his seat in the corner.

The Editor just held his hand up. "I make the decisions

Delancey. Both articles are good. Both are what I want. But I do have something I want to ask you boys. I want a volunteer to go abroad as a replacement war reporter on the front line. Forrester this doesn't concern you. You may go."

Anna began to leave the office and closed the door just as her Editor said, "You two are my most experienced reporters, I need one of you to go and give me the stories as they're happening. It will be the making of one of you."

A little while later, Marcus came back to Anna. "Did you volunteer?" she asked.

"No, Delancey was keen as mustard to go out there. He's ambitious to achieve, that one, so was keen to get on. I'm happy to stay in London."

Anna smiled at him, "Well are you ready for that drink then. Let's find out what happens to Elizabeth at this supposed wedding. I can only presume she gets caught because we know she died unmarried."

They grabbed their coats and went off towards the west end.

A little while later they were sat in the corner of a sophisticated underground bar called Constance Malone that consisted of a tabled bar room and a large bright dance hall room with large sparkling lights on the ceiling.

"I don't often come up here Marcus. One of the girls in my boarding house comes here, but I don't usually find the time."

"I don't either but I know that this one is underground so we can stay here as long as we like while the raids are on, if need be. It's a good spot where you can talk privately, but is noisy enough so you're not overheard by others."

"So," he said. "Let's see what happens to Elizabeth."

She removed the diary from her bag and opened it at the last page she had read and began reading aloud. It seemed strange at first but she soon fell into a natural rhythm.

CHAPTER TWENTY-FIVE
July 1914 ELIZABETH

Harry and I separated at the tree lined avenue that headed towards Leyac House, its brick form peeking through spaces in the branches as the breeze lifted them slightly before letting them down again, to block my view as I strolled alone.

It was fully dusk and the house would have been hidden entirely if it were not for the lights illuminating from the upper windows. I couldn't help but think that they had an appearance of little eyes watching me through the trees. However, I was not afraid. My day had such an air of magic, nothing could possibly stop my smile.

I moved through the gates and across the circular cobbled driveway, ascended the steps and pushed open the heavy front door, smile still lingering. It remained all the way to the staircase, right the way up to the bottom step. My hand hovering above the banister rail about to grasp it when I heard a voice behind me.

"Oh Miss Elizabeth, you're home. Lady Catherine has been asking for you all day. It's Miss Louisa, she's lost the babe."

The thick silence that followed this announcement informed me that whoever they were, they expected some reply or dismissal. "Thank you" I said not turning and stood a moment while the footsteps receded away.

And it was that moment, Dear Journal, that all my dreams and marriage plans smashed into tiny pieces about the floor in invisible fragments. My hand still hovered over the banister rail frozen in that moment. My eyes closed as I willed time to preserve my perfect day.

At Louisa's room I only paused briefly to pray inwardly that Catherine would be too distracted to effect a dispute over my day long absence. Catherine and four maids were fretting around a cushion bolstered Louisa, who had the odd appearance of a miniature doll in a sea of pillows. She appeared pale and tired but her eyes were dark with a wild air about the edges and gave the impression of being more annoyed than distressed at yet another loss.

However, she was not too tired to tell me just how annoyed she was with my absence. "Just where have you been all day? Why were you not there when I had need of you? It is because of you this continues to occur Elizabeth. You cause me upset and see what happens. You should come when I call and have need of you."

I could utter no reply other than to apologise to her and attempt to change the conversation by asking her how she was feeling.

"I am most unwell" she said, her voice tempering and taking on the tone of someone who needed consolation.

I disregarded the distinctly chilly glance from Catherine, took Louisa's cold clammy hand and caressed it. "I am here now and will stay for as long as you have need of me" I spoke soothingly and Louisa appeared to begin to ease her anxiety then and laid her head on the numerous fluffy pillows.

"Well, I believe I need you all the night through. You will sit by my bed tonight will you not Elizabeth?"

She inclined herself forward again as she urgently pleaded, her blue eyes round with that touch of wildness about them.

I kissed her clammy forehead and agreed, driving thoughts of Harry and our wedding from my mind. Louisa's needs were greater in that moment.

And although I had no notion of how to achieve it, I was certain I could fathom a way to get to that church. I knew that if Harry would be absent for an extensive period, it was imperative he left as my husband.

Louisa appeared extremely tired once again so I helped her find a more comfortable position, tucking the starched sheets and blankets around her and smoothing her hair from her face. It did briefly cross my mind that her maid had been extremely neglectful and should have seen to these matters.

It was then that I glanced up and noticed Catherine had crossed to the window. She was drawing the curtains against the night sky. Her blond hair swept up in an elaborate style fashionable in her younger years, but now only sported on ladies of a particular age. Her dress, a deep navy taffeta, rustled as she moved. She insisted on still wearing the heavy dresses and laced corsets that Louisa had refuted an age ago for the new racy above the ankle styles.

Always in white, Louisa had declared it to be her signature style and had become somewhat famed for her white dresses in certain circles. Anyway, I digress from my story, Dear Journal.

It was at this moment, seeming to sense my gaze, Catherine turned and viewed me directly. I saw plain in her face that she desired nothing more than to let loose her anger, but I suspected she was remaining quiet for Louisa's sake. She would certainly retain it for some other forthcoming quarrel, I was sure of that.

I maintained a blank expression and met her gaze for a time, as she attempted to, yet again, intimidate.

After a brief spell, she moved toward the opposite side of the bed and caressed her daughter's hair, her face miraculously full of softness and love. "Louisa dear, I am going to leave you to sleep. Elizabeth is going to remain alongside you all night and if you require, will fetch me. Will you not Elizabeth?" The tone of her voice changing to a *threatening one when she said the last.*

I, having little choice, agreed.

She inclined her head in a satisfied way and departed the room, removing with her the maids and the air of icy distaste. Without realising I had been holding my breath, I released it when the door closed and eased myself then.

I took up the book on the table beside Louisa's bed and opened its hard exterior as my fingers identified the gold lettering of the title Sense and Sensibility. The book is a first edition and the author is simply called 'A Lady'. It creaked as I opened it due to its considerable age and I turned to the page where the marker held our place. I began to read and Louisa closed her eyes with a gentle sigh as she relaxed.

It was about an hour later when the maid brought food for Louisa, who protested that she could not eat a morsel, but in truth managed to eat a good deal of it. There was not a tray of food for me, no doubt due to some punishment of Catherine's. I decided that I did not care. Harry was home. This thought made me smile then, which Louisa noticed.

"What are you smiling for?" Louisa demanded through a mouthful of her half consumed bread.

"Oh it is nothing, Louisa. Would you like me to read for a time more?"

"Oh, yes. I will admit that it is quite interesting. I would not have patience enough to read it myself, but I will concede that some of those dusty old books you adore are quite pleasant. But before you do, I want to discuss something. It is a great secret so you must keep it. You are going to keep it if I share it, aren't you?"

I nodded my head to affirm that I would as I was very keen to discover Louisa's secret.

"I have come to a decision. I am not going to have any more babies." She viewed me with one arched eyebrow waiting for a

reaction.

"Does your husband agree? Have you discussed this with him?"

"No, I have not. It is my figure and mine own existence. I have decided it entirely of my own accord. I cannot abide this ordeal another time Elizabeth. I am wholly fatigued and bored of it. It has happened so often. I am not even distressed by the loss this time, I expected it. And so I simply refuse to do this any longer. It is ruining my health, my figure, I miss my friends dearly and Elizabeth, do view the despicable state of my hair. It will take an age just to fix that. No, I am quite determined."

She held a few strands of long golden hair for my assessment. And although I did not tell her, she did have a pale and unhealthy look about her, and her hair, which once shone, and for which I had always had a degree of envy, with my wild nest of untameable dark curls, did appear limp and dejected, all the shine and glowing colour gone. I was not sure what to say to her announcement, so I asked if she had told Catherine.

"No, I have not but she will not care. She will let me do as I wish. She has never halted me before. Anyway, I have decided that a baby is not worth this trouble. I am missing countless parties in London. Someone will take my place as society queen if I do not return shortly and my friends are going to simply forget me. I cannot have that. I have spent more time in my bedchamber in the last few years than my entire life prior. And what is a child anyway but something that cries and causes trouble. No, I have decided Elizabeth, I do not want this any longer."

I confess to being unsure how her husband would react to the news of this decision but that was of little matter. Once Louisa made up her mind there was no hope of dissuading her. I know Catherine was secretly worried about her mental state following her problems, so maybe this was a good decision.

As the evening drew on, it was not long before Louisa fell into sleep. In the silence that followed as I listened to her soft breathing, I took the time to mentally plan what I would wear to my wedding before I too fell asleep in the chair beside Louisa's bed. It was the darkness of early morning I woke to, much later, my neck and back unyielding from the chair.

Louisa was still in a deep sleep so I slowly raised myself from the chair and moved toward the door, glancing back at her sleeping form as I left.

My own bed was cold, the room had not held a fire all day and, despite the summer season, had a distinct air of chill about it. I shivered involuntarily but did manage to doze for a few more hours.

When the sun began to rise I dressed quickly and endeavoured to pin my mass of hair up, an enterprise I confess, Dear Journal, that I am yet to master. Anyway, after a number of attempts I elected to give up the idea entirely.

I viewed my reflection one final time and gathered my shoes and small bag in my hand, prior to opening the door and peering down the long corridor. Silent darkness greeted me and I inaudibly moved toward the staircase, my stockinged feet muffling the noise of my footsteps along the wooden corridor, the rim of my dress in my free hand.

I mounted the first few stairs and inclined my head over the central rail slightly, which spirals in a square down and around to the ground floor, and listened. The silence continued. I moved down to the next floor pausing slightly to glance toward the round gallery, which led to Catherine's rooms. Silence. Finally, with a degree of pounding of the heart and every step providing me with the feeling of being a thief in my own home, the wooden rail solid and cold beneath my hand, my shoes and dress slippery in the other, I arrived at the base of the staircase. The front entrance and my escape was in view.

I paused, flattening myself against the far wall, so as not to be viewed by any staff moving towards the dining room, through the hallway. I was aware that they would be preparing breakfast, laying the table, making fires and concerned with their daily duties, but it was essential I was not viewed leaving.

However, the longer I halted there behind the wall, the more certain it was that I would be discovered. I peered out, ready to hasten to the door. But, a maid came up from the back hall which led to the kitchens carrying a tray. She headed towards the dining room and I flattened myself behind the wall again, taking in more air to calm my beating heart. I glanced once again.

That was the moment. I ran to the door, which seemed to lengthen in distance more than ever before. But soon I pulled the cold heavy circular handle and slipped out noiselessly, securing the door behind me equally as silently. I moved on tiptoe across the cobbles still in my stockinged feet and slipped into the early morning light. I maintained this pace until I arrived at the secluded cover of the tree lined way which aided by hiding my escape. I halted, leaning against a tree whilst putting on my shoes and attempted to slow my breathing to a standard rhythm, the hard rough bark against my back. I placed my hand on my forehead before fanning myself a little to cool down. My heart had continued to beat rather rapidly so I attempted to distract myself in order to slow its rhythm.

Despite having made this journey countless times, I remained distinctly concerned at being found. The beautiful trees now appeared like claws trying to hold me back. This was my only opportunity to marry Harry and every noise, every rustle had me jumping and looking over my shoulder. I quickened my pace still glancing over my shoulder.

When I reached the fork in the road, Harry was waiting seated on a horse and buggy with flowers in his hand, his uniform pristine. His mother beside him had a flower in her jacket. They both smiled when they saw me and my fears floated away on that warm morning breeze in July.

"My bride." He bowed offering me the flowers.

A cheek aching smile became a permanent fixture as I closed my eyes and breathed the delightful fragrance of pink and yellow roses.

"They are simply beautiful."

"Mother did them for you. Talented isn't she?"

I glanced at her in somewhat of a surprise.

"Thank you, they are delightful."

"Well I decided that if yer what makes my son happy then that makes me happy."

Harry held out his arm and assisted me into the buggy. His eyes twinkling with mischief as he viewed me. I confess to feeling more than a little unkempt and flustered following my escape and, tugged at my dress and poked my hair in somewhat of an attempt to appear presentable enough to be married.

"Let's get married" Harry said as he climbed up and shivered the reins in a practised motion.

The journey was some considerable length and soon the bumping of the buggy combined with the warm sunny day and the charming chirping of birds in nearby trees had the effect of making me feel tired and heavy eyed.

I was shaken awake some time later and it took some minutes to remember where I was.

"We're here Lilly. You slept the whole way. You tired?" Harry caressed a curl from my face with his fingertip, an expression of concern on his countenance.

I told him I was tired from sleeping in a chair. He gave me a questioning glance to which I shook my head dismissively that it was nothing to be concerned about.

Harry's mother stepped in and touched my shoulder. "Elizabeth, we should go an' get ready. Harry yer can go an' see the priest t' make sure everything is ready."

Harry's mother directed me into the little vestry to freshen up. She helped tame my uncontrollable hair with considerably more skill than I possessed. Once ready, she glanced over me and nodded satisfied with her work before leaning in to kiss my cheek and leaving to take her seat in the church.

Alone now, I glanced around the small room, the silence echoing in my ears. I took one final view of myself before turning the cold brass door knob and opening the creaking wooden door.

I paused for a moment before an organ began to play and I began my descent down the aisle. One step, another. My legs shook, another step. I wished there was another to hold onto at that moment. Then I glanced up into Harry's deep golden eyes and he smiled.

Harry's mother was seated in the pew behind him. The other witness was an elderly woman I did not recognise.

As I reached Harry he grasped my considerably cold hand in his large warm one and held it tight.

The priest began to speak and I discovered, Dear Journal, that the process of getting married is much faster when one is the bridal party, than when one is simply a guest. But I am digressing again. What matters is, I was now Harry's wife.

We strolled up the aisle together, my steps now constant and poised. At the church door, Harry's mother produced a handful of rice and threw it over us where it bounced off and caught in Harry's hair. We laughed and he kissed me prior to thanking the priest and the elderly woman, who was the priest's wife, and left with his own wife on his arm.

Harry's mother was travelling back to Heathfield in the buggy, which they had borrowed and required returning. Harry took my hand and glanced in my eyes.

"Lilly, I have arranged a room at a small guest house for us tonight. I'm going back tomorrow an' I don't know when I will see you again. Let us have this one night as husband and wife t' remember while we are separated."

Harry must have read my thoughts as he said. "Don't worry, she won't think t' look here, you're safe. Although, I am concerned for when you do go back and I'm not around to protect you."

"Do not concern yourself with Catherine. I can manage her if she does not discover your existence."

"So, you will stay here with me then, wife?"

"Yes Harry, of course. Let us have this one night as husband and wife. Until your return I will think on it to remember you."

Nothing seemed more essential in that moment, Dear Journal, and looking back on it now, I am so glad I did. I do not know when I will see Harry again and thoughts of a war makes me feel incredibly concerned for him, but he is my husband and nothing can change that now.

Hang Catherine's consequences. I will concern myself with them later. Nothing but Harry is of any degree of concern to me now, Dear Journal. Finally I feel my dreams are coming true.

CHAPTER TWENTY-SIX
October 1940 ANNA

Anna finished reading and looked over at Marcus. She had actually got married. Elizabeth Leyac, the unmarried heiress had had a secret love affair and married a common sailor boy. She thought, not for the first time, that Elizabeth had shown a small sliver of independence. If only she had lived, what would she have become?

"I can't wait to tell the professor." Marcus said interrupting her thoughts.

"He'll be absolutely astounded to read this," she said.

They sat for a few moments unable to speak, both of them thinking of the consequences of what they had just read.

"I wonder if Catherine ever found out?" Marcus said almost to himself.

"Anna?" Anna is that you?"

The voice was familiar but distant and at first she wasn't sure if she'd heard it in her mind or in reality.

But when she looked up she was immediately struck by the face in front of her, a familiar face but one out of place. Her heart lurched.

The two worlds she had kept separate, and which she had so far been able to deal with by keeping them apart, collided into one with one simple word. That word was her name spoken on the lips of someone who shouldn't be there. For a few moments she blinked at the face before looking deeply into those familiar eyes belonging to Doctor Laker.

He looked different. His hair was slicked across more expertly than it had been in the country. His clothes were smarter too. He looked like a different person, not the country doctor she had met. So shocked was she at seeing him all she could manage to say was:

"Doctor Laker? You're here in London."

He smiled down at her then, and looked over at Marcus giving him a cool look. Marcus met his gaze with mild curiosity.

"Well, are you going to invite me to join you?" he asked with that familiar arrogance she hated. How much he annoyed her still. How much she hated this man still.

"Of course doctor, please sit down."

She continued to stare at him without saying a word.

"Are you going to introduce me to your friend?" he asked a little rudely.

"Yes of course, Doctor Laker this is Mr Anthony Marcus. We work together."

She felt it necessary to clarify this although she didn't know why. It certainly was none of his business who Marcus was. She turned to Marcus.

"This is Doctor Laker. He was my mother's doctor while she was ill."

The two men shook hands. "I'm also responsible for

nursing Anna's knee back to health when she was assaulted," the doctor told Marcus, still giving him a cool look.

"Really? Anna you never said?" Marcus asked.

"Anna, you must dance with me. Mr Marcus you don't mind do you?" the doctor said rising.

Marcus shrugged, an amused expression on his face as he lit a cigarette. The doctor forcibly pulled her to her feet.

"Really doctor I don't want to dance," she said.

"Nonsense Anna, of course you do," he said holding her firmly and marching her through to the dance hall next door.

The dance hall itself was bright with a large square dance floor in the centre. At the far end was a band playing and the floor was already full with couples. As they entered the room, the doctor steered Anna towards the centre and the music ended. He joined the other couples in clapping the band and they began to play a new song, that damn nightingale song. It was the same one she had heard that morning after the phone call to say her mother was dying, after that horrific night in amongst rubble and bombs flying everywhere, that morning when the small boy was crying and some fool played this song. Now it was always in her head like a bad memory. It came to her in her dreams and was a symbol of that day. The day everything changed.

"Doctor, I hate this song. Can we please go and sit down. I have much to discuss with Marcus."

"No Anna, just a moment, I wanted to get you alone to ask you."

"Ask me what?"

"Who is that chap?" he asked. His arm firmly around her waist steering her around the floor.

"Who? You mean Marcus? I told you he's someone I work with. We've been working together on something recently."

"And what is he to you?" he held her a little tighter then as they danced.

"Not that it's any of your business, but he's a work colleague, nothing more. Why what's it to do with you?"

"Nothing, I'm just making sure you're not associating with unsavoury types."

"Even if I was, it would be nothing to you." She felt herself stiffen as anger washed over her again.

"I know. I just feel responsible that you have no one to look out for you."

"And you think you can do that do you? I have been taking care of myself for a long while now. I certainly don't need a country doctor, who has only known me a mere few weeks, to come in and save me." Anna stopped dancing and pushed his arms away from her, which had made her feel uncomfortable from the beginning.

"You really aren't like most girls are you Anna? What is it you have against me?" he raised his voice this time.

"Nothing, I have nothing against you. You are just so arrogant." Her voice rose in pitch and she knew she was losing this fight. She needed to get away from him but he persisted.

"For wanting to help, for looking out for you, for trying to be there. How is that arrogant? Tell me Anna, is it really that or is it that you're running away? Or is there really something else going on here?"

The people around them on the dance floor had begun

to notice their argument now, so Anna, unnerved by the attention, started to walk away. He followed.

"You just need to stop. We're not in the Yorkshire countryside any more. This is my world and things are different here" was all she could think of to say.

They reached the table to a perplexed Marcus who, gave her a questioning look. She ignored the look and the doctor sat down opposite her, also ignoring Marcus.

"I'm sorry Anna. I didn't mean to offend you. I am just trying to help," he said with a sigh, running his hands through his hair.

"I didn't ask for or want your help."

"All right then. I won't try to help any more unless you ask me to."

"Does the doctor also know something of our investigation Anna? How many other people are aware of what we are looking into?" Marcus asked.

Both she and the doctor looked at Marcus blinking as if they had forgotten he was there.

"Marcus, you have completely misunderstood the situation," she said exasperated.

"What investigation is this then?" Doctor Laker said looking between them.

"Oh I'm sorry Anna, I thought when the doctor mentioned helping it meant with our investigation, but I can see now it is something else entirely. Would you like me to leave you two alone?"

"Don't worry Marcus, it's an easy mistake. Doctor Laker, it really is no concern of yours," she said quickly before Marcus could say anything else.

"So you're investigating something new. Good. Can you share the details? I suppose not. Let's just hope it has a better chance of a good outcome than that bloody Leyac thing you were interested in when you were in Yorkshire."

He looked at both of them and she felt her cheeks go hot. Marcus looked amused at the whole thing and lit another cigarette.

"Oh no, don't tell me that's it? You're still investigating that? And now you've got poor Marcus involved? Damn it Anna, won't you ever learn? You're like a dog with a mangey bone."

Marcus laughed aloud then shaking the match he had used to light his cigarette. Anna glared at both of them.

"Well doctor you do have an interesting turn of phrase" Marcus said. "We are investigating the Leyacs and Elizabeth in particular. We've been looking at the diary Anna was given by her mother."

"Diary?" said the doctor.

"Marcus be quiet."

"Why not let him know what we're doing. It's not such a secret is it? After all, you shouldn't keep secrets from your…"

"Doctor what are you doing in London anyway?" she interrupted Marcus and whatever he was about to say. She didn't like the amused look he was giving her and the doctor.

"I'm down to see a relative. My cousin has had her house bombed. Completely flattened. I'm here to help her get back on her feet," he said. "But I still want to know about this diary. Come on Anna, you know me. Tell me, I might be able to help. Where did your mother get this diary and why did she leave it to you? She never mentioned it."

She sighed. He clearly wasn't going to give in and even

though it was against her better judgement, she began telling him about the diary her mother had given her. She reminded him of all the newspaper clippings her mother had kept. She then glanced at Marcus who nodded at her to go on and told him of the professor's theory about the missing twin.

"Well, what a story. I must admit the concept of the baby dying at birth and being hidden in the coffin with Elizabeth to save Louisa's sanity is an interesting and very plausible theory."

"It is," agreed Marcus nodding at the doctor.

"You said I should take the professor's theories with a pinch of salt," Anna said to Marcus with indignation.

"Yes I did say that, and you should. But this one has merit and the more I think about it, the more I think that that's exactly what happened. But there is no way to prove it finally. It would be impossible to get permission to exhume a body without the proper licences. In fact it is against the Burial Act of 1857, which makes it a criminal offence to disturb remains without a licence," said Marcus.

"Well, that seems to be a big problem then doesn't it. But I wonder, would you both be willing to meet me again tomorrow evening, here? I may be able to help you out with that. But I need to make enquiries first before I tell you what it is. It may come to nothing but I think I can help," said Doctor Laker.

"How could you help?" Anna asked.

"Sometimes it is a case of who you know rather than what you know. I am a doctor and I meet a great variety of people. Would you be willing to meet me tomorrow Anna?"

She looked at Marcus who looked interested and

shrugged a nod to say he would come but she could see from his expression that he didn't believe there was anything the doctor could actually do. What could a country doctor from Yorkshire do to help such a case? But she agreed to his request all the same.

CHAPTER TWENTY-SEVEN

October 1940 ANNA

The following afternoon, Anna went with Marcus to meet the professor off the train from Oxford. Marcus had telephoned him the night before from the dance hall and told him of the diary entry and their meeting with Doctor Laker. He had been so excited about the wedding entry he insisted on coming to London to examine it himself.

So as they watched he stepped from the tube in amongst the business suits and uniforms looking thoroughly uncomfortable and out of place. His coat was crumpled and button was missing across his middle. His hat was askew and he took no pains to straighten it. He looked slightly vulnerable and nothing at all like the professor they had met the day before.

"Come on professor, let's get you out of this station," Marcus said taking his arm.

"Ah, uh yes. Anthony my boy excellent idea," the professor replied, hurrying off up the stairs behind a crowd of elderly, suited men.

Marcus turned to Anna and said, "He detests the tube

and trains in general really. It shows how excited he is about this diary that he's actually travelled to London in the first place."

"Oh," she said watching the professor's hurrying figure as he ascended the stairs.

The remainder of the afternoon she was distracted from her work and found herself unable to type her article correctly and made so many mistakes, having to begin again so often that she felt she would be demoted to office cleaner if she didn't watch out. It wasn't long before her unproductiveness was noticed and she received a good telling off.

By the end of the day she hardly felt like going to the dance hall again and certainly not to meet the doctor, but the professor had come all this way and had spent much of the afternoon engrossed in Elizabeth's diary while she and Marcus worked.

The bombings each night had become so commonplace that she was beginning to sleep through the noise out of sheer exhaustion. Tonight she was feeling tired and her bed and sleep sounded like a dream. Frankly just about anything was better than seeing the doctor again but she ignored this feeling and went anyway.

They took the same table as the night before but this time a little more squashed together with the one extra person. The professor looked out of place until Marcus put a large glass of something red in a wine glass in front of him. He took large sips from it, humming audibly about how nice it was and how long it was since he'd had a decent glass.

They had to wait for the doctor, who came rushing in apologising for his lateness. Marcus introduced the doctor and the professor and they all shook hands.

Once the doctor was seated, and after he had taken a rather showy gulp of his drink, he looked up at them all staring at him expectantly. Anna rolled her eyes to the ceiling. He was enjoying this. Bloody attention seeker.

"Now I know you are all curious as to why I wanted you to meet me here tonight and what it is that I may be able to do to help your case. But before I tell you what my idea is, I first wanted to highlight the problem."

He paused looking at them in turn.

"You see, the problem is that there is just too much paperwork. It would take months, maybe even years to get permission to exhume a body. We need to fill in why we want to do it, and how we are related to the person whose grave it is, who is not related to us at all. Then they want to know who the nearest relative is and get their permission, which is another difficulty as all the Leyacs are dead so there aren't any relatives to give permission. Nor would they be likely to anyway. Then because we don't know who the nearest relative is, that would hold up the already long process and to top it all, we haven't got any hard evidence to support this theory, just a few letters and other bits, which are all circumstantial evidence and guesswork. We can't prove anything. So what I'm saying is that it's no good Anna trying to get proper permission, you'll never be allowed to dig up Elizabeth Leyac."

"This was my conclusion as well," the professor interrupted cleaning his glasses as he did. "I have spent many years with people thinking my theories are eccentric ideas, and eventually you get used to not being able to prove them." He shrugged and replaced his glasses, squinting to refocus as he did.

"We can't just give up like that. If that baby is in that coffin it will make us Marcus. I won't be shoved cleaning and housewife stories anymore and people like Delancey will have to stop treating me like a silly girl. This missing baby story has been going for years and it's about time someone solved it. That might as well be us," she said surprising herself at her own passion.

"Anna I told you back up in your Mother's cottage, this story is a silly old fools errand. You don't want to get mixed up in it. It won't do you any favours. And it won't bring your mother back," said the doctor.

She gave the him a cold look.

"You said yourself Marcus it all fits. The baby died for whatever reason children do, and to save Louisa any heartache Catherine hid the baby in the coffin with Elizabeth's body and told Louisa and everyone else that the baby had been stolen. She probably didn't anticipate that it would get the press attention it did," she said.

"That doesn't explain the maid," said the doctor.

"Yes it does. Catherine paid her to disappear. It happens. People go missing all the time. I thought you were here to help, not put holes in the theory."

"All right Anna. I can see you are very determined. I just needed to check that you were sure. I don't personally believe any of this with any certainty, but I trust you Anna and if you believe it then I am prepared to go out on a limb for you. But there is one further question I need you to answer first, all of you, before I tell you what my plans are."

He paused again and looked at each of them in turn. "How far are you willing to go to get the proof you need?"

He looked at Marcus, the professor and then lingered

on her for a long time.

"As far as is necessary." She answered for everyone.

Marcus just stared perplexed and shrugged his shoulders lighting another cigarette. The professor blinked and sipped at his now half empty wine glass.

"Well, in that case I can help you. I know some people who can exhume that coffin."

"How? You just said it was a waste of time as we'd never get permission," said Marcus warily.

"During the course of my job I meet a lot of people from all walks of life. Mostly well to do families with good incomes as they have the money to afford medical bills. But sometimes I get to know some other types of people who do very well for themselves financially but make their money through other methods. I know a particular family who are just such people. I have made enquiries and they have agreed to help."

"What exactly are you saying doctor?" asked the professor.

"I'm talking about exhuming the body of Elizabeth Leyac." The doctor said patiently.

"You mean grave robbing?" said Anna.

"That isn't a term we should use, but yes, essentially," he said fingering the rim of his glass.

"Are you mad? You do know that is entirely illegal. And since when were you a criminal? I thought you were a stiff upright country doctor of the community." Anna's voice rose in pitch.

"The Burial Act of 1857 says…" began the professor.

"Yes professor, I am aware of it," said the doctor ignoring Anna's prior comment." My earlier question still stands. What are you prepared to do to get the answers you need?" He shrugged and took another large gulp of his drink.

"And these friends of yours could help us by doing what? Digging her up for us?" She said almost in a mocking way.

"Oh yes, they would be happy to. We'd have to pay them a substantial sum of course, but they could do it discreetly and without anyone knowing. They make a living of it actually. One more for them won't make a lot of difference."

"But then what do we do once we have exhumed the bodies?" said Marcus.

"Well that's where it gets complicated. It would only be worth doing if we could get someone to take and examine the body of Elizabeth and the baby. I know a lot of people in the medical profession but not many who would be willing to do that. I was hoping one of you might have some ideas."

"Interesting. Interesting." said the professor. "I may know someone who can help. I have a friend who is a Forensic Scientist. I've known him ever such a long time. He's working on pioneering new techniques of science. If I ask he might be interested in examining the bodies. We could then take the coffin to him and he can examine the baby and determine if it is the missing twin," said the professor.

"And what if we open the coffin and the baby isn't there?" said Anna.

"Well, in that case my dear, you had better pray that it is there, for all our sakes. Otherwise, we're exhuming the body of a dead girl illegally for no reason," said the professor gulping a rather large mouthful of his ruby liquid.

She could barely believe what she had agreed to when she left that night to return home. And more to the point who would have thought the doctor would be on terms with criminals.

However, she did have the sense that she was going along with the plan before she fully knew what she was doing.

The doctor was to get in touch with the grave robbers and get them to take Elizabeth Leyac's coffin from its grave. From there the doctor would personally see that it was transported to the professor's forensic scientist colleague to examine.

She was certain the baby was in that coffin and was absolutely sure that the risk they were taking was worth it to find out the truth.

The anticipation following that night was almost endless as the bombs continued to rain down and she again had to step over more broken buildings and rubble, once again having to find a new route to work due to bombed streets and blocked routes. The destruction around her appeared almost as if it were happening through glass.

It was, in fact, a frustrating few days later when she next heard from the doctor. Even more irritatingly all he sent was a short telegram.

"Ready Stop Going ahead tomorrow night Stop"

Anna showed the telegram to Marcus, who looked at her with what appeared to be a mixture of trepidation and excitement.

"Do you think we're right about it?" she asked him irritated at her own anxiety now that it was too late.

"Well, the professor believes it, and I certainly trust his judgement generally speaking. Do not worry Anna, all will be well," he said, although she noticed the frown on his face and the way he absently flicked through the notes on his desk without reading them.

She wondered, not for the first time, how a simple diary left to her by her mother had led her to conspiring with criminals to rob graves and spent all that day and the next, fidgeting and unable to concentrate on her work.

The Editor, barked at her a few times and told her to get her head out of the sky before muttering about bloody women and slamming his office door.

When the night finally came, she asked Marcus to go to the dance hall with her for a drink. She knew she wouldn't be able to concentrate on anything at home and would just sit clock watching, wondering what was happening. She pictured the grave site at Leyac House again in her mind. She pictured Elizabeth's grave and felt helpless and nervous being this far away.

They sat at the bar this time. Marcus was running his finger down the side of his glass tracing the drops of water from the coldness of his drink inside its glass. Anna stared into space tapping her finger on the wooden bar absently.

"I hate being out of control of things," she admitted to Marcus.

"I noticed you've been fidgeting. And it's been remarked on at work."

She pulled a face. "I know. I'm not very good at this kind of thing am I? How about you?"

He shrugged, "I'm interested to find out whether one of the professor's theories is actually correct. But the situation happening this evening is out of my control and is happening at the other end of the country. So there is little sense me worrying about it. What will happen will happen. I am content to wait."

"I wish I felt that way," she said with a sigh.

"Well, you must find a way to get through this evening. We are likely not going to hear anything till morning and in any case I need to get going before the raids start again." He looked at his wristwatch, downed his drink and stood up to leave. "I don't want to be caught out again. Can I walk you somewhere?" he asked.

She had hoped he would stay but said no she was fine to walk herself.

Leaving the dance hall and going their separate ways, she decided to go home and try to sleep.

She made it home, but the nightly raid meant she spent another night in the basement of the boarding house. She couldn't recall when she last spent a full night in her bed, probably the night she returned from Yorkshire.

Despite her worry over what was happening in the north, she did fall asleep and Olivia said the following day that she had slept through the most enormous raid. She wasn't quite sure she had slept right through it and had vague recollections of strange dreams and loud bangs.

She woke early to silence, the raid having ended some time through the night. Many of the others around her were still fast asleep, so she crept quietly up to her room and got into her own bed for a few more precious minutes before she had to get ready.

Her thoughts turned to the events of the previous night.

Had they been successful? Had they got Elizabeth's coffin out of the plot safely?

She sighed staring at the ceiling, leaned over to her bag and took out Elizabeth's diary. She flicked through the pages and stopped at a page with another note stuck into it. This note was a small one however and Anna knew without reading it that it was bad news. She recognised the trace and outline of a telegram. The entry was dated October 1914.

CHAPTER TWENTY-EIGHT
October 1914 ELIZABETH

Oh, Dear Journal, I hardly know where to begin. It's such an unpleasant turn of fate. I received a letter from him only yesterday talking about how much he yearned for me and how delighted he was about the baby.

I still cling to that letter, Dear Journal, with one hand even as I write this and my other hand and traces the curve of his letters and the arc of his capitals. His words for me. He held this notepaper in his hands. He penned each cursive letter so carefully. He told me of his optimism for the future. That cannot be gone. It just cannot be.

Such a stark contrast to the printed black type of the telegram, which lays next to his lovingly worded letter. It cannot be.

But, Dear Journal, I feel I am not making much sense, here is what the telegram says:

Deeply regret to inform you that the ship Hawke, Edgar Class, First Class Protected Cruiser, on which your husband, Seaman Harry McKenzie was serving, sank on 15th October 1914. He must therefore be regarded as having

died during active service. Letter follows.

My face is burning and I confess I cannot halt the tears falling no matter how I attempt to. They blur the words as I write this, even as I try to control them. I confess I feel decidedly unusual. It's as if someone has scooped out my insides and replaced it with burning coals. He cannot be gone. We have not yet begun our lives together. We were so happy. He cannot be gone, not yet.

And no matter how much I look at the two letters side by side, willing them to alter, willing them to contain alternative words, willing one of them out of existence entirely, they remain, tormenting me. The print of the harsh type on the telegram seemingly larger and more stark as I look.

There is not a thing for it. I already know what I must do. I must see Catherine. Today is the day she will find out everything, but I am not scared any longer. I have lost Harry. There is not a thing left to be scared of. I no longer care for anything. Wish me luck, Dear Journal, for I have nothing else. I will go to her now.

I have been to see Catherine. She now knows everything, but I confess I don't care what she thinks or what she will do. I want to die and be with Harry. My thoughts jumble and fudge over each other and the only comfort seems to be to keep writing, so I will start from where I left off and lay out everything that happened.

When I lay down my pen I moved first to my hiding place, opened the secret locked box and removed my certificate of marriage. I retrieved Harry's letter and the hateful telegram and left my room. As I went past Louisa's room she stopped me and began to speak, but I ignored her words and said I need to speak to Catherine. She gave me a strange look and studied my face before she asked what was wrong. For the first time in my existence I disregard her and walk on. She followed speaking insistently. I do not give her any attention. I cannot listen. I cared not of what she was speaking. I have no room for anything other than Harry. Harry is gone.

I strode into Mama's rooms directly through her antechamber, bed chamber and to the back room of her private closet without pausing to knock.

She prepared herself to bellow at me until she sees my face and halted.

"Seat yourself" she instructed standing before me expectantly, tapping her foot.

Without an word I simply handed her my bundle of papers and seated myself on one of her high backed red and gold chairs at the rear of the miniature room. I gazed at the floor, tracing the outline of different shaded wood which makes swirling patterns surrounding a central crown design. I confess to never before noticing how pretty the floor was. The tears continued to fall silently down my face.

Even Louisa, who halted her incessant chatter and was hovering by the door, appeared stunned at my behaviour. I heard Catherine shuffling through the documents as she read each one. The certificate of marriage which informs her I have had a secret husband for three months, the telegram informing that he has been killed and finally the correspondence from him informing me how excited he is to discover I am carrying his child.

I cared little what Catherine would do as no punishment of hers could ever be more wicked than the grief I owned in that moment.

There is silence in the room for a time, but after a while she spoke.

"Elizabeth, is this accurate?" There was a tiny twinge of admiration in her voice.

I inclined my head in affirmation without glancing up. The floor was far too pretty to ignore.

"Are you informing me you have covertly married yourself to a common sailor? A low-class individual with no land, title or money?"

"Yes" I said and looked directly at her face for the first time.

Daring her to retort anything against Harry. She looked stunned. Louisa was staring at me, her mouth open in a most undignified way.

"And, as if that were not enough he has managed to go and die on you, but not before he has left you carrying his common baby" Catherine said in indignation and disbelief.

I glanced again up to her face and fleetingly it betrays a touch of sympathy, only briefly, before it departs and her face hardens once again.

I had not seen that Louisa had moved from the door until she had grabbed me by my hair.

"Are you informing me that you are with child by some commoner? You? You. Who are you to think you may have a child?" Louisa spat with anger and wildness.

"Louisa please. I have just lost Harry. I cannot think how I am to survive being deprived of him nor contemplate what I will do with a baby."

She scoffed and slapped my cheek. "How could you do this to me Elizabeth? You know the trouble I have had to become a mother and here you are doing this to me."

She began to weep and fled from the room. Catherine observed her leaving and turned her face again to me.

My silent tears turned to sobs then and I found myself unable to hold off any further. I wept for Harry. I wept for myself. I wept for our child. I wept for all the plans now lost like the scattered rice on our wedding day, and I wept for my poor sister.

Catherine paced the room during my outburst, my clutch of documents still in her hand. I recognised that she was trying to find a solution. I cared not. She could do her worst.

Finally she spoke to me. "You cannot keep the child Elizabeth, you do see this do you not?"

"Harry and I were married Mama."

"Who would believe such a thing. You have been living here as a

maiden girl all the time you were secretly married."

"But it is the truth. I will leave and raise the child with its Grandmother in the village."

"In the Village. In the Village. Are you an idiot girl? Do you imagine I would allow such a thing? You will make me a laughing stock. As if I cannot control my own daughter. No. That will not do. I must think of another way."

She paced the floor once again but halted momentarily when Louisa's husband entered, however when he had nothing advantageous to offer she continued her pacing.

"Louisa is in her room," he informed me with a sneer, coming more than comfortably close to my face and peering down, his pointed nose and small peering eyes gazing at me intently, a pungent smell of Whiskey on his breath.

"How is she?" I asked.

"What do you care? Of course she is unwell, she is suffering extreme distress. You know what she has suffered and you…" He seized my chin and twisted as if inspecting a prize ham he was considering purchasing.

My memory did not fail to remember that it was a mere few months prior he was complaining he had been sold a faulty wife by Catherine because Louisa could not produce an heir. However, I decided it was not a wise course of action to remind him of this. I have little fight remaining and allowed him to twist my face as he would. I cared not.

"You are a little bitch and always have been. Perhaps I ought to take you and show you a thing or two."

He grabbed at my skirts trying to propel me backwards, while he blundered to climb on top of me. I shrieked in astonishment and attempted to force him away, the stench of cigars and Whiskey almost overpowering. I continued to weep unable to control it. Catherine swiftly moved towards him and with one giant swipe clapped him across the rear of the head.

"Remove yourself you oaf. That does not assist our predicament. Help me find a solution. Elizabeth go to your room I will call when we decide what is to be done."

Louisa's husband flopped onto the chaise long and positioned his riding booted feet on Catherine's plush fabric seat, appearing slightly put out at being reprimanded. I rose and left, moving back towards my room in something of a trance.

So now she knows. I do not know how I feel but all I want to do is climb into my bed.

I must have slept for some hours because the sun had changed position and the room was darker when I was shaken awake by Catherine a few moments ago. She came in and told me what plan she had come up with. Here follows our conversation:

"Elizabeth. I have a plan which will allow you to carry on your prior life and will ensure Louisa is given what she so desperately needs. You see, without your husband you cannot provide for your child adequately and a child requires a father in its life. It is simply impossible for you to do this alone. It is not the done thing. Possibly if you were a common unknown girl but you are not, you are the daughter of Lord Leyac. You simply cannot bring a child up alone as a single girl. It is wholly selfish of you and you must think of the reputation of the family and our place in society."

"Mama, you surely cannot expect me to give the child to strangers? I simply cannot. It is the child of my beloved Harry and the only fragment remaining. I am more than certain his family will provide for us. Mama I refuse to give the child away."

Catherine's face looked stunned at my words, and I was more than a little taken aback myself. I had not consciously contemplated the child. The words simply formed and delivered themselves from some deeper consciousness.

However, despite this declaration I was aware that Catherine was correct. *I could not bring a child up alone it was not the done thing.*

"Elizabeth, you cannot as the daughter of a Lord go and live as a commoner. They would never accept you and this whole family would be a laughing stock. You owe it to your father and your late mother to not tarnish the life they provided for you and sacrificed themselves to ensure you could live."

Those words did have an impression on me. I confess, Dear Journal, I have not considered this before and was stunned at the truth of them. Catherine had never mentioned my mother again following the day of my father's death but she was quite correct in her words. My mother had given her life for me, and it was this realisation that made me sit in stunned silence while I contemplated her words.

But when my thoughts once again turned to Harry I again felt confused. My mind a jumble of beads tangled and knotted. I could not think clearly. I grieved for Harry. I only sought Harry and did not wish to discuss an infant that was not yet in my life.

"And you need to consider your sister. You can see plainly what her miscarriages and stillbirth have done to her state of mind. She is fragile and I do not think she could survive watching you carry a healthy child and it not being her own. Please Elizabeth for the sake of the child, your sister and your own poor parents let Louisa be the child's mother. In name only. You will remain a constant in its life and will be able to spend a great deal of time with it should you desire. It will be brought up here as your nephew or niece and will be heir to Leyac House and Estate. Elizabeth, it will have every advantage I can possibly bestow."

"I am simply not certain what I should do Mama. My mind is such a muddle."

"Do you not realise that as far as society is concerned, your child will be considered a bastard. It will be shunned and spat at in the street. People are cruel to such children. It will have the most

miserable of lives. And it matters not that you were married. You will not be believed. You are condemning your child to a life of misery if you selfishly try to retain possession. But if you allow Louisa to be mother it will become heir after her. I will ensure the child receives the very best education and start in life. You owe this to the child to allow it to enjoy the very best. Part of being a mother means you sacrifice your feelings for the benefit of the child. Do you not see this is the only way?"

"And if I consent to this, you promise I can be a part of the child's life as much as I wish and the child will be officially named as heir?"

"Of course Elizabeth, I would not have it any other way. You must see there is no other solution to your problem. This way you can be a part of the child's upbringing. The alternative is misery for both you and the child."

"You are right Mama I cannot raise a child. I consent to your terms. I will give my child to Louisa."

Even as I spoke those words they only served to reinforce the dreamlike state I was in. I simply wished for Harry to return. I do not wish for a child. I want Harry.

"You have made the right decision Elizabeth. Louisa has already agreed and we will begin today. Shortly we will announce that she is with child once more. You will continue your life as normal for the moment. When you begin to grow we shall feign illness. I will personally make a false stomach for Louisa to wear so it appears she is great with child. I have seen it done in the theatre. Once the child is born you will recover your illness and become a doting aunt."

I attended to what she said but only half hearing. "Mama, what if Louisa should actually become pregnant again?"

"Do not concern yourself with that Elizabeth. I have a solution for that situation too."

She patted my arm awkwardly and despite this being the first time she had touched me physically in a number of years, I ignored her.

Harry. I attempted to seek him out with my mind. Perhaps he would respond if I maintained enough concentration. Harry rescue me from this. If you really are departed I wish to be at your side.

I understood then that Catherine was waiting on a response which I could only give with weeping. She rang for a maid telling the girl I was unwell and she should sit beside my bed.

I want to sleep but am damned to stay awake in this hellish nightmare. I cannot stop the tears, there is not a thing remaining, Dear Journal.

CHAPTER TWENTY-NINE

October 1940 ANNA

When Anna got to work that morning there was already a telegram from the doctor, it simply said.

"Got her Stop"

She turned the note over. That was it nothing else. She was disappointed but at least they seem to have got the coffin without any problems. Now it was a matter of waiting again.

She told Marcus of the entry she had read the evening before. Elizabeth's husband had been killed and she was pregnant with his child.

"So. Catherine has arranged that Louisa will be the mother to Elizabeth's child." Marcus spoke as if he was talking to himself rather than to her.

"Yes and that provides a much clearer explanation as to what Elizabeth's illness was," Anna replied.

"But…" said Marcus, getting up from his chair and pacing the room, one hand on his chin. "What if Louisa does get pregnant again, like Elizabeth suggested? What if both sisters are pregnant together? What if one child is Louisa's and the other is Elizabeth's?"

"So the Leyac twins aren't actually twins at all," said Anna.

"Exactly," said Marcus stopping and pointing at her directly. "So, what do we know for certain? Well we know that Elizabeth Leyac died of a long illness around the time her sister was due to give birth to twins." He held up his hands and began ticking off things on each finger. "Well, in that case we can deduce that the long illness was in fact a pregnancy that became complicated at the time of birth and killed Elizabeth; then either Elizabeth's or Louisa's baby became ill and died shortly after birth."

"So..." said Anna. "If Elizabeth gave birth first her baby was kept hidden until Louisa gave birth. The babies would be, as far as anyone is aware, twins. Then following Louisa's birth something goes wrong with one of the infants shortly afterwards."

"But that leads to a more interesting question. Whose baby was Lord Thomas and whose baby is in the coffin with Elizabeth?" Marcus said sitting back in his chair and sighing.

"There's nothing we can do now until we hear back from Doctor Laker," Anna said.

Marcus nodded and she left him contemplating what the answer could be.

They heard nothing else that day from the doctor, or the professor who had arranged to be at the Forensic laboratory with his friend when the coffin was delivered.

Anna noticed that even Marcus found it difficult to concentrate. She was working on a piece on remaking and reusing out of style clothes. It was actually a little more interesting than the usual household ones she was given and the lady she had interviewed for the piece had lots of ideas for restyling old dresses. In fact, Anna had asked her whether she provided a service to do such things and had then commissioned her to make over some of the dresses she had saved from her mother's collection.

However, it still wasn't the gritty journalism she craved. She wanted to report on things that mattered. She wanted to report on the War. If truth be told, she wanted to do what Frank Delancey was going to do. She wanted to go abroad and report on the boys at the front discovering what was really happening out there, but she knew her Editor would never let a woman do such a thing. So instead she hoped to at least get more real stories here. One step at a time, she thought.

That day dragged, like so many of the days recently, despite her being busy all day. Each stroke of the clock took longer to tick past than the last one. She felt she had lost control of her own investigation and not for the first time wondered how she had allowed so many men to get involved.

It was already beginning to get dark as she left that evening, but she didn't yet feel ready to go home. Her mind was whirling, wondering what was happening with the bodies in the coffin. Neither she nor Marcus had heard anything more from the doctor or the professor and she didn't even know whether they had arrived safely at the laboratory.

The evening was cold and she could see her breath as she walked. The clouds were low and a faint, swirling fog wrapped itself around her as she walked along the street.

She walked on to the part of London with pubs; of the kind you could sit in without being asked to dance or bothered. The places she wanted to go tonight were where you find the real people of London. The real city folk who sang songs round a piano through the raids. She had stumbled on one of these places before, and had quite enjoyed her night there. That had been before the phone call. Before everything changed.

The darkness descended further and she began to realise that she would have to find the place shortly before the bombs started, or she would be caught in the raid again and that was not something she wanted to repeat.

As she walked the fog swirled thicker and thicker, and the darkness made it impossible to see where she was going. She walked blindly on. Turning a corner she did not recognise her surroundings and soon realised her mistake. She tried to turn and go back the other way, but somehow ended up walking along a dark alleyway. Exiting the alleyway she bore left, even though she still had no idea where she was.

Cursing herself for her stupidity she heard the siren begin to wail and whine, its eerie sound, the rise and fall of a screeching; a warning. The bombers were coming.

Marvellous, she thought, could this evening get any worse?

Anna felt she had no choice but to continue walking on in hopes of finding somewhere to shelter. She passed small Victorian shops and went through a dark tunnel that was lit in the centre by a solitary dim lantern.

It was then she heard footsteps and was pleased there was another person who may know where she was so she stopped and waited. The footsteps also stopped.

"Hello," she called, "could you tell me where I am?"

A loud bang and a whistling ping noise shot past her ear making her jump in shock. She flattened herself against the wall of the cold damp tunnel. Another bang - this one didn't whistle quite so close to her. She crouched down in the tunnel and the footsteps ran off into the distance. She stayed perfectly still, stunned, for a few seconds listening.

Damn it. Has someone just tried to shoot me?

She immediately thought back to the kidnapping. Was that it again? Was it more trouble from her father? Damn him.

Why would he not leave her alone? What on earth was going on? Why was he continuing to threaten her like this? One thing was certain, whoever he was, he wasn't someone she wanted to get close to. He was clearly someone very dangerous.

She realised she would have to do something about this. She couldn't just keep ignoring it and hoping he would go away. He clearly thought she was doing something to threaten him. But what to do about it, that was the question?

What she did know was that crouching on the floor of a dark, dirty tunnel was not the answer.

As she remained there crouching in the dark, the faint roar of engines above told her that the bombers had arrived.

A light cascaded through the tunnel from a doorway just a little way from where Anna was sitting. A man in a dirty white shirt with sleeves rolled up and open at the collar came out from the lighted doorway.

"What was it Pa?" said a heavy East End accent from behind the man.

"Not sure," said the man peering into the darkness of the tunnel and squinting. "But I know the sound of a bloody gunshot when I hear one."

"Oh, Oh have they come, are we being invaded?" said a shrill voice from inside.

The man peered into the darkness again. Anna stepped out into the light cast by the open door.

"I think the gun shot was meant for me," she said.

"Who are you?" asked the man suspiciously. "We don't want no trouble here."

"I can assure you, I have no idea. I got lost on my way home from work and some fool tried to shoot at me. At least I think it was me he was shooting at. I don't know how he could see anything at all though. I'm sure it was a case of mistaken identity."

The ground shook and some brick dust from the tunnel roof rained down on them.

He looked up at the roof of the tunnel before frowning at Anna. "What is it you do for a job?"

"I'm a reporter, I work on Fleet Street."

"Oh I see, annoyed some criminal have you with a story?" He chuckled then.

"No, I wish I could get stories like that to cover but I'm a woman and I write the cleaning and housewife pieces."

"Oh," said the shrill voice behind him. "Let her in. I know them articles. Highlight of my week those. Let her in. I want some tips."

"Yes come on Stan, you'll have the warden on the warpath if he sees that light," said a distant male voice from somewhere inside.

He looked at her suspiciously before an explosion made the ground shake violently.

"Come on girl, get yourself in here," he said moving aside and letting her in.

Anna thanked the man gratefully and stepped inside. What she had thought was someone's house turned out to be a narrow set of stairs that led down to a tiny pub emanating a feeling of warm cosiness, as if you had stepped into someone's home. There were a number of people cluttered in the small room. Each with drinks and some with blankets ready for the night ahead.

The man who had let her in went behind the small bar and poured a small glass of something amber.

"Here," he said. "You'll need this after what's just happened."

The shrill voice she had heard from the street turned out to belong to an older lady with rosy red cheeks wearing glasses that were perched on the end of her nose. She was dressed in a mismatched outfit but no one seemed to notice.

She came to Anna and said, "Oh my dear girl. It's not right a young woman such as yourself outside wandering all alone with them bombs raining down. And some maniac with a gun is shooting at people now." She tutted and shook her head. "What's the world coming to? My Arthur would turn in his grave he would. Fought in the trenches for this - more of the same." She crossed herself and looked to the ceiling.

Anna sat and found that her hand was shaking as she went to pick up her glass. She shook it to shake away the feeling and tried again to pick up the glass. This time she picked it up and took a big gulp of the amber liquid. It was burning and made her cough but the warm numb feeling that followed was almost instantaneous. She took another gulp and finished the glass.

Someone in the far corner began to sing *Bless 'Em All* slightly out of tune. The woman by the piano, stuck her cigarette in the corner of her mouth and pulled out the stool before beginning to play an accompaniment. Before long they were all singing happily drowning out the bangs and thuds above their heads.

"...We're saying goodbye to them all," sang Anna joining in, now on her second drink. Perhaps this evening might not be so bad after all.

A few hours later, a little less than sober and thoroughly sung out, she retreated to one of the darker corners of the pub and laid out on an empty sofa bench. The curious band of people had also done the same. But before going to sleep she sat and read another entry in Elizabeth's diary. She was impatient to find out whether Marcus's theory about both babies not really being twins, was correct. She skipped ahead nine months to May 1915.

CHAPTER THIRTY
May 1915 ELIZABETH

Well, it is over, and I must say, Dear Journal, it truly was an horrific ordeal. It was exceedingly early, the room shrouded in darkness when I woke with pain in my abdomen this morning. It moved upwards like a wave rising in strength then declining away. It was profound and took my breath away. At first I wondered whether this was the beginning of the process to end my confinement, but having never experienced it before I was reluctant to shout for help if it were not. Especially as the twinges I have suffered in recent weeks were rehearsals, so Sissy informed me. I wondered if this was just another of those. I was inclined to trust in her judgement since she had a degree more experience than I in these matters.

In fact she and I have become the most unlikely of friends, Dear Journal, through the long days of my incarceration in this room. All through those dark desolate days when I imagined I would die if I were not able to escape these walls, she amused me with her witty personality.

I used to adore this room; my solitary space but it has become my prison and Catherine my jailor. My door remains locked as a constant. Catherine possesses a key and Sissy another, but despite whichever of them enters or departs, it remains in a locked state so any curious servants remain ignorant of my true condition.

I had not looked on another soul except Sissy and Catherine for a deal of weeks apart from my doctor, who arrived to monitor my progress regularly. Louisa visited little and found herself bored in my room. She wore the most ridiculously small with-child abdomen Catherine constructed for her. It was simply laughable when compared to my large size, which was at least twice her size if not three times, I am certain. Even Catherine found my size incredulous but the doctor informed me I have an exceptionally large, healthy child.

I am so fatigued of this room, these walls, this furniture. My once beloved room is now most hated. When I think back to the beginning of my confinement and the period when Catherine initially found out about Harry and the baby, I cared little what was to become of me, Dear Journal. I have however, altered this view over the months spent locked in this room with nothing but my thoughts as the child has grown within me. I found that as the baby grew and Sissy explained each new symptom, despite my grief and daily weeping, followed by fits of melancholy, I began to feel more optimistic for the future. Now the weeping has lessened, even though my heart yearns for Harry just as fervently, I can live with the pain more easily.

I have also decided that it makes little difference who the child names as mother. Shortly I will be able to leave this room and stroll the baby around the gardens in its carriage, take it to all the places Harry and I visited and in time, perhaps I will tell it the truth about Harry.

In more recent days the thought that Harry will never get to look on the face of his child has preoccupied my mind and makes me weep. I still find that I just cannot come to terms with the knowledge that I will never again hear the tone of his voice. Will I forget it in time? I am so frightened of losing the memory of his face and his voice, that this makes me weep too.

I am digressing again from my story. Let me return, Dear Journal. The pain, of which I had attempted to remain ignorant was now intensifying and I resolved that I must wake Sissy. I rolled onto my side and, used my elbow and the hand of my opposite arm to force myself to a seated position. I remained for a few moments to catch my breath, which I never seemed to be able to do. It was as if my lungs were only able to take half a customary breath.

As I remained seated, the relaxed sound of the steady breathing of Sissy floated in the silence. She had begun to sleep in my room on a constant basis in case anything should occur. I reached for the wide heavy cool bed post and used its solidness to aid me to a standing position.

My insides and stomach dropped slightly as I stood and the process made me groan in a most unladylike way. I placed one hand across my swollen abdomen as if to prevent it falling off.

I remained standing for a number of minutes in the silent darkness and considered whether I was being foolish. Perhaps it was simply another rehearsal. I should refrain from waking poor Sissy if there was little reason to do so.

So I remained stood in the darkness, breath coming rapidly through my squashed lungs, holding the cool firmness of my bed post. As I stood I began rocking myself in the hips, it was comforting somehow. Although, my rather engorged size made standing for too long rather difficult, so I considered returning to my bed when the pain returned, that same wave motion growing in strength. However, this time the shock of it made my throat let out an involuntary moan, which at first I did not realise came from my own mouth.

"Elizabeth?" came the concerned sound of Sissy's voice. I heard her rush to light the lanterns.

When she succeeded and lights illuminated the room, I was still rocking from side to side holding on to the post and breathing heavily.

"Oh Elizabeth, I think it's time," she said and rubbed my back in a circular motion.

Unable to speak I nodded.

"I'm going to fetch Catherine. She will need to call the doctor. Will you be all right for a few moments?"

I nodded again, the pain had begun to recede so that by the time she left and I listened to her unassuming footsteps descend the staircase, the pain had gone. My feet and legs however, were aching so I moved to seat myself on the bed. As I did I caught sight of my reflection in the mirror on the inside wardrobe door, which had been left ajar.

My stomach was so large you would need to stand two normal sized Elizabeth's in front to hide my extended frame. My abdomen was not a round shape like Louisa's own had been when her poor son had been born deceased, mine was an oval shape like an egg on its side, sticking grotesquely outwards. I viewed myself for a few more moments wondering whether my mother had been so large with me. Maybe that was the reason she died.

The pain began again. So I pulled myself to a standing position and just as I had achieved this, Sissy entered. She hastened toward me and I leaned heavily on her shoulders bending forward slightly. Her hair smelt of soft honey mixed with soap and fresh linen. I closed my eyes as this wave became greater than the last.

I confess I was so preoccupied I barely heard Catherine enter the room but I did however, hear her exclaim with an intake of breath at my size.

After a while, I confess, Dear Journal, I know not the exact length of time, but the wave began to recede and I glanced up to see Catherine with a most un-Catherine-like concerned expression.

"Elizabeth, you need to go to Louisa's room to have the child if we are to keep up the pretence of her being the mother, she is waiting for us there."

I nodded at her. I cared little where we went and frankly to leave this room would be something of a treat, even if it was only to Louisa's room. I had been locked in here for six months.

There was a faint knock at the door and Catherine opened it.

"There is no one about, you can bring her," said the voice from the other side of the door that I recognised as Louisa's husband.

As I was between pains, Catherine decided we would descend to Louisa's room immediately. However, my large figure meant rapid walking was a simple impossibility, so I waddled slowly, as best I was able, holding the base of my abdomen, the weight of it convinced me it was about to drop out.

Louisa's husband had not looked at me since before my confinement. He remained stood in the hall with a lantern, his hair sticking up and his rather cross countenance soon changed to open mouthed shock when he viewed my figure.

"Good God, she's huge," he said.

"Be silent," ordered Catherine.

We journeyed toward Louisa's room but the progress was slow as I was barely able to walk. The stairs, dark and slippery, were an inconvenience and I was certain another pain was starting. Almost at Louisa's room I found I was not able to go any longer. I halted, my breathing heavy as the pain increased. I had need of being seated and sat myself on the cold hard stair. Catherine attempted to force me to stand but I could not. The wave of pain was considerably more intense and I did not believe I would be able to prevent myself from crying out. All three of them lifted me bodily and carried me inside Louisa's room to her bed.

As they lay me down, the pains stronger than ever now, a loud, low continuous moan escaped my throat as it took hold.

When this pain eventually subsided, I caught the tail end of a conversation. Louisa's husband had left and Louisa herself was at her wardrobe with two dresses in either hand.

Sara Thomson

"You want me to do something? But mother, I couldn't possibly," she said to Catherine a wide eyed and innocent expression across her face.

For the first time I was ever aware of, Catherine almost hollered at her daughter in that moment.

"Louisa, you may sit and hold Elizabeth's hand and mop her forehead as she did for you."

Louisa pulled a face but discarded her dresses in the corner in temper and moved to sit by me examining her nails, a bored expression on her face.

Another contraction began then and I once again missed what Catherine had begun to speak of to Sissy. When it subsided I heard the sum of this conversation too.

"Now remember what I said girl. You have proved yourself trustworthy with our secret over the last few months but I will ruin your family if you breathe a word to anyone. Do you understand girl?" Catherine was shaking her finger at Sissy in a matronly fashion.

Sissy nodded affirmation, white faced and wide eyed as she continued preparing towels and linen.

It did not take very long for my pains to take so much of my attention that I was ignorant of most of the conversations carrying on around me.

But I did catch the words Louisa uttered in protest. "Oh mama, does she have to make that noise? Everyone will think that is me."

I however, became too distracted to hear Catherine's reply as in that moment, my body had great need to push. No, that is not correct. I did not wish to push myself, my body had made the decision to push for me, of its own accord, and I was merely a stunned bystander to this proceeding.

Finally, after much moaning, pain and coaxing a tiny baby with screaming lungs was born. His cries however, did not make me smile

316

as the pain remained.

"Oh Mama a boy. He's simply perfect. Give him to me." I heard Louisa say.

"Elizabeth, the afterbirth should be next and the ordeal will all be over." I heard the doctor say.

When had he arrived? I considered in that moment. Why do the pains remain so strong? The answer came as my body began to push once again.

"Twins." I heard Catherine's horrified voice proclaim.

"Twins? Mama? What are we to do?" said Louisa.

I pushed once again and another tiny baby was born. This one miraculously, was screaming louder than the first.

"Hmm," said Louisa indifferently peering at the second child. "That one's not as pretty as this little one."

She was cradling my first born baby in her arms cooing at him. I breathed a long sigh. I had succeeded. Harry and I had two children. I reached forward to scoop the tiny red faced baby on the bed with waving fists of fury, but Catherine picked up the child in a blanket first. I sat back against my pillows and felt a most unusual mix of shock and elation.

Louisa was first to break the silence. "Mama what are we to do? I cannot have twins, no one will believe I had twins, my pregnancy simply wasn't large enough to make it plausible."

"Well Louisa, if you had worn the larger abdomen I made for you, we would not have this complication."

"It is hardly my fault mother. I am not the fool who had twins when one baby would have done perfectly well."

Louisa's raised speech made the tiny boy in her arms whimper and she glanced down and commenced rocking him.

"Do not worry darling I'm sure it will be fine," Catherine said, a clear attempt to defuse Louisa's rising temper.

Louisa, confident that her mother had it in hand, smiled.

"Well, in that case, I had better get ready. I am so pleased to be able to wear my own clothes again."

She moved toward her wardrobe humming, depositing the child on Sissy without an ounce of concern and pulled one of her customary white dresses from her cupboard.

"My darling, you are supposed to have just given birth, you cannot possibly wear a white dress or go anywhere."

"Mother, I have had a night of hell and months of further torment having to wear that awful with-child abdomen. I am going to wear my dress, go and seat myself and wait with my children for my stream of visitors." She waved her arm with an exceedingly unnecessary flourish.

Catherine appeared concerned but resigned. Louisa was not one with whom to begin a quarrel. Sissy and Catherine carefully dressed me again and aided me in rising from the bed. They found that it was almost necessary for them to carry me to my room. The doctor however, protested that I should stay where I was for a time but he was ignored. I found myself too weak to walk unaided and had waves of faintness when standing, my vision turning a strange black. It seemed to take an age to retire up the staircase once more, but once there I confess to a slight feeling of relief at having achieved it, although not thrilled at being returned to my room.

As Catherine turned to leave, her long dress swishing, I stopped her. "Mama?"

She glanced down at me expectantly.

"Could I hold the babies now?"

"Not at present Elizabeth. Later you may, right now you must rest. You've had an ordeal and the children have need of bonding with Louisa."

"How long must I remain in this room?" I enquired to the empty door. She had left without allowing me to finish speaking, the heavy door slamming and locking behind her with a deadening thud.

So here I am, Dear Journal, my children are here. Harry's babies are here and I confess to wishing more than anything to hold them. But I am stuck here in this room again.

But I am so dreadfully tired. I must sleep first then think. My mind is cloudy and I feel like my body is in tatters.

CHAPTER THIRTY-ONE
October 1940 ANNA

Anna rushed from the pub early that morning ignoring the sharp headache pulling at her temples. The whole place looked completely different from the night before.

In the early light of morning she easily found her way home. She quickly changed and put on fresh clothes stopping only to gulp a mouthful of the tea Olivia was drinking. She had just got in from a night shift and was yawning, a smudge of something that looked suspiciously like blood on her cheek. Anna didn't ask. She didn't want to know.

"Well, well. Where have you been all night. I hope he was worth it." Olivia said her eyes twinkling as she raised an eyebrow and gave her a knowing look.

She didn't have time to chat, she just smiled and said she would tell her about it later. Olivia called after her reminding her of their weekend plans. She rushed out, sighing. She had forgotten and wished she could get out of it. She would have to think of that later. Now she had to catch Marcus. They had been so blind.

Elizabeth had the twins. Both babies were Elizabeth's all along. Louisa's pregnancy had been a fake one.

She rushed down to Marcus' office but he was already coming down to meet her in the corridor.

"I've got something important to tell you, "She said excitedly to him.

"So have I." He said grimly.

As they walked back up the stairs to their office, she told him of the diary entry and how it had been Elizabeth who had given birth to twins. He looked grave and distracted as she spoke.

"What is it Marcus? Why do you look like that?" she asked stopping at the top of the staircase, gripping the thick wooden rail.

"Anna, I've heard from the professor. There's been some developments. I've got some bad news." He paused. "Anna, there isn't another body in the coffin with Elizabeth."

"What? Are you sure?"

"Of course I'm sure Anna, it isn't something you can joke about. There is no baby in that bloody coffin," he snapped running his hands through his hair.

"Oh damn it," she said beginning to walk across the hall to the entrance to their office.

He grabbed her arm then to stop her. "But Anna, the professor wants us to come to see his scientist friend straight away. He says he has something to tell us about Elizabeth's body."

"What does he have to say?" Anna asked beginning to walk off again.

"I don't know but he wants us to come and see him in person. He says it's important." Marcus said following her through the doors to their office.

"What on earth can he possibly have to say? We found out what we wanted, there is no baby in the coffin, which means that our whole theory of the baby dying and being put in the coffin with Elizabeth is wrong. Now we need to start again. What bloody happened to that damn baby?" she said stopping again and facing him.

"It's not about the baby, it's about the body of Elizabeth Leyac. The professor says it's vital we come."

"He does realise that it's the other end of the country?" Anna sighed and closed her eyes. "Oh all right I suppose I have nothing on this weekend apart from a dance with Olivia, which I'm happy to get out of to be honest. I'll speak to the doctor and we'll get the train up tonight, providing you can persuade our Editor we are going up north tomorrow for a very good reason?" she said looking towards where his office was.

"I'll think of something. In the meantime, here telephone the doctor and get him to make reservations somewhere in York for us." He handed her the phone receiver from a nearby desk and a scrap of paper with a scribbled number on it.

After a few rings the doctor answered.

She told him that they were coming and asked him if he knew what it was the scientist wanted.

"No, Anna. I know as much as you. All I know is that they want to speak to us face to face. That's it."

"I'll meet you off the train tonight and I can fill you in a little more on what I do know, which I warn you, isn't a lot."

She began to say goodbye, when he stopped her. "Oh Anna…"

"Yes."

"Are you all right?" his voice sounded concerned, which irritated her. She wasn't a child, damn him.

"Yes fine. Why wouldn't I be?"

"Nothing, it's nothing. I'll see you tonight."

She said good bye to the doctor and placed the phone receiver back in its cradle. The faster she could get through today, the faster she could find out what was going on. Blast these men keeping her in the dark. What could be so bloody secret.

As they left work that evening together, she turned to Marcus and thanked him for his help. She knew that without the help of the professor or Marcus they wouldn't have got as far as they had, and even though they had committed an illegal act for something completely unfounded, she was grateful to him.

"He laughed then. I am purely selfish Anna. We might not have solved the mystery of what happened to the baby, but if there is something we don't know about Elizabeth Leyac that her body can reveal, maybe it might help discover more about her."

"Yes that's true. And it'll be nice to get away from the raids for a few nights," she said trying to feel happy about the prospect of a trip north.

"They have raids in the rest of the country you know." Marcus said amused.

"Yes I know that," she said, but she was thinking about the endless darkness and endless silence of the nights back in her mother's cottage.

Later, as the train snaked up the east side of the country, she found that her thoughts inevitably strayed to

323

her mother and the last time she had made this journey north. So much had happened since that night. So many things she would never have believed possible before. She stared at the blackout blind pulled firmly down blocking out the night. She desperately wanted to pull it up and look out.

When they arrived at York Station Doctor Laker was there to meet them. It was deathly dark but Marcus, never having left London before, was more awed at the silence broken only by the distant thuds of the bombings on the coast.

"I've taken the liberty of booking you both into a hotel here in central York. It will save time."

"That's fine," said Anna.

"I'm staying down here too. Now, let's go get a drink and we can discuss what I do know which, as I said, isn't much I warn you."

Not long after, they were seated in a small quaint pub with stone walls and low hanging doors and windows. Marcus brought over drinks.

This time the doctor didn't pause or drag out the attention on himself, of which she was glad.

"I haven't been told much, but what the professor did slip was that his friend was confused about the cause of death."

"What does that mean?" asked Anna twisting her glass in a circle on the table as she spoke.

"It's a well known fact that Elizabeth died from an illness she'd had for a long time, so there shouldn't be any issues with cause of death," said the doctor.

"But if he's saying there is, then it must be important." Marcus replied cautiously.

"Exactly. And if Elizabeth didn't die in the way we think she did, it might mean that there's more to this whole thing than we have been led to believe," the doctor continued.

Marcus and Anna exchanged a look.

"We have reason to believe that Elizabeth died due to complications from giving birth," said Anna looking directly at the doctor.

He looked like he hadn't shaved for a few days and his hair was tousled. The curls, that he usually attempted to tame, now lay however they wished.

"Oh. Really, well that does make a difference," said the doctor surprised. "But in any case it's pointless speculating. We should wait to speak to them tomorrow."

Anna went to bed in her hotel that evening unable to sleep despite the fact that she had relished the prospect of sleeping a whole night through in a bed.

She tossed and turned, until she could no longer lay in the bed and got up, silently walking across the floor to the window.

She opened the heavy blackout curtain and looked out into the starry night, the distant rumble of bombs from the coast interrupting the silence. Here she was again in this city. This city that seemed to draw her back again and again.

She thought of her mother and how she should visit her grave and the Baxters while she was here. The thought filled her with dread, although she didn't know why.

But she had to admit she had been avoiding thinking about her mother, and wondered again whether the problems she seemed to be having with her father would again resurface. She shook thoughts of him away.

Oh mother, why didn't you just tell me, surely that would have been better. She looked up to the sky despite knowing she would never have an answer.

The following morning the doctor took them to meet the professor. His scientist friend had a private laboratory where he was able to carry out tests on the body.

The Scientist himself was a scruffy sort who didn't seem to notice his appearance. He had a focused and intense look about him. Anna noted the quick sharp intelligence behind the grey eyes and despite his appearance, liked him greatly in an instant.

"I thought it important to bring you here in person, because of the nature of my discovery," he said leaning forward in the chair behind his desk in a room that was as stark and clinically tidy as if it were unused.

They all looked at him expectantly. There were a few moments of silence as he paused to realign his pencil's a fraction of an inch so they were all perfectly straight, with perfect spaces between each one.

"When the coffin was opened," he began, still aligning his pencils and not looking at Anna or anyone else "and the discovery was made that there was no baby for me to examine." He looked up into their faces then. "I decided to examine the remains of what was there. It seemed a pointless exercise not to, given the opportunity that was there. It's not often one gets to look at the remains of a Leyac." He smiled at them, his face crinkling as he did.

Anna shifted in her hard, uncomfortable seat.

"Well, my first discovery on getting the body into my lab, was that there was some damage to the skull." He continued.

"What kind of damage?" asked Anna.

She noticed the professor, slightly behind her fidgeting excitedly.

"There was a hole of about an inch wide, with surrounding damage making the whole damaged area about two inches long."

"What does that mean? Did it happen after death?" Marcus asked.

"Well from my examination of the body, I would say not. The injury to the skull happened prior to death. And I would say was in fact the main cause of death." He paused leaning back in his chair then, watching their reaction to this news.

"So what are you saying, that Elizabeth Leyac didn't die of an illness. She died of an injury to her skull?" Anna asked.

"Yes, I'm saying that the body in my lab did not die of an illness. But that's not all I discovered," he said rising from his chair to a standing position. "When I made this discovery, I naturally set about learning more about the body to identify any other markers or reasons to indicate such an injury."

He walked behind them to a set of tall filing cabinets, causing Anna and the others to crane around to see him. He began rifling through the folders in these cabinets and continued to talk.

"Under normal circumstances I get an unidentified body to examine and it's my job to try and find out anything that distinguishes that person. Often we are successful in being able to identify a body that is otherwise unidentifiable, i.e. when there is no face left to recognise it as a known person. To do this we use a number of techniques. One of these techniques is body measurements, so measuring the parts of the body to identify whether they match up with known measurement of the person. Another is the use of dental records, which is a new technique, and is only of limited use as not all of the population have been to a dentist. However, now we come to the crux of the situation. Elizabeth Leyac had been to a dentist, so we have records of this and we have information on her body measurements."

He pulled out a file from his cabinet and took it over to a wall mounted x-ray examiner. Anna didn't know the correct name for the machine but she had seen one once before, so knew what it was for. He held the folder close to his chest and turned to them switching on the x ray light.

"However, you might ask why this is relevant when we already knew the identity of the body. But I thought that due to the nature of the injury to the head, it would be wise to carry out further tests. So, I employed both of these identifying techniques on the body in my laboratory. Now…" he said waving the finger of his free hand at them as if giving a lesson.

"Elizabeth Leyac was 5ft 7ins tall, quite tall for a woman. However the body now in my laboratory was 5ft 4ins tall when alive. That's a difference of three inches. But, body measuring isn't entirely foolproof so I employed the new technique of using dental records and fortunately as we have records of her teeth, I was able to successfully employ this identifier."

He put up two black and white x ray photographs of teeth onto the board behind him.

"These are two examples of the X-rays we can get of people's teeth. Can any of you tell me the difference between these two particular X-rays?" he looked at each of them.

"Yes," said the doctor pointing with his hand. "The one on the left looks to have teeth missing at the back on both sides."

"Exactly." He said. Pointing his finger at the doctor as if in a lecture. "Top marks doctor Laker. Now we get to the crux of the issue. You see…" He said pointing at the image on the left with a stick he produced from beside him. "This X-ray here with teeth missing at the back is the dental records of Elizabeth Leyac herself from when she was alive. This one…" he said pointing at the other one with his stick. "…is the dental X-ray I took of the teeth belonging to the remains now in my laboratory."

"What are you saying?" asked Anna impatient for him to get to the point.

"I'm saying Miss Forrester that in my professional opinion, on the evidence produced so far, the body you brought me, the one that was in the grave at Leyac House is not the body of Elizabeth Leyac."

"Not Elizabeth? Then who is it? And what happened to Elizabeth?" she asked.

The Scientist shrugged his shoulders, balancing his stick back against the wall now his lesson was over.

Marcus was running his hands through his hair, a frown on his face.

The professor, who had been fidgeting all the time his friend was speaking couldn't contain himself any longer. "Anna, Anthony my boy, doctor, don't you realise what this means?"

"It means…" said Anna quietly, "…that Elizabeth didn't die."

"Exactly," shouted the professor jumping up from his chair and beginning to pace.

"Anna." said Marcus, "I think you should update them with what you discovered in the diary."

The professor stopped pacing and turned to Anna. "Has there been a development. Is there a clue to what happened to Elizabeth?"

Anna told the professor and the doctor of the last two entries she had read, about Harry's death, Elizabeth's pregnancy and Catherine's plan to allow Louisa to be the mother to Elizabeth's baby. She told them of her and Marcus' theory that the sisters may have been pregnant together, and finally she told them of what she had read the evening before about Elizabeth giving birth to twins.

"How many entries are left?" asked the professor thoughtfully rubbing his chin.

"Two," Anna replied. "I had assumed they would be the last few before she dies, but now I'm not sure. But the diary does end, so who knows."

"Well come on then girl. Get it out. Let's find out what happened to that girl and the missing twin. She must have the answers," said the professor.

Anna pulled the diary from her bag and cracked the leather binding open to the last few entries and began reading aloud to the whole group. Her voice echoed in the clinically silent room.

CHAPTER THIRTY-TWO
May 1915 ELIZABETH

Things have taken a dramatic turn, Dear Journal. When I stopped writing last time I was going to sleep following the birth of my little twins. Well I did just that. However, when I woke it was some hours later as the sun had moved position. Despite this I did not entirely trust my own judgement and instead glanced at my antique dark wooden clock. It was in reality three in the afternoon. I blinked to clear my vision in case eyes deceived me but the clock remained steady at three. How was I able to sleep for such a long time? Despite the evidence before me, Dear Journal, I persisted in my disbelief .

I knew I must rise however. I had not even looked at my own children and had spent the entirety of the first day of their lives laid in my bed sleeping. I had been a mother for a mere matter of hours and was already neglectful.

My head had a sense of lightness as I rose to stand, my legs decidedly wobbly despite my intention to stand steady. However, one improvement was that I was now able to rise without faintness. Even so, I remained still a few moments holding the bed post as I attempted to decide how my body felt.

I glanced at my wardrobe but the door was shut firmly. Only the dark wood inlayed carvings stared back at me. I was however, not upset at not being able to look in the mirror, it was probably best I did not look at myself just yet. I certainly did not feel my best. I could sense that my mass of wild hair was sticking up in all directions. I attempted to smooth it but as was customary, it sprang back again. Curse my hair. It was the one feature I hated, and so unlike my sister's silky smooth straight blond locks.

Sissy saw me stood holding the bed post, dropped the needlework in which she had been engrossed, pins raining to the floor, pinging faintly as they landed on each other.

"Oh bother," she said and raised her hands to her head in exasperation before letting them fall in defeat. She stood for a few moments undecided whether to pick up the pins and needlework or whether to come to my side.

I smiled at her. She really did provide me with much amusement for the amount of disasters she managed to cause.

"Sissy, it is quite all right. Do pick up the pins and needlework. I am quite well."

She glanced at me once again appearing to decide something, whether I would keel over I suspect, before sighing audibly and kneeling to retrieve the tiny pins and stab them back into the silken domed pin cushion inside the wooden sewing box.

"I'm sorry, Miss. I never was no good with my needlework. I'm a farm girl, born an' bred. I spent my childhood raisin' pigs and milkin' cows, not stabbin' my thumbs with tiny little needles. Ow." She halted briefly and sucked the end of one thumb. "See what I mean?" she said and shook her head.

"Well your needlework has improved considerably in recent months. You should not be so harsh with your abilities," I replied amused at her constant defeatist attitude.

"I'll tell yer Miss, it's a good thing you're s'nice to me. Any other mistress would 'ave thrown me over for a new maid ages ago. I *wasn't cut out for bein' in service."* She shook her head once more.

"Nonsense. You have been delightful Sissy. You are like a dear friend to me rather than my maid. I have spent a vast degree more time with you than with any other. Now come along, I want to visit my babies."

She raised herself and placed the remainder of the pins in the cushion and came to my side. She helped me to the high backed chair in the corner of the room. Once seated comfortably she surveyed me.

"Now. Are you wanting to get dressed?"

"Yes please Sissy. I cannot very well make introductions to my babies in my nightdress. But do remember as far as everyone is concerned, I have been extremely ill, so we cannot dress me up finely. Something simple I think."

Sissy nodded, went to my wardrobe and began removing things for me to choose. I shook my head at each in turn. Then I spied the sleeve of something grey.

"Sissy that one, what is that grey one?" I said pointing directly.

"What this?" She said pulling it out in distaste. *"Miss, it's awful drab."*

The dress was long sleeved with fitted cuffs and little beaded grey buttons. There was a high lace collar that fastened around the base of the neck and twin lines of buttons all down the front of the dress to the floor. It was in the modern style, quite narrow to the body but the material was plain and of a clay grey colour. I was certain it would wash me out and make me look rather ill. *"That is the one. It is simply perfect."*

"Miss are yer sure?" She was still frowning, holding the garment between finger and thumb as if it might reach right up and bite her.

"Yes, that is it."

Once the dress was on Sissy surveyed me again still frowning. She shook her head. *"I'm sorry Miss, it's the ugliest dress."*

"I am aware it is but I have been in my sick bed for months. It

would be unthinkable for me to suddenly rise one day miraculously recovered."

"What will yer say miss? If anyone asks why you're up suddenly."

"I will inform them I have been much improved recently and the news of my dear sister's twins helped me to feel improved enough to rise and visit them."

She did not appear convinced but took my arm and helped me toward the door. Unlocking it with her free hand she steered me down the corridor. Being on the topmost floor, it was the stairs that would take the time. Still, I remained determined to look at my children, even if that was simply as their doting aunt.

As we descended silently to the first floor I began to wonder whether they had announced the birth yet.

Once we began to move across the round gallery with its portraits of ancestors and its large oval shaped cut-out of the floor something made me halt.

Voices from the north drawing room rang clear and loud, due to the nature of this house being such that many rooms lead on to others, which also means that voices travel clearly to other rooms. This was one such place and the voice that made me halt my progress was the deep voice of Louisa's husband.

"Louisa you fool, don't you realise what a problem this is? Why do you think we have not announced the birth yet? It will be impossible for people to believe that you with your tiny abdomen gave birth to twins. You should have had one the same size as Elizabeth's actual one. It is no wonder she was so bloody enormous."

"Oh darling, you are being ridiculous, how will people know? They will not know. Paranoia is a very serious thing my dear. I suggest you enjoy being a new father."

I saw in my mind Louisa's floaty, flippant hand gestures prior to bobbing her hand at the base of her hair absently, as was her habit.

"Louisa dear," this was Catherine's more steady voice. "It is a problem because rumours lead down dangerous paths. We cannot have rumours circulating. Your husband is right. Something must be done."

"Yes it must," answered Louisa's husband. His voice had taken on a degree of anger now. "And another thing Catherine, you promised me, Elizabeth would meet the same fate as her mother and be out of the way. But lo and behold she's still bloody here, causing yet more problems."

Sissy held me tighter as we stood ungraciously eavesdropping. I have always been taught, Dear Journal, that listening at doorways is the absolute height of bad manners but in that moment I was unable to move. My feet firm on the parquet patterned floor of the gallery.

"I made no such promise. I merely said that it may be a possibility and would therefore solve the issue of her wanting to be around but do not concern yourself. I have a plan. The Earl of Somerset is elderly and unmarried, and his estate is very far into the south of England. I will make arrangements to have her married off quickly. Elizabeth is not a problem. I can control her. She is a trusting fool."

"But what about the twins? We cannot have two. We need to get rid of one." Louisa's husband said. "People will become suspicious if they see two babies. What are we to do?"

"I have thought of that too. We can leave one at the foundling hospital. Infants get left there all the time. What is one more?" said Catherine.

"Oh mother, it would have to be the crying one. That one cries constantly, the noise has been fretting my nerves all day. Leave me with this lovely quiet one. He looks just like my lost little boy, do you not think darling?"

"I could arrange for one to have an accident." Louisa's husband said.

There was silence in the room. I could almost see them glaring at him. *This surely was too far even for Catherine. My heart beat wildly out of my chest, I felt nauseous but still could not leave.*

Finally after I was certain the silence would endure forever, it was broken by Louisa who for once seemed to wholly grasp the situation.

"Murdering the child is out of the question. I refuse to allow it. It may be an irritating little thing but it is an innocent. I will not allow you to harm it. You must find another way."

"Do not worry Louisa darling. We would never do such a thing. I promise my sweet. I am sure he was merely jesting." I recognised the tone in Catherine's voice as one she used when her aim was to pacify Louisa.

But surely she would not do such a thing. Catherine was capable of a great many things but child murder? No. I could not believe it. Still, I had to fight every bone not to run into that room and remove both my babies that instant.

I hated the very smell of the house then, Dear Journal. The very air thick with poison I wanted nothing more than to depart immediately.

My head spiralled with blackness interrupting my vision once again, I began to feel faint. On some level I was dimly aware of Sissy removing me silently but urgently upstairs before we were discovered.

It was at this point that my mind called to Harry, something I had not done for a few months. Why did you not return? What am I to do?

Back in my room Sissy sat opposite me and we glanced at each other for a time. The echo of my stunned feelings mirrored in the face before me.

After a while I began to cry but had not realised until Sissy handed me a handkerchief. I mopped at my silently streaming eyes, and was more than aware that weeping would not aid my situation but seemed at a loss to control it.

Sissy disregarded my weeping and remained silent, until in a calm measured tone, which I had never heard from her before, said, "Yer can't let them do this Miss Elizabeth. You know that don't yer?"

I glanced at her face and the stoney serious expression on her usually light hearted features and it sent a thunder of fear through my body.

"I know we have talked before of what 'appened in my past and why I came t' be sent here by mi family. My child was teken from me. There was nothing anyone could 'ave done about that. It was an illness an' was no one's fault. It took me a long time to come t' terms with that. But you Elizabeth can do something about this now. Yer can save your children. From them. Before they destroy their lives and yer own. Believe me, I know what it is t' lose a child an' I warn yer Elizabeth, it isn't somethin' yer can easily live with. Do not let them keep either of yer children."

"Sissy, your counsel is always welcome and I agree with you. I will leave and take my babies with me. They will never stop hunting me though, I will need help to disappear. I wonder Sissy, would you get word to Harry's mother? She resides in the village. I can inform you of where."

Sissy moved across the room and squeezed both my hands in her own.

"Elizabeth, I will do everythin' it teks t' make sure that you an' those babies get away from this dreadful place an' those people. I will go now t' see Harry's mother. Here write the directions on this paper."

She produced a scrap of notepaper from her skirt pocket and I scribbled the directions rather badly, alarmed to observe that my hand was shaking rather violently.

Sissy studied the paper however and nodded, dressed in her hat and coat, kissed me and departed. I was most uncertain how Harry's mother would receive the news. I had not had contact with her since prior to Harry being killed. She would more than likely have come to the valid assumption that I had turned out to be everything she had initially believed me to be.

Recalling the day when I first became acquainted with Harry's mother reminded me of that delightful picnic and our plans to get married. It was not even a year since that day.

Thoughts of Harry made me want to weep until I began to consider what he would do if he were here. I was well aware that he would take himself directly up to the house, punch Louisa's husband on the nose and remove our children without any degree of hesitation.

However, reading those words back, Dear Journal, I am struck with the thought that I have clearly been reading far too many romance novels during my incarceration to believe such a fairy tale.

It seemed an age before Sissy returned and I will admit, Dear Journal, that I had begun to panic because she was my only means of escape. Without Sissy's help I would remain trapped here and my infants would remain in grave danger.

When she did return she was damp from the rain and the fresh smell of outside lingered around her. I breathed her in delightfully. I missed the outdoors desperately and came to the decision that when this was over, I would never be imprisoned again and this is a resolution I am determined to stick to.

Sissy shook herself from her coat and hat. "Harry's mother wasn't trustin' of me at first. But when I said it was about you an' Harry, she let me in. 'er husband is back on leave, a big brute of a man he is. Anyway, I told them everythin', how when you found out about Harry's death Catherine imprisoned yer and kept yer pregnancy a secret. That you gave birth to twins just this mornin' and we overheard the three of them plottin' t' kill one of the children t' make it believable that Louisa gave birth to them. They were surprised an' pleased that you had given birth to Harry's children an' as soon as I told them you wanted to escape yer family, they said they would help, for Harry's sake an' the sake of their grandchildren. We are to escape in the dark of night an' go to them. They will then help us on to London. Harry's father says he knows someone who can help us hide."

I enquired then as to her use of the word 'us'.

"Of course Elizabeth, I'm comin' too, what have I to stay fo'?"

"But Sissy your family? Catherine made threats to ruin them through a refusal to buy their produce if you went against her. Be assured Sissy, she is a woman of her word."

"They survived before the Leyacs an' they can survive after them. After I disgraced them with an illegitimate babe, I don't think anythin' could shock them again. No this is the right thing t' do, yer need me."

"Well I must confess to feeling a great deal of relief to have you alongside me Sissy but I will only consent if you are wholly certain you are aware of what you are doing."

"Just try an' stop me. I will get together a few things t' tek. We can only travel light, so mus' pack wisely. Leave it t' me Miss, I know what I'm doin'. Right now we must act like everythin' is normal. I will go down and get your evenin' meal as usual. I have a plan to keep the wet nurse out the way later on, so yer can go to the nursery and get the babies. Don't look so worried Elizabeth, it's a good plan. It'll work."

I nodded my head in affirmation and she departed the room once again.

It may be a good plan but Sissy did not know my family as I did. Catherine would never stand for this. She would never desist searching for me. But that risk is one I must take in order to protect my infants, Dear Journal. I will never yield and would certainly not abandon Harry's children. Finally for the first time since he went I feel alive. I feel like I have a purpose. I am a mother and I will protect my children from those people, no matter the consequences. I will update you, Dear Journal, once this is over and we are out, if we get out. No. I will remain positive. We will get out.

CHAPTER THIRTY-THREE
October 1940 ANNA

Anna stopped reading and looked up at the faces watching her.

"So Sissy helped plan Elizabeth's escape."

Anna flicked through the pages of the final entry, it was long, much longer than the others.

"The official word was that Elizabeth died from a long illness around the time the twins were born and the child that went missing was stolen by the maid Sissy. But we now know that they were Elizabeth's children, that she and Sissy planned to take both children away and that the body in the coffin is not Elizabeth.

I don't imagine for a moment the Leyacs' would mistakenly put the wrong body in a coffin, so we have to assume they knew about it."

The professor began pacing the floor, one hand on his mouth, his head bent as he talked.

"So Elizabeth didn't die, the Leyacs knew, planted this body and faked Elizabeth's death but we know that only one of those twins disappeared, so we have to also assume something went wrong with Sissy's escape plan."

"But why would they fake her death?"

"I don't know but I have a feeling it has something to do with this missing twin. Someone has worked very hard to keep the truth a secret," said the professor.

The three of them left the laboratory contemplating their new information. The professor staying behind a little longer with his friend.

"What do we do now? Are we going to break the story?" asked the doctor.

"No, not yet," said Anna.

"No? Why on earth not?" We have evidence that the body is not Elizabeth. That's a great story. Surely that's what you wanted?" The doctor said almost indignantly.

"It is, you are right, but there's more to this and I want to find out what that is. If we break the story now, we will never find out what happened to that baby. We're close. I know it." Anna said.

"Anna's right," said Marcus to the open-mouthed doctor.

"Well you two are the reporters. You know better than me what to do. So what now."

"Now we go for a drink. We need to think about where to go from here and what this information means," Marcus said. "And, I could really do with a good stiff drink."

The doctor looked disappointed and kicked a stone. "Who do you think it is that's been in Elizabeth's grave then all these years?"

"I'll bet my right eye it's the maid," said Marcus, turning up his collar as they rounded a corner into the wind.

"What Sissy? The one who supposedly took the baby?" said the doctor surprised.

"Yes," said Marcus.

"Hang on a minute Marcus, the last time you came up with a crazy theory, we ended up digging up a grave and your theory was proved wrong," the doctor said.

"Ah, correction there doctor. It wasn't my theory at all. It was the professor's. But we found out something much more valuable," Marcus replied "Now where's this pub? I need to get thinking."

"Oh Anna speaking of valuable things. Did you ever open that safety deposit box your mother left you? Were there some treasures in it?" The doctor asked with a laughing smile, pushing open double doors to a pub.

"What safety deposit box? I don't have a safety deposit box." Anna said, giving the doctor a quizzical look.

"Yes, you have a necklace with a key on it."

"How did you know about that?"

"I was your mother's doctor. I saw it many times and when you hurt your knee, the chain came out from under your clothes and I saw it again. I knew what it was because my Great Aunt used to have one just like it to store her emeralds in. Her husband was an officer in the military and they lived abroad somewhere when she was young, and he bought her lots of expensive jewellery. Anyway, you never mentioned it so I thought I'd just ask. Sorry I didn't mean to pry," he said.

She felt her cheeks go hot at the memory of the kiss and the irritating way he gave her a knowing look.

Marcus had ordered drinks and handed her one. She made a show of taking a big swig and being distracted before continuing.

"But it's just a necklace. Mama used to wear it all the time, for years. It's just an old trinket, a piece of jewellery. It's not a safety deposit box key." Anna took out the necklace from beneath her blouse and showed them the little gold key on the end of a chain. "See, it's just an item of jewellery."

"It is Anna, it's exactly like the one my Great Aunt used to have, and there's one major place in this city that it might come from," the doctor said.

"What on earth would my mother want with a safety deposit box? And why didn't she tell me she had one? Are you sure about this doctor, because I'm not convinced," she said.

"Come on then, let's go and I'll prove it to you," he said, gesturing with his arm before gulping his drink.

"Well, even if it is, they won't let me examine the box. I could be anyone," she said, taking a nearby seat and tracing the droplets forming on the outside of her glass.

"Do you want to go and have a look Anna?" Marcus asked sitting down opposite her.

"No, I'm not sure I do." She said thinking of the dangerous encounters she'd had with her father's people. She hadn't told either of them about that. But then, maybe it was about time she dealt with the father problem.

"There might be something in there about how your mother knew Elizabeth Leyac. People don't tend to keep any old thing in safe deposit boxes. If your mother took the time to take one out in the first place, then it must be important," Marcus said with an unconcerned shrug.

"I have a feeling it's going to be information about

someone I don't want to know about." Anna thought back to the letter she got from her father.

"You're thinking of that letter again aren't you?" the doctor said, looking down at her from where he was stood.

She looked up sharply, she'd forgotten he knew about that, had read it. Damn him.

"Well I'll tell you what…" he continued. "We'll all go together, we'll open it and take a quick look, if it's about your father we'll close it and you don't have to look. If it's about Elizabeth you can look." said the doctor.

"Your Father? Anna why would it contain information about your father?" Marcus asked.

Anna sighed, she was tired of all this secrecy, maybe she should just tell them. What the hell.

"Get me another drink and I'll tell you both. You might as well know everything."

So a few moments later, sipping her drink Anna paused thinking how to start, watching the bartender polish glasses in the almost empty pub.

She told them both of the letter, she had received at the cottage, she told them how she had always known her mother had never married and how they had moved frequently when she was a child. She told them of her kidnapping and what the kidnapper had asked and finally, she told them of the shooting in the blackout and how she had ended up in an East End pub.

"So you see. He really doesn't want me in his life and is very frightened that I might investigate him. He must have something big to hide. The only reason I'm telling you is that you should both know the consequences of what we may discover. I have no idea who this person is or what he is capable of. However, judging from what he has already done to me, he clearly has no morals at all, so you should be careful. If this key is what the doctor says and his secrets are in it, which is what I believe to be true, knowing that information may have consequences. However, if it is the answers we need about Elizabeth, then it might solve this mystery but solving Elizabeth's mystery might come at a huge price. Are you both prepared for the consequences of what we might find out?"

They both stared at her almost in disbelief.

"Anna how have you kept such things a secret for so long. What if something had happened to you? How would I have found out the reason? You could have been killed you bloody fool?" The doctor had gone quite red in the face and the bartender had stopped polishing glasses and looked over at them.

Marcus, held up his hand. "Now doctor, calm down. Anna you really shouldn't have kept this to yourself."

She waved her hand in an impatient way. "Well that's not important now. Are you both prepared to put up with the consequences of what we might discover in that box?" she said.

"Well I'm not turning back now that I've discovered the danger you are in," said the doctor, folding his arms and looking a little put out. "I'm never leaving you alone again Anna," he said wagging his finger at her and downing his drink. He began moving from foot to foot in an agitated way.

"I am happy to deal with whatever consequences may happen," said Marcus. "But maybe before we do, we should read the last entry of the diary and discover the last thing Elizabeth has to tell us before we go any further."

Anna pulled out the diary from her bag and turned to the last entry, only too glad to stop the doctor's interrogation of her.

CHAPTER THIRTY-FOUR
May 1915 ELIZABETH

I can barely think on what has happened since I last wrote, Dear Journal, and even now I have very little time so I will get straight to it.

When Sissy returned with my meal, she expertly balanced the tray while she closed and locked the door once again. I confess I barely registered the food she placed on my lap and remained lost in the view from my window, attempting and failing to discover a way Catherine may allow me to leave with my infants. It was only when Sissy spoke and I glanced at her face that I recognised the expression of concern.

"What is the matter Sissy? Is it the babies?" I said at once ready to dash to their side, my heart beating with wild fear.

"No, Miss. It's not that. The servants hall is all a twitter wi' news of an intruder."

"What variety of intruder?"

"A reporter, fo' the newspapers. Yer know how Louisa is a high society darlin', well it seems the papers are interested in her having a child. This reporter managed t' get into the house an' take a picture of Louisa an' the babies without anyone stoppin' him."

"And how did this reporter gain knowledge of the birth? I believe

it is yet to be announced?"

"It seems he's been hangin' round fo' weeks, hoping t' catch the first photo of the baby and break the story."

"Did they capture him attempting to depart?"

"That's just it Miss, he wasn't caught at all an' now the staff are sayin' the picture will be in the mornin' newspapers telling of Louisa an' her twins. There's something else Miss."

"What? What is it?"

"There's a lot o' talk as to how Miss Louisa give birth to such strappin' twins an' look so well afterward given her history."

"It is of little concern to us now. The only mild problem is this reporter. However, once we depart and remove the twins it will matter no longer. I shall remain in hiding, or otherwise attempt to persuade the doctor to break his confidence with Catherine, but as this means he must then face being struck off for malpractice and taking bribes it is by no means certain he will assist me. As far as is official I am a mere common thief stealing my sister's infants. What a thought."

"We can't let these worries stop us carryin' out the plan."

"These complications must be considered but will not hinder our escape."

"Good" she said. "I've arranged t' spend time with Polly the wet nurse tonight. I will keep her away from the nursery. Apparently she has a partiality for gin."

"Who told you this?" I inquired.

"Ah never yer mind, I do have some friends on the staff here, not many but some. Anyway, once everyone is asleep, about one in the mornin' I would say is safe enough, you need t' go down to the nursery room take the babies, go down through the back door of the house an' I'll meet yer there. From there, once we're clear of the house it's on t' meet Harry's parents an' off to London an' our new life."

I nodded my head. However, I had little knowledge of how I was to succeed. There was still a great chance of discovery. I realised with some degree of fear that I must rely on remaining unseen in a house overflowing with people.

It was not the first time that day I had longed for Harry. I had always had an enormous sense of safety with Harry, Dear Journal, and have attempted to conjure this feeling again on my own, especially as I was waiting that night, but the fear refused to subside.

I simply could not fail. It was imperative I succeeded. Nothing was more important.

I continued to pace the room propelling myself from one corner to another, all the while distracted by my thoughts. I must succeed.

I was not aware of Sissy until she told me to stop pacing as it was making her nervous. But sitting still took a good deal of effort, so instead I glanced out my window and looked down on the gardens.

The evening sun had begun to set and gave the gardens an orange glow. I was not interested in the gardens this time though. I looked toward the distance, where atop the hills and in the fields, tiny trees were blowing, like hands waving, beckoning me to freedom.

I was so decidedly angry with myself and I still am, Dear Journal. I have been a great fool. I allowed Catherine to manipulate and persuade me into acting exactly as she required. Blinded by grief, I gave no heed to my babies.

I ought to have married Harry and departed when he first asked me and not delayed, because I felt I owed my family some misplaced sense of loyalty.

That I delayed for this is now almost a laughable circumstance were it not so tragic. I am so filled with anger and regret, that now my vision has cleared, I recognise them for what they are - purely out to forward their own interests.

Not one has ever given me any second consideration or thought. Even Louisa. I have wasted years misleading myself and now my innocent babies may suffer the consequences and it would be no fault but my own. I simply refuse to succumb to the will of others any longer.

As rage replaced my fear, the injustice of everything made me wish to scream, Dear Journal, as I stood looking out of that window with such seething anger at my own stupidity. I remained in this dark mood for almost the whole day. Restless and agitated, I paced the floor, seated myself for a time and viewed the window, stood touching the items on my dressing table, fingered the lace on the bed cover. I was restless for it all to be over. My anger was further multiplied by my mood being constantly close to bouts of weeping.

By the time darkness descended, and the time drew near for Sissy to leave and begin the plan of keeping the wet nurse away from the nursery, I had begun to feel like this night would never end. After she departed, I sat and listened to the faint sounds of movement around the house; the distant creak and bang of doors, someone descended the stairs, a dog barked outside and irregular creaks and moans of an old house with no explanation as to the cause.

The room was dim and my oil lamp flickered intermittently in time with the tick of the clock, which seemed to be remarkably slower and take a significantly longer period for each stroke to strike. Five minutes since Sissy departed, six minutes.

I picked up the book from my table and opened it at the first page. It was an Austen novel, one of my favourites, but the familiar script and the heroine who shared my name did nothing to distract me. So, after reading the same paragraph four times over, I closed the book in extreme irritation. It's slightly dusty pages puffed out a little as it snapped shut with a bang.

I returned the book to its original position on the table. Then on further consideration glanced down at it, picked it up and inserted it into the pocket of the rather small bag Sissy had packed. I suppose I would need something to occupy me while we were hiding in the coming months. There was not a soul to miss it and none of them were particularly keen readers.

I confess, Dear Journal, that I will miss the library most of all, but that is likely the only thing to miss of this house Nevertheless I felt a degree of melancholy at leaving the only home I have ever known.

Time dragged at an astonishingly slow rate, I found myself thinking of what they would be doing at any given point in the evening, relaxing in the small drawing room, sitting in the plump high backed chairs with their red brocade pattern, Louisa's husband lounging in the corner lazily, Catherine sitting upright and commanding, and Louisa her usual restless self floating about the room in her white dress. The fire would be lit for the evening chill and the lamplight would give the deep red walls an air of darkness. The staff would bring tea, Catherine would pour, Louisa would let hers go cold, her husband would drink brandy and depart to his rooms - he did not much care for the company of the family. Soon Catherine and Louisa would retire and shortly they would sleep.

I listened to the faint but rather distinct sounds of movement which diminished as the hours of the clock slowly ticked by. When the longed for silence finally descended and the darkness outside reflected my own face through the window, I thought of how out there in that darkness Harry's family were waiting.

When the time drew near to one am, I had already dressed myself in my cloak ready to depart. I stood by the door waiting, watching the second hand of the clock move slowly onwards one, two, three. The house was silent and seemed itself to be holding its breath in anticipation, six, seven, eight more ticks. Damn why was this night so painfully slow? Eleven, twelve, thirteen, the second hand ticked slower as each stroke passed. Twenty one, twenty two, I had almost made the decision to proceed early and held my hand to the cold firm handle, thirty five. I removed it again and seated myself on the chair nearest the door. I could not risk being discovered by departing too early.

It was at this moment, Dear Journal, that I first considered mine and the babies' future. I confess to having been so wrapped up in escaping Leyac House, I gave little attention to where we would go and how we would live. Perhaps a spell abroad, America looked a promising and delightful place to begin a new life. Yes, it must be out of England. Catherine would easily discover us in London, but with Harry's family and Sissy's assistance, it mattered not where we ended up, just that the infants could be contented, as Harry would have wished.

When it was time to go I fetched my bag, took one last glance around my room and opened the door to the dark cool corridor and locked my room after me with Sissy's key.

My body was sore and weak and I confess, Dear Journal, to being desperately tired. However, I could not help but feel stronger with each step along the dark corridor. The sound of my breathing the only distinct noise in the darkness, the air thick with anticipation.

At the end of the corridor I peered over the staircase down through the floors to the darkness of the ground floor.

Taking a deep slow breath, I placed my first foot on the top staircase. This was it. I had begun.

The cool wooden rail was firm beneath my hand as I stepped again to the stair below that one, then another and another, past the war trophies carved into the balustrades, cannons, swords, helmets, armour and each corner post as the staircase turned round and round as it descended. I had never paid much heed to the staircase before, but each balustrade appeared to me then as a warning with their sharp angular depictions of war. Each hauntingly familiar painting still watched me, with eyes that pierced through the moonlit windows.

When I reached the first floor I glanced at Louisa's firmly closed door. There was silence from within. Turning right I gently opened the door to the nursery. It moved with a faint whispering sound, as if it too was aiding me by remaining silent. Hastily I slipped inside and pushed the door closed behind me and stood listening for a time. The sound of tiny breathing and the scent of baby soap and milk lingered in the air.

Propelled forward by some force that I could not control, I moved toward the crib in the centre of the room. Peering through the darkness I could make out the form of a single tiny baby slumbering peacefully. Frantically I scanned the room for indications of life but as I was already aware in my heart, the room was indeed empty.

There was no other child asleep in this room. The nursery itself was small with a long window at the far side, a cupboard against the wall, a rocking chair in the corner and the crib in the centre. Other than these items, the room was empty. Where was the other twin? With a deep sense of foreboding I clung to the dearest wish that Sissy may already have the other child.

However, as panic stabbed me like hot knives I remained undecided for a time before my body, propelled by some other force, moved of its own accord. I gathered up the tiny infant, my heart beating in fear and worry, and cradled the tiny bundle to my chest. The baby was warm and soft, and stirred momentarily before once again relaxing in my arms. I covered the tiny bundle with my cloak and held the little body securely.

I resolved to continue as arranged and with a degree of luck, Sissy would have the other baby.

I paused in the hallway to listen for movement in the house, every sense heightened with the danger of being discovered.

Silently I descended the final staircase to the ground floor and hastily hid by the wall at the bottom of the stairs in the same place I had hidden before escaping to my wedding. After a time, I took a breath and ran across the main entrance towards the rear hall, the baby shifting with the sudden movement.

The rear door was mainly for staff use but this evening it was to be my means of escape. A few more steps and I would be free. In silence I moved nearer to the door, glancing over my shoulder as I got closer. The hall and staircase to my rear were silent and dark.

Now I would discover whether Sissy had been able to get the key and unlock this door as she had promised. Saying a silent plea that it would indeed open, I raised my hand and took hold of the brass door knob. It was ice cold and firm. I paused there not daring to turn the handle. The tiny infant shifted in my arm and sighed. Slowly I turned the handle and the door opened with ease.

The cool night air was sharp and I clasped the infant closer to me. Descending the few steps I moved to hide myself in the recessed alcove, which marked where the side of the house inverts to become to the front.

Waiting there, I began thinking on the stark reality that one of my babies was still within. I listened to the sounds around me, the hoot of owls, the scurrying of night creatures and my own heavy breath. I made a conscious attempt to calm my fretful nerves and breathe steadily as my breath caught on the cool air creating a brief, faint fog.

Despite the chill of the evening, I was perspiring and felt decidedly faint and more than a little nauseous. Using the wall of the house to lean on, its hard bricks a firm constant beneath my back, I closed my eyes and took great breaths of night air until the faintness subsided.

At that moment I heard a new sound, a brushing noise from behind me.

I was instantly aware that this was the sound of the door to my rear being opened. I held my breath and cradled the child with both arms, willing the infant not to stir aloud. Closing my eyes firmly I willed us invisible.

"Elizabeth?" Sissy's urgent whisper made my heart leap. I came out from my concealment and into the clear moonlight.

"Sissy." I said with a great deal of relief. "I only have one baby Sissy, where is my other infant?"

"He's with Louisa an' her husband. They took him t' their room.

It seems she's taken a likin' to that particular one."

I began to weep as my worst fear came true "I cannot leave him. Sissy, how can I? I know not what to do. If I remain this little one is in grave danger, but if I leave I abandon my other child to them."

" Don't worry Miss, I have a plan. I'll stay behind. Yer go on t' London an' I'll come afterward with the other baby. I'll wait a few more hours until they are sleepin' then creep into Louisa's room, tek him an' catch you up. Yer go on now, Harry's mother is expectin' yer. They have friends who are going to make sure yer get t' London safely. Go now Elizabeth. I'll follow on I promise."

"Sissy, it is such a risk. Are you certain you can do this? I dare not put you in danger, but I do not wish to leave without him."

"Miss. Do yer trust me? I promise he'll be all right, I'll make sure of it. Now go. Jack the stable boy is waitin' he's sweet on me an' has promised t' get a horse ready."

I nodded my head at Sissy and tried to ignore the fear and anxiety inside that willed me to return upstairs to my room and abandon thoughts of escape. Sissy embraced me and returned to the house closing the door firmly behind her. Somewhere an owl hooted loudly. I glanced up at the house, windows loomed above like dark foreboding eyes - waiting. Somewhere in there my tiny baby remained.

However, he was the one twin they had wanted. It was the one cradled into my chest that had been in danger. Instinctively I stroked the little body huddled into me before making a decision, that I am aware I will regret for the entirety of my life, Dear Journal. A decision that despite whether Sissy is able to carry out her plan, it would always be a fact that I walked away then and left one of my twins behind. What sort of mother that makes me I do not know, and I confess I am still struggling with that decision even as I write this and it's all over.

Every inch of me told me I was wrong, that I should stay and go to him, yet I continued. Silent weeping tears turned to sobs that came in great gasps, which I was unable to prevent.

Nearing the stables I spied a dim light in the far corner hidden from view unless you were on the immediate approach. My steps faltered but did not halt, my feet slipping on the uneven surface of the dark ground below.

A tall young man moved out from behind the stable wall, in shadow at first, but as I neared his location I observed a warm friendly smile on his face.

"Miss Elizabeth?"

"Jack?"

"Yes Miss, I've got yer horse ready."

He moved toward the stable door and where the light was brightest, the wooden half door creaked a little in the silence.

"This is Molly, she's a quiet thing and will take care of yer and the babies." He said patting the dark brown mare and stroking her under the chin and down her neck.

The horse stood indifferently, her eyes calm as she waited patiently. I had managed to control my weeping briefly but it resumed once again as he spoke.

"Miss what is it? You'll soon be away from 'ere. Where is Sissy?"

He moved to the door once more and glanced toward the way I had arrived.

"One of the twins was moved. Sissy is to fetch him and we are to meet in London."

A frown of concern rumpled his rather smooth forehead but he smiled at me despite this.

"Sissy is a girl of 'er word, don't worry Miss, she can do it. I'm certain. I'm hoping to make 'er my girl, if she'll 'ave me. But Miss, we need t' get you going, the longer we delay the 'arder it is for you to get away."

Despite his attempt at a cheerful tone, the concerned expression had not escaped my notice.

He produced what appeared to be a large long piece of cloth and begun wrapping it around me and the child in something of a practiced manner. I confess to being rather bewildered, Dear Journal, at this performance.

"This will keep the baby tight t' yer chest and allow yer arms free to hold the reins, the baby will be perfectly safe. It's a trick I learnt from a traveller once."

He proceeded to lead the mare from her stall into the cool night air. She tossed her head impatiently and stamped her hoof. Taking my arm he aided me to mount. I confess it was more than a little problematic with the infant strapped to my chest, but before long I was safely seated astride the mare. He then began strapping my bag to the back and as he worked behind me I seized his arm on impulse and held him a moment.

"You must aid her Jack. Make certain she fetches my baby. Promise me Jack."

"I will Miss, don't yer worry." He paused and glanced directly into my face. "Can I jus' say miss. My grandfather used to work here many years ago. He once told me he was here the day yer mother arrived, yer real mother I mean. He said she were the most beautiful thing he'd ever seen an' was such a kind mistress. It were such a shame what 'appened to her."

"I thank you Jack, I have no knowledge of my mother."

He nodded his head and stood back. "God speed Miss. An' don't worry about Sissy. You just get that little one safe."

He smacked the horse's rump and I felt her muscles move and stretch as she trotted along the courtyard gathering speed. The house fell away to the rear with nothing but open country before me. The cool night air blowing my face provided a feeling of flying, with shadows and darkness stretching out in front.

Almost gone from sight at my rear, I halted the mare for a brief moment, turned and glanced one final time at my childhood and the life I had always known, before turning back and speeding onwards once more. My single infant child lying still and silent in a tiny ball. The small weight a degree of comfort as I rode. Be assured I am not leaving you. I silently sent out to the baby I was involuntarily abandoning. I stroked the miniature lump across my chest with one hand.

By what means could you possibly ride away and leave him? A voice in my head asked. A voice, Dear Journal, that continues to incessantly ask that question over and over again.

I simply must, I answered, like I still do, but this does not serve to make me feel any less wretched.

I thought of Harry and how he would have handled this evening. Would he have performed a better rescue of our children? With certainty, I was sure he would have.

I was soon riding alongside familiar hedgerows, the patch of bramble bushes that always yielded the best berries, the cluster of trees where many years ago I crafted rope swings alongside village children. All the places I spent a degree of my time attempting to escape Catherine and Louisa.

I began to feel nauseous again so slowed my pace. The scenery hurtling past slowed and I began to breathe more easily, as did Molly the horse.

As we trotted along in the darkness, I came to realise that my infants required the presence of a strong mother. One who didn't weep at complications. I must finally accept that Harry would not return. He would not assist me regardless of how bitterly I wept. The ache of his loss must be embraced as part of my own new character. I must accept it and live with the longing. Although longing does not seem a strong enough word to encompass what I feel for Harry's loss. I am uncertain there is any word that does not fall woefully short.

These tiny lives required my strength and protection from the people who would be hard on our heels in the morning light.

I am however, certain with a determination I have never experienced prior, that no longer would others bend me to their will. I would be resilient. My twins would enjoy the freedom to choose their own future. Of that much I am gravely determined.

I am going to end the chapter on you, Dear Journal. You will be locked away and buried alongside my previous life, I am a new person now, I will have a new identity.

Elizabeth Leyac and who she was is no more. Now I am simply another woman.

CHAPTER THIRTY-FIVE
October 1940 ANNA

Anna set down the diary and blinked at Marcus and the doctor, her eyes refocusing on them after looking at the words.

"Well at least now we know how only one of the twins went missing," she said.

"But we still don't know what happened to that child or Elizabeth," the doctor said.

"He's right," said Marcus. "There's still a lot we don't know and we know there are no more diary entries."

"Do you think they caught her?" the doctor asked, setting down his empty glass.

"I don't know," Anna said. "But I know there's only one place left to look for answers." She pulled the necklace from around her neck and dangled it in front of them all. It swung there catching the light and twinkling a little.

The doctor put on his hat with a smile and Marcus downed the rest of his drink.

Outside, the wind was blowing again and it had started to rain. Marcus turned up his collar and the doctor pulled down his hat lower.

"It's this way," the doctor said taking them down towards Parliament Street.

But what if it wasn't about Elizabeth. What if it was about him, her father? Details of who he was and where he lived. She knew she was too curious and that if she knew his name, she would investigate him and who he was further.

She didn't want to know about him, but at the same time she wanted to know what could be so important that they were willing to pay her to keep quiet and out of his life, not to mention threaten her life.

She knew she should be doing this alone and not so long ago wouldn't have dreamed of letting two men know secrets like this about her, but she now felt she could trust them both and hoped that trust wasn't misplaced.

When they got to the safety deposit box main desk and she showed the woman her key, she asked for her identity card and took her name before showing them into a single room, with a table in the centre.

Around the walls from floor to ceiling were little doors all locked tight. The woman clicked her smart shoes over to one of the doors in the middle of the room, unlocked it with her key and placed a locked metal box on the table. She left the room and the two men looked at Anna expectantly.

Taking a deep breath Anna put her tiny gold key into the lock and turned it.

Opening the box it was filled with a whole host of things, papers, letters, boxes, trinkets and what looked like legal documents and a number of other items.

She picked up one folded item, printed type on stark

white paper. It was the original telegram Elizabeth had mentioned in the diary.

Deeply regret to inform you that the ship Hawke, Edgar Class, First Class Protected Cruiser, on which your husband, Seaman Harry McKenzie was serving, sank on 15th October 1914. He must therefore be regarded as having died during active service. Letter follows.

She read the words again that she had seen in the diary. As she traced the typed print with her finger the two men had begun to examine some of the other items.

"Anna." The voice was Marcus' and something in his tone made her look up to his face. He was looking slightly shocked and more than a little wary. The doctor stared at him questioningly.

"What? What is it?" she asked.

"Anna, you need to look yourself," he said.

She went around to where Marcus was stood and he handed her the paper he had been holding. The doctor leaned in to get a better look. It was a birth certificate dated 1915. The name was Thomas Harry McKenzie Leyac. The mother's name was Elizabeth McKenzie Leyac and the father was Seaman Harry Arthur McKenzie. Underneath that was another identical birth certificate of a Victoria Eliza McKenzie Leyac with the same parents.

"Anna, one of the twins is a girl not a boy. Think Anna, did Elizabeth mention anything in the diary about the second baby being a boy?"

She paused briefly contemplating the question. "No,

when I think about it, no she didn't. But why was the world told that the missing twin was a boy?"

She reached into the box again and pulled out the birth certificate of Elizabeth Leyac herself and the death certificate of Eliza Leyac, Elizabeth's mother.

Further in was her own birth certificate. Anna Forrester, daughter of Bertha Forrester, the father's name was blank.

Next was an old black and white photo of a seaman with floppy hair, the back simply said 'Harry, 1914.'

She showed it to Marcus and the doctor, "Elizabeth's husband Harry."

Next were some legal looking documents, which she unfolded.

"What is it?" asked the doctor.

"I'm not sure," she replied handing it to Marcus.

Marcus scanned the document for a few minutes.

"Anna, this is a document dated 1918, stating that Elizabeth Leyac agrees to keep her true identity hidden and that of the twin she has in her possession for the remainder of her life. She agrees to never visit Leyac House or reveal that she is the true mother of the twins to either Thomas or Victoria whilst she is living. She agrees to abide by these rules and will be compensated by a monthly allowance from the Leyac estate, and a home to live in wherever she chooses..." He paused then and stopped reading, looking up at her.

"What? What is it?" she asked.

He glanced down at the paper again and began reading further. "It states that Elizabeth Leyac agrees to go under the name of Bertha Forrester, and the twin in her possession, Victoria Leyac, will go by the name of Anna Forrester for the remainder of Elizabeth's natural life." He stopped reading and looked up at her shock and a strange look of something else on his face.

"Give me that," said the doctor taking it from him and scanning the document himself.

Marcus remained frozen staring at her, his hand still in front of him where the paper had been.

"Don't be idiotic Marcus. It doesn't say that," she said. "Good joke though, but I don't think now is the time."

"Anna…" the doctor said gently in a calm voice. "It does say that, he's right."

"This can't be right. Give that to me." She leaned over and snatched the paper from the doctor and read the document herself. And there it was in bold black type. *'The twin in her possession, Victoria Leyac, will go by the name Anna Forrester for the remainder of Elizabeth's natural life.'*

She stared at them both. There must be some mistake. This isn't right. She was a bastard child, her father wanted nothing to do with her.

"Anna," the doctor said slowly, "You do realise, this means that the letter you got warning you to stay away, the kidnapping and the shooting, weren't by your father at all. Your father is Harry McKenzie and has been dead since 1914, so who is it that's threatening you?"

"It's got to be someone from the Leyac Estate, someone who knows the truth - warning you not to reveal your true identity."

She picked up the faded old telegram again and examined the words.

She couldn't take it in. Her father wasn't alive at all. He never had been. All those times her mother had insisted she had been married she had been telling the truth. His name was Harry McKenzie and he was a war hero.

Good God. The woman I've been reading about, the young flighty girl in love was my mother all along.

"Do you know it's funny…" she said looking up at them. "When mother died she left me a note, attached to Elizabeth's diary. In this letter, she told me that in some ways her life had been one big war. She was talking of herself. She was talking of what she lost. She was giving me a clue. The whole thing was her trying to tell me the truth. She wanted me to know who she was. But this." She picked up the legal document and shook it. "Prevented her from telling me directly, so she left me clues and hoped I would follow the breadcrumbs. Damn it, I've been so blind."

"There's two letters here Anna. One for you and one addressed to Thomas McKenzie Leyac," the doctor said fishing two letters out of the side of the box.

"Of course," she said taking both letters and looking at each of them in turn. "This means Thomas Leyac, the Thomas Leyac recently dead, was my twin brother and I never knew him, he never knew our mother. Do you think he knew the truth?"

"No." Marcus said. "He made a great deal of looking for his missing twin, and spent a great deal of money on it by all accounts. He can't have known or he would have simply kept the secret hidden. But what it does mean is that there is someone in that house still connected with that family that does know the truth."

Anna looked at the letter addressed to Thomas and put it back inside the safety deposit box, taking her own letter, she opened it hastily.

My Dearest Girl,

So now you know the truth. I have wanted to tell you so many times over the years and wish I could be there now to answer all your questions.

The diary I left you and the rest of the items in this box should tell you the truth but I wanted to fill in some blanks.

When I first ran from my home with you, I had always intended to take both my children. It was pure chance that meant I could only take you my darling. We remained on the run from my family for three years, buried deep inside the streets of London. However, we were very poor and life was pretty bleak for both you and I. My family finally caught up with me in 1918 and offered me the chance to keep you so long as I remained hidden and didn't reveal who I actually was.

To my personal shame, I took that offer and we have lived in houses owned by the Leyacs and off their allowance to me ever since. I am not proud of this but I needed to provide a life for you and wanted you to go to school. I couldn't have done this without their backing.

I stayed hidden from them at first because I feared for our lives, I knew they had killed Sissy when she didn't come to meet me and when I saw news of my own death in the paper, I feared they meant to kill me and you so ran for our lives for three years.

My married name was McKenzie but Harry's mother's maiden name was Forrester and she was named Anne. I chose to rename you Anna after her, as she helped me so much when we first left that I don't know what we would have done without her help. It is for her you are named - how I always wished to tell you that.

I loved your father dearly and he would have loved you and your brother both. I was devastated when he died and let Catherine take advantage of that. I have regretted that decision my entire life. I never did escape my family and have remained my entire life in their shadow, but you my darling girl have no such affliction. You have all your confidence and sense of injustice from your father.

If you do decide to meet your brother Anna, do so with my blessing. You are all that is left of Harry and I now, and I hope you can find a way to be friends and maybe you can tell him about me. My one lifetime regret will always be leaving him behind, and never getting the chance to be in his life.

With my love as always dear one,
Mama

She showed the letter to the doctor and Marcus with tears in her eyes. "She talks of an allowance coming from the Leyacs. I have been such a fool."

"Why?" the doctor asked.

"That letter doctor, what did that letter say? Do you remember?"

The doctor shook his head in confusion.

"The one in the cottage. Remember?"

"I just remember it being threatening."

"It said that the payment terms already in place would remain. Don't you see doctor, it's them. It's been the bloody Leyacs all along. The letter, the kidnapping, the shooting. It's always been them. Whoever it is that knows the truth is now very worried that I'm going to break this story in our paper."

"But you didn't know anything about it," the doctor said.

"True, but maybe they didn't realise that," Marcus said.

"Oh come on, I've had enough. Let's go back to the pub. I need to think," she said.

They piled all the documents and things back into the safe deposit box. She couldn't stand to find any more secrets. The rest could wait. Right now she must process the facts.

The body in that laboratory was almost certainly Sissy, who had somehow been killed trying to rescue baby Thomas. For some strange reason they had told the world the missing twin was a boy, and that Elizabeth had died from her illness. But they had allowed Elizabeth to keep her baby, me. So many questions. Her head hurt.

The journey back to the pub was a quiet one as each of them was lost in thought. Anna barely registered the doctor taking her arm as they walked. Marcus lit cigarette after cigarette, deep frown lines on his face.

Back at their seats, the now empty pub, was broken only by the sound of a wireless - some drama programme.

With fresh drinks in their hands they sat looking at each other.

"Now what?" she asked because she genuinely didn't know what to think.

Marcus opened his mouth to speak when the door to the pub opened, distracting him. Anna with her back to the door, felt the cold air rush in and blow at the backs of her legs. Marcus was watching whoever had just come in. Anna, curious at what was so interesting, was just about to turn around when she heard her name.

"Miss Forrester?"

She turned to see a face she recognised from her day at Leyac House.

"Julien Flynn, not sure if you remember me." He held out his hand to shake, his stony face looking directly at her.

Anna stared at him. "Yes, Mr Flynn I remember you. You threw me out of Leyac House for trespassing."

"Yes I did. And I've also warned you to stay away, but you seem intent on pursuing your line of enquiry. So, I am here today in person, as a last attempt to persuade you to stop what you are doing."

"It's you isn't it, you're the one who sent that letter to me, you're the one who has been sending people to threaten me."

"Well," he said with an absent flourish of his hand in an unconcerned way. She noticed he was wearing an expensive watch and his coat was thick, heavy and well tailored. "The mugger was just to find out what information you might have been given by your mother, which turned out to be nothing."

"You sent the mugger as well?" Anna asked, shocked.

"Why yes. I do hope you aren't a stupid girl Miss Forrester. I thought you were a reporter. Anyway, the kidnapper was meant to find out any information you knew and get you to agree to the terms, which I am annoyed that you lied about. The shooting was never meant to harm you, just frighten you into doing as you are told. You know I am most upset that I've had to come down here in person. You're not at all like your mother. She agreed without any persuasion, from what I was told."

"Now look here you, I won't have you harming Anna in any way. You hear me?" the doctor stood up and looked as if he might punch him.

"Now, now doctor, you don't want to go getting upset now do you?" said Marcus calming him down.

The doctor did sit then but his fists remained in balls and he stared at the table.

"Yes, do call off your man Miss Forrester," said Julien Flynn.

"Mr Flynn, you completely misunderstand," she said before the doctor could again try to punch him. "My mother told me nothing of who she really was. I knew nothing at all until today. I thought those threats were from my father, who I had thought was some irresponsible fool who had got my mother pregnant with an illegitimate baby."

"Ah, well. I see," he said rubbing the side of his temple in thought before sighing. "Oh well I suppose I should tell you what it is I want."

He sat down and clicked his fingers at the bartender who looked over and gave him an insolent look but poured a drink and set it down on the table with a slight bang. After the bartender had left, he began.

"I am the Manager of Leyac House and was a great friend to Thomas and his mother Louisa. I was told of your true identity and the agreement that had been struck by Catherine and Elizabeth in 1918. For Louisa it was only imperative that Thomas never discovered the truth and I have worked exceedingly hard to keep the promise I made to her that day that he never would discover you.

This was why I wrote advising you to not pursue your claim on the Leyac Estate. I was unsure at the time whether or not your mother may have told you the truth before she died."

He paused and took a dainty sip of his drink. "So now we must work together to find a solution for the future, as I mentioned in the letter. I am keen to continue with the same terms that your mother enjoyed."

"But Thomas Leyac is dead," said Marcus. "What difference does it make now whether the world knows who she really is?"

"The entire country has been looking for a missing boy for 25 years and we select few know what actually happened. No good can come of releasing this information now," Julien said.

"But why?" said the doctor raising his head for the first time and giving Julien a dark look. "I don't understand why you are so keen to keep it quiet."

"For the simple reason that it was set in place by Lady Catherine, Louisa and Elizabeth many years ago. It has served very well so far and should continue to do so. Who are we to upset the balance of things?"

"Can I just ask then Mr Flynn, if the missing Leyac twin is not found, who inherits Leyac House?" said Marcus.

"Well, Thomas set out in his will that in that case it shall be given to Leyac House's trustee to keep for the next heir, which we know wouldn't be found."

"So you'd inherit," said the doctor.

"I'm not at liberty to discuss the Leyac House trustees with you. But don't underestimate me or the means at my disposal, I have kept this secret from my nearest friend for years."

"That means he'd inherit," snapped the doctor. "He's bloody doing it for the money. You make me sick."

"Now now doctor," said Marcus. "Surely keeping the identity of the true heir of Leyac House a secret is withholding evidence. Thomas specifically said he wanted the house kept for his twin."

"Not if no one ever finds out," he said checking his shiny watch. "Now I am a very busy man Miss Forrester, will you finally answer me once and for all? Will you accept my offer and keep quiet about your true identity?"

"I have some questions first before I will answer that," she told him.

He sighed, "Come on then, ask them so we can all get on with our day."

"Did Catherine kill the maid Sissy?"

"No she did not. Louisa's husband did but it was accidental. Sissy was caught trying to steal Thomas and there was an argument and Louisa's husband struck her across the face, she fell and hit her head on something. I believe they buried her in Elizabeth's grave."

Anna nodded, purposely not looking at the doctor's face. "Why did they tell everyone the missing twin was a boy?"

"That stemmed from a misunderstanding. It's actually a very funny story. It seems that there was some conversation Louisa had with the staff that morning the twins were born. Louisa was showing off Thomas to one of the staff members, that staff member asked if both babies were boys, but Louisa didn't hear the question correctly and replied yes. So this staff member naturally reported that the twins were boys to the rest of the house.

When Elizabeth stole you, Catherine decided to use this to help her cover up the fact that it was Elizabeth who had stolen the baby. The scandal of a maid stealing a baby is preferable to a member of one's own family. So to protect their reputation she blamed the now dead Sissy, said Elizabeth had died and told the press that the missing twin was a boy. That way there would be no chance anyone but the family could find the baby or Elizabeth. They were looking for a common maid and a baby boy, not a well spoken lady with a baby girl.

Catherine wanted to be certain there was no way anyone else would be able to find Elizabeth. It was important to protect the family and to do this they needed to find Elizabeth themselves."

"What did she plan to do when she found Elizabeth?""

"I cannot say, whether there was another plan or whether she always intended to allow Elizabeth to stay hidden. But Elizabeth brought the misery on herself, she shouldn't have stolen the baby. However, she has lived very nicely over the years, I know. I prepare her allowance. It paid for your education, Miss Forrester. You are where you are because of me, Louisa and Catherine, not Elizabeth. All she did was take a baby. But I hope you can now see why it is important this secret remains. It would ruin the reputation of the family, a reputation Catherine, Louisa and her husband and now myself have worked very hard to protect."

She nodded again. "I have one further question and then I will give you your answer."

He sighed again. "What is it Miss Forrester?""

"Did my brother really not know the truth?""

"No he did not." His voice changed as he said this from a tone of superiority to one of regret. "It is the one thing that has been hardest, keeping this secret from my greatest friend, but now he is gone, so it is no matter. Now Miss Forrester, will you once and for all tell me if you agree to my terms?""

"Yes I agree. I will stay away and keep quiet. I won't break this story. I will go back to London and won't visit Leyac House."

"What are you saying Anna?" the doctor jumped to his feet.

Marcus lit a cigarette and looked curiously at her.

"Doctor it is my decision."

"But Anna you can't do this. Do you know what you are

giving up?"

"Doctor. It's my decision."

She stood up turning her back on the doctor and shook Julien Flynn's hand, folding her coat over her arm and picking up her hat she walked quickly towards the door.

"I'll prepare the paperwork Miss Forrester," he said to her retreating back.

"Anna. Anna wait," the doctor called after her.

But she ignored his calls, she didn't want to see him, and sped her walk up to a run.

The doctor came up behind her panting and pulled her around by the arm.

"What are you doing Anna?"

"What does it matter? What do you care? Leave me alone doctor, it's my decision."

"But it's a foolish decision. You're making a mistake. You're going to regret it."

"I don't care, it's nothing to do with you. Why, doctor, do you insist on always getting involved in my business like this? Marcus isn't chasing me telling me I'm a fool. Why doctor, why are you doing this?

He grabbed her by the shoulders then. "Why? Why? You ask me why Anna. Good God is it not obvious? Because I bloody love you, you little fool. Did you not realise that. I love you."

"No, don't be ridiculous. I can't think about anything now. I've just had everything I ever knew in life turned upside down. I can't think about you or anyone else."

She turned and ran from the doctor then. She ran from her life. She kept running blindly.

Damn it all. Damn you War. Damn you mother, why didn't you tell me?

She ran until her legs hurt. She ran until the tears came. She ran on and on until she could run no more.

Finally, she sat on a bench overlooking the river and watched the sky. She made out the shape of a Spitfire above. How she wished then, that she could fly with that plane. Fly away from it all, free, high in the sky.

She stood up and began to walk. Tomorrow she would decide the future. Tomorrow was a new beginning.

Want to read the next book in the Home Front Series?

Then join my exclusive readers club to find out when **book two titled,** *The Prisoner* is being released.
Only priority Early Bird Club members get access to the following:

1. The chance to win **free signed copies**
2. **Exclusive competitions**
3. Access to **upcoming release dates**
4. Opportunity to **help with the writing process**
5. The chance to **have your say**
6. **Advance warning** of events, signings and readings

So don't be shy, **get on board and join the early bird club today**

http://sarathomson.uk

About the Author

From being a very young child reading and writing were a huge part of my life and my mother encouraged this through her own love of books. The very first book I ever wrote was a children's story for my younger sister when I was seven. I painstakingly drew (very badly) little hedgehogs and animals and loved creating the story for her to read. I stuck the book together with sellotape and presented my work to a delighted little girl.

Alongside things like this, I kept a diary throughout my childhood and teenage years, and had so many different stories floating around my imagination that sometimes I just had to write them down to get them out of my head.

However, I resisted this urge to write and kept it a secret, because real people didn't become writers; real people got jobs in offices. But I always told myself I would write a book - one day.

Now finally that book is written and I've found what I was meant to do. So if you are like me and have always told yourself you would write 'one day,' make that one day today.

Through taking that plunge and deciding to write, I have found that it is a passion that does not go away with just one book. Instead, like a hungry child, it wants more and more stories that come raging and begging to be written.

Other than writing, I've spent 20 years as a military wife and moved around a lot. I gained a BA Hons degree in English with Creative Writing as a mature student, brought up four children and built a career in content and copywriting.

For the future, I plan to release book two in the Home Front Series and write many more books.

If you would like to connect with me on a personal level, to ask questions or for any reason at all, **email me at** sara@sarathomson.uk I always reply to all my reader emails personally.

Acknowledgements

There has been so many great people, books and events that have helped me to create this book, I find I don't know where to start.

But first I feel I should thank my family, particularly my husband who has taken over duties we would normally share so that I could hide away with my computer and finish writing this book. I also need to thank my four amazing children who have always had unfailing faith in me.

Next comes my mum who was the very first person to show me the beauty and joy in literature and reading, that led to a life long love of words, books and story.

I'd also like to thank my sister, who is the one I turn to when things go wrong and who is always able to cheer me with her crazy smile and outlook on life. And also to the rest of my family, who have fully supported and been excited about my insane dreams and ambitions.

For writing the book, I must give enormous thanks to Andy, who without his patience and encouragement, this book would have remained in a folder on my hard drive forever. I also need to thank my extremely talented mum who did an amazing job line editing and proofing, so thank you very much.

I must thank Calum for the absolutely fantastic cover design. It is exactly what I wanted.

I need to thank all my amazing beta readers for your brilliant feedback and suggestions, so Helen, Holly, Jacqueline and Chris thank you so very much for your help.

I'd like to thank all the successful indie authors who have so inspired me to make this dream a reality and I would especially like to thank Laura who gave me some much needed encouragement.

In researching the book I read a lot of great books both fiction and non-fiction about the period and visited a vast number of museums and events to help me research. There are far too many to list but I am grateful to all of you for your help too.

I really hope you all enjoy the result.

Made in the USA
Charleston, SC
17 October 2016